SOME DAY I'LL FIND YOU

Diana Arnold marries the handsome and mysterious James Blackwell in haste, one summer morning in 1940 — and she is still wearing her wedding dress when her new husband is summoned back to base to fly his next, terrifying, mission. Then fate delivers what is the first of its cruel twists: James, that very day, is shot down over northern France. Diana is left a widow, and pregnant with their child. More than ten years later, living in the south of France with her daughter and new husband, Diana is flourishing in the Provençal sunshine — until one morning, when she hears something that makes her blood run cold: the voice of someone who will set out to torment and blackmail her, and from whom there can be only one means of escape . . .

Books by Richard Madeley
Published by The House of Ulverscroft:

FATHERS & SONS

RICHARD MADELEY

SOME DAY I'LL FIND YOU

Complete and Unabridged

CHARNWOOD
Leicester

First published in Great Britain in 2013 by
Simon & Schuster UK Ltd.
London

First Charnwood Edition
published 2015
by arrangement with
Simon & Schuster UK Ltd.
London

The moral right of the author has been asserted

A catalogue record for this book is available from the British Library.

ISBN 978–1–4448–2239–7

Published by
F. A. Thorpe (Publishing)
Anstey, Leicestershire

Set by Words & Graphics Ltd.
Anstey, Leicestershire
Printed and bound in Great Britain by
T. J. International Ltd., Padstow, Cornwall

This book is printed on acid-free paper

For Judy, who as a fellow first-time novelist forgave me my trespasses as I worked obsessively on this story.

To the men and women of the RAF who, in
1940, delivered this country from an
unspeakable fate.
We owe them everything.

Prologue

Diana sat at her usual table outside the pavement café reading her morning paper. There were still many words she didn't understand, but after two months her French was definitely improving. Everyone told her so.

She searched the pages for the weather forecast. Not that she needed to: it was obviously going to be another beautiful day. The sky above Nice flower-market was an unbroken blue and even though it was only April, the air was warm and still. The cut flowers on the stalls packed into the square around her would be impossible to find anywhere back home, this early in the year.

It had been below freezing for weeks in shivering, rationed-to-the-hilt England. She'd spoken by telephone to her father in Kent the night before.

'You're much better off down there, Diana,' he told her. 'Lots of sunshine and plenty of food. Rationing here just goes from bad to worse. You wouldn't think we'd won the bloody war.'

A taxi came slowly round the corner, past a little grove of orange trees that lined the centre of the road. It was a shabby brown pre-war Citroën, all the windows down in the spring warmth. She stood up to hail it, but realised it

1

already carried a passenger and wasn't going to stop.

As it passed her, she saw the silhouette of a man sitting in the back. He was leaning forward and speaking, in English, to the driver.

'No, not here. I told you — it's much further up. Keep going all the way to the Hotel Negresco. And get a move on — I'm late enough as it is.'

Diana swayed and gripped the back of her chair. *Impossible.*

'Stop! she called at last as the taxi reached the top of the square and began to turn on to the Promenade des Anglais. 'Oh please, stop!'

But the Citroën entered the flow of traffic and disappeared down the long curving road that bordered the sparkling Mediterranean.

'*Madame?*' It was Armand, the *patron*, solicitous. 'Do you have a problem?'

'No, no . . . ' She sat down again. 'Everything's fine, really.'

But she was lying.

Everything was wrong.

Completely wrong.

Part One

1

When she looked back — at all of it, mind, right back to the point where it all really began — she was surprised at only two things.

That she had survived at all and how foolish she had been.

Even in the moments when she had believed she was being clever, she wasn't. Such a silly girl, she thought to herself now. Such a ridiculous, *stupid* girl.

Which is a little harsh. For how many of us would recognise the Devil if he stood smiling at our door?

★ ★ ★

The Arnolds were a family who took a quiet pleasure in using entirely the wrong names for each other. It had started even before Mr and Mrs Arnold were engaged. She was Patricia, he was Patrick; both were known as Pat — potential for confusion from the very beginning. To their mutual pleasure and relief they discovered that each harboured an irrational dislike for the names their parents had bestowed on them. So they agreed to refer to each other by the ones they shyly confessed were their secret preferences.

Patrick had always thought of himself as Oliver; he said he had no idea why.

5

Patricia believed that the *creamy* sound of 'Gwen' somehow magically softened the lines of her lean, angular face — at least, she thought of it as lean and angular — and gave her bony hips and splayed feet — again this was how *she* thought of them — a less prominent form. Of course, she didn't confide any of this to her fiancé. She simply told him that she wished she had been christened Gwen, 'for no more logical reason than you regret not being called Oliver, my dear'.

So they made their arrangement, and their marriage. And when first a son, and then a daughter arrived, the children came, in time, to follow their parents' example. They were intrigued to learn of the pact and when he was eight, Robert gravely informed the family that he would prefer to be known as John. His sister privately thought Robert a much nicer name and was content with her own given one of Rose, but gradually she felt inclined, obliged even, to join the family gavotte.

After much thought and lengthy private consultation with her intimates at school (who were thrilled to be part of the process), Rose reached her decision. She announced it to the family that Christmas.

Her new name was confirmed just in time for a new decade. Rose was left behind in the swirling backwash of the 1920s.

The future belonged to Diana.

6

2

South of England, 1938

Oliver loved the chalk stream that flowed swiftly beneath the ha-ha wall separating his rabbit-cropped lawn from the paddock beyond. In fact, Mr Arnold loved, and was proud of, every aspect of the home he had built — or, rather, bought — for his family.

The four of them lived in an oak-framed Dower House tucked beneath the Weald of Kent. Five, if you included Lucy, the maid, who had a room at the top of the back stairs.

The surrounding countryside was heavily wooded and that summer, as Mr Arnold drove the three miles to the tiny railway station to catch his London train, he compared the thickly timbered lanes to his memories of the previous year's astonishing new feature-length Walt Disney animated film, much of which was set in an extravagant forest.

Gwen and he had been amazed by Disney's artistry. Even John and Diana, reluctantly persuaded to accompany their parents to Royal Tunbridge Wells' largest cinema, found their own cheerful impertinence — 'it's a *cartoon*, Oliver; they're just *drawings*, Mum' — silenced after five minutes of the first reel of *Snow White and the Seven Dwarfs*.

'That was really something, Dad,' John said

afterwards as they walked back to the car. Since their middle teens Mr Arnold's children had called him Oliver when they wanted to tease or annoy him; Dad when he'd earned their grudging respect. It never occurred to either child to call their mother Gwen.

'Some of those tableaux — you know, the backgrounds to the action — were amazing. Mum, you really should think about adapting and developing that style for your next painting. I think you could do something with it.'

Gwen coughed. 'I think Mr Disney might have something to say about that, John. I have my own romantic style, and he has his, dear. But it was very fine, I agree, if a little . . . well, rudimentary.'

There was a slightly awkward silence as they arrived in the side street where Mr Arnold had left the car. Gwen was sensitive about her painting, especially since an unflattering review of her first exhibition had appeared in the evening paper. 'So unfair!' she had cried, crumpling the pages in distress. 'I am my own inspiration! I owe nothing to any of these people he writes about. He's all but accusing me of plagiarism! And oh, all of our friends will be reading this . . . it's too much. Oliver, I want you to do something.'

Mr Arnold was a libel lawyer, and a successful one. He preferred to represent plaintiffs; he had something of a gift for persuading jurors to empathise with his clients. He used simple tricks of rhetoric. 'How would *you* feel if the article had said that about *you?*' he would ask the jury,

8

before turning to the opposing barrister with a look of reproach, as if the man should be ashamed of defending the peddlers of such calumny.

Juries instinctively liked him with his crisp, pleasantly inflected voice and pleasing looks. Mr Arnold wasn't conventionally handsome, but he had an attractive smile and a reassuring air. Jurors felt they could trust him, and were flattered by the subliminal message he managed to convey to them, which said: 'You're a sensible lot, I can see that. Between you and me we'll sort this nonsense out, won't we?'

Crucially for any barrister working in high-conflict court cases, juries wanted to be on his side. It was half the battle won.

Success had brought him great wealth. For years he had been able to charge the highest rates for the privilege of his time, and such was his reputation as a winner that publishers increasingly preferred to settle out of court when they heard that Oliver Arnold was against them.

So he had dutifully taken the offending article about Gwen to his office in Holborn. After careful scrutiny, he concluded that there was nothing defamatory in it. If anything, he thought privately to himself, the piece was a rather adroit dissection of his wife's shortcomings as an artist. It said she owed much to the work of others, and after Mr Arnold had spent an afternoon visiting some of the galleries mentioned in the piece, he was inclined to agree.

Later, at home, he dissembled. 'There's nothing to be done, Gwen. It's what's known as fair comment. Yes, yes, I know *we* think it's *un*fair, but critics must be free to criticise, and all that. I realise it's upsetting, but if I were you I'd just put it behind me and forget all about it. What was it Wilde said? 'The only thing worse than being talked about, is not being talked about.' Something like that, I believe. Anyway, at least they've taken notice of you, darling.'

His wife's face was full of resentment. 'Well, of course, if you're going to take their side, I suppose there's nothing to be done.'

She had been cool with him for weeks.

That was three summers ago and it was only by the spring of 1938 that Gwen had recovered her *amour-propre* sufficiently to return to her oils, brushes and canvases in the attic of the Dower House. Mr Arnold may have had his own (unvoiced) opinion of his wife's ability, but he couldn't fault her new-found self-belief. Indeed, he had been obliged to cancel a long-anticipated holiday to the Lake District after Gwen protested that she 'couldn't possibly, *possibly*' leave her work.

'Not at such a crucial stage, Oliver. Surely you can understand. I've never experienced such a creative *burst*.'

Her husband reflected that one half-finished oil depicting a vase of what appeared to be drought-stricken daisies didn't represent much of a creative burst to him, but nevertheless dutifully wrote to the hotel near Ullswater, and bade a sad farewell to his deposit.

So Mr Arnold spent his two-week holiday taking packed lunches, prepared for him by

10

Lucy, on lonely expeditions into the surrounding countryside while his wife laboured, or, if we are to be honest, postured, at her easel. The house was quiet now the children were away at their studies and for the first time in years, he experienced a touch of melancholy. It did him good to get out.

He was at his happiest up on the Weald, from where he could look down upon the smoke and haze of London to the north, and across to the shimmering hint of the sea to the south. Small powder-blue butterflies exploded from the bushes along the footpaths in front of him as he strode along the ripple of high ground between the North and South Downs. 'Kent's answer to the Malvern Hills,' he would murmur to himself at some point during each visit. It was a knowing conceit, but it pleased him. Yet even the sunniest days were increasingly darkened by the growing threat of war.

Invisible just below the southern horizon lay France. France, which twenty-four years ago had stood toe-to-toe with a threatening, blustering Kaiser, and now stared into the dead eyes of the Führer.

Mr Arnold, munching his ham sandwiches on the slopes above Ashdown Forest, could scarcely believe another war might be coming. He had ended up as a major in France last time. When he'd asked Gwen to marry him he had been on a short leave to London, and although her 'yes, yes of course!' had thrilled and exhilarated him, secretly he didn't expect to survive long enough to see his own wedding.

11

Even today he looked back with genuine astonishment at the fact that he'd come out of the war in one piece. He had been almost four years in the trenches, joining his regiment immediately after leaving public school in the summer of 1914. Plans to read law at university were postponed, although Oliver and his parents were quietly confident that he would take up his place at Oxford within a few months, certainly by the New Year. The war would be won by Christmas at the latest; everyone knew that.

By the end of 1918, Mr Arnold was the only boy from his school year's Cadet Corps to survive the war. He had no idea why he had been spared. It certainly wasn't through lack of exposure to battle; he had fought in so many, and seen so many men killed directly beside him. Some had been shot, others evaporated in an instant by the blast of a shell that somehow left him unscathed. Shellfire did that sort of thing; he'd witnessed men closest to an explosion crawl away while others further back were blown to pieces.

Now, probably too old at forty-five to fight again, his fears were for his son. At twenty, John was at the RAF Officer Training School at Cranwell in Lincolnshire. Nothing was certain, but if he was commissioned, ultimately John could be sent on active duty. The papers said the war would be decided in the air this time. John might be one of the young men pitched into a new kind of front line; a modern battlefield where the enemy, bad weather or bad luck would toss boys like him into gravity's unforgiving grasp.

Mr Arnold tried to keep grotesque images of his son tumbling helplessly through the skies at bay, and confided his anxieties to no one. But as the summer days shortened, and August drifted into September, the secret fear within him grew. Hitler's threats against Czechoslovakia were becoming wilder and more bellicose by the day. Mr Arnold scanned the gloomy headlines in his newspaper each morning on the train to Charing Cross. Britain and France were honour-bound to stand by what Mr Arnold's editorials unfailingly described as 'the plucky Czechs'.

Summer was nearly done and the woods that surrounded the Dower House began to glow with the first colours of autumn. Fires were lit again in the cottages and farmhouses that dotted the station road. Mr Arnold, sitting behind the wheel of his big green Humber (a present from a grateful client he'd represented in a swift and decisive action), noted the wood-smoke rising from chimneys. It was, after all, the last weekend in September. He wondered if it would also be the last weekend of peace. The Prime Minister had that very afternoon announced to a cheering House of Commons that he was flying immediately to Munich to hold talks with the Führer, at Herr Hitler's personal invitation, to 'settle the Czechoslovakian Question . . . once and for all'.

Tomorrow's meeting in Germany, Mr Arnold reflected as he turned into the gravel drive of the Dower House, represented not much more than a last desperate throw of the dice.

Lucy let him into the hall and helped him off with his hat and coat.

'Will it be war, sir?' she asked politely, in the same tone of voice as if she were asking him if it might rain.

'I very much doubt things will come to that, Lucy,' he said. But secretly he was relieved that Diana and John were coming home for the weekend. War felt very close now, and he wanted his children near.

3

'Hitler is absolutely no different from Queen Victoria. No different *what-so-ever*.' Diana pushed her plate away and stared defiantly at the rest of the family.

'Oh dear,' murmured Gwen. 'Not another of these tiresome arguments over lunch, please. Lucy will be serving dessert in a moment.'

Her husband shifted in his chair. 'There's nothing tiresome about these discussions,' he said irritably. 'Nothing tiresome at all, as it happens. I like to hear the children speaking their minds. I — '

'We're hardly children, Daddy,' Diana interrupted. 'I'm at Girton learning how awful politicians are and John is at Cranwell learning how to kill people. Not exactly the occupations of infants.'

Mr Arnold looked at her over his glasses and put down his Sunday paper, from which he had just been reading aloud, and with rising anger, to his family.

'You may be reading politics at Cambridge, young lady, but it's infantile to compare Adolf with Victoria. Surely you — '

'It's infantile *not* to! Victoria and her ghastly prime ministers and gunboats built the biggest empire the world has ever seen, and they did it with threats and brute force, smash and grab. Remind you of anyone? Hitler may be a horrible man and his party a bunch of gangsters, but he's only doing what we've been getting away with for centuries. It's the height of hypocrisy to say anything else. Come on, Daddy, surely you must *see*.'

'I certainly see that you're oversimplifying things. You can't compare British democracy with Nazi thuggery. We built partnerships across the world. We — '

'Oh, give it a rest, both of you.' John pushed his plate away. 'Dad, you know Diana doesn't believe a word of what she's saying. She just likes a good row.'

'I do *not*. Shut up, John. Anyway, Daddy and I agree on one thing — Britain and France have sold the Czechs completely down the river. It's awful. I feel so ashamed.'

Her father threw back his head. 'Well, we're in the minority, my dear. Most people,' he waved his paper, 'think Mr Chamberlain's the hero of the hour; he's saved us from war and stood up to Hitler. Wrong, on both counts. Our PM may have said 'no' to the bully for now, but he's agreed to give him everything he wants in regular instalments in the near future. A sell-out in easy stages. And we promised the Czechs we'd stand by them. Some promise! We've forced them to hand over half their country to Hitler. You're right, Diana. It *is* shameful.'

'But if it stops a war . . . I mean, the PM has at least stopped that, hasn't he, Dad?' asked John.

'Of course he hasn't. Good God, John, haven't you read any of Churchill's articles in the

16

papers? Hitler's a blackmailer, and blackmailers always come back for more. After what we gave him on Friday, he must think we're abject worms. I'll tell you this: there'll be German troops in Prague by Christmas.'

Gwen, who had gone to the kitchen to see what Lucy was doing about dessert, returned in time to hear her husband's prediction. Her shoulders dropped.

'Let's pray you're wrong, Oliver,' she said. 'Otherwise John will have to go to war, just as you did. You can't want that.'

'Of course I don't want that! Why is no one listening properly? What I'm trying to say is — '

John coughed. 'I don't think Dad wants war, Mum. But . . . er . . . a lot of us rather do, you know, if we're being honest. It's obvious Adolf's going to have to be stopped sooner or later. I'm training on Tiger Moths now and the chaps say that could mean qualifying for a Hurricane or even a Spitfire squadron. If Dad's right, we might actually get a crack at showing Hitler where he gets off.'

His parents stared at him.

'You never mentioned this,' said Gwen, after a pause. 'You never said you were training to be a fighter pilot. Isn't that awfully dangerous, Oliver?'

Mr Arnold hesitated. 'Well, up to a point. All flying has its risks, especially in war. We just have to — '

Diana clapped her hands. 'What fun, Johnnie! A girl I know at Girton goes out with a fighter pilot. He flies Gloucester something-or-others . . . Radiators — oh no, it's Gladiators. Anyway, he's *gorgeous* and so is everyone in his squadron. You simply *must* fly fighters!'

She turned to her mother. 'Don't worry, Mummy. Like it says in the song: 'There ain't going to be no war, no war'. Old Adolf won't dare attack us, or France. Especially France. Professor Hislop told us during a lecture this week that the French have a massive army, much bigger than ours. We'll be fine.'

She pointed at her brother. 'When you start flying fighter planes, Johnnie, promise you'll bring home the best-looking pilot in the squadron to stay for Christmas, and I'll bring home Sarah Tweed, that girl you kept making ridiculous sheep's eyes at during the Freshers' Ball. Agreed?'

John smiled. 'I haven't even got my wings yet, sis.'

'Oh, but you will. You have my fullest confidence. Anyway, talking of old Hislop, I ought to be off. No time for pudding. Will you give me a lift to the station, Pa?'

'Me too, please,' said John, standing up. 'I'm due back at camp tonight. Flying first thing in the morning.'

'Certainly,' said Mr Arnold, with forced cheeriness. 'This lawyer can run a one-man taxi-rank with the best of them. No difficulty there. I'll get the car out.' He turned to Diana. 'Come on, Piglet — you open the garage for me while I start her up.'

Gwen said nothing as her children kissed her goodbye. Foreboding had risen from her throat like ash and her tongue was choked.

18

4

Diana slammed the telephone in the hall back onto its cradle so fiercely that a small crack appeared across the smooth brown Bakelite surface.

'Mum! Oliver! Come on! Hurry!'

Muffled exclamations floated from the drawing room and a moment later Mr Arnold opened the door.

'What on earth's all the racket about? What's happening?'

Diana was already halfway into her coat. 'It's John! He's going to be up there in about twenty minutes. Come *on*.'

'Up where? Calm down and tell me — '

Diana stamped her foot. 'How *can* I, when you keep asking silly questions? Up *there!*' She pointed at the ceiling. 'In his thingy, his kite, his Spit, his *plane*, for heaven's sake. You get the car out and I'll fetch Mum.'

'But how do you know he's going to be up there?' Oliver couldn't keep up.

'*Oh!*' Diana stamped her foot again, 'Damn the man, damn him to hell . . . because he *called*, didn't he, and told me. John just telephoned from his aerodrome. He says his squadron's taking off on an exercise any second now and they'll be over the Weald in twenty minutes. He says we should head for Upper Hartfield — they'll be passing directly

19

overhead. Come on!'

Gwen appeared in the hall. 'Why is everybody shouting?'

'It's John,' Mr Arnold said, searching frantically through a set of drawers for his car keys. 'He's going to be up there in a few minutes. We need to leave right now, if we want to see him.'

'Up where?' Gwen looked bemused. 'Tell me what's happening.'

'How can I when you keep asking questions? Put your coat on — we're going to see John fly his Spitfire. Now where are my blasted keys!'

Three minutes later, Mr Arnold and his wife and daughter were hurtling under leafless branches towards Upper Hartfield. Mr Arnold had parked his car there often the previous summer on his solitary holiday excursions.

Today, the March air was cold under a summer-blue sky. Diana and Gwen craned their necks out of the windows as the car raced through the lanes.

'I think I can see them!' Diana screamed when the big green Humber swerved to the south and the north-west sky opened like a luminous page beyond an oak spinney. 'There — look, like lots of little silverfish! No, *there*, Daddy!' as Oliver looked the wrong way.

He pulled to a juddering halt opposite the village church and leaped out, saying, 'Quickly — there's a clear spot behind the spinney at the back of the church. We can look from there.'

A few moments later, the family were standing on an ancient grassy knoll; all that remained of a Crusader's grave, anointed 800 years earlier, abandoned and all but forgotten for centuries.

They stared up at the new Knights Templars: would-be warriors of the skies, untested yet in battle.

'My God,' muttered Mr Arnold to himself as a dozen Spitfires cruised swiftly above them, engines throbbing and sunlight flashing off Perspex cockpits and aluminium wings. 'My God — how long before John will be flying into war?' He shivered as a ripple of disquiet passed through him.

'What's that, Daddy?' asked Diana.

'Nothing, dear,' he replied, trying to shrug off his premonition. 'I was just wondering which aircraft John is flying.'

The squadron moved off to the south-east, the deep rumble of engines dwindling as they swept towards Rye and the Channel. The wonderful moment was over, and the Arnolds walked slowly back to their car.

5

Six months after what Mr Arnold invariably described as 'the son and heir's flypast', lingering hopes of peace quietly evaporated and war was born on a sluggish, late-summer morning as German troops swept into Poland. Gwen and Oliver sat by their mahogany wireless set and listened intently to the Prime Minister admitting comprehensive diplomatic defeat. He sounded desperately tired.

'Well, that's it,' said Mr Arnold, switching off the radio. 'We're all for the high-jump now.'

'I can't bear it,' Gwen said quietly. 'I always thanked God for the miracle that brought you back to me the last time. I always promised Him, when I was praying for you, that I would never, ever, ask for another one. And I haven't. I kept my promise. But what am I supposed to say to Him about John? What? It isn't fair. It simply isn't fair.' Tears rolled silently down her cheeks.

Mr Arnold stared at his wife.

'Look, Gwen,' he said finally, pulling her to him. 'God's mercy is — oh, you know how difficult I find it to believe in all this stuff, after what I saw in France the last time — but surely God is supposed to have infinite compassion? If you believe He saved *my* worthless skin twenty-odd years ago, surely you can believe that He has the power to keep our son safe too?'

'But that's just it,' Gwen said miserably. 'I

don't know if God even heard my prayers about you. Maybe you were just one of the lucky ones. Maybe John won't be. Oh God . . . '

The telephone rang.

John.

'I can't bloody believe it, Dad,' he shouted down a bad, crackling line. 'They're disbanding the entire squadron in some kind of stupid reorganisation. Bloody bureaucrats. We've just declared war and I've been given *bloody* leave. It'll all be over before I get a chance to do anything. *Hell!* I'm sorry, Dad, but I'm spitting rivets here.'

'Yes, I'd rather gathered that,' said Mr Arnold, putting his hand over the receiver. 'It's John,' he whispered to his wife. 'Looks like your unsaid prayers have been answered. He's coming home for a bit. The RAF have put him on standby.'

Gwen grabbed the telephone. '*John!* Are you coming back here now?' She listened for a few moments, then said, 'Of course, darling. We'll see you both tomorrow.' She hung up.

'Both?' her husband repeated.

'Yes,' said Gwen quickly. 'John is bringing his flight commander. Apparently the poor boy's parents are in Canada at the moment and the family house is shut up. He can't stay in camp all alone and John says he's terribly nice and very funny. Now, what did he say his name was? I forget . . . oh yes, it's James. James Blackwell.'

Mr Arnold shrugged. 'A full house for the weekend, then, with Diana coming home too,' he said. 'She'll be most invigorated at the prospect, I'm sure. You'd better go and tell Lucy to make

23

up one of the spare rooms. Actually, let's put Mr Blackwell up in the top attic. You know what these fighter boys are supposed to be like with the girls. Predatory so-and-so's.'

'Don't be disgusting,' said Gwen as she pulled the bell for the maid. 'I'm sure that Flight Commander Blackwell is an officer and a gentleman.'

'Yes, but he's a fighter boy too,' her husband muttered under his breath as he left the room.

★ ★ ★

Diana, as her father had predicted, was electrified by the news that Flight Commander James Blackwell would shortly be arriving with her brother.

'He's bound to be a dish,' she said confidently as she ran upstairs to reapply her make-up. 'All Spitfire pilots are impossibly glamorous. It's practically one of the qualifications for the job. What time do him and John get here?'

'*He*, dear, *he*,' her father called after her. 'So much for the Girton girl. I thought language and politics were your passions, not Brylcreem Boys. In fact, I thought . . . '

Diana's muffled answer drifted down from above, but he could only make out two words — '*absurd*, Daddy' — before her bedroom door slammed shut.

★ ★ ★

'It's absurd, all right,' said James Blackwell, as

24

coffee was served in the Arnolds' dining room that evening. 'Everyone else racing back to barracks at maximum speed, and our lot gets sent home. Hardly the most martial start to a war for us, is it? The whole squadron's furious. It's a total waste of resources. I don't know what Mr Chamberlain would make of it.'

I wonder what Mr Chamberlain would make of *you*, thought Mr Arnold as he passed their guest sugar cubes and silver tongs. James Blackwell was pin-up material; a gift for the RAF's propaganda unit. As Diana had predicted, based more on hope than intuition, he was impossibly glamorous. Indeed, all three of the young people sitting at his table were, in Mr Arnold's view, excessively attractive.

His daughter's dark brown hair and green eyes were a source of initial surprise (and continuing private discussion) between her parents. These features — and her olive skin — owed nothing to their own fairer colouring. Gwen's blonde hair and blue eyes, and Oliver's light brown hair and pale grey irises, had been bypassed in Diana by some genetic resurgence from the past. She looked, her parents agreed, more Irish than English and sometimes even Spanish, especially when the long Kentish summers turned her already burnished skin a glowing brown, a setting from which her eyes glittered with emerald intensity.

'She's a Changeling,' Mr Arnold told his wife at Diana's tenth birthday party, as their daughter raced, screaming with laughter, along the ha-ha with her friends in blazing August sunshine.

'Nothing to do with us. Our real daughter is in Faerie. This? This is a cuckoo-creature from the Underworld. She'll disappear on her twenty-first birthday when they come to reclaim her, you'll see.'

John, though, was a Janus. Tall and slim, fair-haired and blue-eyed, he could be, depending on his mood, the reflection of either of his parents. At his most thoughtful, his expression was identical to Gwen's when she hesitated before one of her unfinished paintings. But when relaxed and amused, he became a young Oliver, suppressed humour dancing behind his eyes. He had inherited his father's smile, but was more conventionally good-looking, with a straight nose and high cheekbones. From his middle teens, John had fascinated the opposite sex. He was entirely unaware of it.

James Blackwell, thought Mr Arnold as he sipped his coffee, was, at a casual glance, not dissimilar in looks to his own son. Like John he was blond, although his eyes were a brighter, almost glittering blue. He radiated a sense of self-possession, speaking in clear, confident tones. But there was something a little odd about his accent. It was public-school, certainly, but tinged with something else.

Mr Arnold tried to place the inflection as James told a wide-eyed Diana about a recent crash-landing at the squadron airfield. Was that a colonial twang he could hear? The boy's parents were in Canada, apparently; maybe the family was originally from there. But he didn't think that was it. James Blackwell's vowels were

26

slightly clipped, rather than drawled. South Africa, perhaps?

Oliver gave it up for now and looked from his son to their guest. Both men were a little over six feet tall, and from a distance they would be practically indistinguishable in their blue RAF uniforms. Closer examination would reveal that one was a flight commander and the other a more junior pilot officer. But, Mr Arnold reflected, that wouldn't count for anything, anything at all, when either boy was in the enemy's gunsights.

At the moment, though, one of them was very much in his daughter's sights. Clearly, it wasn't her brother.

6

Diana was, at nineteen, far from sure of who she really was, or would turn out to be.

'I feel like a walking question-mark,' she told a friend at Girton. 'I don't have the faintest idea how I'll end up. Part of me wants to stay here in Cambridge forever and slowly become a fossilised academic, part of me wants to marry as soon as possible and have millions of babies, part of me wants to have endless *liaisons dangereuses* and be a woman with a certain reputation — you know, like the Dean's wife here at Girton. Actually, maybe that's my answer. I should marry a Dean, have his babies and lots of affairs. What do you think?'

This little arc of reflection was, as it happens, a neat summary of Diana; a character sketch in shorthand.

She knew she possessed a fine mind. She had cruised through exams and her School Certificate, and was universally regarded by her tutors as the brightest in Girton's intake of 1937. Academia called to her. She adored Cambridge and its ancient college buildings. She loved the river that slowly rolled through the town and lazily curled through the fields and water meadows surrounding it. The thought that she might stay here her whole life was, at times, intoxicating, and brought with it a deep sense of inevitability and peace.

Sometimes, during lectures, she would stare at a tutor in full flow and say to herself: 'I *know* I could do what you're doing. I'd do it better, too.' And she would glimpse a future of stately intellectual growth. She would hone her intelligence in the great college libraries, and in lectures to, and exchanges with, the finest young minds in the land. She would compose insightful essays and ground-breaking papers which would be published to academic acclaim. And when she died, peacefully in her study, behind her desk and at a great age, there would be calls for a college to be named after her. The calls would be heeded . . .

There was no room in these fantasies for a husband, or a male partner of any kind, come to that; still less children. So Diana could not understand why, at the most unexpected moments, she was suddenly possessed by a raging desire to have babies, as many as her body could produce. This fierce passion could descend on her without warning, and consume her wordlessly, an instinct so primal and powerful that it overwhelmed her senses and left her unable to think coherently for minutes at a time.

But again, these experiences (which Diana wryly described to herself as 'my atavistic attacks') had no male component to them at all. They never included even the vaguest, shadowy image of a man who would be necessary to the business. Diana felt almost embarrassed after the blazing flames of maternal passion had flickered and died. 'When it takes hold of me and burns me,' she confided to a friend, 'I feel like some kind of towering, fiery goddess with powers to create life all by herself. Afterwards, the whole thing just seems silly — completely ridiculous, in fact.'

But there was a third Diana; the one which unsettled her the most, and about whom she confided in no one. This Diana was erotic, carnal and quivering with sexual curiosity. This Diana, she sometimes thought, her cheeks growing warm as her heart beat hard and fast, was capable of the kind of recklessness and animal lust that, later, when she remembered her dark fantasies, astonished her. The images that caused her to catch her breath never materialised when opportunity was at hand — at a college ball, or on a date with an undergraduate — but only later, in the darkness and solitude of her room. Then, this Diana hungered for a sexual experience that had so far been denied her. Or, to be more accurate, she had denied herself.

7

James Blackwell was the quintessential scholarship boy. Unapologetic elitism had been the making of him since, at eleven years old, he won the Mayor of Hackney's Junior Essay Prize, was plucked from grimy Dalston Lane Primary and installed, on a full governors' discretionary bursary, at the Stones Company Grammar School in Garnford Square, Whitechapel.

Stones Company was a trade school established in the late sixteenth century, just a few years after the Spanish Armada. By the twentieth century it had become a ladder which East End boys might scale to escape London's most economically stunted and deprived community.

Stones, for those able to rise to its academic challenge, was a way you could drag yourself out of the pit.

And James Blackwell wanted out. His father was a faint memory — a coalman who had left forever with a, 'So long, Jimmy!' when James was five — and his devoted mother was an usherette at the Whitechapel Odeon, who smuggled her son in to see the silent films of his boyhood and the 'talkies' of his teens. It was about the only frivolous pleasure of his childhood. An usherette's wages were barely enough to clothe and feed the two of them.

But James's mother compensated for her son's pinched existence with the extravagant praise she

31

heaped upon him as he grew up.

'You can be anything you want to be, Jimmy,' she told him firmly as she dressed him for school. 'You're clever and handsome and the best boy that ever was. You could be Prime Minister or an explorer or a film star . . . you're special, James; really special. You'll see. One of these days you'll surprise the world, just you see if you don't. You'll amaze everyone. And you'll have beautiful, beautiful ladies — princesses, I shouldn't wonder — who'll give anything to be your wife. Mark my words.'

James believed she was telling him the truth. Why wouldn't he? But he also knew that much of what he watched, open-mouthed, on the Odeon's dazzling screen was pure, bewitching fantasy. He gradually realised that the newsreels were much closer to reality — closer in every sense. Many of the glamorous premières, parties and soirées they highlighted offered tantalising glimpses of lives being extravagantly enjoyed just a couple of miles from where James sat in his flea-pit stall. They called it 'the West End'.

By the time he was sixteen, James Blackwell had worked it out. He had drawn himself a map to the glittering world that pulsed less than an hour's stroll from his own poverty-stricken corral.

But he wouldn't be walking or even driving to it.

He was going to fly there.

8

'A place at Cranwell? I hardly think so, Blackwell,' the headmaster murmured as he poured himself sherry from his study's sideboard. 'I gather that a lot of RAF chaps pay for their own flying lessons before even joining the service. Cranwell's a sort of finishing school for them, really. I very much doubt there are any suitable places available. I'll check, of course.'

He took a sip of his sherry, then resumed: 'Anyway, why the RAF? No history to speak of; no regimental traditions — why d'you think they call it the junior service? Because that's exactly what it is. Now, I have some connections in the Guards. I could — '

James stood up.

'I'm sure you have, sir,' he said carefully, 'but I've looked into all that, actually. It's kind of you but I think we both know that someone with my background would hardly have a meteoric career with any of the old regiments, let alone get accepted in the first place. There's only so much that elocution lessons can achieve. I'm grateful for the ones you arranged for me, but there's a limit to how far they'll take me socially. Certainly not to the rarefied heights of the Guards.'

The headmaster sighed. 'Ever the realist, eh, Blackwell? Well, I'll see what I can do.'

'No, sir,' said James. 'You'll do better than that.' He produced a sheet of paper from his

33

prefect's blazer pocket.

The headmaster raised an eyebrow. 'I beg your pardon? I'm not sure I like your tone, boy.'

'I'm not sure I care either way, sir,' replied the teenager. He placed the form on the desk between them. 'This is a typewritten reference from you to the commanding officer at Cranwell, explaining that I am ideal officer material, based on my exemplary record with the School Cadet Corps. It also gives details of my School Certificate results this summer, with special emphasis on my excellent examination score in mathematics. An 88 per cent mark, as I recall.'

The headmaster sat very still.

'Blackwell, you are barely competent in mathematics.'

The boy smiled, and waited. After a long moment, the man opposite him shifted uncomfortably in his chair.

'Look, I'm very fond of you, Blackwell — James — you know that, but I'm not signing this. You simply can't ask it of me.' He picked up the letter and tore it carefully in half.

James smiled again. 'You've got it all wrong, sir. I was your star cadet and I did exceptionally well in maths. You must have me muddled with another boy, I think. But you have a habit of doing that, don't you, sir? Do you remember when you called me Thomas instead of James? You were very apologetic. Mind you, you were rather worked up at the time, as I recall. I put it down to over-excitement.'

The headmaster's voice, when he finally spoke, was barely above a whisper. 'You little bastard. You *fucking* little bastard. I've done so much for you. I paid for lessons to stop you talking like a barrow-boy, I — '

'But sir,' James interrupted. 'You told me you *liked* me to talk like a barrow-boy. Have you forgotten that as well?'

The headmaster sank back into his chair. 'You wouldn't dare. You wouldn't dare say a word. We'd both go to prison.'

James inclined his head. 'No, sir, *I* wouldn't go to prison. I'm much too young — especially when we . . . how did you used to describe it? When we had our . . . 'special lessons'. But you, sir? You certainly *would* end up in clink; there we are in full agreement. And of course, there's the rather nasty business of corrupting a minor, too. That's got to deliver some hard labour into the bargain, I should imagine. But what do *you* think, sir?'

Frightened, shrunken eyes met those of the brightest blue.

'I think — I think you had better write me another letter to sign, you little tart.'

'Ah.' James stood up. 'Now, just for that, you can stick that one back together again, sir, and copy it out in fair hand. I wasn't all that happy with a typewritten version, to be honest, any more than I was happy with our . . . well, transactions, as I suppose we should consider them in hindsight. Anyway, recommendations of this kind are so much more intrinsically *personal* when they're handwritten, don't you agree? And you have such lovely copperplate, sir.'

The headmaster's eyes closed for a moment.

35

'Get out, just get out. You'll have your filthy letter in your pigeonhole in fifteen minutes. Then you can go back to your pigsty of a home and your scrubber of a mother, and never come back here. Term finishes next week anyway. If I see your face at this school again I'll call the police and bring charges for blackmail. I swear I shall.'

James Blackwell walked calmly to the study door. He opened it and turned back.

'No, you won't. You'll write my letter and then you'll shut up. Don't bluster, sir. It demeans you even further, if such a thing were possible. Goodbye, sir.'

9

James Blackwell may have manipulated his way into Cranwell, but once there he found himself struggling to keep up with the other trainee officers. Standards were dauntingly high. With mounting dismay he watched candidate after candidate quietly asked to leave the college after flunking academic or practical tests. His own grasp of mathematics was shaky at best. What would happen when navigation classes began?

Socially, he stood out. His carefully enunciated words fooled nobody. One night in the Prince Rupert, Cranwell College's pub of choice in nearby Newark, as he broodily nursed a beer in an unlit corner, he overheard a Kensington-born trainee pilot in the adjoining booth deliver a damning verdict.

'Blackwell? The ghastly man's a fraud, and common with it. He only got in in the first place because this is the RAF. Anywhere else and the bloody little oik would have been barred at the camp gate. Just wait until we've finished theory and start getting up in the air. He'll be kicked out of here faster than a lance-corporal who's wandered into the Officers' Mess. No *rank*. No *class*. No class at all.'

Later, lying on his iron-framed cot smoking cigarette after cigarette in the dark, James came to a decision. He couldn't make it through Cranwell on his own. He needed back-up, support. Someone with standing who would, by association, enhance his own and offer some social protection, even advice.

In other words, a well-placed friend.

A friend. James smiled faintly to himself. He'd never wanted, nor solicited a friend in his whole life. He wasn't entirely sure how to go about it.

But he wouldn't have to worry, as things turned out.

John Arnold found him first.

10

'Honestly, Di,' John murmured to his sister, keeping his voice low in case his parents and his friend at the other end of the room overheard. 'James was really up against it at Cranwell, poor bloke.'

Together they poured cognacs from the drinks trolley for everyone. John was amused to see that his sister had put on fresh lipstick during the party's move from dining room to drawing room, and changed into new stockings after he'd whispered to her that she had a slight ladder in one of them. He was half-surprised she'd not gone the whole hog and put on a different frock; he was sure she'd been tempted. But she'd returned downstairs in the same dark red woollen dress which she knew showed off her figure at its best.

'I hope James appreciates your efforts, sis,' he murmured, nudging her conspiratorially.

'Steady,' warned Diana, as she slopped a little of the brandy over the tray. 'This might have to last. Everyone's saying the war will be over by Christmas, but that's exactly what Daddy says people thought last time, and it was four years. I've already told Mummy to go easy on the tinned salmon.'

Five balloon glasses were placed on the tarnished silver tray.

'Anyway, never mind me,' said Diana. 'Go on.

39

What d'you mean about James being up against it?'

'Not here,' answered her brother, glancing across the room. 'Fetch some cigarettes and I'll smoke one with you on the ha-ha. I'll tell you all about James there.'

★ ★ ★

John had never seen class snobbery at work until Cranwell. It made him deeply uncomfortable. His own public school, Hedgebury, had operated a generous system of scholarships and assisted places. Most of the boys there were sons of professional men — lawyers like his own father, businessmen, doctors, politicians. The school was run on modern lines as an uncompromising meritocracy. Assumptions of superiority by birthright were frowned on.

True, there had been occasional bouts of trouble with 'town boys' when older Hedgeberians found themselves at a loose end in the local High Street on their half-days off. But these run-ins were relished by both sides, and had more the flavour of sporting fixtures than class war.

John found the patronising of James at Cranwell unpleasant. His own public-school background had taught him that it was usually best to let others fight their own battles, but even so, he looked for a way to offer quiet support.

The chance came after an afternoon's navigation instruction. James went straight to the room he shared with three others and sat alone, surrounded by textbooks on navigation theory. John passed the open door in time to hear a deep sigh coming from within.

He hesitated, then rapped on the doorframe. 'Everything all right in there? Not too much doom and gloom? *Nil desperandum* and all that?'

James looked up from the page. 'Fuck off, mate. Don't give me all that cheery balls. It'll take more than a Latin tag to get me through this lot.' He gestured at the books. 'Trigonometry I can just about cope with. It's these bloody equations that have me floored.'

He rose and moved to the doorway, hand outstretched, to introduce himself. 'James. James Blackwell.'

'John Arnold.' They shook hands. 'Actually, I'm not really John at all — I'm Robert. Don't ask. It's a sort of family tradition. We all change our names. I have no idea why.'

James laughed. 'Well, I've always been James, though right now I wish I were someone else altogether. Someone who could understand this stuff.' He gestured towards the books. 'If I don't crack it soon, I'll be out on my arse like those other poor sods.'

John sat down in a battered leather armchair and swung one knee over the side. 'I could help, if you liked,' he said. 'I don't think we've got the best of navigation instructors, as it happens. He rattles too quickly through everything. But I'm lucky — it mostly comes pretty naturally to me. I could go over things with you more slowly until it sticks. You'll get it eventually.'

The other man stared at him. 'Why would you do that? We hardly know each other.'

John stood up and stretched. 'It'd be one in the eye for those braying idiots who think being born into high society makes them better than chaps like you. Or me, come to that. They'd love to see you booted out of Cranwell; it would confirm all their ghastly prejudices. Let's give them a kick in the pants, shall we?'

★ ★ ★

Diana drew thoughtfully on her cigarette in the darkness. 'You must be a bloody effective teacher, brother,' she said. 'Too effective for your own good, perhaps. He's ended up a flight commander and you're a humble pilot officer.' She giggled and poked John in the ribs. 'You should show him some respect. Why haven't I seen you salute him or call him 'sir'?'

Her brother's glowing cigarette end arced over the ha-ha as he flicked it into the little stream beyond. 'Oh, James isn't interested in any of that nonsense,' he said. 'Obviously on base we observe the proprieties, but not here. We're friends. It was a real stroke of luck that our first posting after Cranwell was to the same squadron. Anyway, I haven't finished telling you about him.'

11

James Blackwell, thanks to long hours of private tuition from his new friend, scraped through his navigation exams. The frightful condescension directed at him by Cranwell's self-styled social elite eased somewhat, but that had nothing to do with the exams. John was popular among the other trainee pilots and his friendship with James conferred a degree of social acceptance on the other man — enough, at least, to mute the more contemptuous comments about him behind his back.

'But here's the thing, sis,' John continued. 'He's actually got more blue blood in him than the lot of them. His mother used to be in service. James won't tell me the name of the family, but I get the impression they're not just well-connected — they're the kind of people half those chinless wonders at Cranwell would give the family silver to be connected to.

'Apparently, the young Miss Blackwell got herself into a compromising position with Lord Whoever-it-was and the upshot was James. She was chucked out without references, ages before the birth — the usual story — and ended up waiting on tables in London. She married a no-good who walked out on her and she had to bring James up alone.

'Now she works in a cinema in Mile End or somewhere. James won a scholarship to a good school and dragged himself up by his own bootstraps. Until he got his commission he didn't have two pennies to rub together. I really admire him.'

Diana frowned. 'But I thought he'd come here for a few days because his parents are in Canada. That's what you told Mummy on the phone yesterday.'

Her brother took her arm and began walking them back to the house. 'That's because James has discovered that telling the truth about his background — well, his real father's family, anyway — usually backfires. People think he's making it all up and either laugh at him or steer well clear from then on. He still won't reveal his father's identity to me and God knows, he knows he can trust me.'

Diana looked up at her brother in the near-total dark as they reached the Dower House's French windows, and prepared to slip inside the blackout curtains that she, Lucy and their mother had hastily put up that morning. 'Yes, but how do you *know* he's not making it up? You seem to have taken an awful lot on trust, John. And why lie to Mummy about that Canada business? Why not tell her, and Daddy, what you just told me?'

John shook his head. 'Because the rest of the chaps have been told the Canada version, that's all. He just wants to keep things simple.'

He turned to his sister. 'Wait until you get to know him, Diana. You'll see. I'm sure he'll confide in you, and Oliver and Mum too, in the end. Trust me, sis, he's as straight as they come.

James is probably the most upstanding chap I know.' He opened the windows. 'Ready?'

They prepared to move quickly through the thick black curtains. 'Ready.'

A moment later they were inside and blinking in the sudden light. Voices drifted from the dining room across the hall.

'And there's something else you should know about him,' John said, lowering his voice and adjusting the drapes so no chink of light escaped outside. 'You asked why he outranks me. Well, I'll tell you. He's the best damn flyer in the squadron — by a long chalk. He might have needed some help with his navigation, but my God, the man can fly. He's a total natural — first one of all of us to go solo, and he was sent to train on Spits while the rest of us were still lumbering around in bi-planes like Gladiators. Christ help the German pilot who comes up against James Blackwell.'

Arm-in-arm, they went in to join the others.

12

Diana didn't have the chance to get to know her brother's friend any better on his first visit to the Dower House. Breakfast on Monday morning was interrupted by a phone call from the men's squadron leader. John came in from the hall, laughing.

'What a muck-up, good people; what a muck-up. Word has come down from Mount Olympus that we're not to be disbanded, after all: it was all a huge mistake in the big flap.' He turned to James, who was loading kedgeree from a silver server onto his plate. 'We're being transferred instead to another group, Jimmy — the best of the lot. Eleven Group, my fine friend. We're going to be a part of Eleven Group!'

'What's Eleven Group, darling?' Gwen asked. 'And why do you both look so pleased with yourselves?'

'You tell them, Jimmy,' said John. 'I'll ring for a taxi to the station.' He hurried from the room.

Gwen, Oliver and Diana stared expectantly at their guest as he joined them at the table, his plate piled high with rice, chopped egg and smoked haddock.

'Eleven Group's the collection of fighter squadrons assigned to defend the south-east corner of England — in other words, here,' he explained, forking food into his mouth. 'It's where pilots like John and I are most likely to see some fun. If Jerry sends his planes to bomb London, we'll have to stop him. Or, as we're closest to France, we might get sent there to support the Army when Herr Hitler invades, which he's certain to do. Then of course there's the Channel, and protecting the shipping lanes. However this war turns out, we'll be at the main party. It's terrific news.'

Gwen stared down at her plate; Diana looked thoughtful. After a short silence, Mr Arnold cleared his throat.

'Well, Mr Blackwell, I can see why this is good news for you both, and I congratulate you, I do, really. Forgive us, but from our side of the matter it will mean . . . well, a good deal of worry about our son.' He inclined his head. 'And, of course, yourself.'

'A good deal of worry? This is terrible news, Oliver — just *terrible*.' Gwen had lifted her head and was glaring at her husband. 'Why does it have to be James? Why can't he go and defend somewhere else — oh, I don't know, *Wales* or somewhere? Why should they put our boy *directly* in harm's way?'

She turned to their visitor. 'And how can you talk about it being 'fun'? I'm sorry, I don't mean to be rude, but surely you realise . . . '

Her husband raised a hand. 'Darling, please stop.' He smiled faintly at their guest. 'Forgive us, Mr Blackwell, we need a little time to absorb this. We've only been at war for three days so there's been a lot to take in. I'm sure your own mother will be as concerned as we

47

are when she hears your news.'

His son came back into the room. 'Taxi'll be here in half an hour, so we'd better get ready.' He stared at them all. 'Good God, why does everyone look so boot-faced? Jimmy, you haven't told them one of your awful jokes, have you?'

Nobody smiled.

'Mr Blackwell's been telling us about Eleven Group,' Diana said in a small voice. 'It sounds rather dangerous, that's all. Mum's a bit upset.'

Her brother walked over to Gwen and kissed the top of her head. 'Nothing to worry about,' he said cheerfully. 'We're flying Spitfires, remember? There's nothing to touch a Spit. I've got eight machine guns to swat the blighters with and a ruddy great engine in front of me to keep the bullets off. Piece of cake.' He turned to his friend. 'Half an hour, Jimmy. The CO says we've got to fly to Upminster by five o'clock. That's our new base. Shame it's in Essex and not Kent, but you can't have everything.'

His father stood up. 'What am I thinking of? I can run you both to the station myself. Cancel your cab, John.'

The young man shook his head. 'Uh-uh. There's a war on. You're going to need every drop of petrol for yourself. It's bound to be rationed sooner or later. Which reminds me — I reckon I'll get myself a motor bike. Upminster can't be more than twenty or thirty miles from here, so when I'm not on flying duty I can roar down here and see you all, even if it's only for an afternoon.'

He turned to his mother. 'See, Mum? It's not

48

all bad news. You'll soon be sick of the sight of me.'

Gwen stood up and kissed his cheek. 'I very much doubt that, dear.' She drew a deep breath and turned to James.

'Mr Blackwell, I must apologise for my loss of control just now. It was perfectly selfish of me. Please say you forgive me.'

'There's nothing to forgive, Mrs Arnold,' he replied. 'But I shall only let it pass if you all stop calling me Mr Blackwell. From now on, I insist you call me James.'

Mr Arnold inclined his head in agreement. James it is, then.

He looked at his watch. 'And now, everyone, war or no war, I must go to work.'

13

When Diana arrived back at Cambridge for the Michaelmas Term, she was disconcerted to see how few male undergraduates now cycled around the town. There were a great many more young men strolling about in uniform, though. It unsettled her and she was glad to retreat to the all-female fastness of Girton.

Her college was two miles from the centre of Cambridge, and kept itself quite separate from the other campuses. Its Victorian founders had decided that a *cordon sanitaire* was required to protect Girton girls from marauding male students. Not that penetrating the establishment's defences was beyond most resourceful young men. As fast as college porters sealed off one illicit point of access, another would be found, usually with the assistance of those inside who were happy to help accommodate a bit of marauding.

'We might as well move into the middle of town lock, stock and barrel now,' complained Sally, Diana's closest friend at Girton. 'We'd be quite safe. At this rate there'll be no chaps left in Cambridge to pester us, more's the pity.'

Diana often wondered if Girton would be quite as much fun without Sally. She was blonde and bouncy; a judge's daughter from York, with a wicked gift for mimicry. There wasn't a lecturer in college she couldn't impersonate. During the summer holidays she had telephoned Diana at the Dower House pretending to be her senior tutor, accusing her of plagiarism in a recent examination paper. An outraged Diana had been on the point of apoplexy when Sally finally broke into shrieks of laughter. 'It's me — Sal — you dodo!'

Now Diana looked at her friend, who was energetically brushing her hair back from a wide brow. 'What about all the soldiers?' she said. 'Don't they count?'

'Never mind the soldiers. It's the RAF boys I like. Those blue uniforms . . . *hello!* I do believe you're blushing, Diana! Am I about to hear a confession? I hope so. It's about time you stopped living like a nun and had some fun.'

Diana sighed. 'I *do* have fun. I've been out with heaps of boys, as you well know.'

'You've been out with precisely three. And you've not smuggled one of them back here, not even for a drink. Anyway, you're avoiding my question. Why did you blush when I said,' here Sally paused for emphasis and waggled her head as she pronounced breathily, 'ARR . . . AY . . . EFFF!'

'Stop it!'

'There, you're blushing again! Come on, tell your Aunty Sal all about it. You know you'll have to eventually, so you might as well spit it out now.' Sally tucked her legs under herself and settled back into her armchair. 'Proceed.'

Diana smiled at her. 'All right. It's nothing, really. Nothing at all. Just that my brother came home last month with another pilot from his squadron. They met at Cranwell last year. Anyway, he's called James and, Sally, he's so attractive. He's exactly what you imagine when you hear the words 'Spitfire pilot'. It's ridiculous, really.'

'Quick, quick! Describe him!'

'Oh, I don't know — tall and fair, with incredibly blue eyes. He's extraordinarily confident, although he's only my brother's age — and there's something . . . oh, I don't know. Something a bit mysterious about him, I suppose. He certainly has a past.'

Sally sat up. 'A past? Whatever do you mean?'

'Well, I'm not supposed to know this and I probably shouldn't tell you, but his mother used to work as a maid or something for a really important family, and she got taken advantage of. I think he was a lord. Anyway, it was a frightful scandal and it all had to be hushed up and she was sent packing before her pregnancy started showing. James is her son.'

Her friend stared at her. 'That's quite a story, Di. And you believe it, do you?'

Diana shrugged. 'I don't know what to think. My brother certainly believes it and he's James's best friend. He thinks the world of him. I've only met the man twice — at dinner and then at breakfast next morning — but he's tremendously impressive. Clever, and really rather funny. My parents obviously liked him a lot. He didn't strike me as the sort to be a fantasist at all.'

Sally nodded. 'All right. So when are you going to see him again?'

'Oh, Lord knows. They're both stationed at

Upminster and that's miles away down in Essex. During the Christmas holidays, perhaps.'

'Nonsense.' Sally shook her head. 'If he's anything like the fighter boys I've heard about, he'll be up here in Cambridge before you can say 'Heil Hitler'.'

Diana burst out laughing. 'What? That's ridiculous. I don't even know if he has the slightest interest in me.'

'Don't be silly, dear,' Sally said dismissively. 'You're beautiful. Of course he'll come.'

14

Upminster was turning out to be a disappointment. As the autumn days shortened, so did the squadron's patience with the war.

'Nothing's happening. Absolutely bloody, disgustingly, boringly, pointlessly *nothing*,' said a young flight lieutenant as he drifted into the Officers' Mess with the morning paper.

'They're calling it the Phoney War and they're damn right,' he continued. 'Why doesn't somebody *do* something? Invade somewhere? Drop some bombs on someone? I had more thrills and spills on the bloody dodgems last August Bank Holiday weekend.'

James Blackwell twitched irritably. He was deep in thought over a post-breakfast cigarette. He had a lot to plan, and a lot to decide. This idiot prattling broke his concentration. He pushed past the fool, slipped outside and began to pace the aerodrome's perimeter. He needed air.

Becoming friends with John Arnold had turned out to be one of the smartest moves he'd ever made; perhaps even better than the business with his headmaster. It hadn't just got him through a sticky patch at Cranwell, it had opened other doors, too.

Specifically, the doors to the Dower House.

Blackwell hated being poor. For the first time in his life he now had a bit of money to buy a

54

few luxuries, but a ten-year-old battered two-seater sports car didn't count as much of one. A flight commander's pay was barely enough to keep him in beer, fags and petrol, the odd night out and a woman's favours. If he didn't have bed and board courtesy of the RAF, he'd be right up against it.

Arnold had things much cushier, the lucky bastard. He got an allowance from Daddy and was able to afford anything he wanted — even to get his bloody uniform tailored. Granted, Arnold had paid for Blackwell's tunic and trousers to be altered too, but that wasn't the point. And that new motor bike of his had cost five times what Blackwell had paid for a sputtering, clapped-out car with a leaky roof.

Then there was the parents' home. Jesus, compared to his mother's wretched flat in Whitechapel the place was a bloody palace. Compared to *most* houses, it was a palace. How many bedrooms were there? He'd counted at least nine and that didn't include the maid's quarters. The fixtures and fittings were of the very best — beautiful furniture, much of it obviously antique, one of the biggest wireless sets he'd ever laid eyes on and what looked suspiciously like one of those new television sets built into it. Not that there'd be any more television programmes until the end of the war, but again, that wasn't the point.

He'd noticed the way the girl had looked at him. Blackwell knew that look of old. He'd been getting it even more since his commission. Even the ugly buggers on the squadron were getting their legs over now simply because they wore the blue uniform of the RAF. He supposed it was because it made them somehow look more modern than the poor Army sods in their boring, khaki-brown tunics. Only the Navy could compete with the RAF when it came to uniforms.

James Blackwell knew that one of the secrets of his success was sizing up a situation early on, coming to a decision, and then sticking to it. He'd worked out how to play his headmaster at Stones like a hooked fish, and then waited patiently for the right moment to reel him in. It hadn't been pleasant — Christ, parts of it were repulsive to him — but he'd got exactly the result he wanted.

Now he had the Arnolds squarely in his sights. Yes, there were richer families out there and who knows, they might have daughters even more gorgeous than this one, but James Blackwell had learned a long time ago that a bird in the hand was worth two in the bush. The Arnolds would do very well, thank you. They were rolling in it; they had a stunning daughter who, with luck, would bring a generous settlement on her marriage. The lawyer might even stump up for a house to get them started in, who knew? He looked the kind of doting, sentimental type who'd do something like that. He certainly had the means, that was obvious.

There was the slight problem of that stupid story he'd told James about his parentage, which James was certain John had repeated to Diana, but he could bluff that one out indefinitely. At

56

least it had the advantage of being half-true, and in the unlikely event of any of the Arnolds meeting his mother (very unlikely) she'd say exactly what he told her to.

If everything went the way he planned — and it would — James Blackwell and Diana Arnold would be walking down the aisle by the summer of 1940.

By the time he had circumnavigated the airfield, he concluded that the next stage in the rise and rise of James Blackwell wasn't merely achievable, it was inevitable.

He went to find the girl's brother. He only needed two things. An address, and a telephone number.

15

Diana did not believe for one moment that James Blackwell would call on her in Cambridge. He would have far better and more important things to do with his squadron, and anyway, the two of them had only exchanged a few remarks during his fleeting visit to the Dower House. It was hardly the basis for . . . for what, exactly? An affair? Was that what she wanted to happen?

After her conversation with Sally, Diana took herself to the college library, selected a book at random, and retreated to a secluded corner to think things through. She had an analytical mind and was impatient with what she thought of to herself as 'drift'. As far back as she could remember, Diana had always wanted to know where she was heading and how she would get there.

This single-minded attitude was what had led her to apply to Girton in the first place, two years ago, despite well-intentioned opposition. Her friends in Kent had told her she would be wasting three years of her life. Most of them seemed content to be launched into society by their well-heeled parents, the chief aim being to find a suitable husband. Quite a few of them were already engaged or actually married.

Even her headmistress had tried to discourage her.

'You have to face facts, Diana,' she'd said.

'Girton isn't a proper university college. They don't exist for women, anywhere. You won't get a degree however hard you study — Cambridge doesn't recognise female graduates. Nowhere does.'

It was true. Ever since opening its doors in Cambridge in 1873, Girton had had to wrestle every concession from the university of which it aspired to be a full member. Even now, more than sixty years later, it was still academically semi-detached from the other colleges.

Diana had read up on Girton's history. She was intrigued and impressed that thirty years before the Suffragettes, women were fighting to be treated on equal terms with men. The battle was still being fought. If she went there, she would be a part of living history.

But the day after she'd dropped her application to Girton into the village post box, Diana was assailed by sudden doubts.

'It's a complete waste of time, isn't it?' she asked despairingly of her parents that evening at dinner. 'Everyone's right. There's no point. I could work twice as hard as the boys at Cambridge but I still won't get a degree. I must be mad.'

Mr Arnold, who had been inclined to this viewpoint from the very beginning, opened his mouth to gently agree but his wife slapped the table with the flat of her hand.

'Don't you dare talk like that, Diana! Don't you *dare!*'

Mr Arnold was surprised. The last time he had seen Gwen this agitated was when he told her she had no case for a libel action against the art critic who had been so dismissive of her first exhibition.

'Even if you don't get a degree yourself, one day other women will, and it'll be because of girls like you. You've read all the stuff Girton sent here when you told them you were thinking of applying. They're almost there! Cambridge University has made heaps of concessions — one more heave and Girton will be in! It might even happen while you're studying there, who knows? Just wait a minute . . . '

She went to the oak Welsh dresser and rummaged through a drawer. 'Yes, here it is. It came with all the other things they sent to you.' She unfolded a single sheet of paper, grabbed her reading glasses from the dresser and jammed them on her nose.

'This was written over sixty years ago. It's about the very first three women to study at Girton. I know it's sentimental and awfully 'jolly hockey sticks', but it's brimful of pride and passion. Listen!' Gwen cleared her throat.

'*And when the goal is won, girls*
And women get degrees,
We'll cry 'Long live the three girls
Who showed the way to these!
Who showed the way we follow
Who knew no doubts or fears,
Our Woodhead, Cook, and Lumsden —
The Girton Pioneers!''

Diana burst out laughing. 'Beautifully read,

60

Mum, and thank you. But that decides it, I'll have to go to Girton now. They're desperately in need of some new songs.'

Gwen laughed too, a little embarrassed. 'Yes, better verses have been written, I grant you, but Diana — of course you must go! Even if you don't get a 'proper' degree, you'll benefit hugely from the experience, and as you yourself have said, you'll be a part of history and progress. I won't hear of any other outcome. Don't you agree, Oliver?'

Mr Arnold smiled at her, spreading his hands. 'You've missed your vocation, Gwen. If some of my juniors in the firm could make cases as succinct and compelling as you just did, I'd take a sleeping partnership.'

So it was settled. In the autumn of 1937, Diana's parents delivered her to Girton. The green Humber swept under the gate-house and past the neo-Tudor red brick and terracotta facades, built around close-cropped grass quadrangles. 'Very nice,' murmured Mr Arnold, glancing around. 'Very grand indeed, I must say. I'm surprised they don't charge for entry — and are you sure they allow us chaps in here? Am I about to be run off the ranch? Should I have dropped you outside the gate-house?'

'Don't be absurd, Daddy. It's not a nunnery.'

Now, two years later, Diana sat in the library and thought long and hard about what she wanted from her life. She was still only twenty. She was coming up to her crucial final year at Girton and knew she couldn't afford any distractions. Yes, she was strongly attracted to

James Blackwell, but so what? He was at war and the two of them were ninety miles apart.

In any case, there was nothing to decide, was there? She hardly knew the man and as she'd said to Sally, the idea that he'd come up to Cambridge to see her was preposterous. She was behaving like a silly schoolgirl with a crush; she had been since the day she met the man. It was ridiculous. She needed to grow up and get down to some hard work.

A few minutes later, Diana crossed the courtyard on her way back to her room. Darkness was falling and as she walked past the porter's lodge, she could see its elderly occupant fussing with his blackout curtain. He seemed to be having trouble with it. She stopped and called to him. 'Want a hand with that?'

He glanced at her through the window and beckoned.

'I've been looking for you, Miss Arnold. No, I can manage this all right, thanks very much. There's a message for you, miss.' He nodded to a table by the door. 'It's on that slip of paper there. Gentleman telephoned about an hour ago. Wants you to call him back. Drat this thing, I can't get it to close properly . . . '

While the porter grumbled, Diana picked up the piece of paper with her name and a telephone number neatly written on it and, underneath, the briefest of scripts.

Flt Cmndr Blackwell. C/O Officers' Mess, Upminster. Please call back.

16

The battered MG Midget pulled up at the camp gate so its driver could show his pass to the guard. James Blackwell had managed to wangle two days' leave, which he reckoned would be enough to take care of everything, for now anyway.

He'd saved up as many petrol coupons as he could for this trip — tricky, as they expired soon after issue to discourage hoarding — but he'd had to shell out for a couple of black-market jerry cans of fuel, all the same. He calculated he'd have just about enough to get him to Cambridge and back, if he went easy on the throttle. Not that the 1932 convertible could do much more than forty without feeling like it was going to shake itself to pieces. It had been a long time since the car had come anywhere close to the 78mph top speed it was originally capable of. Black smoke from leaking cylinder gaskets billowed behind the two-seater every time he pulled away from traffic lights. It was embarrassing.

Christmas was long gone and the little car's canvas top had been up since October. But the fit was poor and it was freezing inside, with a constant forced draught of cold air rushing underneath the tatty, patched-up hood.

James loathed his car. It symbolised everything he wanted to leave behind him. That included the girl who was about to receive an unexpected visit.

Jane Timming worked in the dress shop in Upminster High Street. She had a flair for designing and making women's clothes. Even now, barely seven months into the war, material was becoming scarce, but Jane could work wonders with the bits and pieces she picked up cheap from jumble sales. She had a good 'eye' — she'd even taken a sewing needle to her new boyfriend's already exquisitely tailored RAF uniform, telling him that one side of the expensively cinched-in waist didn't quite match the other. She'd been right. The jacket now fitted perfectly.

Jane had met her flight commander at a dance at the aerodrome. She'd seen him notice her the moment she walked into the hall, and he went straight up to her, just like that. Normally, boys were shy to begin with. They eyed her up from a safe distance, intimidated by her beauty: the glossy, dark brunette hair and the large saucer-shaped hazel eyes. Even the most confident lads stuttered and blushed when they finally got up the nerve to speak to her.

James Blackwell hadn't been like that at all. He'd taken her hand — without so much as a by-your-leave — and bowed, ever so slightly.

'There's something I've got to tell you straight away.' He'd spoken so quietly that she had to lean in close to him to catch the words. 'You must be the prettiest girl I've ever seen in my whole life. You simply *have* to dance with me.'

He'd led her to the centre of the floor,

introducing himself when they got there. 'I'm James, by the way. James Blackwell.' And then he had kissed the back of her hand, just like in the films. No one had ever done that to her before. You'd think it might be a bit — well, *corny*, as the Yanks said, but it wasn't at all. It was lovely. She felt as if she'd been asked to dance by a prince, really she did.

Since then, she'd seen him at least twice a week. He took her to the pictures, or drove her out into the Essex countryside in his sweet little sports car. None of her previous boyfriends had had a car. They'd had to catch the bus or walk to wherever they were going. And a car meant that you could — you know. Do things. Do things she'd never done before, and that she wouldn't dare tell her friends about, not likely. If her mum or dad were ever to find out . . . it didn't bear thinking about. They'd throw her out, bag and baggage.

She introduced James to her parents in the little terraced house she had lived in all her life. They'd both been in absolute awe of him, with his officer's uniform and wings on his tunic and his stories about flying. James had been so sweet to them. She'd seen an expression on her dad's face she'd never seen before. She couldn't think how to describe it, not until she came across the right words in a soppy magazine story the next day. 'Hero worship'. That was it. James was a hero, and everyone worshipped him, including her. She'd do anything and everything he asked of her. In fact, she already had. And that had been lovely too.

Now she was putting on her hat and coat ready to walk home for her lunch, when the shop door opened and the little bell above it jingled. She turned to see James, wrapped in his thick RAF greatcoat, coming in from the pavement outside.

'James! What are you doing here? What a nice surprise!'

'Hello, Jane.' He stepped forward and kissed her on the mouth. 'I'm glad I caught you before you went home. I'd rather tell you this here, and not with your mother around. Are we alone?'

She nodded. 'Yes. Mrs Purbright had to pop out and she left me in charge, didn't she? I was just going to lock up for an hour or so . . . Sorry, tell me what?'

He was expressionless. 'I'll get straight to it. We're finished, I'm afraid. I don't wish to see you any more and I have no plans to do so. I've met someone else and we're to be married, probably in the summer. That's all there is to it.'

She stood frozen. Then a crooked smile appeared. 'What? This is a joke, ain't it, James? You're having me on.'

'Of course I'm not. Don't be ridiculous. I'll say it again: we're finished. There's someone else.'

He glanced at his watch.

'Come on, Jane, I'm an officer and you're — well, you're a shopgirl. Surely you didn't tell yourself you had any kind of future with me?' He saw her eyes widen. 'Ah, you did. Well, more fool you. I never promised you anything, did I? We've had some good times together, but it's over now.'

He looked at his watch again, more impatiently. 'Look — I have a long way to drive and I think it might snow. I should get started. This is goodbye, Jane.'

Perhaps she'd closed her eyes in shock, just for a moment, but when she opened them again, he'd gone. She was reminded of a magic trick she'd seen at the theatre, last Christmas. One minute the magician was standing right there in front of them all; the next, he'd vanished in a puff of smoke, just like that.

James had disappeared as quickly as the magician. She couldn't believe it. After a few moments, she found she was able to move. She rushed to the door, opened it and looked up and down the street. James was nowhere to be seen.

She closed the door again. A high-pitched tone began to hum inside her head.

Alone in the shop, she swayed slightly and then, very slowly, crumpled to the floor.

17

James Blackwell never acted on impulse. He always thought things through before coming to a decision. Afterwards, he rarely analysed what he'd done. He couldn't see the point, unless it was to congratulate himself, as he did now.

He'd timed it and reckoned the whole business of dumping the girl had taken no more than forty-five seconds, if that. A personal best; had to be.

He dismissed the scene from his mind as he looked out for signs to the A11, the road that would take him straight up to Cambridge, and Diana. She was expecting him. With luck he'd be there before dark. One headlight wasn't working; it never bloody had — but if the RAF's Met boys were on the ball, he reckoned he should just about stay ahead of the late-season snow.

He began singing softly to himself. It was one of his mother's favourites. 'Moonlight Becomes You . . . '

He was experiencing a sensation that had become familiar to him over the years, and he welcomed it as an old friend. An unmistakable, satisfying feeling.

Everything falling smoothly into place.

But it *had* been a tricky few months, he had to admit. That phone call to Diana last autumn when she was back at Girton had turned out to be somewhat premature, to say the least. It was meant to be the opening move in his campaign to have an engagement ring on her finger by Christmas, but infuriatingly the war mucked all that up. Without notice, all leave was cancelled, and the squadron flew endless training exercises and boring patrols up and down the Channel. Then January plunged the whole country into blizzards and the coldest winter anyone could remember. Driving all the way to Cambridge was out of the question. He'd have needed a battle tank to get through. The big freeze lasted for weeks and weeks.

One bright spot was that Diana had returned his phone call (that very same evening, in fact — an encouraging sign) and they'd had a most agreeable chat. James had long ago discovered that girls were flattered to be asked questions about themselves and he had shown great interest in Diana's life in the university town. He'd managed to make her laugh, too, and she'd ended up happily accepting his suggestion that he motor up to Cambridge the very next weekend, to take her to dinner.

Cancelled leave had put paid to that. He'd had to telephone another message, explaining. Then came the atrocious weather. He'd never known such a run of bad luck. Of course, he'd written some letters to Diana to keep the pot boiling, as it were, and her replies were friendly enough, but he could hardly move matters forward in any significant way until he saw her again.

He had thought he might get his chance at Christmas — the Arnolds had invited him to spend it with them at the Dower House — but the squadron 'leave lottery' scuppered that, too. To his fury he drew one of the short straws. So he'd been stuck in Upminster with the other saps and losers while John Arnold went down to Kent alone. Another lousy break. It was maddening. If he hadn't had the delightful distraction of that shop-girl over the last couple of months, he'd have gone up the wall.

But now it was the first week of April 1940, and finally, he'd got his leave. He was back in control. Doing what he did best.

James Blackwell always made his own luck.

18

As the MG spluttered its way towards Cambridge, John Arnold was on his motor bike going in the opposite direction, headed for the Dower House. He had a two-day pass too, his first leave since Christmas. Gwen was longing to see her son again, and although her husband affected nonchalance, secretly he was too. When they'd spoken over the phone a day or so earlier, Oliver casually asked if John might be able to get off camp and come down to Kent — 'your mother's missing you rather badly, you know, old son' — and his heart had leaped at the reply: 'Actually, yes, I think I can. Tell Mum I'll try and get there for the weekend.'

John's parents had gradually become reconciled to his role as a fighter pilot. He didn't seem to be in any immediate danger. In fact, this war was developing into more of an inconvenience than a desperate struggle for survival. A few days after New Year, butter, bacon and sugar had been rationed, but that was an irritant, not a cause for despair. Now petrol was 'on points', but that seemed manageable enough too.

There had been a few skirmishes in the air, none of them involving John or James's squadron, and some incidents at sea, but neither side had attempted a lethal thrust. The old battlefields of France and Belgium were dormant and safely under Allied control. Perhaps all the

71

squaring-up of the previous autumn had been a lot of bluster and Herr Hitler would see sense.

'As Diana always says,' Gwen said comfortably to her son over breakfast on his first morning home, 'the French have a huge army and, anyway, our men are there with them too, now. Look at this.' She showed him the headline on the front page of the morning paper: HITLER'S MISSED THE BUS! 'It's too bad, darling. I know you wanted an adventure but your father and I think it's all going to fizzle out.'

Mr Arnold looked up from his own newspaper. 'Hey, I didn't quite say that.'

His son smiled at him ruefully. 'Mum's probably right, Dad. And truly, I'll be glad if you are, Mum, although I'll also feel a bit let down, in a completely selfish sort of way. We've all trained so hard and for so long — and it's so exciting, in the most primitive sense, when you're barrelling along through the air at three hundred miles an hour and you flick open the firing-ring and press the button and eight machine-guns simultaneously burst into life ... It's pretty indescribable. The noise is *incredible*, I can tell you. Like eight great canvas sails being violently ripped in half. The whole aircraft shudders and you feel like — I don't know . . . like an avenging angel.'

His father stared at him. 'My word. And what does the inestimable Flight Commander Blackwell make of it all?'

John shrugged. 'He feels like I do. That it'd be a real shame to have done all these rehearsals and not put on at least one show.'

The breakfast-room door opened and Lucy came in. 'Please, ma'am, it's almost eight o'clock and I've put the wireless on. It should have warmed up by now.'

Listening to the first main BBC news of the day had become an institution at the Dower House since the war began. Lucy was allowed to stay and listen. She had a brother in France with the British Expeditionary Force.

The four of them moved into the drawing room. The radio's speaker issued a promising hiss, and then a deep voice boomed out. *'This is the BBC in London. Please stand by for an important announcement.'*

'Hello,' said Mr Arnold, as John whistled. 'This is new.'

More static. Oliver and Gwen stared at their son, who was pressing a forefinger against his lips. Gwen reached for her husband's hand. The wireless seemed to briefly whisper something they could not quite catch, and then the deep voice was back.

'This morning, powerful German forces invaded Denmark and Norway. It is understood that Denmark is seeking an immediate surrender, but that Norway is fighting on. The Prime Minister, in a statement, said that . . . '

'This is it, everyone,' Mr Arnold said, when the news bulletin was over. He jumped up and began to pace the room. 'This is most definitely *IT*. A classic spring offensive. Hitler is guarding his northern flank and grabbing some extra ports; then he'll attack in the west.' He turned to his son. 'You'd better call your unit. I'd imagine they'll want to — '

He was interrupted by the telephone in the hall.

'That'll be them, pound to a penny. You take it, John.'

As their son strode from the room, followed by Lucy, Mr Arnold and his wife stared at each other. There were tears in Gwen's eyes, and she took a deep, shuddering breath.

'I didn't expect it would feel quite like this, Oliver, when it came to it,' she said.

'What do you mean, dear?'

'That I would feel — well, so enormously proud of him. I'm actually not afraid at all. I'm just proud.'

John rushed back into the room. 'Yup, that was Upminster all right. Immediate recall, as of yesterday! I'm off. I'll ring you as soon as I know what's happening. Bye, Mum. Bye, Dad.'

'Goodbye, darling,' said Gwen, hugging him tight. 'You'll be all right. I know you will.'

'Of course I will. We all will. I keep telling you.'

His father had found his keys. 'I'll open the garage for your bike. Do you have enough petrol to get back? I've a couple of jerry cans you can have.'

'I've plenty. But thanks, Dad.' John hesitated, and then looked steadily at them both.

'Look, you're not to worry, either of you. Practice makes perfect, and I've had heaps of it. Everything's going to be fine.'

The silence that followed this was broken by

Lucy, who almost ran into the room.

'Excuse me, sir,' she panted, 'but I've brought your bag downstairs. You'd only unpacked a few things and I think I've put them all back.'

The three of them came to the door to see him off. There was a light dusting of snow on the gravel drive and Mr Arnold called to his son as he wheeled his motor bike out from the garage: 'Mind you don't skid!'

John grinned, eyes shielded behind goggles. 'Dad, if I can manage not to prang a Spitfire, I can manage this thing, trust me. Bye, everyone!'

And with a deafening roar and a back-spray of snow and gravel, he was gone.

19

Over a hundred miles north, Cambridge was under three inches of snow. It had begun falling in earnest as James Blackwell swung his little car under Girton's gate-house, and pulled up, looking for somewhere to park. A porter came puffing up behind him and rapped on the driver's window.

'Excuse me, sir, you can't come in here,' he said. 'No visitors after dark, without a pass. I must ask you to leave the college precincts immediately.'

'That's all right,' said James. He enjoyed this kind of confrontation with functionaries. All one had to do was speak complete nonsense in a confident tone to assert control.

'I'm here on RAF business,' he said pleasantly, briefly showing his leave-pass. 'The Dean asked me to pop up here personally to discuss the forces' mentoring scheme for quasi-undergrads. It's all covered under section six of the putative war dispensation procedures. Now, where can I park? I'm already late, thanks to this bloody snow.'

The porter blinked. 'Well, if it's like that, sir, I suppose you can take one of the faculty spaces up there to the right — but I'm surprised no one told me you were coming.'

'Not a problem, old chap. There's a war on. Everything's fouled up. You'll get the paperwork

76

tomorrow, rest easy. Park over there, d'you say? Thanks.' The MG chugged away.

Christ, it was just too bloody easy, sometimes.

He pulled up next to a large grey Wolseley — *God*, what were these poncey lecturers *on* to afford cars like this? — and stepped out of his tiny two-seater. The freshly falling snow had an antiseptic aroma and gave the college buildings an added lustre. Even his mother's grimy Whitechapel garret looked better under a fresh covering of snow — until London coal-smoke turned it a dirty grey.

Here at Girton, the transformation was safe from metropolitan grime. Diana's college looked like the illustration on a Christmas card. But where was he to find her? He noticed a figure walking diagonally across the quadrangle, head down against the strengthening blizzard.

'Hello there! Excuse me!'

The figure turned towards him, uncertainly. 'Hello yourself!' came a faint voice. 'Can I help? Sorry, I can't see you too well — my eyelashes are full of snowflakes.'

James laughed. 'Mine too . . . I'm looking for Diana Arnold . . . well, her rooms, at any rate.'

'Then you've come to the right shop.' The figure materialised out of the snow and dusk. She was blonde, rosy-cheeked, short and dumpy, wrapped up thickly in coat and scarf. She looked exactly like a Russian doll, James thought.

'I'm Sally, Diana's friend. Who are you? How did you get past our fearsome gatekeeper?'

James shrugged. 'I lied through my teeth,' he admitted, putting out his hand. 'James Blackwell.

Flight Commander Blackwell, actually. I'm here to take Diana out to dinner.'

Sally gaped. 'You're *him*?. Good grief, I was beginning to wonder if you were a figment of Diana's imagination. She's been prattling on about you since last autumn, but every time you were supposed to put in an appearance . . . '

'I flunked it, I know,' said James. 'Not my fault, I swear. Entirely Adolf's. Well, the Air Ministry's, actually. Anyway — can you take me to her before you and I both turn into snowmen?'

Sally squinted at him through the drifting flakes. 'I won't take you to her. I wouldn't want to spoil the moment. I'll tell you the way, though.' She pointed to an arch. 'Through there, left, and left again at the first corridor. All the rooms at Girton are laid out along horizontal passages. You can't go wrong. Diana's is the first door on the right after that second turn.'

She brushed away the snow from her hair and forehead and stepped forward, looking at him properly in the face for the first time.

'You're . . . well, you're *all right*, aren't you?' she asked, in a flatter tone. 'Diana isn't just my friend; she's damn special. She's special to all of us here, actually. And we all take care of each other. You should know that. You've been a long time coming, Mr Blackwell.'

He stared calmly back at her, holding her eyes with his own until she looked away.

'Yes, I'm all right,' he said quietly. Sally had to lean forward to hear him. 'And I agree, Diana is

78

. . . bloody special. Which is why I'm here. OK?'

She relaxed a little, and raised her eyes to his again. 'OK. But be warned, Flight Commander. You're at Girton. Mess around with one of us at your peril. Here, we've been fighting for over half a century to get women up to the same level that men casually occupy as of right. We're sick of inequality and intellectual snobbery and being looked down upon. We want our due.'

He raised gloved hands in mock defensiveness.

'My dear Sally . . . You have absolutely no *idea* how much you and I have in common.'

★ ★ ★

Diana was expecting James to stop at the gate-house and send a porter to let her know he'd arrived. It hadn't occurred to her that he would talk his way in, so when she heard a knock at her door she assumed it was one of the college servants.

'I'm coming,' she called, pulling on her coat, hat and gloves and dropping a pack of cigarettes into her handbag. She switched out the light and opened the door.

'Miss Arnold, I presume? It's been so long I'm not sure I'd recognise her.'

'Oh my goodness!' Diana stepped back into her room. 'James! How on earth did you get into college?'

'Everyone keeps asking me that,' he grumbled. 'Aren't you glad to see me?'

Diana giggled. 'Of course I am. You took me by surprise, that's all. I was expecting an elderly

79

porter with hair sprouting out of his ears, not a conquering hero.'

'I'm hardly that,' he replied as she put the light back on and motioned him inside. 'None of us are. If it wasn't for the newspapers to remind us, you wouldn't know we were at war at all. Perhaps Mr Hitler's forgotten all about us.'

Diana closed the door and they stared at each other for a moment.

James's cap and shoulders, Diana saw, were white with snow. It was far too chilly in the college corridors for the flakes to have even begun to melt yet. His blue eyes glittered out at her from under the cap's peak, and his cheeks glowed with the cold of outside. He was grinning at her with something like triumph. Diana felt her heart miss a beat.

To James, Diana looked sensational in her belted, French-style raincoat and bright red leather gloves. She was wearing fur-trimmed bootees, and a red cloche hat to match the gloves. Her green eyes were fixed on his and for a long moment, neither of them seemed able to speak.

It was Diana who broke the silence.

'Well,' she said at last. 'This feels rather peculiar, doesn't it? We've only actually met that one time, and here you are in Cambridge, and in my room.'

He looked around him. 'And a very cosy room it is too, if I may say so. Did you bring the furniture and paintings from home?'

'Sort of. Daddy sent a man with a van.'

'Hmm, well, it knocks my Officers' Mess into

a cocked hat, I can tell you. And yes, all right, it *does* seem a bit strange to be here at last, I'll admit. Although if I'd been able to get up to Cambridge last autumn I'm sure neither of us would be feeling the least bit peculiar.'

They sat down a little awkwardly at either end of a pretty chintz sofa. Diana cocked her head. 'Why *were* you so keen to come? I don't think we spoke two words alone together when you came down to the house with John, and the next thing I knew you were ringing me up asking me out to dinner.'

He reached into one of the deep side-pockets of his coat. 'I'll keep this on, if you don't mind. I'm bloody freezing from the car.' He found the cigarettes he was fishing for. 'Want one?'

She nodded. He lit two, and passed hers across.

'OK, well, let's see. Why did I ask to see you again? You know, for a Girton girl you're a bit slow, I must say. I thought you had to be brainy to get in here.'

'Hey!'

'The answer's rather obvious, isn't it? We may have spent only — what was it, three or four hours in total in each other's company? But I thought you were the most interesting, attractive girl I'd ever met. Still do. Simple as that; it isn't complicated. You're funny and clever and absurdly beautiful. There, I wasn't going to say any of that for ages, but you did ask. And now you're blushing.'

'Well, you've made me! What do you expect? Oh God . . . I'm completely lost for words, I'm

81

afraid. No one's ever said anything remotely like that to me before.'

He grinned at her. 'Then it was about time. Anyway, I was wondering how we were going to break the ice, and you just went and gave me the perfect opportunity. We can both relax from here; I've been outrageously forward, you've blushed: now we can get on. Everything after this can be frivolous chit-chat and gossip. Come on, I've booked us a table at The Eagle in town. Shall we leave? I've had nothing since breakfast and I'm starving.'

As they stood up, Diana began to laugh.

'What? What is it?'

'Nothing,' she said, pushing him from the room and locking the door behind them. 'It's just that of all the different ways I imagined this evening beginning, I never once thought it would happen like this. You're extraordinary.'

'Good,' he said as they linked arms and walked to his car. 'I've always thought life should be full of surprises. As long as they're nice ones.' They entered the quadrangle. 'Bloody hell, look at this snow now. I'll be lucky to get back to Essex tonight.'

20

As James and Diana were shown to their places in the old coaching inn's busy restaurant, heads turned.

'Blimey, look at them two,' whispered one young waitress to another. 'They look just like film stars, don't you think?'

Diana slipped off her coat and handed it with her hat and gloves to the head waiter, who was all fussing attendance. Underneath she was wearing a pale blue jumper with a matching silk scarf tied loosely at her throat. Her plaid skirt was a deeper blue and fell just below the knee. Her dark hair swung briefly across her face as she sat down, and as she absently pushed it back with one hand, the man had to suppress a little gasp. This was the most beautiful young woman he could remember ever coming to his restaurant.

Bloody hell, thought James to himself as he watched Diana studying the menu, she's even more incredible than I remembered. Those eyes . . . they're like emeralds. She looks like a fairy queen or a goddess. I must *not* mess this up.

And suddenly, to his surprise, he found himself considering a change of tactics, a rare thing for him. Not in the larger picture, of course, but in tonight's opening manoeuvres.

After they had ordered, and Diana began to tell him about her life at Cambridge, confiding a little of her confusion about who she was and what she wanted out of life, James decided that he should pull back; extend the timetable. This girl was shrewd and quick (she's probably as clever as I am, he thought) and she'd become suspicious if he rushed things. With the war going nowhere in a hurry, he probably had more time at his disposal than he'd first calculated.

Even so, there was no harm in unrolling a little of his strategy tonight.

The chance came when Diana suddenly put her hand to her cheek and exclaimed: 'Oh, my goodness! Here I am clattering on and on about me, and I haven't asked you anything about you! And what you're doing is so much more important. You said you thought Adolf's forgotten about us. I know you were joking, but do you believe the war might just, well, evaporate?'

That was the last thing he wanted her to think. It would remove all the required urgency from the equation. Diana needed to believe he was facing dangers that, if not imminent, were fast approaching.

'Well, don't misunderstand my remark earlier. We are desperately bored and frustrated and longing to get stuck in. But I think things will start to hot up any day now, in every sense. One of the reasons it's been so quiet is because the winter was incredibly long and hard, and even worse over on the continent. But despite this lot,' he gestured at the snowflakes whirling past the window, 'spring is pretty much here. I think he — Hitler, I mean — will make the first move.

Then we'll all be crying our eyes out for the phoney war.'

Diana looked curiously at him. 'Are you frightened? My brother seems extraordinarily sanguine about the whole thing.'

James sipped his wine. This part had to be exactly right; this was where he planted the seed.

'I'm not sure if I'm frightened or not . . . It all seems so unreal. The other day in the mess, my squadron leader said: 'When it starts, boys, it's going to be kill or be killed. Don't forget that. Get the other bastard before he gets you.' And straight away the thought jumped into my head: some commanding officer somewhere in Germany right now is probably saying exactly the same thing to *his* pilots. So no, I'm not quite as sanguine as your John is, I'm afraid. But that isn't the same as being scared . . . Oh, I don't know, I'm blethering on a bit. But I do know one thing for certain.'

He waited for her to ask.

'What's that?'

James took another sip of wine. *Careful, careful.*

He reached across the table and placed his hand gently over hers.

'It seems to me that we can't live the way we used to, people like you and me. There may not be the time. You asked why I was so keen to come up and see you last year and I told you the truth, but I left something out.' He paused. This part had to be exactly right.

'It's simply this,' he continued slowly. 'I didn't want to waste any time. I don't mean to sound melodramatic or vainglorious, but I am a realist and I know it's perfectly possible that I won't come through what's ahead. Before the war we'd have had all the time in the world to get to know each other, to see if we were suited. Now we have to move along more quickly; put things to the test much earlier than we might once have. I think everyone our age does these days.'

Diana stared at him. 'I'm not sure I — ' she began, but he gave her a quick smile and shook his head.

'Don't worry, I'm not making an improper suggestion. Far from it. And I'm not about to tell you I adore you and only want to be with you until the end of my days. You'd think me mad, and you'd be right. I hardly know you. All I'm saying — and I've had the winter to think about this — is that if we decide to see each other, especially when I start flying real operations, not training flights or boring patrols, we might find ourselves wanting to . . . well, speed things up.'

He sat back, drew a deep breath, and then exhaled loudly. 'There. That's the second time tonight I've done that.'

'What do you mean?' she asked him. 'The second time you've done what?'

'Told you something I had no intention of mentioning just yet. First in your room, about how I feel about you, and now this, about how our futures might play out. You're pretty good at getting a chap to reveal his inner thoughts, Diana, I'll give you that.'

'Well, it's certainly not intentional, I can assure you,' she said, half-laughing. 'Mind if I smoke before pudding?'

He shook his head and, once again, lit cigarettes for them both and waited.

'I think I see what you're getting at,' said Diana eventually. 'The war has changed things. Or rather, it *will*, if you're right and things start to happen soon. And in any case, I haven't been quite fair with you.'

He raised his eyebrows. 'In what way?'

'Well . . . ' She took a long pull on her cigarette. 'You've been very honest about what your first impressions of me were, and I've told you nothing of mine about you. My turn, then.'

'OK. Shoot. If it's a bullet to the heart, I can take it.'

'No, that's not it.' Diana was now turning rather pink. 'You made a huge impression on me at the Dower House. I asked my brother heaps of questions about you after dinner. He was — ' she hesitated — 'well, to say 'complimentary' would be an understatement. And he told me the truth about why you'd come to stay with us.'

'The truth?'

'Yes. He said that story about your parents being in Canada was nonsense, and that in fact your mother used to be in service and your father was her employer and took advantage of her. When he realised she was expecting you, he threw her out. Is that true, James?'

He took his time, drawing on his cigarette and staring out at the big, wet flakes driving against the window. Then he turned to her.

'Well now, this was something else I hadn't planned on discussing tonight. But yes, it's true.

And it doesn't matter. In fact, it doesn't signify at all. My mother gave me a good upbringing and I've made my own way. It's irrelevant who my father is. I'm sorry I deceived your parents — and you — but I've found that when I do tell people the truth about my parentage, they usually give me strange looks. They think I'm a liar, or a self-deluding fool, or a bit touched. I find it better to ration the truth. But as I say, I'm sorry. I didn't want to start our . . . friendship . . . with a lie.'

In her own turn, Diana reached for James's hand. 'You haven't,' she told him firmly. 'I asked you something and you told me the truth.'

She smiled at him. 'I'd call this a very good start.'

21

Diana's portable alarm clock went off just before eight o'clock the next morning, as it always did. The Arnold family habit of waking up to the radio news had been transplanted to her Cambridge bedroom. Diana hadn't missed the first BBC bulletin of the day since war began more than seven months earlier. Not that there was usually much to report, thus far. But still, you never knew.

With a small jolt, she remembered she was not alone in her college bedsit. Over on the little chintz sofa lay James Blackwell, tangled in her spare blankets with his blue RAF greatcoat spread across the top. His feet poked out from under the coat and covers and way over the sofa's edge. He looked extremely uncomfortable. But he was sleeping.

Diana switched on her bedside radio, a battery-powered Roberts the size of a small loaf of bread. While it warmed up, she took her dressing-gown from the chair next to the bed, slipped it over her shoulders and went across to the kitchenette and put the kettle on. Then she drew the curtains above the sink.

The overnight snow had stopped; already a thaw was setting in. Indeed, as she watched, a slab of wet snow slid from the roof of the dormitory opposite and thudded to the ground, scattering a small family of starlings drinking from a partly defrosted bird-bath underneath the eaves. James had been right. Spring was arriving, at last.

It had been quite impossible for him to drive back to Upminster the previous night; in fact, they'd had to abandon his car halfway from The Eagle and walk the rest of the way through the snow to Girton. The porter was asleep when they reached the college so there was no difficulty in smuggling James back to her room. She'd wondered if he might try to kiss her — she rather hoped he would, and perhaps go even further than that — but his behaviour had been exemplary. He'd turned his back while she undressed and climbed into bed, and then had insisted she do the same while he disrobed, solemnly warning her that 'the flames of passion may otherwise consume you, Diana, and you would pounce on me without shame or compunction'.

She had gone to sleep laughing under her breath.

Now, pouring boiling water into her small teapot and hurrying back to bed to listen to the news, she decided she was glad nothing had happened last night. That might have made his little speech about 'speeding things up' seem self-serving and cynical. Clearly, he was better than that.

Two minutes later, she was shaking him awake.

'James . . . James . . . wake up. You have to listen to this. It's on the news. Germany's invaded Denmark and Norway. It's started.'

He rolled off the sofa in a single movement and crouched by the little radio. Diana noticed that he hadn't quite taken all his clothes off the night before: he was still wearing a rather frayed vest and long-johns. Thank God for small mercies, she thought to herself. Oh . . . perhaps not so small. She averted her eyes.

'You're bloody right,' James said after a minute. 'This is most definitely it. *Damn*. I should have tried to get back to base last night, after all.'

'Don't be silly, James, you'd have ended up in a ditch after the first two miles. Anyway, it's thawing now. Get dressed and I'll walk with you to the car.'

Twenty minutes later, after strolling insouciantly past an outraged porter on the gate, Diana and James were standing in the slush next to the MG.

'That porter isn't going to get you into trouble, I hope?' James asked her.

'Not him,' Diana laughed. 'He's got a soft spot for me. I'll be fine.'

James hesitated. 'Look . . . I'd hoped we'd at least have lunch before I had to go back,' he said to her. 'Every time I think we have a bit of time to get to know each other, the bloody war sticks its nose in. I'm sick of it.'

She put scarlet-gloved hands on both sides of his face. 'Me too. But we *have* got to know each other. We did last night at The Eagle. In fact, we got to know much more about each other than we ever would've done without this stupid war; at least, I did about you. You were

91

so honest and open.'

He pulled her to him. 'I should have done this last night.'

That first kiss, an astonished Diana realised later, was the point at which, for the first time in her life, all her disparate parts dimly recognised each other. Her yearnings for a sense of purpose, for love, for a child, for passion, were, for a few dizzying moments, almost unified.

Then James Blackwell was stepping back from her, smiling.

'Diana, I don't know when we'll be able to see each other again,' he said. 'I'll phone; I'll write. It may be difficult, I may be in France or, God knows, Norway. But I'll come back to you, just as soon as I can. I promise.'

Then he was swinging into the bucket seat of the little car, the engine coughed into life, and he swerved and skidded away through the melting snow.

It was, he thought to himself as he crunched up a gear and joined the main road south, one of his more effective exits.

22

'No, Dad, I don't think any Spits are going to Norway, not that I've heard, anyway.' John paused to sip his beer and shifted the mess phone to his other ear.

'Well, there's a limit to what I can say, obviously,' he went on. 'Careless talk costs lives, and all that. But according to the papers, an aircraft carrier's gone over stuffed with Gladiators and Swordfish, although how those old bi-planes will manage against Hitler's fast fighters is anyone's guess. There's talk about maybe sending some Hurricanes too, which would even up the odds a bit. But we've had no orders. I think the general feeling is that Norway's just 'opening and beginners', and the real scrap will start, like last time, in France and Belgium. But we're ready for him, Dad. In fact, James and I were saying last night that we wish it would kick off so we can get it over with. Everyone here's had quite enough of this endless stooging around.'

Mr Arnold, listening intently on the other end of the line in his office in Holborn, knew exactly what his son meant. A quarter of a century ago, he too had fretted in a reserve division stationed just behind the Western Front, desperate to go into action. Anything was better than living on jangling nerves, waiting for something to happen. Or at least, that's what they had all believed before they were marched up to the front line that first time. Things took on a very different perspective when you stood on the firing step in a flooded trench, waiting for the whistle to blow to send you over the top and on your merry way. Very different indeed.

'I understand, John,' he said. 'But it'll start soon enough, believe you me. Do you think you might get some leave any time soon? No? I didn't really think so. Well, good luck, old son. Your mother and I think about you all the time. Yes . . . yes, I know you do. Bye for now, then . . . Yes, bye.'

He put the telephone carefully back on its receiver and stared out of the window towards the best view from his chambers, the dome of St Paul's Cathedral. But, as so often these days, Wren's soot-blackened masterpiece failed to register in the smallest way. All he could see was his only son (still a boy, for all his carefully posed urbanity and hard-won professionalism) strapping himself into his cockpit, pulling on his oxygen mask and taking off to do battle with the enemy. To die? Why not? War takes the skilled along with the stupid and those in between. He knew that from the Somme.

Mr Arnold's hands trembled slightly as he lit a cigarette. He could scarcely believe it had come to this, after the sacrifice and suffering last time: 'the war to end all wars'. What a pathetic joke that had turned out to be. All his darkest doubts and fears, which had made their first stealthy approach to him two summers before up on the Weald, were turning into the bleakest of realities.

94

He felt a wave of despair and hopelessness wash over him.

He found himself wishing his son suffered from poor sight, or deafness, or mathematical ineptness: anything to keep him from being chosen to fly in a front-line fighter squadron. John had confided in his father, one evening when Gwen had gone to bed, that although the Spitfire was a remarkable aircraft, so were some of the enemy's.

'I'll be honest with you,' he said over a late-night brandy, 'the new German fighters are as fast as ours and some of us think they're better armed. They have cannon; we've only got machine-guns. And their pilots have operational experience from the Spanish Civil War. We're going to have to work bloody hard not to be caught on the hop. Not a word to Mum or Diana, though.'

Mr Arnold glanced down at the evening paper his secretary had placed on the desk during the phone conversation with John. A large picture of Hitler dominated the front page and Mr Arnold experienced an unexpected surge of loathing. It shook him: until now he'd mostly felt cold contempt for the man. This hot, violent hatred was new, almost animal in its intensity. If he could have conjured the Nazi leader into existence before him he would have choked the life out of him with his bare hands then and there, without a solitary word or a moment's compunction. The blood sang in his ears.

This was no good. He needed to walk; he needed air. Mr Arnold called to his secretary in the outer office, 'Laura, I'm going out for half an hour,' and he could hear the tremor in his voice. He walked quickly down the stairs and out onto a side street through a fire-door. His first thought as he headed towards St Paul's, surrounded by its defending family of gently bobbing barrage balloons, was of his daughter.

At least Diana was safe. Nothing, and no one, could touch her.

23

As Mr Arnold was grappling with unusually dark
thoughts — unusual for him — James Blackwell
was back at the Upminster aerodrome, also
indulging in some rare introspection. He almost
never allowed himself the luxury of self-analysis.
You were what you did, and what you did made
you what you were. What was the point of trying
to work out why? It wouldn't change the past
and he was perfectly happy with his plans for the
future; he always had been.

But in recent days something had begun to
puzzle him, and now he lay smoking cigarette
after cigarette on his bed in the small wooden
hut that was part of the officers' quarters, trying
to work through the conundrum.

Why wasn't he afraid?

John was afraid, he'd admitted it to him a few
days ago. So had some of the others, however
obliquely. Even those who claimed they weren't
frightened of what was coming clearly were, too.
You could see it in their faces, hear it in their
voices, and their weak jokes.

But *he* — James Blackwell Esquire, of
Whitechapel — wasn't frightened at all. Not the
slightest, tiniest bit. It wasn't that he was unable
to grasp the sheer enormity of what was about to
happen to them all. He knew perfectly well that
he was shortly going to be asked to do something
extraordinarily dangerous. The fact that he was

one of the most skilled pilots in the squadron gave him no extra sense of security.

Yes, he was undoubtedly what his instructors had called 'a natural' — someone who had an instinctive feel for an aircraft. Sometimes it almost seemed to him that his Spitfire was an extension of himself; his arms and hands creeping and spreading into the curved wings on either side of him; his legs and feet somehow merging into and becoming part of the flaps and controls that dictated the little plane's height and direction.

But that was pure flying, not fighting. If he was 'bounced' by two or three enemy fighters at once, or even a single German pilot more skilled than himself, he'd be lucky to get out of it alive. He knew that perfectly well.

But the prospect held no terrors for him. Neither did any of the other scenarios of doom that unwound like spools of film inside his head. Why?

Thinking about it, he asked himself, had he ever been afraid of anything? Not that he could remember. It occurred to him, for the first time in his life, that he had always seen himself remotely from the outside and never from within.

James began to get excited. This nascent self-awareness was a completely new sensation to him and he felt a sudden conviction that if he could grasp the elusive truth about himself, whatever it was, he might become even stronger.

He found himself thinking back to that evening with Diana in Cambridge, and his perfectly judged exit the following morning. And those last moments with Jane in the dress-shop in Upminster.

Then there was the final dénouement with his headmaster.

How he'd silently applauded himself after every scene! What did they remind him of? Something to do with his past. Dammit, he was so close! It was . . . it was . . . and then it burst through into his consciousness like a sudden flash of sunlight from behind a swift-passing cloud.

Of course. The films his mother had let him watch at the Odeon, from as early as he could recall. The films that had formed his emerging view of the world. The solitary small boy had watched the characters on the screen with an intensity that the tittering, whispering, chocolate-gobbling audiences surrounding him never did. But because the shades flickering before him were not real — he had always known that, hadn't he, even when he was what, four? — he had never cared about their pain, or their joy, or their fear. He had watched them dispassionately. But never disinterestedly.

Sometimes he had seen the same film five or six times in a single week. Then he had come to feel he was following the characters as closely as their own shadows, and, because he knew exactly what was about to befall them, it was almost as if he was controlling them, nudging them toward their destinies. It didn't matter whether they were heroes or villains; all that counted was how their inner characters and outward actions

dictated their fate. Glamorous; ruthless; successful . . . James had never cared about what
defined them. Even if they were ultimately
doomed, it was their unfolding stories that
counted above everything else.

'That's what I do now,' he whispered to the
empty hut. 'I direct. I'm the sodding director of
my own life and everyone else who's part of it.
Of course I'm not afraid. Why would a director
be afraid for one of his actors? And that's me
too. I'm an actor in my own life-story. And I'm
the lead. I can do what I want. Bloody hell.'

He lit another cigarette from the glowing
stump of the last one and stared, amazed, at the
ceiling. James Blackwell spoke aloud only once
more, and when he did, it was in a voice full of
pride and awe.

'Fuck *me*.'

24

And then, in a shattering instant, it came: the ferocious eruption of total war. The country woke, stunned to find that the long stalemate had evaporated in a single night, in the smoke and fury of an enemy assault so savage, so overwhelming, that all foolish hopes that catastrophe might yet be averted vanished as though they had never been.

Some heard the news from their radios as they tapped spoons on boiled eggs or shook open innocent newspapers that had gone to press a few hours before the convulsion. Others were telephoned by friends or family. Some were woken by bleary-eyed neighbours, still in dressing-gowns and slippers as they knocked on friends' doors.

Oliver and Gwen were in bed drinking tea brought to them by Lucy when they heard the phone ringing in the hall below. They turned to each other. 'Who the hell is *that*, at half-past seven in the morning?' Mr Arnold grumbled.

Gwen gripped his hand. 'Let it not be something's happened to John. Please God, let it not be that.'

Her husband stroked the hand that clutched his. 'I spoke to him yesterday, I told you. His squadron's still waiting for orders. John is perfectly fine, darling.'

Downstairs, the phone had stopped ringing

and they heard Lucy's muffled voice. Then her feet were on the stairs and she was tapping at the door. 'Excuse me, sir, ma'am, but it's Mr John. He says sorry to wake you, but the war's started good and proper.'

Mr Arnold slammed his teacup down on its saucer and kicked the bedclothes aside. 'I'm coming down!'

He overtook the maid at the foot of the stairs and skidded to the telephone on its little oak table. 'John! What's happening?'

'Armageddon, Dad, the Four Horses of the Apocalypse are riding. The gods of war are — '

'Stop that! What's *happening?*'

'Sorry, Dad — everything that you said would, and then some. The Germans invaded Belgium, Luxembourg and Holland at dawn, and they've smashed the French positions too. They're moving like a hot knife through butter, apparently.'

'What? But what about the Maginot Line? The French say their border defences against Germany are impregnable!'

'Not if you nip around the side, they're not. That's exactly what he's done — simply bypassed the whole issue. He's streaming into the countryside behind the Maginot Line as we speak. We've been completely sucker-punched, Dad. His air force is bombing and strafing anything that moves on the roads, civilian or military. At this rate he'll be at the Channel ports in thirty-six hours.'

'You can't mean that.'

'Well, no, perhaps not, but honestly, Dad, this

102

is about as serious as it gets. I could be at a forward base in France by tonight for all I know. Anyway, I don't think I'll be able to phone again for a while, so I just wanted to give you and Mum the news and say — well, bye for now and not to worry. I'll be fine. We all will. But it's exciting, isn't it?'

Mr Arnold held the receiver in front of him for a moment, and stared at it. Then he returned it to his ear.

'Yes — yes, I suppose it is, John. Of course it is. And you do what you have to do. Give 'em everything you've got and then some, old son. We'll show the bastards they can't get away with this nonsense any longer. We're right behind you.'

'Thanks, Dad. Give Mum my love and say that as soon as things calm down, I'll come over. Tell her and Diana not to fret. Oh, that reminds me — James is seeing to our flight's fuelling and can't get to a phone. He wants you to give Diana his best. Will you do that for him? I rather think something's afoot there, by the way.'

'Is there indeed! Yes, I'll do that for him, and you give him our best in return, our very best. Yes, well . . . I suppose you had better go, John. We'll see you when — when we can. Take care, my boy. We love you very much.'

'I know. Me too. Bye, Dad.'

The line went dead. Mr Arnold sat down in the little wicker chair by the telephone table, and slowly buried his face in his hands.

25

That was the last the Arnolds heard from their son, or Diana from James, for many weeks. It was hardly surprising. The speed of the collapse across the Channel was astounding. It was difficult to say which side was more astonished by the rout: the all-conquering Germans or the humiliated British, French, Belgians and Dutch.

Less than a week after John's snatched phone call, Holland surrendered. France had collapsed into chaos. The Arnolds had no idea where their son might be or what he was doing.

'No news is good news,' Mr Arnold repeatedly told his wife. But Gwen impressed him with her calmness and refusal to give in to the monstrous fears that stalked them both.

'It won't help John if we fall apart,' she told him. 'We have to carry on. I'm working on a painting and I intend to give it to him when he gets back.'

Mr Arnold, for his part, continued to go into the city every day. What else was there to do? One sunny morning as he strode along Holborn's pavements towards his chambers, a former associate fell into step beside him.

'Morning, Arnold. Heard the latest? His tanks have reached Abbeville.'

Mr Arnold stopped in his tracks. '*What?* But that's just a cough and a spit from the Channel!'

'Tell me something I don't know — and that's

not the worst of it. It means our forces to the north and south are now completely cut off from each other. All done in precisely ten days. Extraordinary. Do you know, I believe we might lose this war. It's most inconvenient; my wife and I were planning to motor to Bordeaux this summer. Oh well, *quel dommage* and all that. Have you heard from your boy at all?'

Mr Arnold shook his head and began walking again. 'No. Not a peep.'

'Well, I shouldn't worry. I'd be surprised if your John is in *la belle France* at all.'

Mr Arnold halted again. 'What do you mean?'

The other stared at him. 'Surely you can see that France is a completely lost cause? She'll be suing for peace inside a couple of weeks, mark my words. Then we'll need every Spitfire and Hurricane we've got for ourselves. Next stop Blighty for Herr Hitler. It'll be the job of boys like yours to keep the buggers out. No point squandering pilots and planes to buy a few pointless extra days for the Frenchies. Well, this is me. Cheerio. Onward to victory!' He gave an ironic salute and disappeared into his office doorway.

As soon as he was behind his desk, Oliver telephoned Gwen at the Dower House.

'So you see,' he concluded, 'although John must be flying missions over France, he may still be based here as insurance against invasion. Williamson's a canny fellow and he's usually got an ear to the ground. He has contacts in the War Ministry, I know that for a fact.'

After a moment, Gwen spoke. 'But Oliver, if

France falls, doesn't that mean we'll have lost? Would there be any point in fighting on? Risking the lives of boys like John?'

Now *that*, thought Mr Arnold as he rang off, is the burning question of the hour.

26

Barely a week after the shock of Abbeville, the little French seaside town of Dunkirk dominated every conversation and front page. For ten consecutive mornings the Arnolds — Oliver and Gwen in the Dower House, and Diana in Girton — huddled by their radios listening to the unfolding story of a cobbled-together evacuation. Shot-down RAF pilots were reported to be among the exhausted men being brought off the beaches, and Mr Arnold began slipping into the nearest cinema during his lunch-hour to watch the newsreels. He thought he might catch a glimpse of his boy standing in one of the long lines of haggard men waiting patiently for a boat to ferry them to safety.

Meanwhile, Diana was suffering agonies of uncertainty. She hadn't seen or spoken to James since he'd kissed her goodbye at the kerbside that April morning. Her father had passed on James's message to her the day the squadron flew their Spitfires to war, and that had been the last she'd heard of him.

She was desperately worried about her brother too, but she felt increasingly guilty that her thoughts were more focused on the man she was now certain would be her lover — if he ever came back to her.

'I'm going quietly mad here, Sal,' she told her friend. 'One minute I'm sick with worry for the two of them, the next I feel awful because I realise I've been thinking more about *him* than my brother — and then there are times when I feel absurdly happy because I realise I'm in love, for the first time in my life. And then I come full circle again and can't get the thought out of my head that he's been killed.' She dropped her head in despair.

'I know, Di, I know,' Sally soothed, stroking Diana's hair. 'Shhh . . . it's the same for everyone with someone in this fight. You just have to be strong and patient. As your father keeps telling you, so long as your family doesn't receive some sort of horrible telegram or phone call from the RAF, you can keep hoping that — '

Diana jerked her head away. 'Yes, but that only goes for my brother, doesn't it? No one's going to tell me if a James Blackwell has been shot down over France or been injured or captured. It's not as if I'm his wife or anything. No one at the RAF knows I exist. Every morning I comb through the newspapers' lists of men killed or missing in action. It's the only way I'll find out if something dreadful has happened. The other day there *was* a Blackwell on the list and I nearly fainted until I saw he wasn't a James. It's horrible, Sal, just *horrible!*'

Her friend stood up. 'All right, my dear, get your hat and coat.'

'What? Why? Where are we going?'

'To the Fox and Hounds for a *very* stiff drink.'

108

27

The last of the men to be rescued from Dunkirk had arrived in England forty-eight hours before. The first week of June was coming to a close and there was still no word from either John or James.

The Arnolds sat with their daughter in the gardens of the Dower House on a fine, warm evening. The longest day was barely a fortnight away and even now, at eight o'clock, the late-evening sunshine had residual strength. Rabbits were out in force below the ha-ha, and the sparrows in the thick ivy that covered the rear of the house were settling into their bedtime chatter.

The three of them were drinking wine from crystal glasses that Lucy had brought to them on a tray.

'Wedding presents from your grandparents,' Mr Arnold informed his daughter, waving his glass in the air. 'Once there were six; these are the sad survivors. Do you remember the day you broke all the others?'

Diana winced. 'Of course. I was three, wasn't I?'

'You were four. You watched your brother playing with his wooden skittle set and he wouldn't let you join in, so you — '

' — so I went and got your cricket ball,' Diana continued the well-worn refrain, 'took as many

109

glasses as I could carry from the sideboard and put them together in the drive, where I — '

' — scored a full house with the first roll of the ball. I can still hear the exquisite tinkling noise now, and your screams of delight.'

Gwen laughed. 'John was always frightfully mean with his toys, wasn't he? The two of you never really hit it off until he went away to prep.'

Diana shrugged. 'I was an extremely irritating little sister. I never gave him a moment's peace. It was only after he'd gone to boarding school that I realised how much I loved him.'

She put her glass down on the white-painted wrought-iron garden table and looked up at her parents.

'Look, we haven't really discussed it since I came home from Girton. But what do you think has happened to the two of them? Honestly? I'm worn out with worry and I don't think I have another tear to shed.'

Her father put down his own glass. 'I was intending to talk about it over dinner. But OK, here's what I think.' He considered them both. 'I'm optimistic. Truly, I am. The papers have been pretty short on detail, but it's clear our fighter squadrons have been operating over France until very recently, covering the evacuation. I keep saying it, but no news really *is* good news. That was true in the last lot and it's just as true now.

'But here's the thing.' He leaned forward. 'Williamson came to see me this afternoon at the office. All very hush-hush, cloak and dagger. He told me in strictest confidence that the new

Prime Minister was informed in no uncertain terms by the RAF that it's time to stop fannying around in France and keep every last plane and pilot back here at home. Williamson says he doesn't believe a single Spitfire squadron was ever even based across the Channel. Apparently Churchill refused to allow it, in spite of tremendous pressure from the French.'

He looked at his wife and daughter. 'I know it's all been absolutely awful, but I think we're due for some good news about our John,' he nodded towards Diana, 'and your James, my dear, very soon. Let's drink to it, anyway, shall we?'

The three of them touched glasses.

'*To good news.*'

28

Next morning, Lucy entered the garden room to open the curtains, but to her surprise they'd already been drawn. The armchair that faced out on to the lawns had its back to her, but she could see a curl of cigarette smoke curling slowly into the air above it.

'Oh! Good morning, sir. I didn't realise you were up. Would you like some tea?'

'Yes, please, Lucy. I've been sitting here since six, waiting for everyone to wake up.'

John stood up and stretched, turning to face the astonished maid.

'Gorgeous morning, isn't it?'

★　★　★

Diana thundered down the stairs in her pyjamas ten minutes later. 'Where is he?'

Her mother emerged in her dressing-gown from the breakfast room, beaming. 'He's in the garden with your father, darling. He looks very tired but I think — '

Diana careered through the French windows and was running across the dew-drenched lawn towards the two men, who were standing under the great sycamore that stood by the path leading to the kitchen gardens.

'John! *John!*'

Her brother spun round and flapped both

112

arms humorously in the air. 'Hey, sis! It's all right — we're both fine. James is fine. I'm fine. We're both fine!'

Diana leaped headlong into his embrace, as she used to when he came home from school for the holidays.

'Here, you'll have me over!' he laughed, staggering backwards. 'My my, the child grows strong. Morning, young miss. I trust you've been behaving yourself?'

'We've been so horribly frightened! It's all been awful. Just *awful*.' She burst into tears.

John squeezed his sister tight. 'Yeah,' he said, his voice muffled against her cheek. 'That pretty much sums up what it's been like at our end too.'

He partly pulled away, his hand trembling slightly, but perceptibly. His blond hair appeared darker than usual — he hadn't washed it for a month — and his skin was sallow with angry blotches of eczema around the mouth. His blue uniform was creased and stained, and there were suspicious rusty-coloured splodges on the sheepskin tops of his flying boots.

That's blood, or I'm a Dutchman, Mr Arnold thought to himself. My God, look at his face. He's aged ten years in a month.

His son looked at them all. Lucy hovered nearby, listening.

'Well . . . ' John began. His eyes closed for a moment. He suddenly looked overwhelmed by exhaustion.

'If you'd prefer, you can just leave it for now,' Gwen said. 'Don't feel you have to go into any of

113

it, dear. You've only just got home. Perhaps you should go upstairs and rest?'

Her son smiled faintly and shook his head. 'No, Mum, honestly, I'd like to tell you about it. I'm OK, just damn tired. Nothing a couple of nights' uninterrupted sleep won't fix.' He turned to Diana. 'He really *is* OK, sis. I left him sound asleep on his cot. I imagine he'll be down here tomorrow.'

Diana blinked and gave a quick little nod. Her brother led her inside to the drawing room, their parents following.

'It's funny,' he said, sinking into an armchair. The others followed suit. 'It's nothing like you think it's going to be. I bet you discovered that in the last lot, Dad.'

Mr Arnold nodded. 'Oh, yes. War is full of surprises, that's for sure.'

'Yes. Well . . . we didn't go to France. Not as far as being based there, anyway. The government decided weeks ago that Spitfires should operate from here in England. So our lot have been flying across the Channel from Upminster ever since the German Blitzkrieg started. I'm sorry I didn't ring you, but we've been extraordinarily busy, every single day, and anyway we were told in no uncertain terms not to talk about operational stuff to anyone. I don't suppose that matters now, not now that we've been kicked off the Continent.'

The phone in the hall began to ring. John didn't appear to notice.

'We've been on the back foot since the tenth of May, to be truthful. Fingers in the dyke, and all

114

that. It's all been about covering a fighting retreat. The Army say we abandoned them at Dunkirk but that's completely untrue, Mum and Dad. Some of our boys have been beaten up in pubs by soldiers shouting, 'Where was the RAF?' but we were there. We just weren't directly over the beaches.'

John began to speak more rapidly. 'I flew three missions a day over Dunkirk for five straight days. Fifteen sorties, back-to-back. We took off at dawn, patrolled above the Pas de Calais and got stuck into the bastards — sorry, Mum, the enemy — whenever they came in to attack. Christ, there were so *many* of them. Most of the dogfights were inland, away from the beaches. I suppose that's why the Army thought we'd let them down. The whole point was trying to stop Jerry's planes getting to Dunkirk itself. But we didn't have long to engage them. After a few minutes we had to turn back home to refuel, grab a sandwich and a mug of tea, and then it was back over there again, a.s.a.p. It was absolutely bloody exhausting, I can tell you.'

Lucy came in from the hall. 'Telephone for Miss Diana.'

Diana slipped from the room.

'The thing is,' John continued, 'the thing is . . . ' Here, he came to a complete halt.

'It's all right,' his father murmured. 'Take it easy, John.'

'No, I'm all right, Dad — really I am. The thing is, well, we lost a lot of chaps, you see. Someone in Intelligence told me yesterday that at least sixty Spits have been shot down over

115

France and the Channel in the last three weeks. You're not supposed to know that, by the way. And I saw some of them going down . . . heard them, too.'

His parents looked puzzled. 'How could you hear them?' his father asked quietly.

The boy pointed to his throat. 'Over their radios. Some of the chaps accidentally leave their mics open, and when they're hit, you hear — well, noises. You know. A lot go down in flames and . . . stuff. It's pretty horrible.'

Gwen and Oliver stared blankly at their son.

'And we've lost four from our squadron alone. Really super chaps. Two definitely killed, one burned to a bloody crisp and lingering, another shot down and taken prisoner. All that in less than a month.' His head twisted away.

Diana burst back into the room. 'That was James! He's got leave too and wants to come down here. I told him that was absolutely fine. It *is*, isn't it?'

Gwen stood up and took her boy into her arms.

'Of course it is,' she said over his shoulder. 'It's the least we can do.'

29

Brother and sister lay on the lawn behind the Dower House and stared up at the brightest stars that were beginning to appear in the summer night sky.

'That's Venus, isn't it, Johnnie?' Diana asked. 'You know: 'Twinkle, twinkle, little star' . . . '

'Yes. That's the Evening Star all right. Remember the Mad Hatter? 'Twinkle, twinkle, little bat, how I wonder what you're at'?'

''Up above the world you fly',' Diana continued, ''Like a tea-tray in the sky' . . . '

They laughed.

'Bonkers,' said Diana. She turned her head to his. 'Johnnie?'

'Yes?'

'Have you killed anyone?'

'Yes.'

'More than one?'

'Yes.' Her brother sat up beside her, patting his pockets. 'Do you have the cigarettes? I can't find them.'

'Yes. Here.' She lit one for each of them. 'Go on.'

John lay back on the grass. 'I think I've killed three men, actually. Well, that's stupid, I *know* I have.'

A shooting star flared across the sky and Diana grabbed her brother's hand. 'Make a wish, quick!'

He tensed, and then slowly relaxed. 'It's done . . . anyway . . . '

Diana waited. When her brother remained silent, she sat up and considered him in the gathering dusk.

'We're living in extraordinary times, aren't we, John? I can hardly conceive of my big brother killing anyone, let alone three men. Tell me about it, if you can.'

After an even longer silence, he put an arm around her waist and rested his head on her lap. When he spoke, his voice was muffled.

'It's awfully mechanical, actually. Automatic.'

She let him gather himself. Eventually he pulled clear of her and finished his cigarette.

'Let's see . . . ' he started. 'There were about six or seven of their dive-bombers headed for our men on the beaches late one afternoon. I think it was last Tuesday. Maybe Wednesday. They were Stukas. Vile things. They have two men on board, you see, one flying, the other operating the machine-gun, shooting up the blokes on the beach. Stukas are bloody terrifying if you're on the ground; they've got sirens fixed to their wings and they make a ghastly wailing noise when they dive to attack. But actually they're slow and vulnerable in normal flight and I smacked one of them down in my first pass. It was easy. I saw my bullets smash through his cockpit canopy and . . . well, there was lots of blood. I mean a *lot*, sis; it was only a momentary image, but blood was spraying all over the shop. It was horrible.

'There weren't any flames; their plane just

118

flipped over and sliced straight into the sea. The whole thing took less than ten seconds from start to finish.

'A couple of days later I nearly copped it. We were about six miles inland from Calais and suddenly I saw flashes all over my wings and engine casing. Cannon strikes. Terrifying. Next moment, a German fighter roars about ten feet above my Spit and there he is right in front of me. He was a good shot but a lousy flyer. Reflex — I pressed the firing button and he went up like a Roman candle. *Foom!* Sheer luck.

'I have no idea why his rounds didn't do for me. They just went straight through or bounced off without exploding. Duds, I suppose. When I got back to Upminster they patched up the holes and I was in the air again by teatime.'

Diana was silent for a long time before speaking again. She was trying to form pictures from the words he had spoken. She felt rather foolish: over the last few weeks when she'd tried to imagine what John and James might be experiencing, it hadn't once occurred to her that blood — real, human blood — would be a prominent feature. Now she remembered the strange stains she'd seen on her brother's boots.

'Is that blood on your boots, James?'

'Yes. It's not mine though. I helped a chap down from his cockpit after he'd landed. He'd taken a shell in his shoulder and his arm was off. God knows how he landed in that state. Anyway, we managed to stop the bleeding right there on the grass and he's going to be OK. Says as soon as he gets his new arm he'll be back with us.

Knowing him, he will.'

Diana considered this new image; her brother fighting to save a man's life bare minutes after straining every nerve to keep his own and take those of others. She felt a wave of compassion for him, and tears suddenly began pricking her eyes. She bit her bottom lip, hard. Crying would not do at all.

By now the faintest of the stars were joining the brighter ones above them. Diana stared up at them, blinking hard. When she felt able to speak in a normal voice, she cleared her throat and asked: 'Are you all right, Johnnie? I mean, *really* all right?'

'Yeah. I think so, sis. When it's happening you don't have time to think, and when it's over it seems like a completely insane dream. But I *am* worried about James.'

'What do you mean? You told me he was fine.'

Her brother turned to her. 'He had a very narrow squeak, Diana. I'm sure he'll tell you about it himself when he gets here. He's hiding it well, but I think it left him pretty shaken up. It bloody well would me. I'm hoping that seeing you again might give him a bit of a boost.'

He paused. 'Can I ask *you* something, sis?'

'I think I can guess the question,' she said. 'And the answer is 'yes'. Yes, I believe I'm in love with him.'

30

From inside the cockpit, the engine of James's Spitfire sounded to him like a mighty church organ, majestic chords pulsing and vibrating around him. The sound was oddly comforting. He glanced to his left and right. Both the other Spits in his group of three were in position either side of him.

One of the other pilots turned and, catching his glance, flicked him a cheerful V-sign. James laughed and turned back to his instruments. They were almost at the end of what had been an uneventful patrol over the Pas de Calais. The French countryside rolled slowly under their wings and the Channel gleamed seven or eight miles to the north. In five minutes they could turn for home.

His cockpit exploded in fury all around him.
Holy fuck!!!
Instruments evaporated in a spray of glass and smoke as a cannon shell burst with a deafening bang through the canopy just above his head. There were more ear-splitting explosions behind him as his fuselage was raked with fire, and to his horror he saw his aircraft's left wingtip blown clean away by another shell. The plane slewed drunkenly to the right and the joystick was snatched from his grasp as if by a giant invisible hand.

He looked around frantically, but to his

astonishment the other Spitfires had vanished. He was seemingly alone in an empty blue sky, his plane beginning to plunge into an uncontrolled dive.

He grabbed at the stick and pulled it back, hard, into his stomach. The aircraft's nose lifted reassuringly.

Thank Christ. Still flyable.

The thought had barely registered when more thunderous explosions rocked and shuddered his Spitfire, and there was a blinding flash just behind the propeller.

Stop it! Bloody stop it, you vicious bastard! You're going to kill me!

His canopy was hit again and this time most of it was blasted completely away. The airstream instantly tore at his eyes and nostrils and mouth: he could scarcely see or breathe. Where the fuck were his goggles? Vanished, along with his flying helmet and oxygen mask. The nose of his plane dipped down again, more sharply than before.

Right. You want to dive? Good. Let's bloody well dive then. I'll show you what a dive is.

He ducked his head as low into the shattered cockpit as he could, thrust the stick forward and boosted the throttle all the way open. The engine responded instantly with a throaty roar and the Spitfire arced into a near-vertical plunge. The whole aircraft began to tremble, whether from the increasing speed or more enemy strikes, he couldn't tell. Jesus, he must be pushing 500mph, easy. The bloody wings would strip off at this rate. He didn't care. All he wanted was to get away from the maniac who was trying to murder him.

Very close to the ground, he levelled out and for the first time twisted his head to look behind him. Nobody there. He must have outrun the bastard.

He peered along both wings. Hell, the one with the missing tip had definitely been bent backwards in the crash dive. It didn't look right at all. The other had several terrifyingly large holes, and it looked to him as if he'd lost a chunk of propeller — its whirling arc had a peculiar shimmied pattern to it that he'd never seen before.

But, incredibly, the plane was still responding to his controls, and as a long sandy beach flashed under his wings and he shot out over the sea, he began to think he actually might, just might, get back. All his instruments were gone — there was a great gaping hole under the remaining jagged shards of his canopy — but the weather was clear and he could already see the white cliffs of the English coast lining the horizon ahead.

He pulled up a couple of hundred feet and took another quick look around, as best he could in the raging slipstream. Not another aircraft in sight, friend or foe.

All the same he slammed his battered aircraft down again until the Spitfire was almost skimming the waves.

He was bloody well going to make it.

31

Diana heard the sound of tyres crunching up the gravel drive and ran to the front door. The little MG was pulling up next to her father's garage. Its hood was down and there was James Blackwell sitting in the sunshine and grinning at her from behind the wheel.

She ran across and threw her arms around his neck as he climbed out.

'I've been so horribly worried about you! I thought you might be d — ' Her words were cut off by his kiss.

'Very much alive, as you can tell,' he said softly after almost a minute.

She laughed. 'So will I be, if you let me breathe.'

He laughed too. 'Sorry. Just making sure you were real.'

'What do you want to do, James? Come inside, or . . . '

He shook his head. 'No. I want you to myself for a while. Come on, it's a beautiful day — let's go out for lunch.'

'That's a wonderful idea. Let me get my hat. You can say hello to everyone when we get back later.'

He watched her as she ran inside the house. Christ, she was lovely. She was wearing a short-sleeved emerald-green silk dress that matched her eyes, and summer espadrilles. When she reappeared moments later, she was busily setting a red beret to the side of her head. She looked, he thought, enchanting.

'There. Will I do?'

'You'll more than do,' he said. 'Come here.'

A while later she pulled away. 'That's only our third kiss, James,' she said a little unsteadily, 'and each one's been longer than the last. I think we may need to start making appointments.'

'Nonsense. I'm at your disposal round the clock, now and forever more. Well, as long as my leave lasts, anyway. Come on, let's go. I'm absolutely ravenous, and not just for you.'

They found a pretty pub-cum-restaurant tucked under the Weald, and took a table in the apple orchard at the back.

'I've been here before,' Diana told James as he came out of the thatched, half-timbered building with their drinks. 'Daddy brought us all here when he was made a senior partner. I was about twelve and John would have been fourteen, I think.'

She looked around her at the fruit trees, now wearing their freshest green of June. 'That seems like another world now. Sometimes I still can't quite believe that we really are at war, and that it's all gone so horribly wrong, so quickly. Do you think we're going to lose? I suppose I shouldn't ask you that, not after what you've just been through.' She reached out and put her hand on his arm. 'John has told us a bit about what it's been like for you all. He said you very nearly . . . that you almost . . . '

'Got killed? Yes, I did. It's all right, I don't

mind talking about it. I was jumped by one of their fighters over France and very badly shot up. I never even saw the other plane. Actually, I think there were probably two of them. It was the most terrifying experience of my whole life, Diana. God knows how I managed not to have my head blown off. My Spit got me home somehow but it was like flying scrap metal. I think they've broken it up for parts. I have a new one now, anyway.'

She stared at him. 'I don't know what to say, James. I can't even imagine being in a situation like that.'

'Neither could I, until it happened. And to think that until a short while ago I actually decided that I was impervious to fear. I truly did, Diana. Impervious to imagination, more like.' He lit a cigarette.

'As to whether we're going to lose — we might. In fact, we probably will. The Belgians have gone under already and the French are obviously getting ready to throw in the towel. The Dutch are out and Norway's clearly had it, so it'll be just us left. Not exactly a reassuring prospect, is it?'

A waitress came to take their order. When she'd gone, Diana got up and went round to James's side of the table. She sat next to him on the wooden bench and kissed his cheek.

'Listen . . . there's something I want to tell you right away. I've been thinking a lot about this while you've been away and I've come to a decision. What you just told me makes me even more certain it's the right one.'

126

Bloody hell, if this is what I think it is, thought James, she's moved a lot further and faster than I could have dreamed.

'It's what we talked about that night at The Eagle — about how the war changes our perspective; how we can't take things for granted any more. Especially time. How we might find ourselves wanting to . . . speed things up.'

She twisted the ring her parents had given her for her twentieth birthday earlier that year. 'I mean, what if you *had* been shot down that day? Even if you'd survived, you might have ended up in a prison camp, and God knows when I'd see you again. What I'm trying to say is . . . is . . . if we want to — and I do want to — we should . . . '

He took her face in his hands. 'It's all right, Diana, I know what you're saying. I feel exactly the same, you've known that since April. And yes, I want to as well.'

She kissed him lightly, then sat back and considered him for a few moments. 'So — you'll come to me tonight, then?'

'My goodness.' He stared at her. 'You really have made your mind up, haven't you?'

She started laughing.

'What is it?'

'I've just thought of something I said to you back at the house this morning. Remember?'

'Um . . . no, I'm not sure I do.'

'I said we'd need to make an appointment. And so we just have!'

32

They got back to the Dower House in time for tea. It was another fine afternoon and Lucy, helped by Gwen, had set out sandwiches and cakes on the garden table near the French windows. Gwen woke her son soon after James and Diana returned.

'Darling?' She gently shook his shoulder. 'Diana and James are back. You've been asleep for nearly seven hours. Wouldn't you like some tea on the lawn with the rest of us?'

He was near-catatonic. 'Mmm, thanks. I'll be down in a minute.' His head flopped back on his pillow and by the time Gwen had quietly closed the bedroom door, soft snores drifted from the bed again.

Even though it was now late afternoon, the day seemed to be getting even hotter. Diana had gone upstairs to change into a cooler dress while Mr Arnold joined their guest on the lawn. James was drinking tea from a cup balanced on his chest just below his chin, long legs sprawled out from the deckchair he'd sunk into.

'Evening, Flight Commander. No, no, don't get up,' Mr Arnold said as the younger man struggled for purchase against his canvas seat. 'As you were, as you were.'

James sank back. 'Thank you, sir.'

'Oh good God. Call me Oliver.' He sat down in a deckchair of his own. 'Well, how are you,

James? Our boy seems utterly drained.'

'We all are, sir. I mean, Oliver. You'll know what it's like. As long as you're in action you have inexhaustible reserves of energy. When you stop . . . ' He made a pantomime of a puppet whose strings have been comprehensively cut. 'You flop to the floor.'

'Yes, I certainly remember that,' Oliver said.

Lucy emerged from the French windows and poured them both more tea. 'Madam says we'll not be joined by Mr John until dinner,' she informed them. 'He's still catching up on his shut-eye, she says.'

'Thank you, Lucy.'

James and Oliver sipped their tea.

'Why aren't you sleeping too, James? You must be as exhausted as John is.'

James put his cup down. 'For two reasons. I slept like the dead all day yesterday, while John was coming down here, and . . . well, I wanted to see Diana today, as soon as I woke up. More than anything.'

Mr Arnold nodded slowly. 'I see. And, if I may be allowed to sound somewhat old-fashioned, what are your intentions towards my daughter?' He gave an embarrassed laugh. 'I'm sorry, that sounded terribly Victorian and pompous, didn't it? But really, James — what are your plans?'

The question caught James completely off-balance. He realised with a slight shock that, for the first time since he'd met the Arnold family, he was no longer calculating his every move concerning Diana. Even on the drive down to the Dower House that morning, there had been no plots or strategies turning over in his mind. His only emotion had been one of genuine excitement that he was going to see her again.

The admission just now about how much that meant to him had been no careful stratagem to impress her father. It was the simple truth. He *had* woken that morning desperate to see Diana, and for no other reason than . . . than what?

Perhaps it was something to do with his desperate encounters in the air above France. Maybe brushes with death did this to a man — everything was greatly simplified.

Mr Arnold coughed. 'Well, James?'

He looked at Diana's father. James Blackwell was nothing if not an opportunist, and this was a golden opportunity. It didn't matter that, for once, he hadn't manipulated it precisely into being.

He stood up.

'My intentions are to marry Diana, sir. Do I have your permission to ask her?'

33

John was drowsy at dinner, and after only half a glass of wine his head was nodding.

'I'm sorry, good people, I have more serious sleeping to do,' he announced apologetically, rising from the table before dessert was served. 'I'm off. Tomorrow let badminton, tennis, and all other vigorous pastimes be unconfined. I shall be re-invog ... re-onvig ... *damn!* ... Re-invigorated.

'Diana,' he turned to his sister, 'you may, if you so wish, undertake a game of skittles with me on the lawn after breakfast. It will atone for my selfish past behaviour on this matter. It is time. The sins of my youth shall be washed away — and yours too, scourge of the family crystal.' He gave an enormous yawn, and bowed to his friend.

'James, you may ... you may ... I don't know what you may do. I shall decide tomorrow. I'm drunk with tiredness. Night, all.' He tottered from the room.

★   ★   ★

'Good heavens, what did you say to him?' Gwen asked her husband as he climbed into bed beside her.

'I said yes, obviously! What would you have said? Haven't you seen the way she looks at him?

131

She's head over heels in love with the chap.'

'But why on earth didn't you tell me earlier?'

'This was the first chance. We haven't been alone until now; that's why I suggested coming to bed early, so we could talk. Anyway, come on. What d'you think?'

'Oh, Oliver, they're both so young! And he's — well, he's a fighter pilot. I can't even begin to think about the awful dangers John faces, I simply can't. But I *can* bring myself to say that James Blackwell might well be . . . '

'Wounded? Killed? Taken prisoner? Wasn't that exactly the position I was in when you agreed to marry me in 1916?'

She stared at him. Then she slowly put her hand in his.

'Oh my dear,' she said, 'we've come full circle, haven't we? Nothing's changed at all, has it? Nothing. Those poor creatures. How we've failed them. How could we let such a terrible, terrible war happen again?'

Her husband pulled her to him. 'I think it's because we couldn't face our fears,' he said deliberately. 'We were so horrified by memories of the last time that we'd do or say anything to convince ourselves it couldn't happen again. Even when reality was staring us in the face.'

He tilted his head back against the headboard. 'And now it's our children who've got to clear the mess up. Let's hope they can. Let's just pray it's not too late.' He reached for her other hand. 'And let's allow them whatever happiness they can grab hold of, shall we? While they can?'

Gwen nodded. 'Of course you're right. And as for being too young . . . ' she considered for a moment. 'Weren't we the same age?'

'To the year.'

34

They'd left the pair of them downstairs in the garden room. The night was warm and the French windows had been thrown open, chairs pushed to the threshold. Outside, fireflies were hovering above the lawns.

As soon as her parents had said goodnight and closed the door into the hall, Diana jumped out of her armchair and went over to sit on James's lap, arms thrown around his neck.

'What was all that business between you and Daddy at dinner?' she asked, after she had been thoroughly kissed.

'What business?'

'Oh, come on.' She poked his ribs. 'The pair of you looked fit to burst! What's going on?'

He wished he entirely knew. Always the master of his affairs, James Blackwell felt strangely off-balance tonight. Events seemed to be controlling him, rather than the reverse. This was a new sensation and, to his surprise, not necessarily an unpleasant one.

'OK.' He took a deep breath. 'I had a conversation with your father, at tea, while you were upstairs.'

'What about?'

'You. Well, more to the point, us. He asked me what my intentions were towards you.'

Diana laughed. 'Really? How funny! That doesn't sound like him at all.'

James smiled. 'To be fair, he thought it was pretty funny too, as soon as he'd said it — but anyway, he pressed the point.'

Diana's own smile faded. 'What did you say? Oh James, you didn't say anything about our speeding things up, did you? You didn't even hint at it, surely.'

'Of course not! No, I went much further than that.'

'*What?* I don't understand.'

'Me neither, as it happens. Well, not fully, yet. I asked your father to give me permission to do something. But let's do this properly. Let me get up.'

She climbed off his lap and he stood up, motioning her to sit in the armchair. When she was settled, he snapped off his best salute before dropping on to one knee in front of her. Diana gave a little gasp.

'I'm sorry,' he told her. 'I don't have a ring to put on your finger, but I do have a question for you.'

She stared down at him, one hand pressed to her mouth.

'Diana Arnold, would you please marry me? As soon as possible?'

She sat absolutely still for so long he began to think he had somehow paralysed her. Finally, she took her hand away from her mouth, and spoke.

'So *this* is what you meant by speeding things up. I had very different ideas, I have to say.'

'Oh yes, all that too,' he said. 'Most definitely. But what's your answer, Diana? Say it's yes.'

She slid from the chair and sank down on her

135

knees to face him, putting her hands on his shoulders.

'How could it *possibly* be anything else?' And in an unconscious echo of her mother during another war, a quarter of a century earlier, Diana added: 'Yes. Yes, of course.'

* * *

She woke early next morning, as the sun was rising. James lay next to her, one arm flung behind his head, the other across her waist. He was deeply asleep, his chest steadily rising and falling. They were both naked, their clothes scattered across her bedroom floor.

Trying not to wake him, she shifted slightly in the single bed in which she had slept since childhood. It was impossibly narrow for two grown people but somehow they'd managed to fall asleep, afterwards.

She turned her head to look at him before carefully pushing a strand of blond fringe out of his eyes.

Her lover. Her fiancé. Her man.

She had wondered, as they fell asleep together the night before, if she would have any regrets in the morning; might wish they had waited. She considered the question again now. Surely she should be feeling guilty? She hadn't even tried to call a halt to what was happening. She hadn't wanted to; not at all.

Before they had come upstairs together, moving past her parents' bedroom with the stealth and silence of seasoned burglars, James

136

had told her about the special marriage licences introduced soon after the war started. Three days after applying for one, couples in a hurry could be legally married in a register office.

Was that why she had given herself to James? she wondered. Because she knew they would be husband and wife in a few days, so breaking the rules now didn't really count? Diana smiled to herself. She knew a self-serving excuse when she heard one, even if it was only in her own thoughts.

She looked around her room. She had purged it of most of her childhood possessions before leaving for her first term at Girton, but it still retained a lingering atmosphere of innocence. Her dresser with its pink-framed mirror; the twin bookshelves where her old storybooks mingled with academic works she'd brought back from Cambridge; the candlewick dressing-gown hanging on the back of the door . . . how long was it since she had worn that? It must be three years, maybe four.

There might have been better places, Diana reflected ruefully, to lose one's virginity.

Even so, she couldn't summon up the slightest regret. She felt only deep contentment and an indisputable feeling that she had met her destiny. The act of love had overwhelmed her. More than that, it had somehow completed her. She had always known instinctively that it would.

Sexual Diana. Carnal Diana. She had always been there, hadn't she? Patiently waiting. Perhaps that was another reason she felt no guilt: if she was honest, she had to admit she'd found the whole experience last night absolutely wonderful.

They hadn't taken precautions. It hadn't even occurred to her. But here again, she was without regrets. Another completion. She had no idea if there would be consequences, but her deep-seated longing for babies meant she didn't care; rather, she found herself almost hoping she would have a child — and the sooner the better.

She lifted her head slightly from the pillow to look at her bedside alarm. Nearly half past five. Lucy would be up and about soon.

'James.'

He mumbled something and pulled her closer to him.

'*James*.' She tugged gently at his hair. 'Time for you to go back to your room, darling.'

He opened his eyes. 'Oh. Hello.'

'Hello.'

'We're getting married.'

'Yes.'

'Good.' He raised his head and kissed her. 'Thank you for saying yes.'

'Thank you for asking.'

He stretched, luxuriously. '*Must* I go?'

'Must is the operative word, I'm afraid. If Mummy knew you were in my bed she'd have a fit. Daddy wouldn't be far behind her either. Come on, James, seriously. It would spoil everything.'

'Of course.' He rolled out of bed and stood unselfconsciously naked before her, scratching his stubble. 'Where are my clothes?'

'On the floor behind you.'

He looked at the tangled heap unhappily. 'My uniform's going to look awfully crumpled. God knows what your parents will think.'

She laughed. 'Just tell them you fell asleep in your clothes. John can lend you some of his while Lucy irons those.'

'I suppose so.' He glanced around the room. 'Crikey. It looks very different in daylight. Not at all suitable for . . . you know. I'm awfully sorry, Diana. You deserved a petal-strewn boudoir, not the nursery.'

She laughed again. 'Hardly a nursery. Anyway, there'll be time for all that.'

He looked at her as he pulled on his uniform. 'Diana, thank you for — you know.'

'Thank you, my darling — it was wonderful. I'll see you at breakfast. Is that when we should tell everyone, do you think?'

'About the wedding, yes. About their daughter's wanton seduction of a poor, innocent visitor to her parents' house, perhaps best not.'

She assumed mock outrage. 'Innocent? After last night there's one thing I know for certain about you now, Flight Commander. You're about as innocent as . . . as . . . '

He pressed his finger to her lips. 'Shh. You don't know that. For all you know, you bring out the worst in me.'

She grinned at him as he backed theatrically out of the door.

'I certainly hope so.'

35

Oliver and Gwen took the news of the engagement with aplomb. After all, they were expecting it. Their son, on the other hand, was dumbfounded. He dropped his eggy spoon with a clatter and stared open-mouthed at the other four.

'Did all this happen while I was asleep? Am I some sort of latter-day Rip Van Winkle? Have I been kipping for the last twenty years? Blimey, Jimmy, you're a fast worker. So are you, Di. Bloody hell!'

Then he was on his feet and hurrying around the breakfast-table to hug and kiss his sister. He glared at her fiancé over Diana's shoulder. 'Make sure you damn well look after her,' he said. 'Any messing her about and I'll shoot you down myself.'

Then he went over to James and pumped his hand up and down. 'Congratulations, Jimmy. Welcome to the family. When's the happy day?'

Diana answered for them both. 'We're going to get a special licence. They let you get married after only three days now. James is going out straight after breakfast to see to it, once Lucy's pressed his uniform. Today's Tuesday, so I suppose we'll be tying the knot in Tunbridge Wells Register Office on Saturday morning.'

Lucy came into the room. 'I've turned on the wireless for the news, sir, madam. Will you take coffee in the drawing room as usual?'

'No, thank you, Lucy,' said Mr Arnold. 'Let's open a bottle of champagne.' He nodded to Diana and her fiancé, now holding hands on the other side of the room. 'Those two are getting married at the weekend. Fun, isn't it?'

36

Diana and James's modest plans for a short honeymoon in the Cotswolds were comprehensively dashed by events in France. The day before the wedding brought news that the Germans had entered Paris. On the morning of the ceremony itself, the French were begging Hitler for an armistice. Britain stood quite alone. The Continent was lost.

Back across the Channel in Tunbridge Wells, the tiny wedding party arrived at the town's register office just before one o'clock. Mr Arnold drove his daughter in the Humber, white ribbons fluttering from its bonnet. James and Gwen followed behind in the MG, and the best man brought up the rear of the little convoy on his motor bike.

There had been no time to issue invitations. But theirs was not the smallest wedding party that day: as the five of them walked towards the register office, a young couple emerged from its main entrance, laughing. The bride was in white, the bridegroom in the brown serge and Sam Browne belt of an Army officer's uniform. They were quite alone, and as they came down the steps, the husband suddenly pulled a handful of confetti from his breast pocket and sprinkled it above the two of them. The Arnolds' party burst into spontaneous applause, and the couple waved happily to them as they hurried away.

'My goodness!' exclaimed Mr Arnold, pulling out his handkerchief and blowing his nose to mask the treacherous tears that threatened to unman him. 'What times are these, everyone? What times are these.'

Inside, the registrar was waiting for them. He was a short, dapper man in a dark suit. He wore his oiled hair combed back, apart from the cowlick that hung low over his forehead. A small moustache completed the unfortunate resemblance.

'Nice of the Führer to pop over and officiate,' John whispered to his father. 'You'd think he had other things on his mind today.'

But the official turned out to be the soul of kindness and enthusiasm, ushering Diana and James into position in front of his polished oak desk, and beaming at the others as he gestured to them to take their seats.

'Welcome to you all,' he announced, brightly. 'Yes, yes, do sit in the front row, you three, there's plenty of room, ha ha! I must say I find these wartime weddings *so* romantic, don't you? And look at the two of you! How wonderful you both look.' He clasped his hands in an almost girlish gesture and Diana began to giggle.

James turned to look at her. She was wearing the simplest of white silk sheaths, gathered in at the waist by a narrow green satin belt. The flowers garlanded in her hair — tiny wild roses, daisies and buttercups — had been picked from the paddock that morning by Gwen. The toes of white satin shoes peeped out from the hem of Diana's dress. The entire ensemble had been bought by mother and daughter in a hurried shopping expedition to Piccadilly the day before.

'You look bloody sensational,' he whispered in her ear.

'So do you,' she whispered back.

He fingered the cuffs of his RAF tunic. 'Oh, this old thing . . . '

The short ceremony began. Diana was wearing her engagement ring, a modest cluster of three emeralds that James had bought in Tunbridge the morning he came in to see about the licence. When the time came for the wedding ring to be presented, John, also in service blue, came forward.

The gold band that James proceeded to slide onto Diana's finger had belonged to Gwen's late mother. It was old gold, pale and slightly matt. It needed re-sizing; it was a little too big, but there had been no time.

When the happy party arrived back at the Dower House for the wedding breakfast — caterers had been summoned at short notice, much to Lucy's outrage — telegrams were waiting on the hall table.

Both pilots were summoned back to base immediately.

'I'm so sorry, darling,' James told his wife as they held each other beside his car in the drive of the Dower House. 'No honeymoon, not even a wedding night. *Bloody* war.'

'It could have been worse, James; we might have had to postpone the wedding. At least we're married. It's amazing, I can't quite believe we've done it.'

'I can't believe *you*,' he said, stepping back and holding her at arm's length. 'Let me look at you.'

She was still in her wedding dress; there had been no time to change.

He kissed her. 'I'll remember the way you look today until the day I die.'

She fell against him and began to cry.

'I'm sorry, James, I'm sorry. I so wanted not to cry. When will we see each other again?'

He held her tight. 'I won't lie to you, Diana: I have absolutely no idea. We're in completely uncharted territory now. But I will come back to you, I swear. However long I have to be away, I *will* come back to you. You must believe that.'

Before she could answer they were startled by the sudden noise of her brother's motor bike being gunned into life. He wheeled it out from the garage and stopped beside them, adjusting his goggles.

'I'm awfully sorry about this, sis,' he shouted above the crackle of the engine. 'Rotten way to end your wedding day. You too, Jimmy. Bloody Nazis. We're really going to have to do something about them, you know.'

Oliver and Gwen came out of the house, Mr Arnold smart in grey tails. But he was pale, and his wife close to tears.

Their new son-in-law stepped across to the doorway and shook Mr Arnold's hand.

'Well, I suppose this is it,' he said, bending to

kiss Gwen's cheek. 'Goodbye, Gwen. I'm sorry I can't stay for the baked meats.'

She smiled tearfully. 'Burnt offerings, more like. They must be the worst caterers in Kent. Goodbye, James. I'm so sorry you have to leave like this. Just come home as soon as you can.'

Home. James nodded. 'Yes.'

Behind him, the motor bike revved and his friend yelled: 'Come on, Jimmy. I'll lead, you follow.'

'Righty-ho.' He went back to his wife. 'Well, goodbye, Mrs Blackwell, for now.'

Diana had given up any attempt to stop her tears.

'Come back to me, James,' she sobbed. 'Please.'

His heart lurched. He had never felt raw emotion like this before.

'Goodbye, Diana.' He kissed her quickly and swung into the driver's seat of the open-topped car, calling, 'All right, Johnnie, lead on!'

Motor bike and sports car moved away down the drive. The last James saw of his wife was her reflection in his wing mirror. She was trying to wave, but as he watched he saw her sink to the ground in her wedding dress, Oliver and Gwen running to support their daughter.

He pulled out into the lane and accelerated, hard. The breeze strengthened as the car picked up speed and he suddenly found himself blinking back tears. It was the wind that caused them.

Nothing else.

★　★　★

146

Half an hour later, he was stalled in stationary traffic. Almost as soon as they'd set off, an impatient John had roared ahead and out of sight, after giving him a backwards wave. James didn't blame him; the whole point of a motor bike was getting there quickly.

He drummed the steering wheel with his fingers. Something must have happened up ahead. After a few minutes he turned the car round and picked his way through the countryside along back lanes, finally emerging on to the main road ahead of whatever was holding things up.

The aerodrome was buzzing like an angry hive of bees when he got there. All the Spitfires were at dispersal, engines throbbing as mechanics checked them over.

'Blackwell — about bloody time!' shouted his squadron leader when he spotted James walking across the tarmac. 'You should have been back hours ago! Where's Arnold?'

'I don't know, sir,' yelled James over the roar of a dozen Merlin engines. He hesitated. 'I just got married, sir,' he shouted. 'Pilot Officer Arnold was my best man. We didn't get the telegrams recalling us until we got back from the wedding. But John should be here by now — he was on his motor bike.'

The commander strode across and shook James by the hand. 'Congratulations, Blackwell! You picked a hell of a day for it. Is she pretty?'

'Yes, sir! Very. What's happening here?'

'Big flap on. We're taking off in half an hour.

147

Get your gear straight away. I'll give everyone the flight plan when we're in the air but I can tell you now we're going across the Channel. All except your bloody best man. Maybe he's had a puncture. Now get weaving!'

37

Diana had taken off her wedding dress. She felt strangely numb as she did so, and she hadn't quite known what to do with it afterwards. In the end she hung it on the back of her bedroom door, where it sagged forlornly from the hook.

She tried not to start crying again as she unpicked the flowers from her hair. She was determined not to feel sorry for herself, not on her wedding day. When she'd finished, and put her hair back in an Alice band, she threw on slacks and a cardigan, and wondered what to do next. She had never felt so restless.

'I can't settle,' she said breathlessly when she found her mother, who had gone upstairs to her studio to distract herself with painting. 'I don't know what to do with myself. I feel so lost and peculiar.'

Gwen put her brush down and went across to her daughter. 'I know exactly how you're feeling, darling,' she said, hugging her. 'It was the same after your father and I got married — except that at least we had our wedding night before he had to go back to France. If I were you, darling, I'd — '

The phone began to ring downstairs.

'That might be him!' said Diana. 'He must have got back to Upminster hours ago!' She ran from the room, her father's voice drifting up from the hall as she clattered down the stairs.

'Yes, this is he. Yes. Well, no, we call him John, but his birth name is Robert. Yes, I've told you, I'm his father. This is Oliver Arnold speaking. What is this about, please?'

It obviously wasn't her brand-new husband on the line, Diana realised. This was some business to do with her brother. Disappointed, she turned to go back upstairs when a sudden note of concern in her father's voice made her pause.

'Yes, that's correct, Officer; he owns a Triumph two-fifty. He left here on it — oh, three or four hours or so ago. Look, our boy's not in any kind of trouble, is he?'

There was silence in the hall as Mr Arnold listened to the reply. Diana saw her father sway a little, then put out his free hand against the wall to steady himself.

'What? What kind of accident? Has he been hurt?'

A terrible sensation begin to creep over her.

Her father turned slowly around and stared through her. 'When? When was this? How, exactly?'

Another pause for the answer. Then: 'Are you telling me that . . . Is my son . . . ?'

'*Oh-oh-oh-oh-no, Daddy, no! No no no!*'

Now Gwen was coming down the stairs behind her. 'Dear God, what's happening? Diana, whatever is the matter with you? What's all this commotion?'

'I see — yes, I do quite see. Mr Arnold was speaking again, very quietly. 'Thank you for telling me. What? Yes, of course, I shall expect them. I'll meet you there shortly. Yes. Goodbye.'

150

With infinite slowness, he replaced the receiver on its cracked cradle, and looked up at his wife and daughter. The two women gripped hands and stood motionless together, choked into silence by a fearful apprehension.

'That was Sidcup police station,' he said at last, his voice thick and slow. 'There's been . . . an accident. They're going to send a car for me. I have to . . . I have to . . . ' He stepped towards the two women and gave a helpless shrug.

'I have to identify John. He's been in a motor bike accident. It happened a couple of hours ago. Some sort of collision with an Army lorry.'

Gwen gave a low, animal moan. 'Identify? Isn't that . . . doesn't that mean . . . ?'

Mr Arnold took a deep, juddering breath. 'Yes. Our son is dead, my dear. John is dead.'

He sprang forward and caught his wife just in time. A trembling Diana helped him lower Gwen into an awkward, half-sitting position on the polished wooden floor.

The three of them huddled there together for some time.

They spoke not a word, nor made any sound.

And so, presently, Lucy found them.

★ ★ ★

It was nearly dark when Mr Arnold was delivered back to the Dower House in a police car. A swollen-eyed Lucy let him in. He hugged her, wordlessly, and then walked slowly through to the drawing room. Gwen and Diana were clasped in each other's arms on the sofa. They looked at him through reddened, bruised eyes, almost as if he were an enemy.

'Well?' Gwen whispered.

'Yes. It's John.' Mr Arnold rubbed his face in his hands. 'We'd all better have a drink.'

Diana crossed slowly to the sideboard and filled three glasses to the brim with scotch.

'Listen to me, both of you,' her father told them heavily after they'd all swallowed a finger of neat whisky. 'It's important you both know that John didn't suffer. It seems he was overtaking a car when the lorry came out of a side lane. The police say it must have been over in a split second.'

Before he could say any more there was a loud double-knock at the front door.

Mr Arnold threw his head back. 'Christ. What now?'

He walked back into the hall. The women heard the door open, and a murmur of voices. It went on for some time before there was an exclamation from Mr Arnold. The voices came louder now, from inside the hall itself.

Instinctively Diana and Gwen stood up.

Mr Arnold came back into the room, closely followed by two men, both in RAF blue. The younger man wore a chaplain's collar.

Gwen hesitated, before giving a helpless shrug. 'Oh. It's kind of you to call on us so soon, but we're only just . . . our son has only just . . . '

Mr Arnold shook his head. 'They're not here about John, darling.' He faced his daughter. 'Diana . . . '

She froze.

'I just don't know how to tell you this, my dearest child. Come to me.'

'Tell me.'

He stared at her, and then ran his fingers through his hair, almost violently. 'Oh God! This is a terrible, terrible day.'

'*Tell me.*'

He stretched his arms towards her. 'James has been shot down, Diana. Over France, this afternoon. Two other pilots saw it happen and they say — apparently they say there was no parachute.'

Diana stared at him, then turned calmly to the two officers.

'Are you here to tell me my husband is dead?' she asked, almost conversationally.

The men exchanged glances, before the older one stepped forward. Kind eyes met Diana's and when he spoke, it was with great gentleness.

'I'm Captain Blake, Flight Commander Blackwell's Squadron Intelligence Officer.'

Diana nodded wordlessly.

'I'm very sorry to tell you it's as your father said, Mrs Blackwell. Your husband has been shot down, over the Pas de Calais this afternoon. Other British pilots in the vicinity say that his aircraft exploded when it hit the ground, and it seems he wasn't . . . in a position to bail out. There was no sign of a parachute, you see.'

Diana stared at him. 'So he's dead.'

The officer nodded. 'Yes, we believe so.'

'He and my brother.'

The man turned and frowned faintly at his

colleague, a prompt to the younger man to speak, but after an awkward silence, the intelligence officer sighed and turned to Oliver and Gwen again.

'Yes. We learned about your son,' he nodded sympathetically to Diana, 'your brother, Mrs Blackwell, shortly before leaving Upminster to drive down here. It's . . . well, it's a very bad business. The whole squadron is extremely cut up about it. Your boy was exceptionally popular, as was Flight Commander Blackwell.'

He hesitated, and then added: 'As a matter of fact, I might as well tell you that we lost another chap over the Channel this afternoon. That's three good men in as many hours. It's been the squadron's worst day of the war so far.'

Mr Arnold swallowed and nodded. 'That must be extremely hard for all of you. I'm very sorry.'

The intelligence officer inclined his head in appreciation. He seemed to have run out of words. After a long, defeated silence, the young chaplain finally cleared his throat.

'The RAF offers you its sincerest condolences.'

His colleague closed his eyes. The Arnolds stared at the chaplain, before Diana gave a short, brittle laugh.

'Well, thank you. Yes. Thank you very much indeed.'

For the first time since the men had entered the room, she moved, stepping quickly to the cigarette box. With shaking hands, she extracted one and fumbled to light it.

'I only married him this morning, did you

know that?' she asked in a strange, high voice. She drew hard on the cigarette. 'Not much of a marriage, was it? Not much of a marriage at all, I'd say.'

Diana turned to her parents, tears suddenly streaming down her face.

'What are we going to do now, Mummy and Daddy? Whatever are we going to do?'

Part Two

38

Nice, South of France, April 1951

This damned coffee-maker sounds just like a buzz-bomb, Diana thought as she switched on the chrome-plated machine in her gleaming American kitchen. This morning, as the device bumbled and crackled its way to producing the steaming black coffee that still had the capacity to jolt her senses at the first sip, Diana struggled, as she always did, with the blinds that screened her from what she was certain would be another dazzling sunrise.

Eventually she found the critical angle where the drawstrings reluctantly engaged the fickle pulleys, and the Venetian blinds smoothly rolled up to reveal a Mediterranean dawn.

Diana blinked as the slanting light fell on her face. This was no English sun; even this early in the year — it was still the first week of April — she could feel the latent strength beating through the glass. It would be better to drink her coffee outside in the shade, where the early morning breeze still carried something of the cool of the night.

As she stirred preserved cream into her coffee — preserved cream was still virtually unavailable back home — Diana glanced around the kitchen of her new home. Everything sparkled and shone; everything was twice as big as its equivalent back in England.

Giant fridge encased in shiny chrome. Chromed toaster, which could accommodate six slices of bread; chromed juice-maker which Stella loved playing with, stuffing freshly picked oranges into its gaping maw and laughing delightedly as surprisingly paltry amounts of liquid dribbled into the steel beaker underneath; brushed-steel coffee-maker, now growling and burping in a sulky undertone after yielding its first drink of the day; shiny white washing machine with built-in tumble-dryer which Diana had yet to place her faith in (so far, she had hung all the family's laundry out to dry from the iron balustrade that ran the length of the sunterrace at the back of the villa) and, most wondrous of all, the enormous television which sat in its own walnut cabinet set to one side of the door that led into the vast refrigerated pantry.

The television, like everything else in the villa with a plug attached, was American-made. The previous occupants had shipped everything here to Provence from their house in Cape Cod, and then back again to Massachusetts when they left — everything but the kitchen appliances and the TV.

'You might as well keep the goddamned thing,' the departing tenant had told them with a shrug as he showed them crossly round the villa, all the while incongruously twirling a golf club in his hands. 'It'll cost me more to ship it home again than to buy a new one. Anyway, it's no goddamned use, no use at all. Back home it'd give you forty channels. Here I can only get one,

160

and that's in goddamned French.'

But Diana liked watching French television. It was limited to about three hours each evening. Stiff, formal programmes, most of them — news bulletins, political discussions, dull farming documentaries — but they helped her steadily improving French. Only the evening before she had watched an interview with the American President, Harry Truman, coming live from a studio in Paris, and she had correctly interpreted at least two of the questions before the President's translator did. She had thought the interviewer rather rude and offhand with Truman; you wouldn't have thought America had helped liberate France from the Nazis barely seven years earlier.

Now, Diana put her coffee cup on her usual tray, stencilled with abstract designs in the vibrant colours of Provence: blue, to represent the sky, yellow, the sun — and green, for the lush vegetation that thirstily drank the winter rains and then stood verdant and defiant in the scorching summer heat.

Indeed, summer was almost here. There were little more than ten weeks to the solstice. The strengthening sun was almost as high in the sky at its zenith as it would be on an English midsummer's day. Diana slid open the double doors leading on to the south-facing patio and stepped outside.

As she'd hoped, the air remained cool from the night, although the sun, rising above the hills to the east, licked her skin as soon as she left the villa's shade. She retreated under the terrace's white and yellow striped awning. It was going to be another warm day. Away down the long valley that led to Nice, Diana could see the Mediterranean, a hazy bowl of blue flecked with white; distant fishing boats returning from their night's work.

She sat in one of the terrace's rattan chairs and stared out across her little corner of Provence. Even now, six weeks after the three of them had arrived, she could hardly believe she was actually here, and likely to stay for the coming two, perhaps even three years.

Diana had changed little in the past decade. She still preferred to wear her dark hair down, although instead of being swept back from her forehead, now she had a fringe. It added to her youthful appearance; she could have passed for someone in their mid-twenties.

A casual caller at the villa coming across Diana this morning could be forgiven for addressing her in French. She looked French, her naturally olive skin darkened by the light tan she invariably seemed to acquire after even the briefest exposure to the sun. As always, the darkened skin made her eyes appear extraordinarily exotic: at times they seemed almost to flash and flare in electric bursts.

Her choice of clothes added to the Gallic illusion. Almost the first thing Diana had done on arriving in Provence was to shop for new outfits in the smart dress shops of Nice and in the ritzy neighbouring port of Antibes.

She had left almost her entire English wardrobe behind. Britain still laboured under

162

what the papers called 'The Age of Austerity'. Everything seemed grey and drab and hopeless. Near-colourless clothes. Weary queues waiting patiently outside almost every shop. Bombsites that seemed permanent fixtures in the urban landscape: depressing expanses of shattered brick and glass, weeds poking through the rubble. Smashed building timbers had long since been removed for winter fuel.

Women did their best to dress well but it was difficult. Material was in short supply, and by the end of the 1940s the contents of most women's wardrobes had been re-cut, re-sewn, altered, mended and cannibalised to the point of exhaustion. Diana's was no exception and it had been a relief to leave it all behind, packed into cardboard boxes she was quite certain she would never open again.

One of the few items to remain on its hanger was the wedding dress she had worn the day James and John were killed. It was pristine: Diana had never considered altering it so it could be worn again.

This morning she was in a simple cream short-sleeved cotton blouse matched with a pleated skirt, belted at her narrow waist. She looked like one of the smart Paris wives who had only recently returned north, after spending Easter at their family villas in Provence. They would be back in force in August.

Diana finished her coffee, and gave a slight shake of her head. She still couldn't quite take it all in; there had been so many changes to her life in such a short time.

It was Douglas who had made it all possible. Douglas, with his patience, his indefatigable patience, who had slowly chipped away at her defences and gently but remorselessly pulled her into his life. And not just her.

There was Stella, too.

* * *

Stella had never known her father. Conceived the week before he was killed, for Stella, James Blackwell represented something between a legend and a fairy tale. That was nothing particularly unusual for her generation; almost half her classmates at school in England were fatherless.

'Mummy! Bridget and Janice and Peter all don't have daddies either!' Stella breathlessly told her mother one day soon after she started school in Kent. 'Mrs Roberts made us all stand up and tell the class about our mummies and daddies, and lots of us don't have daddies. Peter's was drownded and Janice said her daddy was exploded up in a desert! When I told them my daddy died in his aeroplane Peter put his hand up and said his daddy did too. He dropped bombs on the Germans. Mrs Roberts said they were all heroes but I said I knew that already.'

Stella was ten now, but she still slept with a photograph of her father on her bedside table. In it, James Blackwell was grinning out at the world, head tipped slightly to one side in faintly sardonic style, RAF cap pushed well back from his forehead and a cigarette in his hand. The child's grandfather had taken the snapshot on the lawn the evening before the wedding, and in the background Diana could be seen walking carefully towards the two men, carrying a tray with a jug of lemonade and glasses.

Now, whenever Diana looked at the photograph — which was every night when she tucked her daughter into bed — the same thought unfailingly occurred.

He had less than twenty-four hours to live, and none of us knew it.

Diana had only one other photograph of James. It stood on the marble mantelpiece in the villa's main lounge, or *salon*. It showed him standing next to her brother. Both men had their arms draped around the other's shoulders, and clasped brimming pints of beer in their free hands. They were in the bar of their squadron's pub of choice in Upminster, and the flashbulb burst made the panes in the men's beer glasses twinkle with tiny points of brilliant light. John looked as if he was in the middle of saying something vaguely insulting or challenging; his companion's face was half-turned towards him and wore an expression of amused disbelief. Behind the men was a folded newspaper whose headline was partly obscured, but the letters NKIRK could clearly be seen. The photo must have been taken a week or two before both men were killed. A squadron pilot had given it to the Arnolds at their boy's funeral.

Douglas had no objection to these photographs being on permanent display in his home. He was not a jealous man; indeed, he

165

encouraged 'my girls' to talk about James. 'After all, my dear,' he told Diana when, early in their marriage, she had asked if he genuinely didn't object to the photographs, 'without my illustrious predecessor I would have no wee stepdaughter to love, cherish and care for, would I?'

Douglas spoke like that. A son of the Manse, his sentences were old-fashioned and over-ornate, like the heavy wooden furniture in his parents' home outside Inverness. Plans to follow his father into the Kirk had been dissolved by the war. Douglas's head for figures — he had won a prestigious Scottish Schools Award in the mathematical equivalent of a spelling bee — had seen him parachuted into the supplies section of the War Ministry as soon as he achieved his double-first in Mathematics at Edinburgh.

Safe in his Whitehall bunker, Douglas had swiftly risen to the top of the department. The stupendously complex business of keeping Britain's war machine supplied and running smoothly didn't faze him in the slightest. Where other men could spend an entire morning pondering flow charts, graphs and shipping tables, and be no closer to making a decision by lunchtime, Douglas could size up the whole multi-sided equation in the time it took for him to drink his first cup of tea of the day.

By the end of the war Douglas Mackenzie — now Sir Douglas after accepting a knighthood for services rendered to his country — had a grasp of the import-export business that was second to none. He bade farewell to the Civil

166

Service and was snapped up by a City firm that had made a killing, in every sense of the expression, trading in metal during the war.

Inside two years he had been promoted to Managing Director, just in time for the Berlin Airlift.

The Soviet Union, in the opening shots of the Cold War, had blocked land-supply routes into Allied-occupied West Berlin, and the only way to keep the population and its garrison fed, watered and warm in one of the coldest European winters on record, was to fly everything in. Hundreds of thousands of round-the-clock flights began and there were fortunes to be made.

Douglas cornered the market in cereals, and by the summer of 1949 when the airlift ended, he had made his first million. His first two million, to be exact.

He met Diana the following year when he agreed to present the annual prize-giving at Stella's exclusive boarding school in Kent. Eight-year-old Stella Blackwell had come up on stage to shyly accept the Most Promising Pupil of 1950, and as Douglas casually watched her skip back to rejoin her mother in the front row, he stiffened.

He couldn't take his eyes off Diana. Douglas, still unmarried, thought he had never seen a more beautiful woman in his life. He wasn't the only man in the room to think so. Just turned thirty, Diana had more than fulfilled the promise of her youth. She was sometimes compared to the actress Vivien Leigh, who had burst into stellar fame with *Gone with the Wind* ten years earlier. Douglas thought she looked enchanting in her little pill-box hat and elegant black suit. He wasn't to know that it was the last remaining outfit Diana possessed that could possibly be described as smart, nor that she had spent the morning carefully ironing it under a sheet of brown paper and a sprinkling of vinegar, an old trick to dull the shininess of worn, ageing fabric.

Douglas wasted no time introducing himself to her at the little reception afterwards for prize-winners and their parents. He noticed her wedding and engagement rings at once, and asked politely if her husband was present.

'I'm afraid not,' Diana said calmly. 'My husband died in the war. It's just Stella and me — and my parents, of course. They've been wonderful; we couldn't have managed without them.'

Douglas's heart leaped, and then immediately he felt a wave of Calvinist guilt wash over him. It was sinful to take pleasure in the fact that this woman was a widow. But still . . .

'So you never remarried?' he asked her, declining a sherry offered by the headmaster's wife.

She shook her head. 'No.' Diana nodded towards her daughter, chatting excitedly with friends on the far side of the room. 'I come as a double order, you might say. Not many men would want to bring up another man's child . . . but what about you, Mr Mackenzie? Are you married?'

Douglas smiled. 'Dear me, no,' he said. 'I

never found anyone who'd have me. Well, there was someone once, but she told me I was married to my job and she went off with another chap. Quite right, too, I might add.'

Diana reached inside her handbag. 'Mind if I smoke?'

'Not at all. No, I won't have one myself, thanks,' as Diana offered him the packet. 'I was brought up to see it as one of the Deadly Sins. I'm afraid I still can't quite shake that one off.'

Diana put her unlit cigarette back into the pack. 'Then it would be rude of me to smoke in front of you. I'll have it later. So . . . your parents were strict, then?'

'You could say that. My father's a Scottish Methodist, a priest, if you like. He and my mother had a . . . well, a rather straightforward outlook on life. They passed that on to me to a considerable degree, I'm afraid.'

As he told her about his upbringing, and his escape from the Manse to make his way in London, Diana relaxed. She liked his sing-song Highlands accent, the serious brown eyes set in a large face with pale, freckled skin, and his apparent lack of pushiness. He seemed solid and reassuring, and reminded her of a big shambling bear. She could tell his suit was expensively cut, but somehow it refused to co-operate with his frame, the jacket hanging from his shoulders more like a potato sack than a bespoke product of Savile Row.

There seemed to be no pretence about him. She was weary of men who, once they discovered she was a widow, 'tried it on' with her. This one

169

seemed different, and when they had said their goodbyes and she drove home with Stella, Diana was surprised that she felt a slight regret he hadn't asked to see her again. She had, she realised, felt safe with him.

Two days later, a letter arrived. Written on paper embossed with *Mackenzie European Trading*, she read the three handwritten paragraphs beneath with an unexpected frisson of excitement.

Dear Mrs Blackwell,

It was a pleasure to meet you yesterday at your daughter's school.

I hesitated to ask because we had only just become acquainted, but I have plucked up the courage to write to you now. The head-master was kind enough to furnish me with your address. I wondered if you would do me the honour of joining me for dinner one evening soon?

I hope the answer will be yes.

Yours cordially,
Douglas Mackenzie

And so it began. It was an assiduous courtship, at least from Douglas's side. He was unfailingly polite, respectful and attentive.

'You don't have to be quite so formal with me, you know,' Diana teased him on their sixth or seventh date, after he had asked her for the first time — almost with a little bow

170

— if he might kiss her goodnight.

They were outside the front door of her home in the Kent village of Hever, which stood in the shadow of a Norman castle. The house — more of a large cottage — was too big, really, for Diana and Stella, and since the day they moved in, three of the bedrooms had been left unused.

Her father had bought it for her during the war, about a year after the boys were killed. 'I was always going to do this for you, Diana,' he told his daughter at the time. 'It was going to be my marriage settlement on the two of you. Well, now there are two of you again, with Stella, so you must allow me to do this.'

Tonight, Diana suffered herself to be kissed. Douglas wasn't a bad kisser, she thought; at least he didn't try to eat her up like some of the men she had agreed to go out with since the end of the war. It had taken her all of five years before she felt ready to do that; it was only the insistence of her mother — *'Darling, you're still in your twenties. You have to try to start picking up the pieces, for Stella's sake as much as for your own'* — that had made her finally take the plunge.

But each time she had driven home alone to the Dower House, to collect Stella from her mother, whose eager: 'Well, darling?' was invariably met with a smile, but a shake of the head.

Douglas was different. He could never, ever match James in charm and fun and wit and passion, let alone looks, and yet . . . and yet . . . he was clearly head over heels in love with

171

her. He was kind and attentive to Stella, too, insisting that the child occasionally come with them to a restaurant or on a trip to the cinema.

And there was the undeniable fact that Sir Douglas Mackenzie was rich. Very rich. One Sunday, after he had joined Diana and her parents for lunch at the Dower House, arriving in a sumptuous Rolls-Royce which he drove himself, Gwen took her daughter aside.

'You know he's worth fifty times what your father is, don't you?' she said gently. 'Now, I'm not saying that should directly influence your reply, but — '

'Hang on, Mummy! What reply?'

'To his proposal of marriage, of course. I can see he's a slow mover, but I predict our Mr Mackenzie will be on bended knee by the end of the month. The thing is, darling . . . well, I know it's a terrible cliché, but you could do worse. A lot worse.'

'I realise that.'

'Daddy's happy to go on giving you and Stella the annual allowance indefinitely, you know that too, so this isn't about your father and I looking to get you off the books, as it were. We just — '

Diana carefully put her fingertips over her mother's mouth.

'It's all right, Mummy, I know exactly what you're trying to say and I understand perfectly. And just so you know, I've been thinking about this long and hard, and . . . well, I think I know what my answer's going to be. Don't either you or Daddy worry about it. I'm going to do the right thing — the right thing for *all* of us.'

172

39

Diana waited for Maxine to arrive at the villa while she got ready to leave for Nice, less than twenty minutes' taxi ride away. Maxine was Stella's language tutor and erstwhile nanny. She lived in the neighbouring village of St Paul de Vence with her parents, and worked part-time in one of the many patisseries there, on the pre-dawn shifts helping to knead and shape dozens and dozens of croissants. She was usually finished by eight o'clock and at the villa by nine, almost always carrying a paper bag of warm, freshly baked pastries. Maxine was a natural tutor; after only a month of coaching, Stella's French was impressive, almost as functional as her parents'.

Douglas and Diana had had intensive private lessons in written and spoken French in the months before they left England.

'If I'm to make the most of this opportunity down there, it's no good my relying on translators and interpreters,' Douglas had told Diana. 'I'll simply be cheated blind. And you must speak the language properly too, darling, otherwise you'll be terribly lonely. Most British expats still haven't returned to the South of France, even though things have been getting back to normal since the war ended.'

Douglas had spotted an opening in a string of import-export markets, with Nice and Marseilles the twin hubs. He sold his British company for the kind of money that made front-page headlines in every newspaper, as well as dominating the *Financial Times* for almost a week, took a train to the South of France, and pounced.

Diana hadn't needed much persuading to move to Provence. When Douglas first tentatively raised the idea with her, she had gone out and bought every guidebook to the Côte d'Azur she could find. Most of them were old pre-war editions, but she was thrilled at their descriptions of the Mediterranean coast, from Monaco to Marseilles. The climate sounded too good to be true. Mild, sunny winters, early springs with properly warm days beginning as early as March, and long, hot summers lasting all the way through to October. The coldest months were December and January, but even then there were plenty of fine, sunny days.

She lingered over photographs of orange trees lining the Promenade des Anglais in Nice, the fruit falling with casual abundance onto the pavements, while the Mediterranean surf washed the curving, scimitar-shaped beach just a few yards across the road. Diana was utterly seduced.

There was more to wonder at. Inland lay great sweeping fields of lavender, vibrant and stunningly beautiful under the almost violent summer sun. And further north and east, rising like jagged teeth towards Italy and Switzerland, lay the Alps: colossal peaks which dwarfed anything Britain had to offer, glittering white

174

with snow in winter; bare rock flushed in the sunrises and sunsets of summer. Diana's favourite photograph showed a grinning boy eating a freshly picked orange on the beach in Nice, with the Alps filling the horizon behind him like a chorus of giants.

The contrast between the sleepy, densely wooded countryside in which the Dower House dozed, or the flat fenlands that lay around Cambridge, could hardly have been greater. Diana was genuinely fond of the English landscape that had formed the backdrop to her youth, but they didn't quicken her pulse as these exotic images of Provence did now.

She showed the books to Stella. Her daughter was solemn.

'It looks lovely, but what about all my friends in Sevenoaks? I'll miss them like anything, Mummy. And what if I can't speak French properly? I won't be able to make new friends.' She sighed. 'Do we *have* to go?'

Diana was ready for this.

'No, we don't have to go, but I think we should. It'll be an adventure. And you will learn French; it's much easier for children to speak another language than it is for grown-ups. I'll make you two promises, though, Stella. First, your friends can come and stay in the holidays as often and for as long as they like. Douglas and I will arrange all of that, their trains and things . . . and two, if you really are unhappy there, we'll come back home to England. All I ask is that you give it a try. Is that fair?'

Stella had cautiously agreed and now, six

weeks after the family had arrived in a deluge, the irony of which was not lost on anyone, she seemed to be settling in. She had yet to begin school but as Diana had predicted, Stella was picking up good, idiomatic French with astonishing speed. In a few months she would be fluent. Meanwhile Maxine had a younger sister about Stella's age and the two girls had, shyly at first, become friends.

It was going to be all right.

★　★　★

Douglas had been up earlier that morning than any of them, and would now be sitting in his beautiful new office on the Croisette in Cannes, just a couple of hundred yards down from the Carlton Hotel. It wasn't his main office — that was 100 miles away in the port of Marseilles — but with imaginative use of telephone and telegram, he was able to spend Mondays and Tuesdays in Cannes, Wednesdays and Thursdays in Marseilles and be home in time for dinner with his wife and stepdaughter on Friday evenings.

In any case, he loved the Cannes office, with its picture windows offering views straight out over the beaches and the sea on the other side of the Croisette. Sometimes Diana joined him there for lunch and they would eat at one of the beach restaurants affiliated to the grand hotels opposite, or even on the terrace of the Carlton, the grandest of the lot.

Like the rest of the Côte d'Azur, Cannes had

had a 'good war'. Safe in the southern de-militarised zone of Vichy, most Germans to come there were tourists, officers on leave from Occupied France to the north. Some of them even brought their families with them. France may have fallen, but it was business as usual on the Riviera. Hotels like the Carlton had thrived.

Nobody mentioned those days now.

Back at the villa, Diana let Maxine in through the heavy oak door that opened onto the shady front porch, jasmine covering the tiled roof and lemon trees in giant terracotta pots flanking the broad steps that swept up to the door.

'*Bonjour*, Maxine.'

'*Bonjour, madame.*' Diana couldn't persuade the young woman to call her by her Christian name. She was discovering just how punctilious the French could be about their social manners; Maxine, at twenty, simply felt too young to be on first-name terms with an older woman who was also her employer.

'It is not suitable,' was all she replied when Diana raised the subject, and that was that. But Maxine was far less formal with Stella, embracing her, kissing her cheeks, and asking whether she wanted her lesson in *le salon* or by *la piscine*.

'Oh the pool, the pool,' cried Stella, and the two of them hurried down the stairs that led to the pool terrace outside.

'Wear a hat and be careful not to burn,' Diana called from the *salon*, but her daughter was gone. Distant giggles floated up from the stairwell.

Diana's gaze fell on the photograph of James and John on the mantelpiece. Stella was the image of James; it was odd how firstborns so often took after their fathers. She had inherited James's piercing blue eyes, straight nose and ironic smile. And the resemblance was not just physical: the child had many of her father's mannerisms, including his tendency, when he wished to make a particular point, to lower his voice rather than raise it.

Diana saw James in her daughter every single day.

She sighed, picked up her keys and handbag, and left by the front door, remembering to double-lock it behind her. One of the things the guidebooks had carefully omitted to say was that petty crime and burglary were common all along the Côte d'Azur. The villa's previous occupant had been vociferous on the point.

'The li'l bastards come in through the front door when you're down by the pool,' he said. 'So you have to lock the door, even when there's folks in the house. They even come in through an open window when you're having lunch or supper or suchlike in another room. That's why I had to put these goddamn bars all over the place. One night after supper I came into the kitchen and one of the li'l bastards had his head in the fridge. But he was too quick for me — back out of the window like a scalded cat.'

He swung his golf club. 'That's why I walk around with this thing. Next time it happens I'll be ready!'

Diana walked down the paved drive that

opened onto the single-track lane leading to St Paul de Vence. She pressed the concealed button on her side of the electric gate and it slid slowly open on its runners. She walked through and a few moments later heard it quietly rumble back into place behind her.

St Paul was less than five minutes' walk away. As she rounded a screen of cyprus trees, the village came into view on her left. In some ways it reminded her of Hever Castle. Like her home village in Kent, St Paul was defined by its massive fortifications. It crouched on a steep hill, enclosed by a colossal medieval wall topped with ramparts. The village houses clustered within, like sheep in a pen. Narrow streets rose steeply to St Paul's crown jewel, the fifteenth-century church with its tall, sleek belltower of pale stone. Diana had yet to climb the tower but she had heard that the views from the top were breathtaking: to the north, the Alps, to the south, the glittering sea; Africa hidden below the distant blue-hazed horizon.

She walked through the remains of the outer fortifications and into the main square, where already local men were playing *boules* outside the Café de la Place, the village's principal meeting-point. Others sat at the café's tables along its shady terrace, reading newspapers and sipping small glasses of beer.

Diana couldn't understand how anyone could drink anything stronger than coffee at nine in the morning, but here it was routine. She watched a waiter delivering a tray bearing three glasses of wine and what looked like two small cognacs to a

179

group of women at an end table. They were off-duty hotel cleaners, dressed in pink pinafores and caps, their mops stacked neatly against the café's wall.

No wonder so many people here succumb to cirrhosis of the liver, Diana thought as she walked across the square to the taxi-rank on the far side. The driver of the car at the head of the line saw her coming and stubbed out his cigarette.

'*Oui, madame?*'

'*Bonjour, monsieur.* Nice, please. The Cours Saleya.'

'*Mon plaisir, madame.*'

She saw him looking at her legs as she climbed into the back of the cab and sighed inwardly. The man must be seventy, if he was a day.

The Cours Saleya was the street that bisected Nice's Old Town, just behind the eastern end of the Promenade des Anglais. All the city's best restaurants and cafés were there, many of them clustered around the old flower-market, where Diana was headed. She came here almost every morning. It had become something of a ritual for her. She would read the local paper, listen to the conversations that flowed and pulsed around her, and thus improve her French.

Even by the time she got there, well before ten o'clock, most of the day's business would be over. Stallholders were busy hosing down the cobbles around their pitches, and many were preparing to meet up at one of the cafés for a stupendous, and very early, lunch. If one had been up and working since before three in the

180

morning, the stomach decreed that lunch should be taken no later than half past ten.

The taxi dropped her off at the Opera House and she walked the rest of the way, keeping to the shady side of the street. The sun was properly up now and she didn't want her make-up to run.

Sure enough, the flower-market was pretty much done for the day when she arrived. For a few centimes, she managed to buy an enormous bouquet of pink and white lilies just before they were tossed into the back of the trader's evilly smoking diesel flatbed Ford — at this time of day stallholders were practically giving away what remained of their stock — and crossed the road to her favourite pavement café.

The *patron* looked up from his newspaper as Diana stepped up onto the low wooden terrace which kept customers' feet dry when the market was being hosed down, and waved to her. He'd grown fond of the beautiful Englishwoman who had been coming to his café for the past month. She looked enchanting this morning, he thought, carrying her flowers and manoeuvring her way delicately between the little tables to her usual place. He half-wished he had bought the bouquet for her, before reminding himself he was a married man on the wrong side of fifty and long past such foolishness.

He was in the habit of greeting Diana each morning with a little joke, which he insisted on delivering in heavily accented English.

'*Bonjour, madame!*'

'*Bonjour, Armand* — go on, then.'

The café-owner mopped his bald head with a

pristine white handkerchief, which he replaced in the front pocket of his apron. Then he folded his hands carefully over a round belly, his waxed and pointed moustache twitching as his mouth made a little *moue* of excitement.

'*Alors* . . . ' He gathered himself theatrically, tilted his head back and announced: 'Last night, I tell my wife I have bought the dog with no nose.'

He cantilevered his body sideways from the waist, swivelled inwards and adopted a simpering expression.

'*Oh Armand,*' he quavered in a falsetto, 'but how does this dog smell?'

He snapped back into position. 'Completely *terrible*, my dear!'

Diana laughed despite herself. 'Armand, that joke probably arrived here with the Romans.'

He nodded. '*Absolument*. And they left it here especially for you, *madame*. Now, I get your *café* and *le journal*.'

A few minutes later, Diana put down her copy of *Nice-Matin*. She had heard somewhere that no newspaper, however worthy, printed more than a thousand different words in any one edition. She was certainly finding it progressively easier to understand Nice's morning paper; her French vocabulary was steadily growing.

She loved this morning routine. The smell of cut flowers lingered on the warm air, and every now and then a passing stallholder would give her a little wave of recognition. She felt completely at home here, and was surprised not to have experienced even a trace of homesickness since arriving in Provence.

It had been a vile journey down. England was in the grip of yet another freezing winter when they left — almost as bad as the one of 1947-48. The pipes in her house had burst the night before she left and the new tenants — Diana had decided to keep her cottage after marrying Douglas, and was renting it out — had been furious.

'Haven't you heard of lagging?' shouted the young husband down the phone the next morning. 'This is 1951. There's no excuse for burst pipes these days, you know.'

In between marshalling trunks and cases in the hall of Douglas's Kensington mansion, looking for her passport which had inexplicably gone missing, and reminding Douglas to bring the envelope stuffed with high-denomination French banknotes from the safe, Diana had somehow managed to organise a plumber to go to Hever. Then came news that there was a rail strike, and three taxis had to be booked to take them and their luggage to Dover. They got there too late for the last ferry and ended up having to stay in a horrible hotel for the night. Diana had forgotten the family's ration cards so their last meal in England had been one of stale bread, a suspicious omelette made with what she was certain was wartime-vintage powdered egg, and staggeringly weak tea laced with milk that was definitely on the turn.

Next day they arrived, famished and exhausted, at the Gare de Lyon in Paris. They boarded the waiting Nice train, and as it was lunchtime, walked straight to the dining car. By the time they were leaving the Paris suburbs behind, Diana was enjoying what she, Douglas and Stella agreed was probably the best meal of their lives. If there was food rationing in France, it didn't extend to the first-class express from Paris to Nice. Goose pâté with warm *brioche* had been followed by tender flash-fried steak served on potato slices lightly tossed with rosemary, with freshly made *crème brûlée* to finish. Wine, brought without being ordered, was a light, fresh rosé from Provence. Stella had some with mineral water, and summed up the general feeling as coffee, again unasked for, was served.

'That felt like a dream.'

Indeed it had. In fact, reflected Diana as she finished her coffee and prepared to leave the café, Nice displayed none of the kind of post-war privations that shivering, flat-broke Britain was still experiencing. A telephone conversation with her father the night before had left her with the distinct impression that things there were getting worse, not better. 'You wouldn't think we'd won the bloody war,' he said gloomily.

She must invite her parents down to stay, Diana decided as she stood up. They'd love it here and the light would be perfect for her mother's painting. She'd phone them today to arrange it all.

She'd hated saying goodbye, back in March. Gwen had insisted that the three of them come to the Dower House for a farewell Sunday lunch, two days before they left for France.

It had not been a happy occasion. Douglas and Oliver respected each other but could never seem to quite hit it off. Douglas had a tendency to become stiff and formal when in Mr Arnold's presence — he told Diana he simply couldn't help it — and Oliver's attempts at humour usually fell on stony ground.

So lunch had been a stilted affair, the imminent departure hanging like a cloud over all of them. Her parents had tried to put on a brave face, but it was obvious they were going to miss their daughter and granddaughter enormously. Diana had formed the closest of bonds with her mother and father after John and James were killed. Not at once; in fact, during the year after the double tragedy, Diana had sometimes wondered if her parents might separate, so isolated from each other by grief were they. She herself was beyond comfort or solace; for a miserable few months the Arnolds barely spoke to each other.

The arrival of Stella had changed all that.

★ ★ ★

Diana left a few coins on the table for her coffee and walked out onto the pavement.

A taxi came slowly round the corner, past a little grove of lemon trees that lined the centre of the road. It was a shabby brown prewar Citroën, all the windows down in the spring warmth. She stood up to hail it, but realised it already carried a passenger and wasn't going to stop.

As it passed her, she saw the silhouette of a

man sitting in the back. He was leaning forward and speaking, in English, to the driver.

'No, not here. I told you — it's much further up. Keep going all the way to the Hotel Negresco. And get a move on — I'm late enough as it is.'

Diana swayed and gripped the back of her chair. *Impossible.*

'Stop!' she called at last as the taxi reached the top of the square and began to turn on to the Promenade des Anglais. 'Oh please, stop!'

But the Citroën entered the flow of traffic and disappeared down the long curving road that bordered the sparkling Mediterranean.

'*Madame?*' It was Armand, the *patron*, solicitous. 'Do you have a problem?'

'No, no . . . ' She sat down again. 'Everything's fine, really.'

But she was lying.

Everything was wrong.

Completely wrong.

Tentatively, Armand touched her shoulder. '*Madame*, are you quite yourself?' he asked in a low voice. The Englishwoman's sudden pallor alarmed him.

Diana wheeled round. 'I know that man,' she stated.

'Who, *madame?* The man in the taxi?'

'Yes. I'm sure of it. But he can't be . . . I can't have . . . ' Diana looked back at the point where the taxi had disappeared, before turning to the concerned *patron* again. 'Did you hear him, Armand? Did you hear him speak?'

The man shook his head, his pointed

moustache ends quivering. 'Non, madame. I only heard you cry out.'

'He was speaking English. I know his voice. Knew it, rather.'

'I see. And who is this man?' Armand sat down beside Diana. The other clients had barely looked up; they were busy smoking, talking, eating and drinking.

Diana looked into Armand's kind face. How to answer him? She hesitated.

'I think — I think he is someone I once knew. Knew rather well, in fact.'

Armand stared at her, now more curious than concerned. 'Oui, madame, as you say . . . but forgive me, you seem to be not quite yourself. Is there anything I can do?'

Diana shook her head. 'No, I'm quite all right, really I am.' She touched her temple. 'I think I must have a touch of the sun, that's all.'

'Perhaps madame should go home and rest, non?'

'Yes, that would be best. Thank you, Armand. Vous êtes très gentil. À demain.'

'À demain, madame.'

Diana somehow managed to walk away from the café with a semblance of normality, but she felt as though her legs might give way at any moment. Then she heard Armand calling after her.

'Your flowers, madame!' He was waving the lilies in the air. 'You have forgotten them!'

She gave a weak smile. 'You keep them, Armand. Put them in a vase on your counter. That way, we can all enjoy them.'

He shrugged and went back inside his café.

Only after Diana had turned the corner where the taxi had disappeared did she stop, and lean heavily against the building. Her head really did begin to throb now, and quite suddenly she felt violently ill. She mustn't be sick here, she simply mustn't. After a few moments she was able to walk on, taking deep breaths and fighting to quell the nausea that gripped her.

It wasn't until she saw the distinctive dome of the hotel half a mile away that the obvious course of action presented itself.

'The Negresco,' she told the first taxi driver to stop. 'As quickly as you can.'

The driver shrugged, and indicated the heavy traffic. 'It will take me a few minutes, *madame*.'

Diana didn't hear him. She was listening to that voice, over and over again, in her head. ' . . . *Hotel Negresco. And get a move on — I'm late enough as it is.*'

The same clipped drawl; the same hint of London accent under the vowels — the confident, slightly arrogant tone of a man used to getting his own way.

James. *Her* James.

She had never been so certain of anything in her life.

★   ★   ★

The Hotel Negresco's lobby was crammed with Americans that morning, fresh off a cruise liner that could be seen towering above the harbour tucked in behind St-Jean-Cap-Ferrat.

188

The hotel's interior design veered wildly from Art Deco to Louis XIII. Today, the lobby was also stuffed with potted palms, an experiment by the current manager. It made the place look even more crowded.

Diana fought her way through to the reception desk. She caught a glimpse of her face in the gilded mirror behind it, and barely recognised herself. Her hair was in disarray; she had been unconsciously running her hands through it while her taxi made its agonisingly slow progress along the Promenade. There was a wild look in her eyes, and under the tan her face looked almost grey.

'Excuse me,' she said. 'I'm looking for someone. A man.'

The smooth, *café au lait*-skinned receptionist behind the counter raised his eyebrows. 'But of course, *madame*. Which man?'

Diana paused. It seemed ridiculous, now that she was going to have to say it aloud. Perhaps she should just leave. Then she mentally replayed that clipped drawl, which kept repeating itself over and over inside her head.

She took a deep breath. 'His name is — was . . . ' Still she hesitated. 'He's an Englishman. He would have arrived here by taxi a few minutes ago. He was wearing a hat — a Fedora, I think.'

'*Oui, madame* — but his name?'

Diana closed her eyes for a moment. 'James Blackwell. His name is James Blackwell.'

There. She had said it. Diana felt a wave of

vertigo sweep through her and she swayed slightly.

'One moment, please.'

The receptionist opened the reservations book in front of him and ran a slim finger down the page.

'*Non.* This gentleman is not staying with us at the Negresco.' He clicked his fingers and a bell-boy in a smart blue and gold uniform and pill-box hat hurried over.

'*Marcel! Cherchez un Monsieur Blackwell. Dans le restaurant, ou le bar . . . vite!*'

The boy scurried off, and the man smiled at Diana. 'If this *monsieur* is here, we will find him for you. He is a friend, yes?'

'Yes, he is. A close friend.'

'Of course.' The man nodded as if he had known this all along.

Diana looked around her more carefully. Nothing but Americans, most of them extraordinarily fat. You hardly ever see fat people in England any more, she thought abstractedly. Not enough food to go round.

There was no one in a hat, or a suit, come to that. She didn't quite know why, but she was sure that the man — James — had been wearing a suit, a dark one. There had been the glimmer of a white shirt, too. But everyone around her was in holiday clothes — slacks and golf jackets for the men, billowing floral-print dresses on the women.

The bell-hop reappeared and spoke in rapid French to the receptionist before hurrying away again.

'I am sorry, *madame*, but my boy says we have no one by the name of Blackwell in this hotel. The restaurant is empty after breakfast and there were only three people in the bar, two French and one American.' He shrugged. 'Perhaps your friend has gone to a different hotel?'

Diana stamped her foot in frustration. 'He *must* be here! I heard him say so, just now!'

One of the American women glanced curiously over to them.

The receptionist spread his hands. '*Madame*, you must calm yourself. There is nothing more I can do.'

'Of course. I'm sorry.' Diana's shoulders dropped and she sighed. 'You've done all you can.'

She stood there a moment longer, considering. Then she took a ten-franc note from her purse. The receptionist looked at the little leather pouch with approval: Chanel.

'Would you give me change for this, please, in one-franc coins? I wish to use the telephone.'

'*Bien sûr.*'

A minute later, Diana stepped inside one of the hotel's beautiful polished wood-and-glass phone booths that lined the rear of the lobby. She slid the door closed behind her and picked up the delicate ivory handset. After a moment the earpiece crackled and she heard the voice of the operator.

'I wish to place a call to England.' Diana gave a number which she knew by heart.

'How long do you wish to speak for, *madame?*'

Diana thought. 'It might be five minutes

— perhaps a little more.'

'Then I suggest you put in three francs, *madame.*'

Diana did so, and as the last coin dropped through the slot, she heard the familiar double ringtone of a British telephone.

40

Oliver and Gwen's marriage had survived the double hammer-blow of that terrible day, but only just.

They dealt with their grief in entirely different ways. For Mr Arnold, a kind of salvation and peace was to be found in ceaseless activity. After the first few weeks of deep mourning for his son — a period spent almost entirely in the Dower House and which he now struggled to recall with any clarity — he had compulsively taken on any responsibility which would distract his thoughts and prevent them from dwelling on what had happened.

But the dreadful reality broke through often enough. The senselessness of his son's death caused him much pain. To some extent, he and Gwen had prepared themselves for the worst during Dunkirk, and as Mr Arnold watched the subsequent Battle of Britain unfold in the skies above him, he sometimes thought that John's death would have been a little easier to bear if he had died in his cockpit defending his country, rather than in a random, meaningless road accident. At least James's end had a degree of purpose to it. Heroism was conferred on the steadily rising number of pilots killed in battle; poor John had been denied even that.

His grief was mostly for his son, but like Gwen, his heart ached for Diana. He and Gwen hadn't really had long enough to get to know James, but they were fully aware of how much their daughter had loved him.

In many ways, the double tragedy hit Diana hardest of the three of them. At a stroke, she had lost two men that she adored. Her grief for her husband and brother made her almost catatonic. She was indifferent to her developing pregnancy and lost interest entirely in her studies. Diana hadn't returned to Girton.

Her parents had taken the news of the coming baby with initial enthusiasm, even atavistic relief that amid so much death, new life was growing. Diana had told them her news one evening over supper when she was quite sure of the matter, but her tone had been listless and resigned. She felt completely in the thrall of fate, powerless to shape her own destiny. After a few weeks her almost complete disinterest in the pregnancy infected her parents too, and they gradually abandoned their attempts to raise her spirits. Their own were low enough.

Sally had come down from Cambridge during the Christmas holidays to comfort Diana, and try to persuade her to return with her to Girton.

'I'm sorry, Sal, I know you mean it for the best, but the thought of going back to college just seems pointless,' Diana told her after listening to her arguments. 'James is dead, my brother's dead, I'm nearly six months' gone now . . . everything's utterly changed. Anyway, how would I manage university with a baby in tow?'

'You could leave it here with your parents, Di,' Sally said. 'You've only a few months left to do now. I'll help you catch up on everything you've missed this autumn.'

Diana shook her head. 'It's no good, Sal, really it isn't. I don't even *want* to come back. I feel utterly miserable, and the thought of opening my books again makes me slightly sick. Anyway, you know neither of us will get a degree; none of us girls will. It's ridiculous. I can't think why I ever got involved in the whole absurd process in the first place.'

It was a difficult weekend and Sally departed, defeated, promising to write.

★ ★ ★

Gwen withdrew into her own world after the deaths. She was distressed beyond measure to see how her daughter was suffering, but felt helpless to alleviate it. She was in so much pain herself.

Gwen experienced terrible guilt over her son's death. She knew she was being irrational, even superstitious, but she couldn't help believing that if only she had finished the portrait of John she had begun when he was fighting above Dunkirk, he wouldn't have been taken from them.

'It was because I was lazy and didn't finish his painting,' she repeatedly told Oliver. 'I said I would paint something special, just for him, and give it to him when he came back to us. But I didn't, did I? I didn't keep my side of the bargain.'

What bargain? Mr Arnold silently screamed at

195

his wife. He seethed with anger and resentment, and one awful afternoon a month after John and James were killed, he vented his rage in a terrible scene after Gwen again blamed her unfinished portrait.

'What possible bloody difference would one of your stupid paintings have made, Gwen? What are you *talking* about? Can you hear yourself? How typical of you to put your damned painting at the heart of the situation, any damned situation, let alone one as wretched and God-awful as this . . . dear Christ, the *vanity* of it! Do you seriously believe your oils and brushes and canvases have the slightest bearing on how the universe functions? Even unto the power of life and death? Your . . . your *conceit* . . . well, it takes my breath away.'

Utterly crushed, Gwen left the room without a word. When her husband tried to apologise later, she covered her ears with her hands, and when he persisted, she walked out of the house. She wandered the surrounding lanes for hours before returning. Neither of them exchanged a remark of any kind for weeks.

It was at this time that Mr Arnold began an almost manic phase of activity. He took on far more work at his chambers than he needed, and was one of the first men in line at his local police station to sign up for the newly formed Local Defence Volunteers, which would later become the Home Guard. He was scarcely at the Dower House at all and the three of them could have been on different continents, so seldom did they speak to each other.

The Christmas of 1940 passed almost unnoticed in this bleakest midwinter for the Arnolds. Oliver volunteered for Christmas Day guard duty at the local electricity sub-station ('someone's got to do it') and Gwen and Diana spent most of the day in their rooms. Lucy the maid went home to her mother and brother who had made it safely back from Dunkirk. She was gone for a week.

The dam holding back the lake of suffering had to be breached at some point, though, and with almost biblical resonance, it did so the day Diana's waters broke. Her parents, galvanised by one of nature's unstoppable events, drove her into Tunbridge Wells Hospital and stayed with her there — Gwen holding her daughter's hand, Mr Arnold patrolling the corridor outside — until, just after dawn on a frosty March morning, Stella Blackwell was brought into a world at war.

The impact of the birth overwhelmed all three of them. Diana felt a wave of intense, maternal love and possessiveness wash over her from the first moment her baby was placed on her breast.

For Gwen and Oliver, it was as if a glorious, roaring fire had suddenly been lit in a vast, freezing room. Their interior worlds were transformed, and unified, by the arrival of new life.

Smiling shyly at each other for the first time in almost a year, the Arnolds could scarcely credit their newfound happiness.

'It's as if James has sent her to me from wherever he is now,' Diana said, staring at the tiny face that lay in the crook of her arm. 'He's saying, 'It's all right . . . you can start again, start again with our little girl.' Can you feel it, Mummy and Daddy? I'm not being ridiculous, am I? This is real. This feeling is real.'

And it was. It was elemental and unmistakable and irresistible. Much later, lying in the bed next to his wife where they had been sleeping like two strangers, back to back, for so long, Mr Arnold was astonished to find tears suddenly coursing down his cheeks. He had not once been able to weep for his boy but now grief and pain and loss poured unstoppably from him. Gwen lay holding him tightly for what seemed like hours, until the torrent gradually subsided.

'I'm so sorry, Gwen,' he finally managed to say.

She knew he wasn't speaking of his tears.

'So am I, Oliver,' she whispered. 'We haven't been much use to each other, have we?'

He shook his head in the darkness. 'No. We haven't. I wasn't. I was just so . . . *angry*. I took it out on you. I've behaved appallingly.'

Gwen held him tighter. 'I don't think either of us had any choice in how we behaved, did we? I know I didn't. It was like being possessed, I think. Possessed, utterly and completely, by a monstrous shadow.'

He stroked her head as they lay silent for a while.

'Stella won't cure everything, you know,' he said eventually.

'I know,' Gwen replied. 'But look at us now.

198

She's given us a start, hasn't she? We've made a start.'

★ ★ ★

Mr Arnold heard the phone ringing in the hall from where he sat in the breakfast room, reading an air-mailed letter that had arrived that morning from California. It was from Lucy. Immediately after the war she had married an American army sergeant and was now living in Los Angeles, from where she wrote the Arnolds frequent letters extolling the virtues of life on 'the coast' as she had taken to calling it. In her latest letter she was describing her father-in-law's orange groves that her husband had returned home to tend, after surviving unscathed the carnage of the American D-Day landings on Omaha Beach.

Everywhere seemed sunnier, warmer and more prosperous than England, Mr Arnold thought grumpily to himself as he tossed down Lucy's letter. He was sick of hearing about oranges, be they Californian or Provençal. Maybe it was time he and Gwen took a cruise somewhere hot. They could certainly afford to.

He moved quickly towards the jangling telephone. Considering that he was now the wrong side of fifty-five, Mr Arnold was in good shape. Five years' service in the Home Guard had a lot to do with that. In the years after James's death, Mr Arnold had thrown himself vigorously into his part-time military life, volunteering for the more demanding training courses and assignments. By the time the service was stood down at the end of the war, he felt fitter and healthier than he had when he returned home from France in 1918. Hardly surprising, given his gruelling years on the Western Front.

He'd ended up as Area Commander, after getting off to a chequered start on day one in the LDV. Like many former World War One officers, Mr Arnold had 'forgotten' to return his service revolver and ammunition to stores after the Armistice, and rather nervously produced them, complete with leather holster, on the evening of the first LDV roll-call and parade. He knew it gave him a certain cachet, even authority, amongst the other men, but there had been a sticky moment.

The local police sergeant, who was signing volunteers into a register, gave Oliver a measured look.

'Have a permit for that, do you, sir?'

Mr Arnold felt slightly clammy. 'Er . . . no. No, Sergeant, I'm afraid not.'

'Hmm. Well, see about it, would you? Let's do everything right and proper from the start, shall we?'

Mr Arnold nodded with relief. 'Right you are, Sergeant.'

But the other wasn't finished. '*Army* property, I take it, sir?'

Mr Arnold felt his queasiness return. 'Um . . . yes. Yes, I s'pose it is, really.'

The policeman nodded slowly. 'Then just you be sure to return it when we've won the war, sir.'

'Yes, Sergeant.'

He reached the telephone on the fifth ring. The hairline crack in the Bakelite was still there, a mute reminder of Diana's excitement on the day her brother rang to tell them all to come and watch him fly his Spitfire.

'Sevenoaks two-three-six.'

'Daddy!'

'Diana! To what do I owe the pleasure? We only spoke last night. Don't tell me there's some problem with the oranges down there? A freak frost, perhaps, that has overnight withered them on the trees?'

'Daddy, stop. Listen to me. Something's just happened. Something so peculiar I truly don't know what to think.'

Mr Arnold dropped his bantering tone and sat down on the little wicker chair next to the telephone table.

'Where are you calling from?'

'The Negresco — the big hotel on the promenade in Nice. It's — '

'Yes, yes, I've heard of the Negresco. Why are you there at this time of day?'

There was a silence at the other end.

'Diana? Are you still there?'

'Yes. Just give me a moment to collect myself, Daddy. This is incredibly difficult for me.'

Mr Arnold waited, giving his daughter time. He listened to the occasional pop and crackle of static on the copper line that stretched, continuously and unbroken, from the Mediterranean, over the Alps, across the great plains of France, under the English Channel and all the way to the Dower House.

He heard her sigh before she finally spoke again.

'Right. Oh dear, this is going to sound insane. It's about James . . . he *is* dead, isn't he?'

Mr Arnold pulled the receiver away from his ear and stared at it for a moment. Then he put it back, and said very gently, 'Yes. James is dead. You know he is. What is this?'

'It's just that something *so* strange has just happened here. About twenty minutes ago, if that. I hardly know where to begin. I'm wondering if I am not going mad, to be honest.'

'You don't sound mad to me, Diana, but you do sound upset. Start from the beginning, darling. Take your time.'

And so, shakily to begin with, but in a voice increasing in confidence, Diana described her experience outside the café that morning. Her father listened patiently, and with growing understanding.

'They said he isn't here,' Diana finished, 'but I heard him tell the taxi driver to bring him here and I *know* it was James. But of course he's dead; of course he is . . . I can't think straight. I keep feeling I'm going to be sick, and back at the flower-market I nearly fainted on the spot. What's *happening* to me, Daddy?'

'I can tell you exactly what it all means,' Mr Arnold said. 'You've just had a very, very common experience, my dear. It happens all the time; it's happened to me too, more than once, since John was killed.'

'What? What do you mean?'

'Part of you never stops looking for the person that's gone,' Oliver continued. 'Your rational mind knows they're never coming back, but sometimes the heart seizes the moment and rules the head.' He cleared his throat before going on.

'A few months after your brother was killed, I could have *sworn* I saw him striding towards me from the ticket barrier at Victoria. He was in his uniform, smiling and waving at me. Just remembering it now brings back some of the pleasure and shock I felt — but it turned out to be another young, fair-haired pilot; in fact, when we passed each other, he didn't even look particularly like John. And of course, he'd been waving at someone behind me — his girlfriend.'

Diana burst in. 'No, no, Daddy, it wasn't like that *at all*. I've had moments like the one you described. Remember that evening we were in the crush bar at Her Majesty's during the interval? I was guarding the drinks while you and Mummy were in the watchamacallits, you know, and I suddenly saw James coming into the bar with a woman. For a few moments I was certain it was him, but as he came closer the illusion disappeared.

'The same thing's happened to me at other times, Daddy, so honestly, I know what you mean — but understand this: *I heard his voice.* It was unmistakable, and . . . '

'But you didn't actually *see* him,' her father interrupted in his turn. 'You said that.'

'But I sort of *did*, though. When the taxi was at the end of the road I saw his silhouette clearly through the open window. It's hard to put into words, but everything about the way he moved his head, the way he tilted it back as he spoke to the driver, the way he tapped on the back of the man's seat, it was *typical* James. And although he was much too far away for me to hear him, I *knew* he was telling the man off, telling him to get a move on and stop fannying about.'

'Just a minute,' said Mr Arnold after a thoughtful pause. 'I'm going to light a cigarette.'

'Good idea — me too.'

After a few moments he spoke again, smoke billowing from his mouth and nose. 'Still there?'

'Yes, Daddy.'

'Right. Look. I accept you've had . . . well, an extraordinary experience, my dear. Naturally you've been left flustered and confused. But you must listen to me when I say: *it wasn't him.* Your husband — forgive me, your *first* husband — was shot down and killed over France almost exactly eleven years ago.'

'But — '

'Wait, Diana. This is what I'm going to do. You'll remember that you were far too upset at the time to read the official RAF report into what happened — the witness statements by the other pilots who saw the whole thing, all the rest of it?'

'Yes,' Diana said in a small voice.

'I'm going to send you those documents now. Can you bring yourself to read them after all this time?'

'I — I think so.'

'Good. And when you do, you'll realise that

what you thought you heard and saw today was impossible. James is dead, Diana. Ghosts don't exist, and I must say I've never heard of one haunting a Nice taxicab.'

Diana gave a small laugh. 'I must sound pretty stupid and emotional, mustn't I?'

'Not at all, you've simply had an unusually intense example of something many others experience. Promise me you'll read the RAF report when it gets there.'

'I will. Listen, Daddy, I could really do with seeing you and Mummy, especially after this. I know it's only been six weeks, but would you both come down here and stay? Get away from all the gloom and doom back there? I was thinking of at least a fortnight; longer if you can manage.'

'We'd love to, on one condition.'

'What's that?'

'We can talk about ghosts as much as you like, but there will be no conversations, whatsoever, about oranges.'

Diana's laugh was interrupted by a burst of tone on the line and a moment later, it went dead.

The hotel receptionist covertly watched the young woman with the green eyes and stunning legs leave the phone booth. He had a good idea what the missing 'friend' must be up to, wherever he was, the idiot. Some men didn't know how lucky they were.

★ ★ ★

Diana told no one else of her encounter with the doppelgänger, or ghost, or ... what? What exactly had she heard and seen? Her thoughts veered wildly from extreme to extreme; from absolute certainty that she had encountered her first husband, very much alive and in the flesh, to an almost equally firm conviction that her father was right, and the whole thing had been a trick of the mind.

Both interpretations were finely balanced. But they were not quite equal and opposite. If there *was* a tipping of the scales, if she *had* to make the call, one way or the other, it was towards the conclusion that she had, incredibly, inexplicably, encountered the living form of a dead man. Her own Lazarus.

★ ★ ★

The RAF report arrived three days later in a thick manila envelope covered in stamps.

'One for you,' Douglas said as he tossed it to her on his way back from the mailbox at the end of their drive. 'Looks like your dad's handwriting.' He sat down opposite her at the breakfast table. 'Where's Stella?'

'Gone for an early-morning dip,' answered Diana abstractedly.

'Aren't you going to open it then?' asked Douglas as he sliced the top off his boiled egg.

Diana extemporised. 'No, I know what it is,' she replied. 'Daddy has a French client living in London who claims he's been libelled in some letters to the papers. Daddy thinks he's wrong

206

and he wants me to translate them into proper idiomatic French to show the man. I'm going to ask Emile — you know, the clerk in the villa rental agent's office, to help me.'

Diana rarely lied but when she did she was astonished at her facility for it.

'Lucky Emile,' Donald said, smiling at her. 'He's taken quite a fancy to you. When he was going through the rental paperwork here last month he went pink every time you spoke to him.'

'Don't be silly, he's just a boy.' Diana wanted to close the conversation down. She hated lying and Douglas was so trusting. She changed the subject. 'Is it Marseilles today?'

'Aye.' Douglas nodded. 'I'm *this* close to landing that shipping contract I was telling you about.' He looked sadly at his egg. 'I don't really have time to finish this — I'm late as it is. I'd better be off. Bye, darling.' He kissed her cheek and left the kitchen.

Diana stared at the big brown envelope. Time to lay this to rest, she thought, and then smiled ruefully to herself. That was certainly apt. James would have liked that.

As she weighed the envelope in her hands, she felt apprehensive. It seemed almost as if she was about to disturb the bones of her dead husband and commit a kind of sacrilege.

But this was all nonsense. All the envelope contained was a dry, military report — something she should have had the courage to read more than ten years ago. Diana snatched a knife from the table, pushed it under the gummed-down flap of the envelope, and sliced the package open. She upended it and shook out the contents: a thin file of two — no, three — sheets of lined brown foolscap, held together with a slightly rusty paperclip. She slid the top sheet free and held it gently by her fingertips.

The heading, in faded red capitals, was direct enough.

LOSS OF SPITFIRE MK 1, PMF 27A, AT APPROX 16.00HRS SATURDAY 30TH JUNE 1940 DUE TO ENEMY ACTION. AIRCRAFT PILOT, FLIGHT CMNDR JAMES BLACK-WELL, D.O.B. 13/04/19, MISSING PRESUMED DEAD.

THIS DOCUMENT IS CLASSIFIED.

Presumed dead? What did that mean? The Arnolds had always been told that the fact of James's death was in no doubt.

Diana began to read.

The first paragraphs briefly explained the squadron's mission that afternoon. They had been sent to patrol the French side of the Channel between Dunkirk and Boulogne-sur-Mer. A mix of Royal Navy ships, two destroyers and a gaggle of Corvettes were attempting to slip through the Channel at full speed, and the German Luftwaffe was expected to try and bomb them. Another RAF fighter squadron was providing cover above the convoy itself, ready to take on the bombers; James's squadron had been told to intercept the inevitable German fighter escort.

Enemy aircraft had duly appeared, and the Upminster Spitfires had quickly found themselves in a series of dogfights with a pack of Messerschmitt 109 fighters. They were estimated to be about thirty in number — more than two-to-one against James's squadron. Having absorbed this, Diana turned to the second page.

WITNESS STATEMENTS

Diana felt suddenly cold. She'd never wanted, or needed, to know the precise details of James's last moments. Even now she wasn't sure she wanted to. She put the sheet of paper back on the table and walked to the brushed steel fridge, where she poured herself a glass of water from a jug.

What on earth was she doing? Why rake up the past because her over-active imagination had made her act like an idiot? She stared at the musty RAF report on the other side of her gleaming American kitchen and sipped the water.

. . . *presumed* dead.

Diana went back to the table.

The second page began with the name, rank and number of one of the pilots who had made it back home that day. Underneath was his sworn statement.

Bracing herself, Diana began to read.

P.O. Franks and I had just succeeded in

shooting down one of the enemy in a joint attack. The fighting had taken me several miles inland over the Pas de Calais and the sky suddenly seemed entirely clear of aircraft.

I was headed back to the coast at approximately 16.00hrs when I saw F.C. Blackwell's aircraft slide under my own, about 300 feet below me. He seemed to be in a fast, shallow dive and as he banked hard to port, I was able to confirm his identification markings. Then he took a burst of fire to the rear of the fuselage — I did not see where the attack came from — and part of his tail section was shot away. The aircraft took further strikes to the nose, including the cockpit, and the engine immediately caught fire.

F.C. Blackwell's aircraft went into an immediate vertical dive. We had already lost a lot of altitude in exchanges with the enemy and were at less than 2,000 feet. F.C. Blackwell's plane seemed to pull up a bit at about 500 feet. At the same time I noticed another Spitfire in the vicinity, which I now know was flown by P.O. Hobson.

F.C. Blackwell's aircraft dipped down behind some tall trees and I lost sight of it. After a few moments there was a bright flash visible beyond the trees and a considerable amount of black smoke.

It is clear to me that F.C. Blackwell's plane was brought down as a result of enemy action and I regret to say I saw no signs of a parachute. It is my belief F.C. Blackwell was either killed or wounded while in his cockpit, or killed when his plane exploded on the ground.

The statement was signed in a boyish scribble, executed in fountain pen. Underneath was a separate note in a different hand and in a darker ink. Diana peered at it.

This officer killed on active duty 9th July 1940.

Diana's hands shook slightly. Behind the professional detachment of this young man's statement lurked the scent of fear and death. Pity, too; for all the attempt to remain factual and unemotional, the word 'regret' had managed to penetrate the dry text.

What must James have gone through in his awful last moments? She half-hoped he had been killed outright in his plane, rather than suffer the terror of that last dive, struggling with the useless controls of a burning aircraft.

Presumed dead? Of course he had been killed, Diana thought, almost brutally; the presumption could hardly have been more reasonable.

She picked up the third and final page, which was somewhat shorter than the others. This was the second witness statement.

Again, the pilot's name and identification number were quoted at the top of the page. It was P.O. Hobson, mentioned in the first statement. Diana thought she recognised the name as one her brother and James had both mentioned in conversation. Hobson. Yes, he was the squadron joker. Diana had a faint but distinct memory of some prank involving the squadron leader's car and a giant pair of knickers — something to do with a riotous night out in the West End.

This time Diana's eyes went straight to the bottom of the statement but there was no annotation to say that Hobson, too, had been killed, just the man's moniker, signed in large, flowing italics that managed somehow to convey a jaunty spirit, despite what was written above.

I had been forced quite a long way inland by three Me 109s which kept me pretty busy for several minutes. I managed to lose them somewhere near what I now believe was the village of Guines, and was hedge-hopping my way back to Cap Blanc-Nez. I was still a couple of miles from the coast when I saw what I was able to identify as F.C. Blackwell's aircraft passing not more than 100 yards in front of me, moving from port to starboard. The engine was on fire and trailing a lot of smoke. F.C. Blackwell was still in the cockpit and he seemed to me to be making an attempt to land, although I cannot be certain of this. He flew over a screen of poplar trees and disappeared from my sight. Shortly afterwards I saw the flash of an explosion and a large plume of smoke. I would have turned back to investigate, but I was very low on fuel and not certain I would make it home, so I flew on to the coast. It is my firm belief that F.C. Blackwell died when his aircraft struck the ground. I noted the time as 16.00hrs.

Diana turned to the final paragraph.

CONCLUSIONS

Taking into consideration the enemy's official claim to have shot down one of our aircraft at the time and in the location referred to above, and the fact that there has been no enemy report of F.C. Blackwell being taken prisoner, nor any communication from the French regarding his whereabouts, we conclude that this officer lost his life as a result of enemy action.

There was a smudged official stamp underneath 'MISSING PRESUMED DEAD' and yet another scrawled signature. Nothing else.

Diana carefully replaced the pages in their envelope and pushed it to the back of a drawer. Douglas was a stranger to the kitchen; he'd never find it there. Then she made herself a pot of tea and took it out onto the terrace. She opened a large yellow parasol and sat in its shade for a long time, barely moving in her rattan chair.

He's not dead.

Two words — 'presumed dead' — were the fixed point around which her thoughts swirled. Why 'presumed'? The men who saw what happened to James were clear enough on the question. One could describe them as expert witnesses; fighter pilots used to dealing in matters of life and death on a daily, even hour-to-hour basis. If they thought James had — what was the expression they would use? — 'got the chop', then he had.

Perhaps it was the absence of a body. Diana shivered slightly. The report had said that the Germans hadn't taken James prisoner, but clearly they hadn't found a body either. They would have reported it to the Red Cross; that was how such things worked. But there must have been some remains in the burned-out wreckage of James's plane; surely? Something to identify him?

He's not dead.

The cicadas were starting to sing now as the sun grew hotter. The lawn beneath the sun terrace was dotted with small olive trees and that was where the insects hid, signalling their presence to each other with their endlessly repeated *chi-chi-chi* calls.

You could never actually see them, but you knew they were there.

* * *

Diana went back into the kitchen and returned with a pencil and pad. For the next few minutes, she bent over the little table under the parasol, making a series of notes, her brow furrowed with concentration. Her eyes glittered fiercely and her mouth was closed in a tight line, almost a grimace. When she had finished, she sat back to consider what she'd written.

214

1) *James still alive in cockpit as plane nears ground? YES, was trying to land.*
2) *Why no body found/reported in wreckage?*
3) *Who saw plane crash? NO ONE. Behind trees.*
4) *'Presumed dead' = doubt: can imply nothing else.*
5) *I'VE SEEN AND HEARD HIM HERE IN FRANCE*

Diana wrote the last sentence so firmly that the pencil broke.

She sat back, taking short, shallow breaths. A light sheen of perspiration had appeared on her forehead, and one foot jiggled restlessly under the table. She got up and walked to the terrace's wrought-iron balustrade.

Normally the view of picturesque St Paul, nestling on its hill opposite, claimed her attention. But this morning her eyes slid south and east to the distant Mediterranean. Nice was hidden behind the hills that folded their way down to the sea, gradually petering out in the narrow coastal plain where the city stood.

But just because you couldn't see it, it didn't mean it wasn't there.

Like the cicadas in the olive trees.

Like James.

Hidden.

She was going to find him.

41

It never occurred to Diana to take Douglas into her confidence.

She was certain he'd think her a fool — or worse, an obsessive. It would be impossible for her to communicate her certainty that James was alive, based as it was on scant evidence. Douglas would tell her she was being ridiculous.

But there were other reasons to keep silent. If she told Douglas what she thought she'd seen and heard at the flower-market, he would immediately detect her hunger to see James again. It would be impossible for her to conceal it from him once the subject was broached. Douglas would be hurt, and almost certainly feel threatened.

Would he be justified in considering that his marriage might be in jeopardy? Diana's thoughts shied away from the question.

Of course, she knew that if she was right and, incredibly, her first husband was alive and actually here in Nice, the consequences of finding him again would be enormous. But Diana refused to allow her thoughts to travel any further in this direction. Subconsciously she knew that too close an examination of her motives in searching for James would probably cause her to call off the whole exercise.

So she ignored her inner fears and told herself that it was simply none of Douglas's business.

The thought that she might be behaving selfishly, dishonestly or even dangerously didn't enter her mind.

She wouldn't allow it to.

★ ★ ★

She dreamed of James constantly, from the very first night after the incident in the flower-market. Usually these dreams were profoundly frustrating, involving endless pursuits of him, always one step behind as he disappeared through doorways, around corners, and into the backs of dark cars that bore him away, oblivious to her desperate cries of, 'Stop! Oh please, stop!' She often woke with tears of frustration fresh on her cheeks.

Other dreams of James were altogether different, and even if Douglas had been in her confidence, she would never have discussed these with him. They were deeply erotic, almost always concluding in convulsive, physical pleasure which jolted her awake, confused and fearful that her involuntary cries had woken Douglas. Fortunately, he was a heavy sleeper.

Outwardly, Diana's behaviour did not change. She still waited for Maxine to arrive each morning to give Stella her French lessons, before walking into St Paul and taking a taxi to the flower-market.

Armand continued to greet her with what he considered the epitome of English wit, before bringing her coffee and *Nice-Matin*, which Diana affected to read.

217

A close observer, however, would have noticed a change in her behaviour. No passing car or taxi went unscrutinised. No tall, suited and hatted man hoving into view went unremarked. And Diana stayed at the pavement café for far longer than she used to, sometimes for more than two hours, lingering over a third *café crème* when once a single cup was all she drank.

In fact, there was one such close observer; Hélène, a woman in her late fifties who owned the flower-stall opposite Armand's café. Diana had never really noticed the woman who worked quietly at her bouquets and arrangements most mornings. She was an unremarkable figure in her plain, neat dresses, greying hair invariably tied back in a conventional bun.

But Hélène had noticed Diana from almost the first time she visited the market, admiring her beauty, which reminded her greatly of her own daughter. Marie too had dark looks, and the same green eyes, and like the Englishwoman opposite, she knew how to dress. Hélène had missed her child since she had left Nice to work in Paris, and took a secret pleasure in pretending to herself that the girl opposite was her own beloved daughter, come to visit.

Now, Hélène saw that something had changed in the Englishwoman's demeanour. It was obvious she wasn't paying her newspaper the attention she once had, and she seemed obsessed with passing traffic, particularly taxis. Men, too. The young woman was constantly on the look-out, giving sharp glances to almost any

218

smartly dressed man who approached. Her expression flickered from hope to disappointment throughout her sojourn at the table and when she finally left, she appeared sad and defeated.

Hélène, already minded to feel maternal towards the young woman, became increasingly concerned. Finally, one morning, when Diana had been fidgeting at her usual table for more than an hour, Hélène came to a decision. She smoothed the front of her apron, propped a painted wooden *Fermé* sign against her stall, and crossed the street to the café. She walked straight up to Diana's table on the corner of the little wooden terrace.

'*Bonjour, madame* . . . you are English, I think?'

Diana, who was staring in the opposite direction at a suspicious taxi that had, in fact, just disgorged two elderly ladies carrying tiny dogs, gave a slight start.

'Oh, my goodness, you gave me a fright. Yes, I'm English. How did you know?'

The woman gestured to Armand, who was washing glasses inside, behind his tiny bar. 'I sometimes come here for lunch and Armand likes to talk about you.' She smiled at Diana. 'He is a little in love with you, I think.'

Diana smiled back. 'Won't you sit down? My name's Diana.'

'And I am Hélène.' The woman sat opposite.

'Would you like a cigarette?' Diana asked, offering her the packet. 'Your English is frightfully good.'

Hélène took a cigarette and Diana lit one for each of them.

'*Merci*, Diana.'

'*Je vous en prie.*'

'Your French is good, too, *madame*.'

Diana blew out a thin jet of smoke. 'Thanks. It's coming along. Where did you learn English?'

'From my late husband. He was from Manchester.'

'Well, that would explain it.'

The two women sat smoking companionably for a minute before Diana spoke again.

'*Madame* — Hélène — what is it that you want?'

The older woman nodded slowly. 'But that is the question, my dear, is it not? What is it that *you* want? What — or perhaps who — are you looking for every day when you sit here?'

Diana looked slightly haunted. 'Is it that obvious?'

Hélène gestured over her shoulder to her flower-stall, which at this time of the morning was almost bare. Only a battered metal bucket containing a dozen white roses remained.

'It is obvious to me from over there each morning. I noticed you weeks ago, when you first came here. Truly, you remind me of my daughter. You are much the same age, I think. My Marie is in Paris now and I miss her greatly.' Hélène tapped ash from her cigarette into the little tin ashtray between them before continuing.

'But, *alors*, it is to you that my . . . ' Hélène searched for the word. 'ahh . . . *ma curiosité* — '

'Curiosity — it's the same.'

'Of course . . . my curiosity is directed to you. There has been a change, *madame, n'est-ce pas?*'

'What do you mean? And call me Diana, please.'

'There has been a change, Diana. Armand says that some days ago, a mysterious event took place. You saw a man in a taxi you thought you knew, and since then you have not been yourself.'

Diana felt a sudden overwhelming desire to unburden herself to this woman, but she resisted a little longer.

'But we have not met or spoken until this moment, Hélène. With respect, how would you know what my normal self is?'

Hélène blew her cheeks out and gave a little shrug. '*Écoutez*, my dear, I am a woman like yourself. Such matters are clear to us. No, you are not yourself and that much is plain to see.' She placed her hand on top of the young woman's. 'Tell me. Who are you waiting for?'

The unexpected physical contact and the sincerity in the Frenchwoman's voice were enough to breach Diana's already shaky defences. She dropped her head low over the table. Glittering teardrops fell from her eyes and she plunged both hands into her hair, and then down to cover her face.

'I can't stand it . . . I can't stand it any more,' she wept through her fingers. 'I don't know what to do — I'm in complete *limbo*.'

Hélène swiftly moved her chair next to

Diana's, and put both arms around her. The younger woman fell on her shoulder, wracked with sobs.

Hélène let her weep, making occasional sympathetic noises and clucking softly. Armand watched, transfixed, from behind his little bar.

Eventually Diana regained control and Hélène passed her a napkin, on which Diana noisily blew her nose.

'I'm terribly sorry, Hélène . . . It's been such a strain. Goodness, you must wish you'd never come over to me.'

'Nonsense, my dear . . . but, please, where is this limbo you speak of?'

Diana laughed despite herself, and then hiccuped.

'Limbo is a word that means, oh I don't know . . . lost; in the middle of nowhere . . . you're stuck there and time seems to stand still.'

'Ah, *la salle d'attente* — the waiting room.'

Diana nodded, hiccuping. 'Yes, that's it exactly.'

Hélène nodded slowly, and then lifted Diana's chin with one finger.

'And so now, *ma chérie*, you will tell me who it is that you have been waiting for.'

★ ★ ★

Diana told her everything. How her brother had brought James Blackwell home to the Dower House; his visits to Girton and their whirlwind engagement after Dunkirk; the double tragedy that crowned their wedding day; and how she

222

and Stella had begun to build a future under Douglas's protection here in Provence.

At first Diana started off at a rush, and more than once Hélène was obliged to ask her to slow down. But gradually, the more Diana spoke, the calmer she became. The jerky hand movements that had accompanied the opening of her story died away, and she found it increasingly easy to look directly into the older woman's kind eyes as she unburdened herself. The only remaining sign of strain was the series of cigarettes that she lit for herself, one after another.

Hélène listened mostly in silence, until Diana told her about the taxi that had driven past Armand's café over a week ago. Here she stopped the younger woman and asked a series of sharp questions. When she was satisfied, Diana carried on, finishing with the findings of the RAF report into James's death.

By the time Diana finished her story, Armand had wiped down all his tables and covered them with white tablecloths. The café was ready to serve lunch. Knives and forks with pretty blue handles, and glasses — green for water, plain for wine — shone and sparkled in the sunshine. It was only a little past noon, but already the chairs around them were beginning to fill up.

Armand bustled over to them, tying a fresh white apron around his tubby waist.

'I trust *madame* is feeling quite recovered?' he asked, looking shyly at Diana.

'Yes, Armand, completely,' Diana replied. She was surprised not to feel any embarrassment about her tears earlier. As she watched Armand nodding and bobbing in front of her, twirling his waxed moustache nervously between finger and thumb, Diana realised how fond she had become of him in the few short weeks since arriving in France.

'*Très bien*,' he said now, and conjured a menu seemingly out of thin air. 'Will *mesdames* be staying for *déjeuner, peut-être?*'

Diana raised her eyebrows at her new friend. 'Shall we?'

'Why not?' Hélène replied, standing up. 'You order for us both, *chérie* — I must close my stall properly. It is the only one left open. Order anything you like, everything is good here.' Armand bowed at the compliment.

While Hélène sluiced down the pavement surrounding her pitch and brought the sun-bleached wooden shutters clattering down on her stall, Diana, with Armand's assistance, ordered their lunch.

'*Salade niçoise* to start with,' she told Hélène a few minutes later when she returned, 'and then I was going to order us *sole grillé* but Armand says it's nicer cooked *meunière* and finished off so it's golden-brown — how does one say that in French again?'

'*Bien doré*,' Hélène provided. 'An excellent choice. And now, my dear, don't you want to know what I make of your remarkable story?'

'Very much.'

'I must warn you, Diana, I am going to be direct.'

Diana nodded. 'Good.'

'Very well. But I want you to . . . how did my

husband used to say it? Ah, yes — 'hear me out'. No interruptions, yes?'

Diana nodded again, and noted the past tense, concerning Hélène's husband.

'So,' Hélène began. 'I do not think for one moment, my dear, that your first husband is alive.' She held up a hand as Diana drew breath to speak. '*Non! Silence, s'il vous plaît.* You promised.'

Diana subsided. 'Sorry,' she mumbled. 'Go on.'

'Yes . . . as I say, I am quite sure he is dead and that he died on the day of your wedding. That much is clear to me. Think about it, Diana. Let us assume, for a moment, that your husband survived the terrible plane crash. Let us also assume he was not captured by the Germans. He would have needed help to survive, and only the *Maquis* — the Resistance — could have given him that. But they would have sent a message to England, *non?* They would have explained that your husband was safe. But no such message was received, was it?'

Diana lips were tightly compressed. 'No,' she managed.

'But let us continue to pretend. He survives, and somehow lives out the rest of the war here in France. That is five years, Diana. Five years! Why does he not manage to send any message to you? But most important, why does he not come home to you as soon as the fighting is over? *Mmm?* Why have you never received a letter or message of any kind from this man? Why would he abandon the love of his life like this? It makes

225

not any sense to me. Does it to you?'

Miserably, Diana shook her head.

'Now let me ask you a question,' Hélène continued. 'Until two weeks ago, did you have any doubt at all that this man is dead?'

'No.'

'*Non, absolument pas.* That is the correct reply, *chérie.* And did anyone else consider the possibility he was alive?'

Another shake of the head.

'No. I thought this would be your answer.'

Hélène paused as Armand brought their starters.

'Eat,' she ordered Diana when the *patron* had gone. 'That is something else that is changed about you, my dear. You are getting rather thin, I think.'

'I'm not hungry.'

Diana jumped as Hélène rapped the table with her knuckles. 'Eat!'

She obeyed, forking small amounts of tuna, boiled egg and anchovy to her mouth. The oil and vinegar and lemon juice dressing was delicious, and to her surprise, Diana felt her appetite stirring.

'Now, where were we . . . ah, yes. The morning of the taxi, here in the flower-market. Your father tells you he has similar moments concerning your brother. He thinks he sees him alive once more, yes?'

'Yes, but he didn't *hear* him too, like I did James. He — '

Hélène raised her hand for silence again. 'Yes. And now, my dear, I am going to tell you

226

something about myself.'

She paused to eat some of her own salad and pour them both a little of the rosé wine from the *demi-carafe* Diana had ordered.

'So.' Hélène dabbed her mouth with her napkin. 'I told you I was married to an Englishman. His name was Gerald. We met in the war, the first one. Your own father fought in it, you said?'

Diana nodded. 'Yes, he was an infantry officer for almost the whole of the war in France.'

'Then he was very lucky to survive and you were very lucky to have been born, my dear. I think he does not talk about his time in France much, yes?'

'Hardly ever. He once told me it was more or less indescribable.'

'Yes, well . . . that is certainly so. Diana, I was a nurse in that time. I worked in a field hospital just behind the lines, near Rouen. That is where I met my husband. He was brought in with three machine-gun bullets in his shoulder. He was . . . how is it said . . . shocking.'

'You mean in shock.'

'Yes, he was in shock, and the doctors thought he was going to die, he had lost litres of blood. But I was determined not to let him die. I was not a very good nurse, Diana; I lost many of my patients, although I am not certain now that any of them could really have been saved. Their wounds were so . . . ' Hélène fell silent for a few moments before continuing: 'But with Gerald I had a feeling *here*', she gestured to her heart with her fork, 'that he was a man sent specially for me. It was my destiny to save him, you see. I *knew* this.'

Diana was intrigued. 'What sort of man was he?'

Hélène laughed. 'Was he a handsome officer, you mean? No. Well, he was an officer like your father, but Gerald looked like a little frog. I told him so, when he started to get better and tried to flirt with me. 'You are a little English frog,' I told him, so many times. But he just laughed. He told me he was a teacher and he would teach me English, and he did. He was very patient with me and one afternoon, when he had fallen asleep in his bed, I looked at him and I discovered that I had fallen in love with him.'

Diana was absorbed in the story. 'Where did you get married — in France or England?'

'Oh, in England — in Manchester. Gerald's parents lived there. My parents were so angry, first when they discover I was engaged to an Englishman, and then when I told them I would be married in England!' She smiled. 'But at least they were happy he was a Catholic.

'We were married in a beautiful little church in the heart of the city — the Hidden Gem, it is called. Next day, we caught the train back to London, Gerald transferred to a troop train to the boats and I went back to Rouen on my own.'

Hélène sipped her wine. 'I never saw him again. He was killed a few days later in a bombardment. All the men in Gerald's trench were killed too, and they never found their bodies. Not one. I received the news on the day that I discovered I was with child. My Marie. It was a little like you and your James, I think, Diana. We managed to make a new life before . . . before . . . '

She fell silent. This time it was Diana who reached for Hélène's hand. 'I'm so sorry, Hélène . . . but why are you telling me this, please?'

The other sighed. 'Because I had *exactly* the same experience as you, my dear, and not just once. When I went to England to visit Gerald's parents, I saw and heard him everywhere . . . in trains, on buses, in cafés. I thought I was gone mad. Once in a restaurant I heard him laughing behind me in only the way Gerald could laugh, and then he said, '*There* you are!' and I turned round and just for a moment I saw my little frog, but then he turned into a quite different man altogether. I cried and cried. Yet I had been *so certain* — just as you are, Diana. Just as you are.'

Diana finished her wine and filled the glass again from the carafe, thinking hard.

'It's because Gerald's body was never found, isn't it,' she said at last. It was a statement, not a question.

'Yes. You have quite taken the point, my dear. I believe that it is most important for one to see the body . . . or at least speak with someone who has. It makes the death a *realité* . . . one can accept it more easily, I think.'

Diana sat in silence for a long time. 'Thank you, Hélène,' she said eventually. 'I feel as if you've woken me from a very strange dream. It hurts . . . it hurts a lot . . . to let go of what I felt so *sure* was real, but everything you said about James never making any attempt to come back to me or send a message, and everything you say about your experiences after your own husband was killed — well, of course, you're right. I've been living in a fantasy.'

Hélène smiled at her. 'Many women like us do, Diana, for a time at least. But we must help each other to accept the truth. I know I will never see my Gerald again; perhaps you can accept the same about your James.'

'Yes, I think I can.' Diana stood up. 'I'm not going to stay for the rest of the meal, Hélène. I want to get home to my daughter. Will you tell Armand to put this on my account? I settle up with him at the end of each week.'

'*Bien sûr.* Thank you.' Hélène rose too. She cupped Diana's face in her hands and kissed her on each cheek. 'I hope I was not too hard.'

Diana smiled. 'No, Hélène. On the contrary, you've saved me, that's what you've done.' She began to walk back to the Promenade des Anglais.

'Will you come back here, Diana?' the older woman called after her.

'Of course,' Diana said, turning around. 'This is where I come to improve my French, isn't it?' She waved, and walked on.

42

Hélène was late to market the following morning. She hated that; it meant that most of the day's business would be lost — if, indeed, there were any suppliers left to buy stock from. They'd probably all gone home by now.

As she hurried through the back streets leading to the Cours Saleya, Hélène ran her tongue over her newly filled tooth. She'd woken in the night with a raging toothache. As a former nurse, she had no fear of dentists and was waiting outside the surgery when the practitioner arrived to open up.

Hélène's friends sometimes teased her that she 'looked' like a nurse. It was true. There was something very capable about her; Hélène wore her competence like sensible clothes. As Diana had discovered, it was easy to place one's trust in those grey eyes that looked out kindly from beneath a wide, smooth brow. Auburn hair, now streaked with grey, was habitually tied back in a neat chignon. Even Hélène's work-clothes had something of the hospital ward about them; she favoured green or pink striped cotton dresses with formal white lace collars. She had never been seen in high heels of any description; Hélène always chose sensible flat, lace-up brogues.

She didn't know why she was hurrying now. It was past ten o'clock and she might as well use what remained of the morning to do the repairs to her stall that she had been putting off all spring. Both hinges on the wooden fold-down display top needed replacing, and the iron handle on the roll-up shutters was a disgrace, bent completely out of shape by a carelessly driven delivery van last autumn.

Hélène opened her purse. Yes, she had enough francs to buy what she needed; there was no necessity to go to the bank. Hélène was not in any way well-off, but she was not poor. She still had Gerald's small British Army pension — Hélène had never remarried — and her daughter, conceived on their wedding night in a Manchester hotel, was doing well in Paris, where she worked at one of the new fashion magazines that had sprung up after the war. Marie sometimes sent her mother cheques 'just to help things along, *Maman*' and Hélène was perfectly happy to accept them.

All in all, there was enough money for her to keep her long lease on a two-bedroom apartment just off the Rue de France, which ran parallel to the Promenade. It wasn't as fashionable as the residences along the seafront, but it was respectable, and one of the bedrooms had a partial view of the Mediterranean, if one stood in the right place.

Hélène headed for a *quincaillerie* she knew of just behind the Rue de la Préfecture. It was one of the oldest ironmongers in Nice; people joked that if you wanted replacement handles for a sedan chair, they'd have a choice of styles and sizes.

It was while she was rummaging through a loose box of hinges ten minutes later that Hélène felt it. It had been a long time since that unmistakable sensation had troubled her.

She froze. There was no mistaking it: this feeling of deep lassitude, as if she were about to succumb to a fever. A nameless dread stealthily began to envelop her, like a dark cloak wrapping her in its folds.

She managed to find a chair and sat down heavily. The shopkeeper, who had been selecting some new shutter handles for her to look at, returned with them at that moment and regarded her with concern.

'Is *madame* quite well?'

'I'll be all right in a minute. A glass of water would be very kind, if you could manage . . . '

'Of course.' He hurried away to fetch it.

Hélène's friends teased her about something other than her nurse-like appearance. Sometimes they called her a witch. They were only half-joking.

Hélène had what her grandmother had called '*la talente*' — the gift of second sight. It ran in her mother's side of the family, although by no means everyone inherited it. Her mother and grandmother certainly didn't, but the old lady said that her own grandmother had, and that she had spoken of earlier generations of women in the family who had possessed the gift, too.

People called it many things: clairvoyance, the third eye, prophesying . . . Hélène simply knew it as 'the voice'.

The voice took many forms, and was master of

itself; Hélène was unable to conjure it up, even if she had wanted to. It came and went of its own accord, seemingly randomly and without warning.

Sometimes she knew precisely what someone was about to say to her, word for word. Only the other evening in her apartment, the phone had begun to ring, and Hélène had known at once it was Marie calling to say she had gone down with flu and had been forced to cancel a much-anticipated visit to the Louvre. So it proved.

Such predictions that announced themselves in her head could be about anything at all, and they were always correct. A few years earlier, Hélène had been passing a church in what used to be the old Roman quarter, and thought to herself, with perfect clarity: That church is going to fall down tonight, but it will be all right, no one will be hurt. And it had happened just so, when one of Nice's occasional earth tremors had struck the city, and the church had collapsed.

But the sensation that gripped her now was one she had learned to dread. It was an infallible sign that something bad had befallen someone she knew.

There had been many such incidents over the years, some of them indelibly burned on her memory. The worst had been the evening Gerald and all the other poor boys had been killed in their trench. She'd been eating her evening meal with the other girls in the nurses' mess-tent, and she'd known with a horrible certainty that something terrible had just happened to her husband.

Now, as Hélène sipped her water and felt the black cloud around her begin to break and lift, she wondered what ill-fortune had just befallen someone.

She would know soon. She never had to wait long to find out.

★　★　★

Armand was beside himself with anxiety. What was he to do? he kept asking himself. What *on earth* was he to do?

If only he had been able to stop it, to intervene in some way. He cursed himself for his cowardice, for that was what it had been, he told himself. Sheer cowardice. When he'd realised who the person was, he'd been frozen to the spot. He simply watched the whole thing happen. He was a pathetic excuse for a man.

Not that there would have been a great deal he could have done, he reflected, his *amour-propre* refusing to take this self-inflicted beating lying down. How would he have explained himself? What could he have said that would have made a difference? Anyway, it had all taken place so quickly, and was so unexpected, that he'd hardly had time to think clearly.

If only Hélène were here; she would know what to do. Where *was* the dratted woman, anyway? It wasn't like her to be this late. Soon it would be time to clear away the little bowls of sugar and small plates of coffee-biscuits, and lay the tables for lunch.

It was while he was busy with this a few

minutes later, distractedly and with frequent interruptions to peer anxiously up and down the street, that Hélène at last appeared at her stall opposite.

Armand ran straight across the street to her, narrowly missing being run over by a spluttering, smoking three-wheeled delivery van. The driver shook his fist at Armand and bellowed insults at him as the little vehicle swayed wildly, its load of empty wooden beer-crates almost toppling into the road. It stuttered on and disappeared in a cloud of black exhaust fumes around a corner.

'Hélène, Hélène!' shouted Armand, oblivious to both his nearmiss and the abuse. 'I have terrible news! *Terrible!*'

Hélène put down her cardboard box of ironmongery with a heavy heart. Here it came, then. Some awfulness, just as she'd expected. She glanced across the road to the café. Her new friend, the Englishwoman, was not at her usual table.

Even before a breathless Armand had begun to gabble his story, Hélène knew with a grim certainty that Diana was in trouble.

★　★　★

She had arrived at her accustomed time, Armand said. She'd seemed lighter of spirit than of late, and he'd noticed almost immediately that 'all that damned looking up and down' and the obsession with passing taxis had gone. It was, he told Hélène, like

236

getting the old Diana back.

He'd only just brought her coffee and newspaper, he said, when it happened. He saw the whole thing from behind his bar.

A perfectly ordinary taxi had pulled up outside, and a tall man wearing a suit and hat had emerged from the back. He was facing away from the pavement, leaning through the open front passenger window, saying something to the driver. The street was quiet, otherwise Armand would have been unable to hear that English was being spoken.

The effect on Diana had been instant, electrifying. Armand said she had leaped to her feet, almost run across the wooden terrace, crossed the pavement and seized the stranger by his shoulders, dragging him around to face her.

The two had simply stared at each other without saying a word. 'Not a word, Hélène. Not a sound from either of them.'

At last the man had leaned forward and said something very slowly and quietly. Armand couldn't make out what it was. After a moment Diana nodded — she still hadn't said anything — and the two of them walked slowly off together towards the Promenade des Anglais. That was nearly two hours ago, and she had not returned.

Hélène felt slightly relieved. She began to say that Armand's news didn't sound all that terrible to her, because she was quite certain who this stranger was. Diana had been right all along, it would seem. Incredible. Quite incredible. But Armand interrupted her, waving his arms and shouting that he was not finished.

'The man! The man, Hélène!' Armand had seen his face clearly for the first time as the pair moved out of the shadow of the café's canopy and into direct sunlight.

He could barely believe his eyes. How could Diana possibly know such a man? It made no sense.

Foreboding began to seep into Hélène's veins like iced water.

'Who? Who was this man, Armand?'

The *patron* wiped perspiration from his forehead with his handkerchief.

'*Le Loup, Hélène. Le Loup Anglais!* The English Wolf!'

Hélène's eyes widened in disbelief. Was this who Diana's first husband had become? It scarcely seemed credible, based on her tender description of him only yesterday.

'Are you quite sure, Armand?' she asked. 'It was definitely the English Wolf?'

He nodded. 'No doubt about it.'

Hélène gave a low whistle of surprise, a habit she had acquired years before from Gerald.

'Well, well. This rather complicates things, I must say.'

'What do you mean?'

She sighed. 'He's not just the English Wolf, Armand — he's her first husband.'

'That bastard was *married* to her?'

'I'm very much afraid so. What's more, he's supposed to be dead.'

★ ★ ★

Diana had arrived at Armand's café, experiencing a peace of mind she hadn't felt in weeks. She had Hélène to thank for this. Diana resolved to buy the woman some sort of gift. Not flowers, obviously. Perfume, perhaps. There was a wonderful *parfumerie* in the Rue Pastorelli that sold lovely scents made in nearby Grasse.

Diana was surprised and disappointed to see Hélène's stall shuttered, with no sign of its owner. She had just decided to ask Armand if everything was as it should be, when a taxi pulled up at the pavement a few yards from her table. Her eyes turned to it in a reflex reaction before she remembered: all that was finished now. She forced herself to look away as the passenger door swung open. She must start as she meant to go on.

Two seconds later Diana felt as though she had been hit over the head. Points of light danced before her eyes. Dizzily, she wondered if she was about to pass out.

That voice.

The unmistakable, unforgettable drawl.

The East End undercurrent.

The old, easy authority.

'I want you back here in twenty minutes, OK? This won't take long. If I'm not here, don't wait for me — keep circling the block until you see me and then pick me up. Got that?'

Without even realising it, she had leaped to her feet and was rushing past empty tables, catching a chair with her knee and sending it spinning to the ground. She crossed the pavement at a run, and with both hands, she wrenched the astonished man violently around to face her.

Diana gaped at him. She had made a mistake. This man wasn't James. He didn't look anything like him.

The illusion lasted for less than a second. Then the man's shock and anger — and something very like fear — faded from his eyes. The animal snarl left his lips, and the contorted facial muscles slackened.

The stranger's face disappeared and that of James Blackwell took its place, the reflex aggression replaced by an expression of utter astonishment.

He's not dead.

I knew it.

I knew it.

Afterwards, she couldn't have said how long it was before he spoke the first words she had heard from him since their wedding day, more than a decade before.

'Well, Diana . . . ' He gave the faintest smile. 'I think we could both do with a drink, don't you?'

★　★　★

The hotel receptionist with the *café-au-lait* suntan sent another silent prayer of thanks to the Blessed Virgin.

'*Holy Mother of God, thank You for keeping my thoughts and deeds pure with the beautiful Englishwoman,*' he inwardly intoned for the third time in five minutes.

What if he had attempted to flirt with her?

Suggested they meet for a drink after his shift, as he had done with so many other women at the Negresco who'd taken his fancy. His palms went clammy at the mere thought.

She'd come back into the lobby just now, but this time she was accompanied by a man — presumably the 'friend' she had been searching for the last time he'd seen her.

What was the name she had given for him? James something-or-other . . . Bakewell? No, *Blackwell*, that was it. Well, that was a new one. God knew how many aliases the man had. Everyone in Nice simply knew him as *Le Loup*, and the idea of moving in on his woman . . .

The boy shuddered. The only reason he hadn't made a move on her was because his manager had recently pulled him up short for flirting too heavily with the female guests. Some American woman had made a complaint. Bitch. You'd think she'd have been grateful for some attention, given the state of the fat slob of her husband. In fact, thinking about it, it was probably her husband who'd gone running to the manager . . . The boy became lost in resentful reverie. He forgot all about the Wolf.

*   *   *

James and Diana sat on the Negresco's sun terrace. High glass screens cut out much of the noise from the traffic moving up and down the Promenade des Anglais. They had just been

241

served espresso coffees and freshly baked croissants, which lay untouched on the table in front of them.

'Do you mind sitting in the sun like this? Would you like me to ask them to bring a parasol?'

Diana slowly turned her head towards him. They had barely spoken during the ten-minute walk to the hotel. In fact, Diana had yet to speak at all. She was still in shock. James had said something about going to the Negresco, 'where we can collect ourselves', and she'd simply nodded. She felt numb. The impossible had just happened and her world had exploded into tiny fragments. She felt light-headed and strangely vacant.

'No.' Her voice sounded husky and she cleared her throat. 'No,' she repeated, more clearly. 'No thank you. It's still quite early. The sun isn't that strong yet.' There, she thought. They were having a conversation about the weather. And she was talking to a dead man whose bones, if the official records were to be believed, lay in a field in northern France.

Their waiter reappeared with two cognacs in tiny glasses.

'*Merci.*' James picked up both glasses and handed one to Diana. 'Down the hatch, then.'

Diana drained her glass in a single gulp and a few seconds later felt more light-headed than before. She bowed her head.

'I think I'm going to faint.'

'No, you're not. Deep breaths, Diana.' He moved his chair closer to hers and gently rubbed her back with the flat of his palm. Diana shivered.

'Keep your head down. Keep taking those breaths. You'll be fine in a minute.'

They sat like this for some time, before Diana finally raised her head with a sigh and eased herself back in her seat. She stared listlessly at him.

He was a little older, obviously, but barely noticeably. No grey yet in his hair or at his temples — well, he was still in his early thirties, as was she. No apparent weight-gain since she'd last seen him. A few more lines here and there, perhaps, but these were mitigated by his tan. The whites of his eyes remained clear and his teeth were white too. He smiled at her.

'Hello, Diana.'

'I knew you were alive,' she replied.

'From the beginning? From the day I was shot down?'

She slowly shook her head. 'No. Only during these last few weeks. I heard your voice, coming from a taxi in the flower-market. You were telling the driver to bring you here. I knew it was you, I was absolutely certain. I followed you here but I couldn't find you.'

He nodded apologetically. 'Yes, I think I remember that day,' he said thoughtfully. 'I was picking someone up from here. We went on somewhere else.'

'How long have you been in Nice?'

'Nearly eleven years. I came here pretty much straight after I was shot down.'

She nodded to herself. He made it sound so

243

reasonable, so normal. 'I see.'

He stared at her. 'Are you all right?'

She laughed at that, a high, wheezy giggle. 'Oh yes. I'm absolutely fine. I meet people back from the grave for coffee at the Negresco most mornings.'

He held up his hands in apology. 'I'm sorry . . . This is difficult enough for me. I can't imagine what it must be like for you.'

'No. I'm sure you can't, James.' There. She'd called him by his name. It felt familiar and normal, and yet completely otherworldly too.

Her first husband pulled a slim gold cigarette case from the inside pocket of his jacket. 'You?'

'No, thank you.' Diana shook her head. 'I'd probably throw up.'

He nodded and lit one for himself. 'Yes. Looking at you, I can see you probably would.'

'Thanks.'

'Sorry, I only meant . . . well, you've had a shock.'

'You could say that. Everyone thinks you're dead. So did I, until we came to Nice.'

He drew on his cigarette. 'We?'

She stared at him. 'Do you know *anything* about what's happened back home since you disappeared, James? Anything at all?'

He shook his head. 'No. Not a thing — not about you, I mean. I read an English newspaper from time to time to keep up, but as far as you're concerned . . . ' He shrugged helplessly. 'How could I?'

Her eyes widened. 'What do you mean, 'how could I?' '

'It's a long story.'

'I'll bet it is.' Diana felt the first stirring of anger. 'Why didn't you send me a message of some kind? The war ended six years ago, James. God knows what you were doing here until then, but why didn't you come home afterwards?'

He drew slowly on his cigarette and looked out to sea, considering his answer.

Suddenly, Diana wanted to hit him. She wanted to punch and kick and scratch him, and pull at his expensively cut hair, so hard it would come out in bloody clumps in her hands. She began to quiver with suppressed rage.

'You bastard,' she hissed at last. 'You utter, utter bastard. Do you have *any idea* what you put me through? The slightest comprehension?'

He looked calmly at her. 'Please try not to be angry with me, Diana, I can explain all of it. I'll answer all your questions, I promise. You must have heaps of them. I'll tell you everything, I swear, and when I'm finished I know you'll understand.

'But before I begin . . . what did you mean by 'we'?'

★   ★   ★

When Diana had finished, James turned his face and stared out at the glittering Mediterranean.

It had been obvious from his expression when she began to explain about her pregnancy that the thought he might have left her with child had simply never occurred to him. He'd even protested a little. 'But we only did it a couple of

245

times. Are you sure?'

She had silenced him with a look.

'Why did you call her Stella?' he asked now.

'Dickens. *Great Expectations*. I always liked the name Estella but she's not a very nice person in the book, so I shortened it to Stella . . . What would you have wanted to call her?'

'Good God, I have no idea — I'm still coming to terms with the fact that I have a daughter. Does she look like you?'

'People say so. She's definitely got your smile. Only a few of us can see that, of course — me and Mummy and Daddy.'

He paused. 'What about *my* mother? Did you make contact with her after I was shot down? Has she seen Stella?'

Diana looked sadly at him. 'You really did cut yourself off from everyone, didn't you?' Then: 'Your mother is dead, James,' she told him after a pause. 'She died in the blitz, before Stella was born. My parents wrote to her after you died — ' she shook her head — 'I mean after you went missing. There was a plan for us to meet her in London, take her out to lunch. I was so looking forward to it, but she was killed before we could do that. I'm sorry.'

James was whey-faced. 'Do you know what happened, exactly?'

'Yes. She was in one of those above-ground community shelters. It took a direct hit — you'll know they weren't designed to cope with that. Everyone was killed outright. She wouldn't have known a thing, James.'

'Yes, I can see that. Poor old girl, she was a

good mother. At least she didn't have long to grieve for me, did she?'

'No, that's true, I suppose. About five months. She was killed in November when the raids had got really bad.'

'Is there some sort of grave?' he asked her after a while.

'Yes, a mass one. There wasn't . . . there wasn't much left, not of any of them. I told you, it was a direct hit.'

He blew out his cheeks. 'So my mother's dead, and I have a daughter . . . It's quite a lot to absorb in one morning. Diana, can I please see Stella? She doesn't have to know who I am. We could — '

Diana interrupted him. 'Just a minute, James. You're running ahead of yourself, aren't you? I've had a lot to take in, too! I have no idea if you can see Stella. I can still scarcely believe we're having this conversation. This is the strangest day of my life. I keep thinking I'm going to wake up from a . . . a preposterous dream.'

They sat in silence for a minute before Diana spoke again, less sharply.

'I'll have that cigarette now.'

He lit one for both of them.

'James,' she said quietly, 'I don't suppose you're aware of what happened to my brother either, are you?'

He shook his head and blew out smoke.

'He died the same afternoon you were shot down.'

James looked astonished. 'What? He *can't* have been! He didn't get back to base in time for

247

the mission. He didn't fly that day!'

Diana sighed. 'No, he didn't. It was just awful, James. John was on his way back to Upminster when his motor bike was hit by an Army lorry. It happened near Sidcup. He didn't stand a chance.'

'Hang on a bloody minute.' James was lost in thought. 'Yes, I remember now. John and I left the Dower House together after the wedding, didn't we? I couldn't get past Dartford that afternoon — there was a complete jam. Nothing was moving. That must have been John, I suppose. The poor sod. I owed him. He saved my skin at Cranwell, did you know that?'

He brooded over his cigarette for a while before continuing.

'When I arrived at Upminster I couldn't understand why he wasn't already there. I assumed he'd broken down or got a flat tyre or something. Jesus . . . poor old John. I often wondered if he made it through all right. But to die in a stupid road accident . . . '

He looked keenly at her. 'Christ, that must have been a gruesome day for you all. Did you get the news at the same time?'

'About the two of you? Yes, more or less. First the police rang to tell us about Johnnie. Daddy had to go and identify his body. It was dreadful for him. Then almost as soon as he got back, the RAF arrived to tell us about you.'

He reached across for her hand but Diana drew back. She looked at him accusingly.

'James, they were certain you'd been killed, even then, before the official report. I've read it.

It said you were dead. Two pilots from your squadron both made statements. They said there was definitely no parachute, and both of them saw your plane explode on the ground.'

She stared at him, as if she were seeing him properly for the first time. 'What are you doing here, James? How on earth did you survive a terrible crash like that?'

He took a deep breath.

'All right. All right, Diana. Where do you want me to start?'

43

He was exhilarated.

He was exhausted.

Three kills in as many minutes.

The first encounter had been over almost as soon as it began. The German fighter exploded the moment James's bullets struck it. The plane transformed instantly into a ball of flame and black smoke — a sudden blemish in the summer sky which until that moment had been blue and clear and without stain.

Bloody hell. I must have hit his fuel tank or a magazine full of shells, he thought, banking sharply to avoid the tumbling wreckage of his own making.

The second and third kills were unexpectedly conflated. His aircraft and a German Me 109 had been flying head-to-head on a direct collision course. He could see the other plane's gun ports emitting little puffs of smoke as they twinkled and flashed, both aircraft closing at over 600mph.

Glowing cannon shells whipped past on either side of his cockpit, somehow missing everything. His own answering tracer bullets were dipping just under the other plane's belly. James adjusted his trim slightly and grunted with satisfaction as he began to see the flash and sparkle of hits all over the enemy's nose-cone.

A strange calmness settled over him. One of us

is going to have to pull away soon, he thought dispassionately.

His thumb stayed stubbornly on the firing-ring.

Actually, I couldn't give a toss either way.

The 109 broke first, corkscrewing wildly up and to one side. It was a disastrous move: the plane smashed into another German fighter that was diving to help out. Both aircraft vanished in a giant fireball.

Christ. Poor bastards.

He scanned the sky. He couldn't see any other aircraft at all, friend or foe. For the first time in minutes, James had a chance to get his bearings. He looked down and around him for the coast.

Whoa!

He'd drifted a long way inland during the fighting. The Channel was a blue shimmer away to the north. Below him, French villages and farmland moved swiftly beneath his wings.

OK, that's enough. Time to go home.

He pushed the stick forward, kicked the rudder and made a diving turn towards the sea. If he kept his nose clean and stayed low, he should be landing at Upminster in about twenty minutes. He peered at his fuel gauge. Low.

Or maybe ditching off Rye.

His Spitfire bucked like a startled horse and sheared sideways, shuddering horribly. He twisted violently in his seat and looked behind him. A 109 was just above and to his starboard, weaving from side to side like an angry wasp.

Fuck. It had shot most of the tailplane away. His plane was now practically unflyable.

This heart-stopping realisation had barely registered when more cannon shells slammed into his engine. The Merlin coughed and stuttered before giving a metallic shriek of agony. Shattered piston-rods and chunks of metal flew in all directions and orange flames shot out of the engine compartment.

Fire began to lick along one side of his cockpit and there was the stench of aviation fuel. Sooty black smoke mixed with the oil that was spraying onto his windscreen from some rupture, and at once the Perspex canopy was comprehensively blacked-out. He couldn't see a bloody thing. It was like trying to fly in a blindfold.

He couldn't believe how fast it had all happened — four, five seconds? — and he felt his plane begin to curl into a dive. Gravitational force pushed him upwards in his harness and his head pressed against the canopy above him.

Christ, what a bloody horrible way to die, in the dark like this.

He wrenched at the black Perspex above him and tried to force it back on its runners. It jammed (*of course*) and he punched it repeatedly with his fists. At last it jerked open a couple of inches and light flooded back into the cockpit. He tried again, fear lending him frantic strength, and the damnable thing reluctantly grated back a little further. Then, suddenly, the slipstream did the rest, snatching the whole wretched business up and away. Wind roared into the cockpit, forcing its way into his eyes, mouth and nose. He could hardly breathe.

Just like the last time. Except that today,

gentlemen, we are crashing.

He poked his head over the side and looked down. *Shit.* He was barely at 300 feet, if that, and dropping fast. It would all be over in a few moments.

A line of tall poplars rushed towards him and instinctively he hauled back hard on the stick and worked the flaps. Incredibly, the aircraft responded, just a little. The nose lifted and he somehow cleared the trees. Then the Spitfire wallowed, juddered, and plunged into its valedictory dive.

This was it. The little plane would meet its end in the meadow below.

Not with me in it.

In one fluid movement James released his harness and heaved himself over the side, yanking at the ripcord of his parachute as he fell. The meadow was less than 100 feet beneath him.

Bloody hopeless.

He had the impression of poppies dotted in a mist of yellow flowers. Buttercups? Dandelions?

He screwed his eyes shut. He didn't have to watch his own death.

There was a sharp crack above him as his canopy opened and the webbing jerked hard between his legs. He opened his eyes again. The burning plane was barely thirty yards in front of him, almost on the deck. So was he. His feet hit the ground, hard. Simultaneously there was an enormous explosion and searing heat. His scalp felt as if it had been dipped in acid.

After a moment, he realised his hair was on

fire. He beat frantically at the flames with his gloved hands and then saw that his flying jacket was alight too. He tried to roll on the ground but inexplicably, he stayed upright. Looking up, he saw that his parachute had snagged on the top of the last poplar on the meadow's edge. The taut lines kept him dancing on the balls of his feet, like a fiery marionette.

Jesus Christ.

He thumped the metal release catch on his chest. The lines snapped away and he fell to the ground like a sack of coal.

Still on fire.

He rolled over and over in the grass, smothering the flames on his jacket and beating frantically at the ones in his hair. Finally they were out. He lay there, panting.

His aircraft was still burning fiercely. Acrid smoke billowed over him and he heard the ominous popping of exploding ammunition coming from inside the plane's wings.

He had to get out of this.

He struggled to his feet and immediately screamed in agony, almost falling over again. His spine felt as if great bursts of electricity were being passed through it. The pain was overwhelming.

Bullets were zipping and cracking through the air in all directions; he *must* get away from what was left of his Spitfire.

He had only staggered a few steps when he felt a tremendous blow to his left leg. It flew up in front of him in a parody of a chorus girl's high kick and his whole body followed it, arcing through the air before slamming back down to the ground. Badly winded, he lay there for a minute or so trying to get his breath. Eventually he worked his way into a sitting position and eased off his flying boot.

He'd been hit all right. There was a neat hole in the back of his calf and a much uglier exit wound at the front, just beside the shinbone. In fact, he could see the gleaming bone itself, looking like a stamen in the heart of a flower that blossomed around it, blood-red petals symmetrically curling away.

He was surprised to see that the bleeding wasn't all that heavy, and there was almost none at all from the entry wound. Grimly, he unwound his silk flying scarf — a present from Diana, she'd given it to him just before Dunkirk — and wrapped it tightly around the whole mess. Then he stood up again.

The plane's exploding machine-gun bullets had worked to a crescendo; it sounded like the finale to a fireworks display. One round sang past so close that he felt a ripple of air brush his cheek.

You'll have your fucking head taken off in a minute, mate, never mind a hole in your leg. Move it!

He limped as fast as his leg and back would allow to a low stone wall at the edge of the meadow and tumbled over it onto the other side, screaming again as his back went into violent spasms.

Wisps of smoke were still rising from his head and jacket. He just wanted to lie there but was forced up and over on to all fours as nausea overwhelmed him, and he vomited, copiously.

So this was what it was like to be shot down.

★ ★ ★

Diana sat in silence for a while. There was nothing she could think of to say that wouldn't sound trite, or silly. Eventually she passed a hand over her eyes and down the side of her face.

'I don't know what to say, James — except that it's a miracle that you're alive. I mean . . . But there's something I don't understand. The pilots who saw you shot down were certain there wasn't a parachute. They both said so in their statements. I've read them.'

He shrugged. 'I can't help that. If they saw my plane go down they should have seen my parachute open too.'

Diana frowned. 'Wait a minute. They didn't actually see your plane crash, James. They said it went down on the far side of some trees. They saw it disappear behind them and then the flash and smoke of the explosion.'

James nodded as he lit a cigarette. 'That would explain it. I told you, my parachute snagged on one of those trees. I don't even think it opened properly. If the boys were on the other side of the trees, they couldn't have seen any of that.' He grinned at her. 'Lucky for me, eh?'

'Yes! If you'd been only a few feet lower when you — '

He laughed. 'No, I don't mean that. I mean that they never saw the parachute, so everyone assumed I was dead. I always reckoned they'd think that anyway when I didn't show up anywhere, but it's nice to know for certain.'

She stared at him. 'Why is that so important, James?'

He stared back at her. 'I should have thought that was obvious. You can't hang a dead man for desertion.'

★　★　★

He came round in the dirt under the drystone wall. He could hear the crackle of his Spitfire still burning, but the popping of exploding ammunition had stopped now.

James struggled to his feet and stifled another shout of agony. The pain in his back was exquisite. What the hell had he done to it? He knew it couldn't be broken; he could walk. Strangely enough, his injured leg was almost pain-free, just the occasional dull ache.

He needed to clear out before a German patrol came snooping around. For the second time that afternoon, he cast around for his bearings. Across the fields, about a mile to the south, he could see the roofs of a village.

It was going to be agony, but he would have to walk, there was no choice. With any luck there would be a friendly welcome, perhaps even a doctor to clean and stitch his leg and give him painkillers for his back. And his tongue, too; it was grossly swollen where he had bitten it, and it hurt like the devil. His mouth and chin were covered in drying blood; he could feel it

257

plastered slickly all over his lower face. Vomit too. He must look an absolute fright.

Slowly, his bloodied face set in a rictus of pain, James Blackwell hobbled over to a farm-track on the other side of the field. It appeared to lead towards the village; he would probably soon pick up a proper road.

The skeletal remains of his downed plane burned quietly behind him.

He didn't look back.

He was finished with all of that.

★ ★ ★

'So that's when you decided to run away.' Diana sounded harsher and more judgemental than she intended to. She flushed.

James shrugged. 'You can call it what you like. Running away, deserting, going AWOL — it's all the same to me, Diana.'

He leaned across the table, his face suddenly taut, eyes narrowed. 'Look. I'd just had enough,' he said quickly. 'Enough. I'd nearly been killed, twice in two weeks. I just couldn't face the thought of going through any of that again.'

'But why desert? Why not just give yourself up to the Germans and spend the war in a prison camp? It would have been pretty ghastly, but you would have been safe.'

He sighed. 'Give me a minute, would you? Talking about this makes me really thirsty.' He snapped his fingers and a waiter appeared at the table at once. Diana thought the man looked extremely nervous.

'Water,' ordered James.

The waiter hurried away and Diana stared out at the surf breaking along the beach opposite.

She turned to him. 'Is that man frightened of you, James? Do you know him?'

He lit another cigarette. 'Nope. Never seen him before in my life. He must be the nervous type.' He inhaled deeply. 'Where were we?'

'You were telling me why you didn't want to spend the rest of the war in a POW camp.'

'Yes . . . Well . . . back in 1940 a lot of us thought we'd lost the war. France had fallen and it looked like England was going to be next.'

Diana frowned. 'But surely the Germans would have sent you back home if that had happened, once the fighting was over. We'd have exchanged prisoners, wouldn't we?'

He burst out laughing. '*What?* Are you serious? Once the Nazis had won, and got their own prisoners back, they would have treated us exactly the same as they did everyone else they crushed — the Poles, the Czechs, the Russians . . . haven't you read Hitler's blueprint for Britain after we'd been subjugated? The newspapers got hold of it last year. It made for grim reading, I can assure you.'

'Of course I read it. Don't patronise me, James.'

'I'm sorry, Diana, I don't mean to. But think about it. The Führer's master-plan for a smashed Britain would have done for every British POW this side of the Channel, me included. Hitler decreed that every able-bodied British man between the ages of seventeen and forty-five be transported to the Continent to work on German war and construction projects.'

'I know,' she interrupted. 'I told you, I read about it. And I agree, it would have been horrendous. Our POWs were to be offered a choice, weren't they . . . Fight for Germany in special British units, or be drafted into factories.'

He nodded. 'Exactly. The Todt industrial complex. It was huge and it took slave labour wherever it could get it. Most conscripts didn't survive the war — they were starved and worked to death. Of *course* I had to stay out of German hands.'

'Yes, but . . . ' Diana gave him a frank look. 'All this is with hindsight, isn't it, James? You couldn't have known any of that back in 1940. Why didn't you try and contact the French Resistance? They would have helped you.'

'Because I thought we'd lost the bloody war! You're not listening! Anyway, helped me to do what, exactly? Get back to Britain? For Christ's sake!'

She flinched.

'I'm sorry, Diana.' He took several deep breaths as he calmed himself. 'Look. Even if I *had* managed to get back home — and it's a bloody big if — and Britain had somehow struggled on for a few months more before collapsing, I would've been given a sodding medal, paraded in front of the newspapers, and then shoved back into another Spitfire to be shot down again, and die a hero's death or be taken prisoner. You have to understand, Diana — the very idea of flying missions again seemed totally mad to me. It *was* mad. Out of the question. I didn't even have to think about it.

'Anyway,' he went on, more gently, 'there was no Resistance, not at that time. France was collapsing. It was utter chaos here. Army chaps wandering about like lost souls and civilians trudging from here to there in random groups or in mass refugee columns or hiding indoors waiting for the Apocalypse . . . I know. I saw it. I was a bloody *part* of it for a while. You've never seen anything like it in your life. It was like the End of Days, I'm telling you.'

There was a long silence.

'How many of my squadron made it?' he asked eventually.

She shook her head. 'Not many. Quite a few were killed. One of the boys who saw you crash was shot down the very next week. Others were taken prisoner, of course. I think one pilot was executed by the Gestapo after he tried to escape.'

He squinted at her through sunshine and cigarette smoke. 'Hmm. You must think I'm a bloody coward.'

'I haven't really had time to consider the question, actually.'

The nervous waiter was back, refilling their water glasses.

Out on the Mediterranean, a distant ferry was returning from Corsica. Diana watched it for a while, struggling with her thoughts. She decided she did not have the right to judge anyone who had gone through the kind of trauma the man opposite her had endured. Perhaps she should accept his reasons for deserting.

'I don't believe that you're a coward,' she said finally, still staring out to sea. 'You fought very bravely, James. My brother thought you were the best and most courageous man in the squadron. Even so, every man has his limits — I realise that. But there's something I need you to explain, now I know you're alive.'

'What's that?'

She turned to him. 'After you were shot down . . . where did you go? What did you do? And why didn't you come back to me when the war was over? I thought you loved me. I thought we were happy.'

'I did love you,' he said quietly. 'And we were — we were so happy, weren't we? But how *could* I come back? As soon as the authorities caught up with me — and they would have, Diana — I'd have been tried for desertion. They'd have hanged me. Probably still would. I made my bed in the summer of 1940 and I've had to lie on it ever since.'

She looked at him bleakly. 'You could have come to me. I would have protected you.'

'No, you couldn't, however much you tried. I would have been a curse on you. Can't you see that?'

'Not really, no.'

He threw his head back. 'I think we need to take a break from all this.'

She shrugged. 'If you say so.'

'Well, I think we should eat, anyway. D'you mind? I don't know about you, but I'm starving.'

Diana looked at her watch. It was almost one

262

o'clock. She'd promised Stella she'd be back at the villa for lunch.

'I have to make a phone call.'

'Of course. Look, Diana . . . ' He reached for her hand. She let him hold it for a moment before she withdrew it. 'I'm going to tell you everything. You deserve that, at least.'

★ ★ ★

She crossed the marbled lobby of the Negresco. It was so much cooler in here than on the hot terrace, in spite of the sea breeze. As she made her way to the telephone booths, Diana was intercepted by the hotel manager, bobbing and smiling and intertwining his hands against each other as though he were washing them. He could be Uriah Heep, she thought.

'*Madame.*' He bowed. 'May I say what a very great pleasure it is to have *monsieur*' — he bowed in the direction of the terrace — 'and his companion with us for lunch today. May I — '

'I'm his wife.'

The little man's eyes widened and she saw fear flicker in them.

'But of course, *madame*, I should have known. A thousand apologies. As I was about to say, if there is anything I can do to make your visit more enjoyable . . . ' He bowed again and scurried away.

Diana's mind reeled. Why on earth had she said that? Douglas was her husband, not this ghost she hadn't seen or heard from in more than ten years. What was she doing?

She realised that she'd been in a state of shock for the last two hours. Now she was away from him for a moment, it was evaporating, and the reality of the situation came crashing in on her. He had been alive all this time. Alive. He'd been hiding in France, and if she hadn't come here — to Nice — she'd never have known.

What was he doing here, anyway? How did he live? He looked prosperous enough, and even after spending such a short time in his company, she could see he had some kind of hold over people here. That waiter, and the manager just now . . .

Diana felt a faint but unmistakable premonition of danger.

Abruptly, she changed her mind. It was madness to have lunch with him. She would go straight home, now, and wait for Douglas to get back from work. She would tell him everything, starting from that first day in the flower-market when she'd heard James's voice floating from the cab.

Overwhelmingly relieved by her decision, she walked briskly to the hotel's side entrance where she knew there was a taxi-rank.

'Diana!'

She turned round. He was on the far side of the lobby, looking at her with a slightly puzzled, hurt expression. Even though she'd been sitting opposite him for almost two hours, she experienced fresh shock at the very sight of him.

Something else, too. She was suddenly and fully aware, for the first time that day, of how attractive he still was.

She felt as if she was looking at two subtly differing images, each one similar, but shifting and overlaid. The James she remembered with such clarity from that last day at the Dower House — crisp in his freshly ironed uniform, handsome despite looking haggard after weeks of gruelling warfare — and *this* James, still lean, but robust, and completely at home in his new environment. From the little French she had heard him speak, she suspected he was more or less fluent in the language.

He walked quickly across to her and after a moment, placed a hand hesitatingly on her shoulder.

'This must be so difficult, so impossibly hard for you. I'm sorry, darling.'

Don't call me that! You have no right to call me that, not now!

It was almost as if she had spoken aloud.

He took his hand away. 'Forgive me. I had no right to call you that.' He looked around them. 'Please don't go. Stay and have lunch with me. I promise that everything I tell you will make perfect sense. I want you to understand the whole thing. At the moment this must seem utterly surreal to you . . . I bet you feel like Alice in bloody Wonderland.'

Seeing him standing there, solicitous and concerned, and so unutterably *real* and solid, Diana's resolve began to fade. It *was* only lunch, after all. She was being silly and superstitious.

He gestured to the phone booths. 'Look, call home. If you can't work it out today, never mind — we can meet here tomorrow, or the next day, or wherever and whenever you like. I'll leave it completely up to you.' He pointed to the men's room. 'I'm just off there. See you back at the table and you can tell me what's happening.'

He smiled at her as he walked away, and then turned over his shoulder and called: 'I hope it's a yes, though. I've already ordered for both of us. Sea bass. It's rather good here.'

* * *

'It's all right,' she said, sitting down at the table. 'Stella's tutor can stay for the rest of the afternoon. They're off to play tennis.'

'Splendid.' James didn't look especially surprised, Diana thought. He was busy with the wine list. She sat back and studied him.

He was still her James, she decided. Completely relaxed, given the extraordinary circumstances. She wondered if anything ever really threw him off-balance. She could hear him humming to himself as his slim brown fingers moved down the *carte du vin*. He glanced up and grinned at her.

She shivered. He was gorgeous.

Once, he'd been hers.

He ordered their wine and turned to her. 'What? What are you thinking?'

'I'm thinking that this is the strangest day of my life. I can't believe this is happening, James. I can't believe you're alive and here in Nice. I swear I wouldn't be surprised if my brother materialised at the next table.'

'Christ, I would,' he replied. 'I'm not one of

266

the undead, Diana, although I almost felt like it the day I was shot down. I was absolutely certain I was about to die when I jumped. In fact, all the time I was staggering to that village, I kept wondering if I *had* died and it was just my ghost wandering around. I remember thinking — '

'Of me? Did you think of me, James?' she interrupted.

He looked steadily at her. 'I won't lie to you, Diana. No. No, I didn't. And we'd been married that very morning, hadn't we?'

She turned her head away so he wouldn't see the tears that suddenly pricked her eyes.

'I didn't think of anyone other than myself, not that day, and not for a long time after. I felt I'd been given a second chance, a new life. I knew I couldn't go home so I suppose I blocked you out of my mind. For a time. Only for a time.'

'How much time, James? Until today? Until an hour ago?'

His head fell to one side and he gave her a crooked smile. 'No, my love,' he said. 'From almost the moment I arrived here in Nice, ten years ago. Don't diminish yourself through my eyes, Diana.'

Two waiters arrived with their food and wine. One filleted the fish at a little side-table next to theirs, the other poured rosé. Their course served, the waiters hurried away.

Diana and James ate in silence for a while. James took a swallow of wine before continuing.

'The village was called Licques,' he said. 'I remember thinking that was appropriate. I was feeling pretty licked by then.' He smiled faintly.

'But I'll always remember it, whatever it was called, until my dying day.'

He gestured to her glass. 'Go on. Have a drink, Diana. Trust me — you're going to need it.'

44

The village street was almost deserted. Brick-built terraces faced each other, divided by a procession of lime trees planted down the centre of the road. The only person in sight was a girl of about seven, sitting on the kerbside playing with a doll. She proffered it to James as he stopped in front of her. She didn't seem the slightest concerned by his scorched and bloodied appearance.

He politely declined the toy before asking her: 'Can you tell me, *ma petite*, does a doctor live in your village?'

She pointed instantly down the street. 'There. The big white house on the left. Dr Lain lives there.'

'*Merci.*'

She gave him a little wave as he lurched away, and returned to her doll.

Sure enough, 100 yards or so further on there was a drive set at right angles to the street. He could see elm trees sheltering a solid white stone-built house at the bottom of the drive. A polished brass plaque on one of the twin gateposts at the entrance announced that this was the *Résidence et Cabinet Médical de Dr Hubert Lain*. He staggered down the drive until he reached a wide front door, which stood between modest whitewashed pillars.

James yanked the bell-pull, and when no one

came, he hammered on the brass knocker. Then he jerked at the bell-pull again.

At last he heard footsteps approaching from the other side of the door and a man's voice called out gruffly, '*Oui? Qui est là?*'

'It is I, *monsieur* . . . I have an injury. I need urgent assistance.'

After a moment he heard bolts being shot back and a key turning in the lock. The door opened a fraction and a big man of about sixty peered out. He was rubicund and fleshy and sprouted extravagant nasal hair. A stained napkin was tucked into his shirt collar; the man must have been having his supper.

The moment he set eyes on James the doctor's face contorted in panic and he tried to slam the door shut again.

He's clocked the RAF uniform, thought James. *Doesn't want to get involved. Can't say I blame him*.

He managed to jam his good leg into the gap and forced his shoulder against the door. His back blazed with pain.

The Frenchman was pushing hard against the other side, shouting at the top of his voice. '*De rien ici pour vous ici. Je ne peux pas vous aider!*'

'OPEN THE DOOR!' James bellowed. 'You're meant to be a doctor! OPEN IT!'

'*Non!*'

Ah, thought James, so you understand English then. Right. He reached down into his flying boot, where he kept his service revolver. A lot of the boys carried them when they knew they might be flying over France. He pulled it out and shoved it into the gap above the doctor's head.

'OPEN THE DOOR, YOU BASTARD! I NEED HELP!'

'*NON!*'

James pulled the trigger and there was an earsplitting bang. The man on the other side screamed and fell backwards, and James shouldered his way in. They were in a little vestibule, the Frenchman trying to squirm away from him into the main hall behind.

'*Ne tirez pas!* Don't shoot!'

'I will if you don't bloody well pipe down!' James dropped awkwardly onto one knee and shoved the barrel of his gun hard against the man's temple. The doctor immediately lay still. 'You speak English, don't you?'

'Yes.'

'You're the doctor, aren't you?'

'Yes.'

'I'm RAF. Spitfire. I've been shot down and I'm hurt. My leg's been hit and my back's bad. I want you to dress the wound and give me painkillers for my back. Understand?'

The man scrambled to his feet, James covering him with the revolver. 'How dare you come into my house in this way! You must leave immediately! I insist that you — '

James clicked the hammer back. 'If you don't do exactly as I say, I'll put a bullet in *your* leg, all right?'

The doctor glared. 'Yes, of course — you have the gun, *monsieur*, do you not? Very well. I will go and get what I need. Wait here.'

'Bollocks. I'm coming with you.'

The doctor led the way through the house to his surgery on the other side, James's gun at his back. When they got there, the Frenchman turned around to face the pilot.

'*Monsieur*, I refuse to work under these conditions. I will not treat you at the point of a gun.'

'Yes, you damn well will.' James hauled himself up on the narrow brown leather examination couch that was bolted to the wall.

'OK.' He ostentatiously put the gun down by his side. 'But this stays here — and remember, it's cocked.' He stuck his bloodied leg out and winced. 'Take a look.'

The doctor pulled a wooden stool from under a desk and propped James's foot on it. He carefully unwound the sodden silk scarf and dropped it on the floor.

The gleaming shinbone had vanished. It was now covered by a large clot of congealed blood. The entry wound remained clean, but had turned almost black. A strange rippling bruise circled the dark hole.

The doctor grunted and stood up, turning to a zinc cupboard on the wall behind him.

'It is not so bad, I think,' he said over his shoulder. 'The wound is clean. The bullet has passed through so there is no need for an operation. And the bone is not broken. You have been lucky, *monsieur*.'

He turned back clutching boxes and bottles. 'Iodine to wash the flesh — this will hurt — then powder to sterilise and disinfect. I will not make stitches; the wounds will close by themselves in time.'

'Fine. Get going, then.'

Now the man was all business, swabbing, dusting, and pressing thick gauze wadding into the pulverised flesh. He took a long cotton bandage and wound it expertly around the whole area, tying it off with a flourish.

'*Voilà!* We are finished, yes?'

'No, we're not. I told you — I want painkillers for my back.'

The doctor nodded and gestured through the doorway of the surgery to a room on the other side of the corridor. 'Of course. I will go to my dispensary. Please wait here.'

'I'm coming with you.'

The Frenchman stamped his foot. '*Monsieur!* Enough of this nonsense! My dispensary has no other door than the one you see, and look,' he pointed to his desk, 'my telephone is in here.'

James looked at the ancient ebony instrument with its beautiful pearl inlays.

'So you must understand,' the doctor continued, 'I can go nowhere and speak to no one. May I now please be allowed to do my job?'

James nodded reluctantly. 'All right. But I'll be watching that door. And I want you back here in two minutes.'

'Certainly.' The doctor exited the surgery and vanished into his dispensary.

James could hear the opening and shutting of drawers and the sound of general rummaging. Then all fell silent, except for the doctor's tuneless humming.

'Hey! What are you doing in there?'

'*Mon Dieu!*' came the exasperated, muffled response. 'I am making up your pills, *monsieur*! A little patience, if you please.'

'Well, hurry up.'

More silence. Now, even the humming had stopped.

Then he heard it.

The faintest click from the telephone on the desk.

The lying bastard. He's got an extension.

Gripping his revolver, James slid off the couch and crossed the surgery and corridor as quietly as he could, gently nudging the dispensary door ajar.

The Frenchman was ten feet away, on the opposite side of the room. He was hunched and, sure enough, held a telephone to his ear. He was whispering into the mouthpiece. '*Bonjour? Bonjour? Il y a quelqu'un?*'

James could hear the tinny response but wasn't able to make out what was being said. But he saw the doctor's shoulders sag with relief.

'*Ah, Dieu merci, Capitaine! Je suis le docteur de Licques. J'ai un homme* — '

If he'd been closer to the man, or able to rush across the room, he would have pistol-whipped him to the floor. That's what James told himself afterwards. But now he pulled the trigger without hesitation or compunction. The doctor's face smashed into the wall, his back arching under the terrific impact of the bullet that struck him just to the left of his spine, blowing out most of his heart through his chest. The man slid to the floor in total silence.

James lurched across the room and, with a single blow of his gun-butt, smashed the wall-mounted telephone into pieces. The wires hung limply from the plaster. The *gendarme* on the other end must have heard the crash of the gunshot, but there was nothing James could do about that. Nevertheless, he cursed the body that lay motionless at his feet.

The doctor of Licques had treated his last patient.

★　★　★

'I said I'd tell you everything.'

Diana had gone very pale. She sipped her water and watched James carefully over the rim of her glass. Putting her tumbler down with care, she spoke at last.

'That man helped you, and you shot him in the back. You didn't have to kill him, James. You could have tied him up, or something.'

He sighed, and pushed his hair back from his forehead with both hands. 'You couldn't be more wrong, Diana. He was turning me in! The French police wouldn't have hesitated to hand me over to the Gestapo for interrogation. I killed him just as he was about to tell them he had a British pilot in his house. He gave me no choice. If I'd waited one more second I'd have been done for. The man was a collaborator.'

She thought this over for a few moments, before her eyes suddenly widened.

'Oh my God. You were *always* going to kill him, weren't you? Once he'd given you what you wanted. You wouldn't have tied him up; you knew he would have got free eventually and called the police. That's true, isn't it?'

He inclined his head. 'Very good, Diana. Yes, I realised from the moment he forced me to draw my gun that I'd have to kill him before I left. But don't you see how your mind just followed *exactly* the same logical path that mine did that day? The stakes were incredibly high. You're beginning to understand that now, aren't you? Come on — aren't you?'

She nodded reluctantly. 'I suppose so.'

James took another long, reflective draw on his cigarette. 'Of course,' he went on, 'if he'd helped me willingly, and not had to be forced into doing it, everything would have been completely different. But he was a very stupid man. He made the wrong choices. And it was wartime and I had every right to avoid being captured.'

'Yes, if you were planning to fight another day. But you weren't. You were running away.'

There was a long silence between them. James's eyes had hardened and his mouth was set in a tight line. He was clearly not going to argue the point.

'Anyway,' Diana continued after a moment, 'how did you know there was no one else in the house? Would you have killed them too?'

He looked calmly at her. 'Actually, there was someone else. And no, I didn't harm a hair of her head.'

★ ★ ★

James's mind raced as he stood over the doctor's body. The fat fool had obviously phoned a *gendarmerie*, but where? Then he noticed a small leather-bound notebook clutched in the dead man's left hand. James bent down and lifted it carefully away. It was the doctor's personal list of telephone numbers, opened under entries beginning with the letter G. The third listing down said *Gendarmerie* and was followed by *St-Omer* and a number.

James closed his eyes and tried to draw himself a mental map. The town of St-Omer was roughly fifteen miles due east of Licques. About three minutes by Spitfire, half an hour by car, probably longer with all the refugees and wandering soldiers clogging up the roads. That didn't give him much time.

But of course, there might be a smaller rural police station closer by. The St-Omer man might be alerting them right now, reporting a phone call that had been abruptly terminated by what sounded very like a gunshot.

He chewed his lip. He'd just have to take the chance. Even if there was such an outpost, it probably wasn't manned these days. France was falling apart.

He shoved his revolver back into his flying boot and bent down over the dead man. With difficulty, he managed to turn him onto his back. The doctor's face was bloodied from where it had smashed into the wall, but James was still able to detect the man's last human emotion. He wore an expression of intense surprise.

James began going through the jacket pockets.

A wallet. He flipped it open. Identity card, an old theatre ticket, and about thirty francs in five-franc notes. James grimaced. That wouldn't get him far. He patted the trouser pockets and pulled out the doctor's keys. One for the house, and one for the ignition of a car. This was better. He'd spotted a wooden lean-to on the right of the house when he'd come up the drive earlier. That was probably the garage.

He stood up and crossed back into the surgery. Two minutes of rifling through the desk drawers in there yielded nothing more than medical forms and the doctor's prescription pad. He stuffed the latter into his pocket with a vague feeling that it might come in useful, and was about to head back to the central part of the house when he remembered his blood-soaked scarf. He grabbed it from the floor and stuffed it in a pocket.

When he got to the main hall he looked at his watch. It was exactly six o'clock. He'd give himself twenty minutes here, not a second more. Assuming the police were only just leaving St-Omer, they couldn't possibly be here before half past at the earliest. If a more locally based unit was coming, he'd just have to shoot it out with them.

There was a wide staircase in front of him, leading to a gallery that ran all around the hall. The bedrooms would surely open off that. To his left were double doors, thrown wide open, and he could see the main *salon* beyond them. He'd start in there.

He *had* to find some cash, or something that

could be readily turned into cash. He was already forming the outline of a plan for his next move, and it wasn't going to come cheap.

The *salon* was an elegant room, with a baby-grand piano next to French windows. They reminded him of the Dower House. On the other side of the room was a large bureau, the kind with a slatted roll-down lid. He hobbled over to it — *Christ*, his back was hurting — and pulled the handle upwards. The bureau was locked.

He turned around. The fireplace opposite had dried flowers in a sort of pewter basin, and on either side were black iron fire-dogs. One of those would do. He carried it back to the bureau, raised the heavy metal cast above his head and brought it crashing down on the roll-top. Several slats burst and already he could see the drawers inside. Two more blows did it and he ripped away what was left of the cover.

The bureau was a disappointment. He snatched out drawer after drawer but found only pens, notebooks, diaries and several half-empty bottles of ink.

He was about to turn away when he noticed a glimmer of white in one of the drawer sockets. He peered closer. It was an envelope, taped to the underside of the little space.

Hello.

He pulled the envelope free and ripped it open. A heavy steel key fell out. It was shiny and struck him as being quite new. A long serial number ending in three letters was stamped clearly on the shank. A master-key, then.

'So why are you hidden away, little one?' He

spoke the words aloud in the empty room, weighing the key in his hand, thinking hard. It was twice the size of the doctor's door key. This had to be for locking something substantial in both size and value, that was obvious.

'I think I know what you are,' he said at last. 'You're the key to a safe, or a strongbox — or my name's not Blackwell.' He glanced at his watch. Five past six. Fifteen minutes left at most. Not much time to find a safe in a strange house.

He tried to remember anything he knew about safes. Hadn't he read somewhere that most people with a safe preferred to install it in their bedroom? Something about an instinctive wish to sleep with one's valuables close to hand. A search of the master bedroom was clearly his best shot — indeed, his only shot, with the seconds ticking away.

James decided that he'd stop looking for anything else and concentrate on finding the safe. He just had to hope he was right about the key.

He left the salon and began climbing the stairs, like an old man with a gammy leg — dot one, carry one, dot one, carry one. *Dammit*, he wished he could move faster.

When he reached the gallery, he saw there were six bedrooms leading from it, their doors facing an ornate oak balustrade. It was obvious which was the master bedroom: it was the only one with double doors, directly in front of him at the head of the stairs.

The doors were ajar and it was very dark inside. James slipped into the room, almost gagging as he did so. The smell in here was appalling: a mixture of sweat, faeces, and something else — a sour medical odour.

He could see at once why it was so dark. The main window was shuttered, although thin bands of late-afternoon sun gleamed in parallel lines through the wooden slats, illuminating floating dustmotes like aeroplanes caught in searchlights.

He crossed the room, still trying not to gag, raised the catch on the shutters and thrust them wide open. Light flooded into the room, along with fresh air. He gulped it in.

Someone behind him coughed.

He spun wildly round, fumbling for his gun.

There was no one there.

After a moment, he heard it again: a dry, papery cough. It was coming from the bed.

Gun drawn, James walked cautiously to the foot of an enormous four-poster. Light gauze curtains enclosed it, and outside them, on the bedside table to his right, were several dirty glasses, a medicine flask, and a bottle of tablets that had fallen on its side. A few shiny red tablets had spilled out.

Very slowly, he drew back the curtain at the foot of the bed and dipped his head under the canopy.

She was an old woman. Old, and clearly very sick. James thought she looked almost as dead as the doctor downstairs. Yellow skin was stretched tight over her skull and her breathing was fast and shallow. Her eyes were closed and as he looked at her, she gave another cough, much quieter than the first one.

He relaxed. *She doesn't even know I'm here.*

He turned to look at the room, which with the shutters open was beginning to smell more tolerable. There were two armoires, side by side, a smaller demi-wardrobe, and a fireplace with an oil painting hanging above it; some sort of seascape, all crashing waves under a dark, doom-laden sky.

He started with the armoires, yanking them away from the wall, suffering more crippling bursts of pain in his back, and checking for a safe behind. There was nothing, just smooth wallpaper.

The wardrobe may have been small, but it was extremely heavy. James could hardly move it and the thought suddenly struck him that perhaps it contained a strongbox. The door was locked, and the key was missing. He decided it would be quicker to force the lock rather than waste time looking for a key. He had a penknife in his tunic pocket, but it wasn't nearly big enough for the job.

Cursing, he limped back downstairs and returned two minutes later with a heavy chopping knife he'd found in the kitchen. He used it like a jemmy, twisting it into the narrow slit between the lock and the frame. After a few moments the lock burst out of its seating and flew across the room.

He threw the door open.

The wardrobe was stuffed full of old leather boots and shoes — dozens of pairs, crammed in anyhow. Some of them looked as if they belonged to the last century. He dragged the incongruous hoard out by the armful, but they were hiding nothing apart from dust and a few mouse droppings.

He cursed again, before remembering that at least it would be easier now for him to drag the wardrobe away from the wall. But when he'd done so, it was the same as with the armoires. More blank wall. He thumped it with his fist in frustration, then looked at his watch. *Hell*. It was now a quarter past six. He decided to extend his self-imposed deadline to the half hour. The police couldn't get here from St-Omer that soon, and if local officers had been despatched, they would surely have been here by now.

There was only the oil painting left. If the safe wasn't behind that, then either it was under the floorboards, or somewhere else equally inaccessible, or it simply didn't exist.

He went over to the fireplace and gave the painting above it a hard shove to one side. It swung heavily on its creaking wire. Good. Not screwed into the wall, then. He grasped it firmly on both sides and lifted it up and out, tossing it on to a nearby chair.

He was looking at the safe.

It was quite small, about nine inches square. Like the key, it looked new, the door of brushed steel sitting in a heavy iron frame. The lock was in the centre of the door. James pulled out the key from a trouser pocket, and slid it into the lock. It clicked easily into place; it was obviously the one.

He licked his lips, and turned the key clockwise. It moved a fraction, and then jammed. He tried again. Still no luck. Trying to keep calm, he twisted the key in the opposite direction. Again, after a tiny movement, it refused to budge. He rattled the key from side to side and up and down, and tried again.

The safe refused to open.

He smacked both palms against the door in frustration, cursing aloud.

'Hubert?' It was the old woman. He'd woken her up. James moved towards the bed.

She struggled for breath, before calling the doctor's name again. Presumably the dead man had been her son.

'Hubert?' Her eyes were still closed. He tried to recall the doctor's gruff speech earlier at the door, and managed a throaty '*Oui*'.

Her lips cracked into the faintest smile and she drew breath to speak. When she did so, it was in a high, breathless squeak.

'Hubert, always you forget! You must touch the spring *before* the key, remember?'

James's French was patchy but he got the gist of what the old woman had said. Something about forgetting to do something, to touch something, and *then* the key.

'*Merci, chère Maman*,' he said. He hoped that was how Hubert addressed her.

She didn't react.

He hurried back to the safe, but he couldn't see anything to press. He tried pushing on the lock itself but it was totally solid in its seating. He ran his fingers around the iron frame, feeling for any depression or slight protuberance. Nothing.

Sucking his teeth in frustration, he stepped back and tried to think of something else. He was so close! He'd found the key, he'd found the safe . . . what the hell did he have to do to get the bloody thing open?

He looked more closely at the door. It closed into the frame snugly, but there was a hair's breadth of a crack running all around the join. He licked his index finger, then slowly ran it round the edge of the door. As his finger passed directly above the lock, he felt it. A tiny catch against his skin. He stared at the spot.

There it was. An almost invisible sliver of metal, between the door and the frame. It was less than an eighth of an inch wide. Whistling in admiration, he fished out his penknife. He opened the smallest blade, and put the point against the fragment of steel. Then he pushed, gently.

There was a whirr and a sharp click.

Trying to keep his hands steady, James put the key back in again. He turned it firmly to the right. This time there was no resistance. The key rotated through ninety degrees, and he heard the magical sound of metal moving smoothly against metal. There was a dull clunk, and the door swung open.

He almost cheered.

The safe was a black hole and he didn't have time to find a torch. He simply stuffed his hands inside and dragged everything out on to the floor in front of him. The safe was less than a foot deep and he emptied it in seconds, crouching down to see what he'd got, like a fisherman inspecting his nets.

This was much better. Oh, this was *so* much better.

Two bricks of high-denomination banknotes, still in their unbroken seals. A green silk drawstring purse, which when opened and upended, yielded a cascade of gold necklaces, bracelets, two strings of pearls and several jewelled rings. But, best of all, a teak box, about the size of a large bar of chocolate. It was extremely heavy and he could guess what was inside.

He opened the lid. Sure enough, he was looking at a little tray of gold coins, nestling in their individual beds of pressed felt. There were a dozen of them. There must be at least three more such trays underneath. Nearly fifty coins in all. He whistled to himself.

The old lady started coughing again. James looked at his watch. Almost twenty-five past now. He was running late.

He moved quickly back to the bed, going to the head this time and pulling back the curtains there. The old lady's eyes were open now and she looked at him in confusion. 'Hubert?'

'No. I'm sorry.' He reached under her head and eased one of her pillows away. 'I'm sorry,' he said again as he went back to the safe, pulling off the pillow's silk case.

Faint mewing noises came from behind him.

He stuffed the cash, the jewellery and the box of coins into the pillowcase and was about to leave when he thought of something else. He went to the armoires and opened them. Arranged on hangers were Hubert's clothes. They smelled of damp and mothballs. James guessed the doctor had moved his newer, better stuff to another room when the patient took residency in here. These would have to do. He grabbed a suit and a couple of shirts and ties and threw them over his arm.

He moved swiftly to the door and looked back at the bed. The old woman was now clearly agitated, and making feeble attempts to sit up. James hesitated, but he'd run out of time.

'Someone will be here soon.'

He went back down the stairs as fast as he could manage, crossed the hall and went out through the front entrance. He turned left along the front of the house and found the lean-to where he remembered it. It was a shabby affair, with sagging doors and a corrugated iron roof. There was no padlock on the doors and he dragged them open.

Inside was a shiny black car. It was a medium-sized Citroën, and it looked pretty new to James. He took out the keys he had found in the doctor's jacket and opened the passenger door.

He cursed. Of course. Left-hand drive in France.

He crossed to the other side of the car, tossed the clothes and the pillowcase into the boot as he went, and slid behind the steering wheel. He switched on the ignition and pressed the starter button.

The engine caught on the second turn. He

watched the fuel gauge slowly creep up from empty. *Come on, come on.* It passed the halfway mark and finally stopped just below the yellow line that told him he had three-quarters of a tank, or very nearly.

This was excellent. Enough petrol to get him over 200 miles away, by midnight if he was lucky.

He let out the clutch and drove back along the drive, pulling up when he got to the entrance to the village street. He looked carefully to left and right. No sign of life, not even a dog. The little girl had disappeared.

He turned left, away from the village. He checked his rearview mirror. Nothing. No car, no bicycle. No one had seen him leave.

The setting sun was on his right. Good — that meant he was driving south, the direction he wanted. James had an increasingly clear idea of his ultimate destination.

The road stretched Roman-straight before him. Trees had been planted on both sides every few yards, and as he stared at a point far ahead, they seemed to merge into infinity.

Infinity. For now, that was as good a direction to head for as any he could think of.

45

'How much longer before you have to go?'

Diana looked abstractedly at her watch. 'About half an hour.'

He nodded. 'OK, I'll skip the boring details then — the bits about bribing farmers and sleeping in barns. I'll just supply you with the headlines.'

He clicked his fingers and a waiter was with them immediately. '*Deux limocelles, s'il vous plaît.*' He grinned at Diana. 'You have to try one of these, Diana. They're a sort of cognac made from lemons. They taste unbelievable.'

'*You're* pretty unbelievable.'

'What? What do you mean?'

She stared coolly at him. 'James. You're in the middle of telling me how you murdered someone — no, don't speak, it was murder and you know it — and then how you stole from a helpless old woman . . . and you break off *to order cocktails.*'

'*Digestifs,* actually.'

'Don't be stupid, you know what I mean. You don't seem to feel at all guilty about any of it. How much more killing and stealing did you get up to on your way down here to Nice? I assume that's where you were headed.'

James smiled faintly at her. 'How judgemental you've become, Diana. Are you sure you don't want to call the police and tell them you've solved a ten-year-old murder?'

She flushed angrily. 'That's ridiculous, and you know it.'

'Do I? You were very quick to call me a murderer just then. But yes, you're quite right about one thing; I decided almost as soon as I left the villa to head for the Côte d'Azur. I reckoned that the fleshpots of Nice would keep themselves semi-detached from the war and the Occupation, and I was bang right about that. Once the Nazis had divided France in half and left the South pretty much to get on with it, life went on down here more or less as before. The only Germans you saw were on holiday, though they pretended they had special business in Nice or Cannes. No one wanted to rock the boat, least of all the Jerries.

'As to whether I continued in my new life of crime, Diana, I didn't need to. I had more than enough cash and valuables to keep me going for a good while. Incidentally, quite how a country doctor could amass such a stash is an interesting question. I sometimes wonder if he had a sideline in illegal abortions or something.'

He broke off as the waiter brought their drinks. When the man had slipped away, James appeared to hesitate, and took his time before continuing, sipping his drink and watching the people passing up and down the Promenade. Diana began to feel uncomfortable.

'Aren't you going to go on?' she asked at length.

He turned back to her, drumming the table lightly with his fingertips for a few moments.

'I'm not sure, actually,' he said in a voice colder than before. 'I'm just reflecting on your remark about guilt. It's rather annoyed me.'

'I can't help that,' she replied evenly. 'You seem remarkably free from it, considering.'

He rubbed the bridge of his nose. 'You think so? I'm sorry, Diana, but do you have any idea how holier-than-thou you sound? Have you the slightest understanding of what it was like to be in France in the summer of 1940? After France threw in the towel, it was every man for himself. I saw things that would turn your hair white if I told you about them.'

'I don't doubt it, James, but that doctor, the old lady . . . something like that would be on my conscience forever. I just can't understand how you can be so matter-of-fact about it.'

She looked at him unhappily. Diana did not think of herself as judgemental but she was repelled by James's description of shooting the doctor and the way he had cold-bloodedly gone through the dead man's pockets. And what of the sick old lady? James had taken advantage of her without any compunction at all.

He seemed to read her thoughts.

'Look,' he began, 'I realise how it all must appear to you. But try to put yourself in my shoes that day. I'd been in battle only a few hours earlier. I'd killed three men in the air; I'd seen them die right in front of me. Then I'd been shot down — and truly, Diana, I believed I was going to die too. When I jumped from my plane I thought it was the last thing I'd ever do. When I eventually got to the village I was in a very

291

. . . well, I was in a very *extreme* state of mind. Anyone would have been.'

Diana nodded, almost to herself. 'Yes. I suppose I can see that.' But her tone was grudging.

'*Damn it*, Diana!' She jumped as James brought the flat of his hand down hard on the table. Nearby diners turned and stared at them.

'I *couldn't* be taken prisoner. I've explained all that to you. For me it was literally a matter of life and death.'

'Don't raise your voice to me. And the old lady? What does your conscience tell you about her, James?'

He grimaced. 'Yes. That was awful, I admit it. But I didn't hurt her; I did my best not to even wake her up.'

Diana gave a short laugh. 'If she hadn't, you'd never have got the safe open.'

'Obviously. But she was dying, Diana, that was perfectly clear. The stuff in the safe was no use to her any more. My need was greater than hers and I bet a lot of men in my position would have done the same.'

'My father wouldn't have.'

He clicked his tongue in frustration and annoyance. 'All right, but your father wasn't a deserter, was he? Look, Diana, let's not be under any illusions. I've tried to make it as clear as daylight: I've been totally honest. *I'd had enough*. I couldn't take any more.'

'My father took four years of it.'

'His was a *totally* different war! Totally! I was in a *completely* different position to him. I wasn't in a trench with a bunch of mates to help keep my spirits up. I was utterly alone, surrounded by the enemy and a terrified civilian population who knew they'd be shot out of hand if they were caught helping or harbouring a British officer. I only had myself to rely on. I'd just been blasted out of the sky and I was probably still in shock. I acted on pure instinct.'

He stared angrily at her before fumbling for his cigarettes. The carton was empty. 'Damn. I'm all out.'

'Here.' She pushed her own packet towards him, and he lit cigarettes for both of them.

When he spoke again, it was in a softer tone.

'Of course you're shocked by what I've just told you. I was pretty traumatised myself that day, believe me. But we're talking about something that happened in 1940. It's more than ten years ago. I've had a decade to come to terms with it, and even now I truly don't think I had a choice in killing that man, or stealing from him, actually. You must believe that.'

'Why?' she asked, raising her eyebrows in surprise. 'Why must I, James? Why would you care what I think about you after all this time?'

He blinked at her. 'I'm not quite sure . . . but I do. I've never told a living soul what happened that day in Licques. You're the first person I've ever spoken to about it. I wanted to, somehow. It never occurred to me not to tell you what I did there.'

They fell into a long silence.

Diana tried to gather her thoughts. Old feelings and memories were stirring in her.

Seeing James had brought back a sense of who she used to be; the argumentative Girton girl with the quick mind. Now, she did her best to analyse his confession.

Was she being too harsh on him? He wouldn't be the first brave man to desert, overwhelmed by what was being demanded of him. And if she removed that part of it from the equation, she could begin to see things from James's point of view. The doctor had been about to betray him. And France, she reminded herself, was supposed to be an ally. Britain had gone on fighting alone partly in order to deliver the French from Nazi occupation.

She looked at the man opposite her. He appeared lost in his own thoughts, staring blankly out to sea and smoking his cigarette. He genuinely seemed to care what she thought of him. Why? Had she begun to rekindle old emotions in him, too?

She tried to imagine what her life would have been like if James hadn't been shot down; hadn't run away to Nice. Supposing he'd survived the war? Pilots did. Would the two of them still be together, have had more children? She recalled how happy she'd been on the day of her wedding, the day she lost him, seemingly forever.

The memory flickered and grew stronger. Suddenly it was almost a physical sensation. Diana caught her breath.

This had to stop. Now.

'I'm going to go soon,' she said in as normal a voice as she could manage. 'But you're right, James, I'm being too hard on you. Anyway, it isn't for me to judge. As you say, the circumstances were exceptional and I can hardly begin to imagine them. I apologise.'

He looked surprised and relieved. 'Thank you, Diana. That means a lot to me. But don't go just yet . . . I haven't even told you how I got to Nice.'

She needed to get away from him, she knew that, but her curiosity was stronger. She pushed her rising emotions firmly back down again.

'All right, but I really can only spare another few minutes. And I don't want to argue with you any more, James. I'm exhausted. Just tell me the rest of it as quickly as you can. I want to go home.'

★ ★ ★

He drove for fifty miles before stopping. It was getting dark and he pulled over at a village which boasted a communal fountain for drinking and washing. He cleaned himself up as best he could, sluicing the dried blood and blackened hair from his face and head, and with no one in sight, peeled off his filthy flying gear. The doctor's clothes weren't a bad fit, if a bit baggy, and the trousers covered his tell-tale flying boots.

He chucked his uniform in a ditch, careful to keep his RAF identification tag. He had no intention of being shot as a spy.

He slept in the car that first night, parked up an isolated lane, and worked out his cover story. To anyone who asked, he'd say he had been attempting to salvage his British company's

295

interests in Northern France and had been overtaken by the speed of the German advance, and was now trying to get back to England via Spain.

It was a thin tale, he knew, but he was never asked to offer it. As he forged south-east he drove past the occasional cluster of parked German tanks or armoured cars, but after the French surrender their exhausted crews lay almost motionless in the shade of their vehicles. Many were asleep, even under the staring day. Continuous campaigning had left them utterly spent.

He kept to the country lanes and steered a zig-zag route around Paris before turning due south to Orléans. Garages were now completely out of petrol but the canny farmers had kept their own supplies back. If most grocery shops were now empty, farms were replete with cheese, bread, milk and wine. Their prices were outrageous but for those who had the money, it was possible, for now, to keep a well-stocked larder and one's car on the road.

James bought enough food and drink to last several days, and filled his car's tank to the brim. He acquired a number of ten-gallon jerry cans of petrol too, and stacked them on the back seat of the car. He felt increasingly confident that he could make it all the way down to the Mediterranean coast under his own steam.

He skirted Orléans and decided to take a chance on the main D-route to Bourges.

It was a mistake.

The road was crowded with French soldiers

milling about, most of them without weapons. They didn't seem to have any orders; James decided that most were simply trying to get home. They looked utterly crushed and defeated. He was reminded of newsreel footage of the British at Dunkirk.

There had been a couple of half-hearted attempts to commandeer the Citroën as he drove slowly through the crowd, but the soldiers had backed away when he produced his gun.

The going got easier for a few miles but after he passed through an apparently deserted village, the road ahead was blocked by a multitude: hundreds and hundreds of civilians, carrying suitcases or pushing carts piled high with possessions. They stared at him dully as he picked his way through them, occasionally sounding his horn. Some of them looked so old or unwell he didn't think they'd see the day out. From time to time he saw a body left behind on the verge, like a piece of rubbish.

★ ★ ★

James paused. 'It did make me wonder, Diana — you know, about what it would have been like if the Germans had invaded England.'

Diana, who had been listening intently, sat up straight. 'We would have gone berserk,' she said simply. 'Almost as soon as France fell, the British organised themselves into official resistance groups, the Local Defence something-or-other. Anyway, later they were called the Home Guard. It was all pretty amateurish to begin with, but they were deadly serious and everyone wanted to be a part of it. Daddy had to queue for hours to join.

'I honestly believe we'd have done just about anything we could think of to fight the Germans if they'd invaded. When Churchill made that speech about fighting on and on and never surrendering, he spoke for an awful lot of people. He certainly spoke for me.'

'Hmm.' James drained his glass and beckoned to the hovering waiter for another. 'I'm not so sure. Total defeat — you don't know what it's like unless you've seen it. People might have just given up. It was an absolute breakdown here, I'm telling you. I've never seen anything like it. It felt as if the world had ended. Looked like it, too. All those people, just walking and walking. It was like something out of the Bible.'

'You're quite wrong, James,' Diana said. 'Not about what you saw in France, I mean, but about how we might have responded to an invasion at home. But as I said, I don't want to argue with you. Go on.'

★ ★ ★

Eventually he tired of driving at a snail's pace through the endless lines of refugees, and cut across country towards Dijon. A farmer along the way told him that south of Dijon, life was going on more normally. James calculated that if he could reach the town that dominated Central France, he could ditch the doctor's car and take the train the rest of the way to the coast.

298

He reached Dijon after eight hours of cross-country driving and went straight to the railway station.

His heart sank as he approached it. At least half a dozen *gendarmes* guarded the entrance to the station, flanked by German soldiers toting sub-machine guns. All travellers' papers were being checked and a little huddle of people had been weeded out and stood miserably to one side. As James watched, they were bundled into a police van and driven off.

That decided him. Twenty minutes later, he had left Dijon behind and was on the road south. Traffic was almost non-existent and he was emboldened to try the main D-route again.

It was another mistake. About thirty miles south of Dijon the Citroën rounded a corner and almost ran straight into a French military checkpoint. Soldiers with slung rifles stood moodily alongside *gendarmes* with holstered pistols. At least no Germans seemed to be around.

He had no option other than to stop. As a tense-looking officer approached his window, pistol now unholstered, James remembered the night he'd bluffed his way into Girton to see Diana. This was a somewhat more challenging situation and he decided to take the initiative from the start.

'*Monsieur* — ' the man began, but James cut him off.

'How *dare* you interfere with me! I'm the British Consul in Lyon and I'm on my way back from a reconnaissance trip to the North. I've had enough trouble with you lot already. Bloody well look at this!'

He had taken off the flying boot from his injured leg because it was pressing increasingly painfully on the bullet wound. He opened his door to reveal the bloodied bandages.

'You trigger-happy bastards hit me taking wild pot-shots at a German patrol. I could have been killed! My government's already made a formal complaint to the French Ambassador in London, and if you don't let me through without any more nonsense there'll be another one. What's your name and rank?'

He was hurriedly waved through and took the first side turning he came to.

He stayed away from the D-roads after that.

About 100 miles north of the Mediterranean, James steered the car into a quiet wooded lane and took out a battered map of France from the Citroën's glove box. He studied it closely. He needed to work out how much further he could get with his dwindling supply of petrol. Luck and bluff had got him this far, but he was urgently in need of false papers and proper clothes, plus a shave and a haircut.

Nice, he regretfully decided after some mental arithmetic, was beyond reach. But there was a better option for the time being, and considerably closer to hand.

Marseilles: a city that was pretty much a law unto itself.

He pulled the last remaining jerry can from the back seat and carried it round to the car's filler cap. As the petrol gurgled into the Citroën's tank, James shaped his plan.

When he got to Marseilles, he drove directly to the docks.

★ ★ ★

'Why the docks, James?'

He smiled. 'I had an East End upbringing, remember? The docks were where people went to buy things they couldn't get hold of above board. Everyone knew that.

'All big ports are the same, right around the world. A man goes down to the docks, finds a rough old bar, slips the bartender a couple of big ones and tells him what he's after. The barman makes a call and fifteen minutes later you're doing business with his friends. Nobody gives a shit who you are, what you've done, or what you're running from. If I'd been German, they wouldn't have turned a hair. Money talks in those places. Always has, always will.'

'And what did you want to buy in Marseilles?'

He looked surprised. 'Papers, of course. A new identity. It didn't come cheap, either, but at least I wasn't short of the readies. I stayed in a sailors' doss-house on the waterfront and within forty-eight hours I had a new me and a whole new cover story. I was a Portuguese English teacher with a very bad sense of timing. I'd sailed to Marseilles from Lisbon just as it was all going pear-shaped for France, and now I was stranded, waiting for a ship home. I chose Portugal because no one speaks the language and I could talk gibberish with confidence. Also,

Portugal was neutral, which made things a lot easier.

'In fact, I had quite an international war, Diana. I was always neutral, though — Portuguese, Swiss, Swedish. The most expensive papers of all made me American, until Pearl Harbor, of course. That was both unexpected and annoying. For me, I mean, not just the Americans. That particular identity had cost me a small fortune and it was meant to be good for at least five years. Then overnight the USA declared war on Japan and Germany and I was up the spout. I must say, I gave a little cheer when the Yanks dropped their bomb on Hiroshima.'

Diana's earlier sense of unreality was returning. He was describing a way of life she could barely imagine. She looked at him afresh. His light-grey linen suit, she realised for the first time, was exquisitely tailored. His shoes were probably handmade by the look of them, and he wore a slim gold watch on his wrist. He was obviously well-off, probably even rich. The subservience of the hotel staff made that pretty obvious.

He noticed her scrutiny. 'What? What are you thinking?'

'To be honest, James, I'm not sure what I think. One moment the fact that I'm sitting here talking to you seems the most natural, normal thing in all the world, and the next I think I'm going off my head. At times during lunch I felt almost dizzy with happiness to be with you again, and at others I've been so angry I wanted to hit you.'

'You've every right to be furious. I just hope that when you think over everything I've told you, you'll understand and forgive me, Diana. But you *are* pleased to see me?'

'I just said so, didn't I? And what about you? What's this like for you? You seem to have taken it all rather in your stride.'

He sighed. 'Well, I never thought you were dead, did I? It was a shock to see you again, but nothing like as big a one as you must have had.' Tentatively, he reached out and took her hand. She began to withdraw it but he held on more firmly.

'No. Don't pull away, Diana, please. Just let me hold your hand while I answer your question.'

She relaxed slightly. It was incredible to feel his touch again. 'All right . . . Go on.'

'The truth is, I can hardly take my eyes off you. I never thought I'd see you again; I believed I'd lost you forever. But to be with you like this, to hear your voice . . . even when it's angry with me . . . it feels almost as if the last eleven years never happened.'

They looked at each other for a long moment in silence before she slowly slid her hand free.

'I'm sorry.' She stood up. 'I'm finding all of this extremely hard to take in.' She glanced at her watch. 'I really must go.'

'Of course.' He rose to his feet. 'But when can we meet again? I've been talking non-stop about myself, I've hardly asked you a thing. There's so much I need to know — about Stella, about Dougal . . . '

'Douglas.'

'Of course, Douglas . . . why you're all living here in Nice. Heaps of things.'

Diana hesitated. 'I'm not sure we should meet again.'

His mouth dropped open. '*What?* You're joking! Of course we have to meet again, Diana! We have a daughter I've only just found out about. I want to see her. We have over ten years' catching up to do too — we've barely started. I have a house here in Nice; I want you to see it. And I suppose at some point I'm going to have to meet your husband, don't you think?'

Diana was horrified. 'Oh, no, no! I can't even think about that now, James. He'd be *appalled* at this. I don't even know how I'm going to tell him.'

James put the back of his hand gently on her cheek. This time she did not try to withdraw from him.

'All right, all right Diana, I completely understand. You've had one heck of a shock today, I can see that. I realise I need to give you time to adjust. But we *must* see each other. Look . . . ' He pulled a leather-bound notebook from an inside pocket and slid out a gold pen from the spine. 'Let me give you my telephone number, and my address.' He scribbled for a few moments before tearing out the page and handing it to her. 'Give yourself a day or so to take all this in and then call me. If I'm not in, a woman called Roberta will answer. Leave a message with her.'

She stared at him. 'Is Roberta your wife?'

He threw back his head and roared with laughter. 'Roberta is my sixty-nine-year-old housekeeper and she's the size of a Dutch barn.' He stopped laughing, and looked at her. 'I'm not married, Diana. Well . . . I suppose I am, come to think of it.

'I'm married to you, aren't I?'

46

Oliver Arnold climbed the stairs to the converted attic in the Dower House and tapped on the door of his wife's studio. She discouraged him from visiting her there while she was working, but after wrestling with his thoughts for the best part of an hour after breakfast, he had been compelled to rise from his deckchair in the garden — it was the sunniest June anyone could remember — and climb the four flights of stairs.

'Gwen? Gwen, can I come in, please? I need to talk to you about something.'

He heard her mutter of annoyance, followed by the clink of brushes being dropped into a jar. A few moments later, the door opened and his wife stood before him.

She was in her mid-fifties now, slimmer than ever. She had never regained the weight that she lost in the year after their son's death. Both Gwen and Oliver had recently been greatly amused to hear a diner at a nearby restaurant table whisper to her companion: 'Look over there.' The woman had nodded surreptitiously in their direction. 'Isn't that Wallis Simpson?'

She looked at him now with undisguised irritation. 'What is it, Oliver? Couldn't it have waited until lunch?'

'Perhaps. Look, I'm probably being silly, but I have to talk to you, Gwen.'

Her face softened. 'You do look worried, I

must say . . . Come in then.'

He wondered how long it had been since he last crossed this threshold. Years, probably. Her portrait of their son was still unfinished, propped on an old easel. He stared at it as he sank down on a battered sofa under the attic window.

'You should finish that one day, you know,' he said. 'It's the best thing you've ever done.'

He was not flattering her. Gwen had perfectly captured John's insouciant good humour. He smiled at them from the canvas, blue eyes slightly hooded as if he were reflecting on a private joke. His blond hair was combed back from his brow, darkened by oil, Brylcreem, probably. He looked terribly young, the RAF jacket he had slung over one shoulder a seeming joke. Boys like him weren't old enough to be allowed to fly aeroplanes.

The painting petered out just below the fifth button on his pale-blue cotton uniform shirt, Gwen's brushstrokes giving way to a few vague charcoal and pencil outlines. If completed, it would be a full-length portrait.

'Actually, I've been thinking . . . I'm not sure I should do any more with it,' Gwen said as she settled beside her husband. '*He* was unfinished, wasn't he? Perhaps that's how the painting should stay. Unfinished. Like our boy.'

He considered. 'Yes . . . yes, I must say, I've never thought about it like that. I think you may be right.' He squeezed her hand. 'I'm going to seize the moment, Gwen. Please say we can hang it in the hall — you know, the empty place we've spoken about.'

She hadn't taken her eyes off the painting.

'Do you know, I think it really might be time, Oliver. I really do. I believe that I'm ready, at last. Maybe I have been for a while, and didn't know it. He mustn't stay up here hidden away any longer.' She squeezed his hand in return. 'We'll hang it tomorrow, just as it is. And all because you came up here this morning. Thank you.'

She turned to face him. 'Now, what's troubling you, my dear?'

★ ★ ★

Diana made it to the villa just in time. As her taxi disappeared back down the drive she fumbled with the front-door key, trembling fingers making her clumsy. At last she had the door open and ran across the hall to the little washroom on the other side. She lifted the toilet lid, dropped to her knees, and was violently sick.

★ ★ ★

'I must say I'm surprised that the Negresco's the guilty party,' Douglas said as he came into their bedroom, holding a damp face-cloth wrapped around crushed ice. 'Did your fish taste peculiar? You should have sent it back.'

'Mmm.' Diana closed her eyes as her husband placed the cold compress on her forehead. 'Thank you, darling . . . no, the food was fine, Douglas. It must have been the sun. We were sitting outside on the terrace for an awfully long

308

time and I'd forgotten to bring my hat.'

'Yes, well, we're not far from the solstice now,' he told her, sitting companionably on the edge of the bed. 'Just a few weeks to go. No wonder you got back home with a thumping headache.'

'Migraine, more like. But it's definitely going now.'

'Good.' He put his hand behind her shoulders and helped her into a sitting position, plumping up the pillows behind her. 'I'll heat up some of that chicken soup Sophia made yesterday. I think there's still some in the fridge.' Sophia was their Italian maid who occasionally, but always grumpily, cooked for them, before tramping back to St Paul and the tiny apartment in the medieval walls where she and her parents lived.

'Anyway, if you're feeling a bit better, tell me more about this chap you had lunch with,' Douglas went on. 'He sounds a most interesting fellow.'

Diana looked directly at her husband. She'd been watching him covertly since he entered the room. She couldn't help comparing him to James; they were so unalike, she reflected, that they could almost be two quite different species of man.

Like James, Douglas wore an expensive suit but the sheer bagginess of his body defeated the finest tailoring, rendering the cut more or less shapeless. In any case, Douglas had put on weight since coming to France and his jacket could no longer be buttoned without looking uncomfortably tight under the arms.

The waistband of his trousers was under strain

too, and heavy jowls were beginning to flow over the collar of his shirt. His fair skin meant he tried to keep out of the sun but nevertheless, his freckles had become more noticeable in recent weeks, and his wispy reddish hair had gone a shade paler.

Diana felt ashamed of noticing these things and, worse, contrasting them unfavourably to the man with whom she had spent the day. She reminded herself how kind and generous Douglas had been to her and Stella.

But for the first time in their marriage, it suddenly mattered to her that she had never found her husband in any way physically attractive. She began to feel a long-denied restlessness awaken, and with it a tingle of anxiety. Or was it excitement?

Earlier, she had lain stricken with the worst migraine she'd had in years, trying to decide what to tell Douglas. Part of her wanted to unburden herself of the entire thing, starting with that April morning in the market when she had first heard James's voice. But when she struggled to find and rehearse the words, her resolve crumbled.

'He sounded like my first husband . . . James . . . I simply had to go back and find him; you can see that, darling, can't you? Those papers Daddy sent me weren't what I told you they were; they were the official RAF report into James's death . . . I had to read them eventually . . . but I didn't believe they proved he was dead, I can't say why . . . I'm sorry, darling, but I just knew he was alive and I had to find him again.'

She had squirmed. She would sound needy and desperate and secretive and . . . something else.

Disloyal.

Even worse would be the questions Douglas was certain to ask her.

'*What is he doing here?*'

'*What does he look like now?*'

'*Will you see him again?*'

'*Do you still love him?*'

It couldn't be borne. Not yet, not now. She needed time to reflect on the impossible thing that had just happened. Absorb it, and decide what it meant. She must find a middle way with Douglas for the time being; an abridged, acceptable account she could give him, that later perhaps could be expanded and corrected. She promised herself that in time she would tell him everything.

But now, with her husband sitting unsuspectingly on their bed beside her, Diana censored and skimmed and lied.

'He's called Peter. He was a friend of my brother — they were at Cranwell together, and in the same squadron during the war. They both flew sorties over Dunkirk.'

'I see,' Douglas said. 'It was just after Dunkirk that your first husband was shot down, wasn't it?'

'Yes . . . Anyway, I was in the flower-market as usual this morning, at Armand's café, and this chap got out of a taxi more or less in front of me. I thought I recognised him but I wasn't sure . . . He knew me though, right away. He came straight over to my table. He shook my hand, said he remembered me from his and John's passing-out parade at Cranwell, and from a squadron Christmas party. Apparently we danced together a couple of times.'

She paused to readjust the cold cloth on her brow. Douglas nodded slowly.

'My. What a coincidence. And, naturally, he'd have known James.'

She'd been expecting him to make these connections, but not quite so quickly. Douglas was being unusually beady.

'Yes, of course . . . but they weren't especial friends, and Peter wasn't one of the chaps who saw James shot down. But they were both in the air over France that day. He — Peter — told me that he nearly bought it himself; their squadron was horribly outnumbered, he said.'

'Did this Peter know James well?'

'No, I just told you they weren't particularly friendly. I certainly don't recall James ever mentioning him.'

'No? Well . . . what did you talk about over lunch?'

Diana breathed a little easier. They were on safer ground now.

'Oh, all sorts. About the war, about my brother . . . what I'm doing down here, and him too. He's something to do with exporting wine from Provence to London.'

Douglas looked interested. 'Really? I've been dabbling in that a little myself recently, did I mention that? What's his full name? I might have come across him.'

Damn.

'D'you know, I simply can't remember. I think he only mentioned it once, at the café. Dodgson . . . Dobson . . . something like that.'

'Well, I'll keep an eye out for him. There can't be that many English businessmen operating in Nice at the moment.' He stood up. 'Right, I'll go and see about that soup. Hungry?'

She smiled at him, trying to keep the relief out of her voice. 'Yes, I am. Thank you, Douglas. You're so kind to me.'

★   ★   ★

Gwen looked perplexed. 'But I thought all that nonsense about James Blackwell being alive was over and done with months ago, Oliver, after you sent Diana the RAF report.'

Her husband sighed. 'Perhaps it was. Perhaps I'm imagining things. I just think something's wrong down there. It could be anything, I suppose, but all my instincts tell me it's something to do with him — with her first husband, I mean.'

Gwen folded her hands in her lap. 'Surely she's not clinging to the belief he's still alive, somehow, and floating around Nice?'

He gave a helpless shrug. 'You wouldn't think so, not after she'd finally made herself read the report,' Oliver said. 'But looking back, I think we — I should say I — missed something when she telephoned to talk about it.'

'What do you mean?'

He had taken the call that chilly April

morning, which seemed so long ago, now the warmth of June was here. On the face of it, Diana had seemed to accept the RAF's formal conclusion that James had died in his Spitfire.

'You're obviously right, Daddy,' she had said. 'I must have had some sort of delusion the other morning in the market, however convincing it seemed at the time.'

But there was something else about their conversation; something that hadn't seemed important at the time.

'You know what she's like with words and language, Gwen — so picky and precise. It's one of the reasons she was doing so well at Girton until . . . until . . . ' He paused.

'Until the two of them were killed. Come on, Oliver, what are you trying to say?' Gwen asked bluntly.

'Bear with me, Grace. I hardly understand it myself.'

He sat deep in thought.

'OK,' he said eventually. 'Diana agreed that the man in the taxi couldn't possibly have been James. But then she asked me why I thought the RAF had used the word 'presumed', you know, in the part that says he must have been killed.

'I said I'd never really thought about it but it was probably because no actual body was ever found. I told her I didn't want to upset her, but that James's remains were probably still in the wreckage of his aircraft, buried a few feet under some French field. You know how they keep digging them up, Gwen, crashed fighters, British and German, with the pilots still at the controls.

314

Anyway, I can't remember exactly what she said to that, but looking back, I *do* recall how she sounded, the tone in her voice.

'It was hopeful. She sounded *hopeful*. Even as she agreed that James must be dead, there was a kind of disbelief at the same time. I didn't pick up on it then, I suppose I didn't want to. I just wanted the whole rather disturbing business over and done with. And she hardly ever rings us any more, does she? She used to call at least once a week. Now, whenever we telephone her, she seems preoccupied, and she's always making excuses to cut the conversation short. Half the time she's not even there. Douglas says she's signed up for classes in French, some kind of intensive course, he said. And she's completely stopped writing letters, hasn't she? We haven't had one in as long as I can remember.'

He fell silent and looked at his wife expectantly. Gwen appeared to be lost in thought.

'Well?' he asked at last, a touch impatiently. 'What do you make of it?'

Gwen sighed. 'She's hiding something. That's obvious, and it's extremely unusual for her. Her life's always been an open book, hasn't it? Diana's never been able to keep a secret, not since she could talk.'

He nodded in agreement. 'Absolutely. Something's happened to make her so distracted and withdrawn. On the rare occasions we do speak, I can hear something in her voice I've never heard before. It's hard to describe . . . it's sort of part-fear, part-elation. She's totally off-balance.'

Gwen looked at him directly. 'Do you think she's having an affair?'

'Completely.'

'So do I.'

They sat without speaking for several minutes.

'What makes you think it has something to do with James Blackwell?' she asked.

Oliver weighed his reply carefully. 'All right . . . here's what I think has happened. I think the illusion that she saw and heard him had a profound effect on her. It was a particularly vivid hallucination, by the sound of it. I think it's reminded her of her feelings for him, how passionate they were for each other.' He gave a half-smile. 'Remember how they thought we didn't know they had slept together on the top floor, the week before their wedding?'

She smiled back. 'Yes, well, Stella was proof of that, if there'd been any doubt about it.'

'Quite. Anyway, I think that her illusion or fantasy, or whatever it was, that day in the market has reignited something within her. Some deep need. Let's face it, Gwen, Douglas may be a wonderfully kind and generous man, but he's no Romeo, is he? I always worried about that for Diana.'

Gwen nodded. 'So did I, but I never admitted it to myself. I was so keen to see her and Stella settled.'

'Me too. But we didn't push her into anything, Gwen? Diana made her own choices. Anyway, we are where we are. I suspect her search for James, her refusal to fully believe he's dead, is really a search for someone *like* him — someone who'll

316

excite her and romance her again. And I think she's found her man.'

Gwen leaned forward, both hands around his face. She held his gaze.

'You're a clever man, Oliver. You know I've always thought so. Everything you've just said is almost certainly true. But listen to me, my dear; listen to me very carefully when I say this to you: '*It's got absolutely nothing to do with us.*'

* * *

When she woke up next morning, lightheaded and dizzy after her migraine, Diana spent a few muzzy moments wondering if the events of the previous day had been anything more than an extraordinarily vivid dream. Had it really happened, any of it?

She sat up. The other side of the bed was unslept in; Douglas must have used one of the spare rooms in order not to disturb her.

After a few moments' thought, she reached down for her handbag at the side of the bed. She fished through a side-pocket, found the piece of paper, and read what was scrawled on it.

James — Nice 4673. Villa Raphael, 24 Rue de Palmes, Nice.

47

She would use the phone in the kitchen. Douglas had already left for work when she came down from their bedroom, but she felt more comfortable making the call from here, not the lounge. She wasn't sure why. She told herself she didn't want Sophia blundering in while she was on the phone. The kitchen had already been serviced — it was the maid's first port of call in the mornings — and Stella was even now outside on the terrace with Maxine. Diana could hear the tutor's voice drifting through the open kitchen windows. '*Non, non, Stella, encore, s'il te plaît,*' and heard her daughter dutifully repeating an exercise in tenses. It was the future that tended to confuse her. Diana smiled ruefully to herself. Like mother, like daughter.

She poured herself a cup of coffee from the electric pot that Sophia had filled before leaving the kitchen, and sat down at the bleached wooden table. She was fully awake now, and realised she had a lot to think about.

Foremost was Stella.

Diana had married Douglas principally for her daughter's sake. She knew Douglas understood and accepted this. He had once said to her: 'I treasure Stella because I fully realise that if it were not for her, I wouldn't have you.'

Yesterday, James had said he wanted to see his daughter. What did he mean? Just 'see' her — a glimpse from a safe distance — or actually meet her, talk with her?

Diana shook her head, almost violently. 'Impossible,' she muttered aloud. 'Impossible.'

How to explain to Stella the very fact of her father being alive? It couldn't be done, at least not without being brutally frank. James was a deserter and — Diana realised this with a little jolt — he was technically still on the run. If the authorities in England discovered he was still alive, he'd be a wanted man.

A fine father for a young daughter to be introduced to, out of the blue.

Granted, James had only learned of Stella's existence yesterday. But if he had made the effort to get in touch once he'd settled in Nice, he would have known years ago that he had a daughter. Back then, perhaps something could have been worked out. Now, it was simply too late.

Stella had grown up believing her father died a war hero. She slept with his photograph by her bed. To tell her the truth now would be unbelievably cruel. And of course, there was no question of introducing her to James under the pretence that he was someone else. The child would recognise him at once from the photograph. He had barely changed over the last eleven years.

Even if she could see some way to bring Stella and her father together, there was Douglas to consider. He would have to be included in any arrangement.

Diana knew with complete certainty that

319

Douglas would be appalled at the arrival of this fugitive in their midst; a man who had lived under so many false identities that even James himself probably couldn't remember them all.

Then there was the whole question of the validity of her second marriage. Was she technically a bigamist? She pushed the thought away.

To Douglas, Stella's father would be a criminal. And he'd be right. James must be breaking multiple French laws, masquerading as he was on forged papers. But if he went home to England, anything could happen. What if someone recognised him? One of his former RAF comrades, for example? The game would be up: James would almost certainly be arrested for desertion and, if he was using a false identity, fraud too.

Then a new fear came to her. It occurred to Diana that Douglas might turn James in to the authorities. She wouldn't put it past him. Of course, he was a man of scrupulous morality: he'd genuinely believe it was his duty to make sure justice was served. But he'd also do it because he felt threatened by the reappearance of his wife's glamorous first husband. He would conceal the motive behind a screen of Calvinist moral rectitude, but they'd both know the truth.

Which was a very good reason not to tell Douglas anything at all about this. She couldn't compromise James's safety.

'*Why* can't I?' Again, Diana had spoken aloud. She considered the question. It was a good one, and she lit a cigarette, the better to think it through.

James had been remarkably honest with her, she decided. He had admitted murdering a man, and making off with a small fortune. He had confessed freely to living completely illegally here in France. He had trusted her to listen with an open mind to his reasons for deserting, and for not coming home after the war. He had placed his fate in her hands.

He had trusted her.

And she, Diana now realised, had been honest with him. She had meant it when she told him that in war, she thought every man had his limits. James had been pushed very, very hard. He clearly hadn't plotted to desert. He had, in fact, gone down fighting. Literally. He'd destroyed three enemy aircraft before a terrifying ambush and encounter with violent death. It was the second such ordeal for him — he'd almost been killed over Dunkirk, his plane so badly shot up it had to be scrapped.

He hadn't gone AWOL after that first brush with death, had he? And on the day they got married and he and John were summoned back to their base, he'd gone without a murmur.

Running away later that same day after such a traumatic experience had been an instinctive, animal response to extreme circumstances. And by the time he'd established himself in Nice, there was no road back. The die was cast.

But he was still James — *her* James. He might have a new name — she realised with a slight shock that she had no idea what it was — but he was just the same as on the day he'd married her: charming, full of zest for life. Incredibly, he had even made her laugh despite everything.

And — she had to admit this to herself — she was hugely attracted to him. She tingled slightly when she recalled one of her recent dreams about the two of them. Those hands . . .

She decided that she was simply going to have to see him again. But the moment the thought occurred, fear and anxiety instantly followed. The consequences of discovery were appalling. The repercussions on her marriage to Douglas, to begin with. What would the effect be on Stella, if her mother's secret came out? And what would her own parents think of her?

Diana was so immersed in her thoughts she didn't realise the phone was ringing until Stella rushed past her and snatched the receiver from its cradle.

'Hello? I mean *bonjour*,' she said, looking at her mother with raised eyebrows. '*Qui est là?*' Stella paused a moment before saying: 'Oh, hello! No, don't start talking in French, I'm getting quite enough of that from Maxine, thank you very much. By the way, you realise you forgot your hat this morning, don't you? You left it on the hall table, I came running out after you with it but you'd driven off. Yes . . . she's here. Yes, I think so, although she seems to have gone a bit deaf.'

Stella held out the phone to her mother. 'It's Douglas. He wants to know how you're feeling.'

Diana took the receiver. 'Hello?'

Douglas's deep Highland brogue burred down

the line. 'Hello, darling . . . Stella says you're feeling better. What's all this about being deaf?'

'Oh, she's just trying to be funny. I'm fine. Thanks for letting me sleep in this morning.'

'Yes, well . . . now look, Diana, I've just been doing some ringing around here in Nice, speaking to my wine people. I have to tell you that I think this Peter chap of yours might be . . . well, not quite as advertised. A wrong 'un.'

Diana's heart hammered. Had she and James been seen at the Negresco? What on earth had Douglas discovered?

She tried to keep her tone neutral. 'Really? In what way?'

'Well, it turns out I was right. There *is* no British chap trading in Provençal wine, or any other kind of wine, here in Nice. Apart from me, that is. The last fellow packed up a couple of years ago when he retired, and he wasn't even English. He was from Scotland, too.'

Diana's heart slowed. She managed to keep the relief from her voice. 'I see. So you mean he was telling me a story?'

'Yes, it looks like it, and one has to ask oneself why, Diana. I've told you before what Nice is like: it's a nest of vipers. You've got the Italian Mafia, the local gangsters and the smugglers too. They're all mixed in together, and the police are hopelessly corrupt. There are only a few of us trading legally and above-board. This Peter chap may be mixed up in something; in fact, he probably is. I don't want you seeing him again.'

Diana controlled a spurt of anger. This was one of the prices she paid for her marriage to

Douglas; every now and then, he felt he had the right to tell her what or what not to do — for her own good, of course. It made her feel as if she were one of his possessions, something that had been bought and paid for.

She swallowed hard before replying. 'Of course, Douglas. You're quite right. I'll steer clear if I see him again.'

'Good . . . Well . . . See that you do. Are you going out today?'

'I wasn't going to.' She took a deep breath. 'But, do you know? Now I think I shall.'

★ ★ ★

James, so gifted at lying to others, was always brutally honest with himself. Now, sitting on the balcony of his apartment on a street just behind the Promenade des Anglais, he sipped his orange juice in the morning sunshine and reflected on the extraordinary events of the day before. He was trying to evaluate the situation and work out how to turn it to his advantage. Sentiment or misplaced romanticism had no place in his thoughts.

He had always known he would see Diana again; for some reason it had been an abiding certainty for years. But when it had actually happened . . . he shook his head slightly. It had taken all of his self-control not to step back into the taxi and tell the cabbie to drive away. For a few moments he had been completely at a loss as to what to do or say.

Now he offered himself congratulations on the

speed with which he had recovered his poise. And on his decision to tell Diana the truth about his life since the day he was shot down. Well, most of the truth. The business of the bedridden woman in the doctor's house . . . that had ended rather differently from the way he had described it.

If only the old girl hadn't opened her eyes as he was taking the pillow from under her head, he would have left her unharmed, really he would. But he'd seen immediately from her expression that she'd emerged from her earlier confusion and now realised there was a stranger in the room — one she could probably later describe to the police.

He didn't know if she recognised his RAF uniform as such, but it was a chance he just couldn't take. His only emotion as he smothered her was irritation that his escape from the house was being delayed.

Diana would want to know how he was supporting himself here in Nice, and in such style. His apartment was one of the most expensive in the city; he'd bought it outright for cash and furnished it beautifully. Somewhat to his surprise, James discovered he had an eye for antiques, and the apartment's spacious drawing room and four bedrooms looked more suitable for a titled Grimaldi in nearby Monaco than an ex-RAF fighter pilot on the run.

He decided to tell her he dealt in antiques. He had enough knowledge and genuine interest in the subject to get away with that for a fair while; certainly long enough for him to execute the plan that was beginning to form in his mind as the morning traffic surged four floors beneath his sunny terrace.

James's thoughts were interrupted by his maid. 'Telephone, *monsieur*.'

'Thanks, Roberta.' He walked into the *salon* and picked up the receiver. 'Yes?'

'*Did you get it?*'

'No. I was . . . diverted.'

'*Will you get it today?*'

'Yes.'

'*You have until the end of the month to get it all. That is our agreement.*'

James hung up without speaking again and went back onto the balcony. He was going to have to move fast.

It was clear from the little that Diana had told him already about her marriage to — Dougal? Donald? He was damned if he could remember. Anyway, whatever he was called, the man was obviously seriously rich. Diana had spoken of what sounded like a mansion in Kensington, and — *Douglas*, that was it — Douglas plainly had the means to buy their second home down here in France.

And, of course, to buy himself a beautiful wife too. James's intuition told him that theirs was not exactly a love match. Diana made him sound more like a father-figure than a husband. James guessed that she'd probably married the man as much for Stella's sake as for her own.

Stella. He was curious about her. He had no intention of assuming any kind of responsibility for the kid — Douglas was on the hook for that

— and had no desire to get to know her, even if that turned out to be possible, which he seriously doubted. But he'd quite like to take a look at her. Something told him she might come in useful; a wild card he perhaps could find a way of playing.

His thoughts moved back to Diana. She had clearly been in a state of shock for most of the time they were together. But he could tell that she found him attractive; in the periods where she'd relaxed, her expressions revealed that. He'd kept his voice low and that had obliged her to lean forwards, and she'd done so unhesitatingly. When he touched her cheek he felt her give a little start; he could feel the sexual tension vibrating within her.

Talking Diana into bed was going to be the easiest part of the equation.

It was the other business that was going to be tricky.

And he had barely a week.

48

Hélène and Armand kept an anxious watch for Diana all morning, but there was no sign of her. By lunchtime it was obvious she wasn't coming to the flower-market, and Hélène joined the café-owner at one of his tables. The pair were despondent.

'How can we get word to her, Armand?' Hélène asked, stirring the large bowl of milky coffee he had brought her. 'We even don't know where she lives.'

Armand was thoughtful as he sipped the tiny cognac he had poured for himself.

'Well, it's certainly somewhere near St Paul de Vence,' he said at last. 'I know she usually walks to the taxi-rank there before coming down here in the mornings, and she quite often arranges for the cab to pick her up from here and take her home. There are only about five drivers working the rank. I'll bet they all know where she lives.'

Hélène stared at him. 'How clever you are, Armand! I should never have thought of that.'

He ducked his head modestly. 'Ah well, I have my uses. *Alors*, what are we waiting for? I'll shut up shop and drive us up to St Paul.'

'No, that's impossible, Armand.' Hélène shook her head. 'The situation is very complicated. We must tread carefully.'

He looked at her in surprise. 'But surely we have to — '

She held up a hand for silence. 'Listen to me,' she said firmly. 'Pay me your fullest attention, old friend.'

Armand nodded. 'I'm listening, Hélène.'

'Good.' She took a long swallow of her coffee before continuing. 'I believe there has been a terrible accident of fate. *Madame* — Diana — may very well be married to two men. The husband who works in Cannes and Marseilles, and the man you saw her going off with yesterday.'

'*What?* You mean Le Loup is her *husband?* I can't believe it!' Armand poured himself more cognac.

Hélène pointed a finger at him. 'Believe me when I say I am certain of this. I told you before, don't you remember? Yesterday's man is thought by the world to be dead. He was a British fighter pilot and he was shot down over the Pas de Calais less than a year into the war. But it seems he did not die, and for reasons of his own he came here to Nice, and never returned home to his wife. Now she has found him again — but she can have no idea what he has become, what he does here. We have to warn her, but we can't just go walking into her house. What if her husband — her second husband, I mean — is there? What would we say to him? This is a matter of great delicacy. No, Armand, somehow we have to get word to Diana by other means.'

Armand rubbed the bridge of his nose. 'You are right, it is very complicated. I can't think what to do. We can't just sit here every day hoping she'll turn up.'

'No,' Hélène agreed, 'that's no sort of plan at all. Let me think . . . '

Across the road from them, a teenage girl slipped out of the doorway to her family's apartment. She was clutching several letters, and as Hélène watched, the girl skipped to the post box on the corner of the street and dropped them through the slot.

'That's it, Armand!' Hélène exclaimed, banging the table with the flat of her hand. 'We'll write her a letter, explaining everything. You can take it in your car to the taxi-rank in St Paul and ask one of the drivers to deliver it. Get the address while you're at it, we may need it later.'

He beamed at her. 'Now who's the clever one, eh? Well done!' He paused, and an expression of concern crossed his face. 'But wait a moment . . . What if her husband — the new one — opens the envelope first?'

Hélène shook her head. 'That is most unlikely. Diana told me he is a gentleman, very kind and proper. He would not do such a thing with a letter addressed to his wife, I am sure. Anyway, it is a chance we must take.'

'All right. But you write the letter, Hélène. I'm no good with words. I'll sign it with you, though.'

'Of course, it must come from us both. I shall go and buy paper and an envelope immediately. We mustn't waste any more time.' She gathered her bag and stood up.

'We have to save her.'

★ ★ ★

An hour later, Hélène looked up from the table where she had been writing their letter. Armand was watching her from inside the café. She beckoned to him. 'Come — it's finished. Read it and tell me what you think.'

The *patron* hurried over, fumbling with his reading glasses. 'You have been frank, Hélène?'

'I don't think I could have been any franker.'

He took the letter and sat down opposite her. 'Give me a little time. I am not a fast reader, and my English is limited. I may need some assistance.'

Armand bent over the pages, and his lips began to move silently as his finger traced the words which Hélène had written to their friend.

Madame (or perhaps I may address you as 'Diana'. After all, this is, as you will see, a most personal letter)

Dearest Diana, then. It appears my advice to you earlier this week was quite wrong. Your first husband is alive and well and living here in Nice, just as you thought. Armand saw your encounter yesterday outside the café, and from his description of your reaction, it is plain that this is the man you have been searching for.

So your instincts were correct all along, my dear, and mine were not. I apologise.

We truly wish you had come to the flower-market this morning, as we have much to tell you about the man you met yesterday. My dear: what or who he was when you married him, he cannot be now, it is quite impossible.

The man you described to me two days ago is not the man who lives in Nice today. I can only think that he hid his true face from you when you knew him in England, or that he has changed, and changed so completely it is beyond any understanding.

Here in Nice, the man you described to me so fondly is known by the name *Le Loup Anglais* (the English Wolf, of course). It is a terrible name, for what I must tell you, my dear Diana, is a terrible man.

No one knows where he came from or exactly how long he has been on the Côte d'Azur, but all are afraid of him. Even the *gendarmes*, whom he pays to close their eyes to what he does.

There are many rumours and stories about him, not all of which can be true, but I will tell you what Armand and I know to be so. You must please prepare yourself to be very shocked, Diana.

This man's business is what we in France call 'extortion'. He threatens to do terrible things to anyone with a business who does not pay him for his 'protection'. Poor Armand for years had to pay thirty francs a week to *Le Loup*; now it is fifty francs.

He picks on the smallest businesses, the ones the Nice Mafia cannot be bothered with. I am lucky he has not come to me for money. I think my little stall is too small for him to notice. But his threats must be taken with the utmost seriousness, Diana. He and those who work for him do not hesitate to make an example of those who refuse to pay.

There was a man who owned a patisserie just off the Rue de France, near the station. It was very profitable, people catching their trains to and from work would stop and buy their croissants and pastries from this man. *Le Loup* offered him his 'protection', but the man refused. He told *Le Loup* that he had fought in the Resistance against the Germans and was not frightened of a 'Merde Anglais'. He said this in front of his customers, Diana, shouting at *Le Loup*. He told him that if he ever came into his shop again, he would shoot him like a dog and that Nice would thank him for the favour.

The next morning this man was found dead in an alley behind the Gare de Nice; he had been stabbed in the eye. It is not thought *Le Loup* did this personally, there are plenty of men in Nice who would do such a thing for money.

People said even the Mafia would have given the baker a warning of some kind, a chance to see sense. The man's wife took over the running of the patisserie; she had herself and her children to clothe and feed. Now this woman pays *Le Loup* forty francs a week. Forty francs, Diana, to the man who had her husband murdered.

I must tell you that there is worse. Armand had a great friend who owned a small café in Cagnes sur Mer; it's not even in Nice, Diana, but *Le Loup*'s territory grows each year. This man was paying him sixty francs a week but asked for a meeting with *Le Loup*, where he explained it was too much and would eventually put him out of business. He offered forty francs.

Le Loup let it be known amongst what he calls his clients that this conversation had taken place. A few days later, Armand's friend disappeared: he has never been seen again. The talk is that his body is buried at the bottom of one of the gorges high in the Alpes Maritimes, but of course no one knows for certain what became of him and the police just shrug their shoulders and blow out their cheeks.

There are more such stories, Diana, too many for me to write here. But I know them to be true.

One more thing, my dear. Recently there have been rumours in Nice about *Le Loup* having a disagreement with the Mafia here. Perhaps you are aware how much of this city is controlled by the Mafia. They came here from Sicily many years ago. Even our mayor is known to be under their influence.

Now they have realised *Le Loup* is making a great deal of money and they want their share, or they will simply take over his business for themselves.

It is all meant to be a secret, but people talk. They say he has proposed an arrangement where he will pay them what they ask, but in return they must be responsible for his financial arrangements with the police.

Armand has heard that the Mafia have agreed, but are insisting *Le Loup* give them a large sum first for the privilege of being allowed to join their organisation. Everyone is frightened he will raise the money by demanding large special payments from his so-called clientèle.

Diana, Armand and I have no way of knowing if you plan to see this man again, or perhaps are even with him as I write this. Please believe me when I tell you that the man you married is now very, very dangerous; truly one of the cruellest men on the Riviera. Do not believe any of the lies I am certain he will tell you.

I am also certain he will want to take advantage of you in some way. Be on your guard. When you read this, show it to your husband, your real husband who cares for you and your daughter.

Also, please come to the flower-market as soon as you can. Armand and I wish to do all we can to advise and help you.

Sincerely yours,
Your friends, Hélène and Armand

Armand laid the pages on the table. Hélène looked questioningly at him. 'Well? What do you think?'

He smiled at her. 'It's a *tour de force*, my dearest Hélène. She must take heed of it. She *will* take heed of it. You've only made one mistake that I can see.'

She bridled slightly. 'Really? And what is that?'

He sighed as he folded the letter and slid it into the envelope, marked simply *Diana*.

'I don't pay the bastard fifty francs a week. Since January, it's been bloody sixty.'

49

The medieval church that sat at the very top of St Paul de Vence's fortified hilltop was striking one o'clock as Diana walked into the village. For once, she ignored the taxi-rank, heading instead for an unobtrusive wooden door set in a high stone wall. Opposite was the Café de la Place, busy with lunchtime customers. Some of them glanced at the young woman on the other side of the square as she approached the door and pushed it open.

A girl nudged her boyfriend and gestured urgently with her cigarette. 'Quick! Over there! Do you see her? That beautiful woman in the white lace dress? Look at those gorgeous shoes she's wearing! They're by Roger Vivier, or I'm a nun. I'm sure she's a film star.'

Her partner grinned at her. 'You say that about every beautiful well-dressed woman you see going into La Colombe d'Or.' He swung round in his chair in time to see Diana smile at someone in the doorway, before she slipped inside and disappeared. 'Wow. You're right about one thing though — she's a peach.' He winced as a stilettoed shoe made sharp contact with his ankle under the table. 'But not as lovely as you, chérie, truly . . . '

Diana was standing on the sunlit terrace of one of the most famous and exclusive restaurants on the Côte d'Azur. It attracted locals, tourists and a constant stream of writers, actors and artists. She loved coming here, and when James had asked her where she would like to meet for lunch after she had impulsively phoned him earlier, she hadn't hesitated.

'Oh, La Colombe! They've been serving lunch on the terrace for weeks now and it's such a glorious day. Let's meet there in an hour — if you think we can get a table at such short notice.'

This is all Douglas's fault, she'd told herself as she made her way to the kitchen to phone James. Telling her who she could and couldn't see.

She knew perfectly well that she was deliberately inflaming her irritation into anger in order to justify phoning James. But she was glad of any excuse, however contrived. Her misgivings of the day before had faded during the night, and she had woken hungry to see him again.

James had promised her he would have no trouble getting them a reservation at La Colombe d'Or. He had an account there, he said, and often took his more valued clients to the restaurant to finalise deals.

He chose not to add that the last time he had dined there, his guest had been a man close to the very top of the Nice Mafia. The agreement they'd hammered out would elevate James into the top drawer of organised crime in the city. Assuming he could get the entry fee together, of course. It was astronomically high and he was still working on the problem. But he knew he'd come up with something. He always did.

Now Diana looked at the busy tables that were

sheltered from the sun by large white canvas parasols. Others were shaded by ancient fig trees that lined a low wall opposite, from where diners enjoyed stunning views across the valley that fell steeply away from the village walls.

The dark doorway that led into the cool interior of the hotel seemed to wink and flash as white-coated waiters moved briskly in and out of the sunlight, carrying plates and bottles and menus. The air hummed with the sound of dozens of conversations and occasional bursts of laughter.

She was tingling with excitement.

She couldn't see James sitting at any of the tables and was beginning to wonder if she was the first to arrive when he suddenly came out of the hotel doorway and stood in the sunshine, shading his eyes with one hand as he looked around for her. He began turning the wrong way.

'I'm over here!' She waved at him.

He spun round and saw her at once. For a moment they stood and smiled at each other, and then he was moving swiftly across the terrace.

She looked quickly around her. She didn't expect to see anyone she recognised; she'd only been in France for a couple of months. But if somebody she knew did turn up, she'd think of an excuse of some sort. She was, she reflected, getting rather good at that.

'Hello, Diana.'

'Hello, James.'

He bent forward and kissed her lightly on each cheek. 'Thanks so much for coming.'

'I had to,' she told him simply. Impulsively she leaned forward and kissed him quickly on the mouth. 'Where are we sitting?'

'Over here. Come on.' He took her arm and guided her across the terrace. 'You'll never guess who's at the table next to ours.'

They sat down under one of the fig trees.

'No — who?'

He brushed her hair behind her ear so he could whisper into it. 'Picasso. Pablo bloody Picasso. Don't turn round, though, he doesn't like being stared at. Do it casually later. There's plenty of time. He's only just arrived and he always sits at his table for ages.'

Diana stared at him. 'What, you mean you've seen him here before?'

James nodded. 'God, yes, I come here all the time. I told you, I have an account. Mind you, at least I pay for my meals with good old-fashioned money — old Pablo just dashes off the odd painting to settle his summer accounts here. You must have a look around inside later. The walls are covered with art — Picasso, Chagall — all the big names come to this hotel. Some of them stay for weeks. The Colombe's private collection must be worth an absolute fortune.'

A dark-haired waiter appeared beside them. '*Bonjour, monsieur. Ça va?*'

'Christien!' James grinned up at him. He turned to Diana. 'This is Christien. He always looks after me here. Best damn waiter in Provence, and the best-looking too. Film-star material, wouldn't you say?'

Diana looked at the young waiter as he

340

handed them menus. He was certainly handsome enough with his jet-black hair, straightened and gleaming with oil. And he had a lovely smile, she thought, as they formally shook hands — 'Christien, Diana; Diana, Christien' — but his dark brown eyes troubled her. They flickered with anxiety, even as he bowed and smiled.

She remembered the waiter at the Negresco the day before. James seemed to have quite an effect on people here. She'd never noticed it before, back in England. Perhaps the French didn't know what to make of a successful, wealthy British man in their midst. Maybe it was something to do with the war; lingering French guilt at being so quickly routed while her ally struggled on alone.

James had ordered their wine before Diana had arrived and now Christien drew the dripping bottle from a silver bucket at the side of the table, and poured ice-cold Chablis for both of them. Then he hurried away with their order.

The faint atmosphere of tension lifted as soon as he was gone, and Diana felt herself relax as she eavesdropped on the conversations that ebbed and flowed around her.

James lifted his glass. 'A toast, Diana, to finding each other again. It's incredible, isn't it? A kind of miracle. You thought I was dead and I . . . well, I never dreamed I'd set eyes on you again. Here's to us.'

'To us.'

They touched glasses. *Something's happening,* thought Diana. *I shouldn't have come here, but*

I'm glad I did. I haven't felt like this for so, so long.

She realised he was staring at her. 'What is it, James?'

'You look different,' he told her. 'From yesterday, I mean.'

'In what way?'

He shrugged. 'Happier, I suppose. Definitely more relaxed, but that's understandable. You must have thought you'd seen a ghost when I got out of that taxi.'

He reached over and took her hand, squeezing it gently. Without thinking, she returned the pressure. 'Can you ever forgive me, Diana, for running out on you? Tell me that *something* I explained to you yesterday made any kind of sense.'

Diana drank some of her wine as she considered. 'Well, yes. Yes, of course, otherwise I wouldn't be here now and I wouldn't be . . . feeling like this.'

'Like what?'

'Happy. Incredibly, unbelievably happy. I woke up this morning feeling like a different woman . . . No, that's not quite true — I feel like the woman I used to be. I can't deny it, James, not to myself nor to you. Being here with you now is just like a miracle, as you said. I feel that a part of me which went to sleep a long time ago is waking up again.'

He laughed. 'My very own Sleeping Beauty.' He gestured at the sun-dappled terrace around them. 'And here we are, in our own fairy story. Who knows what's going to happen to us next?'

Diana couldn't think quite what to say to that and was grateful for Christien's reappearance with their starters. They were both having *bouquet de crevettes* and Diana wished she hadn't worn her cream lace dress; one false move in dead-heading the juicy prawns that were perched all around the rim of a small cut-glass salad bowl would leave her spotted with indelible orange stains.

James noticed her hesitation and understood at once. 'Ah yes, the timeless exploding prawn dilemma. Here — give them to me.'

He drew her starter towards him and deftly removed the heads, tails and scales before washing his fingers in a finger-bowl of lemon-scented water brought by Christien. He pushed the prawns back to her. 'There. All done.'

'Thank you,' she said, and then, barely realising what she was doing, she took his hand in hers and raised it to her lips, kissing his fingertips.

'Thank you,' she said again.

He smiled at her. 'Well, I suppose it's a start. Preparing your prawns for you, I mean. I have to start making up for the last decade somehow, don't I?'

They ate in silence for a minute or so before Diana looked at him, and sighed. 'I'm sorry, but I have to ask you a question. You can probably guess what it is.'

'Yes, I think I can. You want to know if I've found someone else, as you have, and precisely how I make my way here in Nice.'

'That's two questions.'

'True, but you were planning on asking me both of them, weren't you?' He paused while Christien took away their dishes. James then poured more wine for them both.

'Right.' He looked up at her. 'Firstly, I am not involved with anyone at the moment. In fact, I haven't been for some time. Of course I've had liaisons over the years, but nothing ever came of them.'

For a second time he reached for her hand. 'I admitted yesterday that in the days and weeks after I was shot down I didn't really think about you much, if at all. I was just too damned busy staying alive and keeping out of either French or German hands.'

'I can understand that.' She squeeed his hand. 'Really, I can.'

He nodded gratefully. 'But once I got to Nice and found my feet,' he went on, 'I thought about you more and more. I kept wishing that somehow things had turned out differently. That I'd been shot down over England, for example, and perhaps wounded in a way that stopped me flying again. All hopeless, foolish fantasies; I knew that. But you were always on my mind.'

'It was the same for me, James. A day never passed when I didn't think about you.'

They stared at each other for some time, before he continued: 'As for how I live, it's not complicated. Even after I got my false papers in Marseilles, I had a lot of money left over. Most of the hard cash and all the gold and jewellery. As I told you, there was far more in that man's safe than he could possibly earn as a country doctor. Did I mention that in the same bag as the banknotes there were embossed business cards giving his name and the address of another surgery in Paris?'

Diana shook her head.

'No? Well, I had a lot of ground to cover yesterday, I suppose. Anyway, when I got to Nice I decided to invest in some local businesses. There might have been a war on but as I said, you'd hardly have known it. I bought stakes in shops, bars, hotels — even a taxi-rank. That cab you saw me getting out of yesterday is one of mine and the guy driving it is basically my personal chauffeur.

'Eventually I was able to buy most of my partners out entirely. I did pretty OK during the war, Diana, but now,' James waved expansively at the packed restaurant around them, 'the South of France is really booming. I'm making serious money. I deal in antiques. I don't know how much your Dougal is worth, but — '

'It's *Douglas*,' Diana corrected for the second time. For some reason she wanted to smile.

'Dammit! Douglas! Sorry, Diana, I'm not doing it on purpose. I was always rotten with names, you remember that . . . Anyway, I was going to say I'd be happy to meet him at any of the tables in the casino at Monte, win or lose. I'm bankrolled. In fact, I'm putting the money together to close my biggest deal so far, but I won't bore you with that now. I don't want you to think I'm shooting you a line.'

She allowed herself a smile. 'No, you're not

doing that. I can see you're a local VIP by the way people treat you. Christien, for example. But he reminds me of the waiter at the Negresco, James; something tells me he's frightened of you.'

'*Frightened* of me?' James burst out laughing. 'I just stand out a bit because I'm an Englishman and I don't talk about my past. Man of mystery, that's me. I reckon they're just curious.'

50

The brown Citroën pulled away from the villa's front door and Maxine took the white envelope the taxi driver had handed to her and propped it on the marble mantelpiece. The fireplace below was laid with logs and kindling, but they were hidden behind a large bowl of flowers that had been placed in front of the grate. The fire would not be lit again until late October.

'Come along, Stella!' she called, her low heels clicking on the stone slabs of the entrance hall. 'Our lessons are over for today. We are going out.'

A few moments later, the girl appeared at the top of the stairs that led to the villa's bedrooms.

'Are we? Who was that at the door?'

'A letter for your mother. Come down and put your shoes on, I have a treat for you.' Maxine scooped car keys from a side table and fumbled in her bag for the scrap of paper with the villa's burglar-alarm code scrawled on it. She could never remember the random series of numbers and letters.

Stella ran into the room. 'What about Mummy? Where is she?'

'She's having lunch with an old friend she bumped into. She just rang to say she won't be home for a couple of hours yet.'

'*Again?*' Stella looked surprised. 'But she was out quite late yesterday afternoon, too. She promised she'd take me to the fair at Villeneuve Loubet today. It just opened for the summer.'

'I know,' Maxine said. 'That's where I am to take you. We will have fun together, won't we? And Mummy says maybe she can join us there later. It is not a large fair and she will find us quite easily, I think.'

Stella was mollified. 'All right. Let me get my pocket money and put my shoes on, and we can be off.'

* * *

Diana shivered under him and James leaned back towards the foot of the bed to pull the sheets up over them both. Then he drew her to him and kissed her forehead.

'Cold?'

She shivered again, and gave a small laugh. 'Hardly . . . not after that. It's just that I — oh my goodness, James!'

He held her tightly until another, exquisite convulsion had passed.

'Well,' she said, when she felt she could speak with reasonable composure. 'That was . . . ' Diana made a small fanning gesture in front of her face as she gazed up at the ceiling. 'That was . . . I don't know . . . exactly like it was, you know, that week at the Dower House.'

He slid one arm under her waist and pulled her gently on her side until they were facing each other.

'For me, too. You're lovely, Diana. Lovelier than you ever were. Let me look at you properly.'

He pulled the sheets away again and sat up, gazing at her.

'You're perfect . . . unchanged. Except for this.' He looked at the neat horizontal scar below her navel and stroked it gently with a forefinger. 'But this makes you more real, and oh . . . I don't know, complete.' He stroked the silver line again. 'That's Stella, I suppose?'

'That's Stella,' she confirmed.

She felt completely comfortable under his scrutiny, in a way she never did with Douglas. Dear, kind, generous Douglas. She knew he couldn't help it, but Douglas always seemed to devour her with hungry eyes before they made love. And even afterwards, when she slipped out of bed to go to their bathroom, he followed her every movement with a relish she found increasingly difficult to bear. Soon, she knew she would think it repellent.

They had never once made love in the dark. Douglas always insisted on keeping the light on 'so I can see you properly'. Surely husbands could desire their wives without being so openly lecherous? Douglas didn't make her feel desired; he made her feel gloated over. For some time now she'd increasingly found pretexts to avoid the act of love. She could tell Douglas had noticed. A certain coolness had begun to form between them.

She had made no such excuses an hour ago to James.

★ ★ ★

349

As their lunch progressed she had found herself reaching for his hand more often, and detaining it in her own for longer. She had always loved his hands, from that first night they slept together in the Dower House, and the shuddering, involuntary responses that they drew from her. And then later, when they made love . . . she trembled slightly at the memory.

And as they talked and laughed about the time they'd spent together all those years ago, she began to understand her hunger to see him today for what it really was.

She craved him. She longed to take her erotic dreams of that summer, and turn them into a consummate reality.

He noticed the change in her. Her lips became slightly parted, her cheeks gently flushed. At last a pause fell; a silence that slowly filled with unmistakable expectation and mutual, unspoken understanding.

Eventually he'd leaned forward, and brushing her hair behind her ear as he had earlier, whispered to her, 'Diana.'

'Yes, James?'

'When you saw me coming out of the hotel earlier, I'd been to Reception. I booked us a room here this afternoon. I know that was incredibly presumptuous of me, but I — '

She pressed the tips of her fingers against his lips. 'No. I'm glad, James,' she whispered. 'Really, really glad. Can we go there now, straight away?'

* * *

In the room, they undressed each other wordlessly before falling on to the bed. He entered her almost at once.

'I'm sorry, Diana,' he gasped. 'I have to have you right now . . . Later, I promise I'll — '

She silenced him again, this time with her lips. After a moment, she turned her head away a little and drew her arms tightly around him, pulling him still further in.

'This is *exactly* what I want, my darling, darling James. I couldn't want anything more.'

★ ★ ★

He continued to stroke her Caesarean scar. 'What happened? Was it an emergency?'

'Sort of. She was in completely the wrong position and nothing the midwife or doctor did could turn her. Stella was stubborn right from the start. It would have been a breech birth and they're awfully dangerous. The surgeon was quite sweet about it before they put me under. 'I'm going to make Baby a little front door so he can join us,' he said to me. Except that it wasn't a 'he', was it?'

James propped himself up on one elbow and stroked her hair. 'Did you think you were having a boy?'

Diana nodded, taking his hand and kissing the palm. 'Oh yes. We all did — me, and Mummy and Daddy. It's obvious now why. We'd lost both you and John less than a year before, and a son would have seemed incredibly symbolic. I convinced myself you'd left me with a boy.'

'So what did you think when you came round and they handed you a baby girl?'

Diana lay back on the pillows and smiled at the memory. 'I burst into tears of sheer happiness. I completely forgot all thoughts about having a boy . . . There was something so sweet and — oh, I don't know — almost *funny* about having a little girl. We all felt it. My parents doted on Stella from the day she was born.'

James reached down to the side of the bed and groped for cigarettes inside his jacket. He lit one for each of them before asking her: 'I don't suppose you have a photo of her on you, do you? I'd love to see her.'

'Not so fast, *père* Blackwell,' she replied. She sat up and looked at him with mock seriousness. 'How did you know I'd want to come to this hotel room with you?'

He dipped his head and kissed each of her breasts in turn before answering.

'Because I heard something in your voice when you telephoned me at my apartment this morning. Remember, you're my wife, though I suppose our marriage must have been dissolved or annulled or whatever, years ago. But that doesn't alter what we had — what we *have*, together. We know each other instinctively. That doesn't go away, does it? Do you see?'

She smiled at him. 'Of course I do. I'm only teasing. I know exactly what you mean. I feel it too.'

He put his cigarette on the ashtray by his side of the bed, and took hers, placing them carefully side by side. Then he held her face in both his

352

hands and kissed her gently on the lips.

'There's one more thing that I have to tell you, Diana. It's more important than anything I've said yet.' He pulled her gently down beside him, and began to stroke the curve of her waist. 'I still love you. I never stopped loving you.' He kissed her again. 'And I think that you still love me.'

She kissed him back. 'Yes, I do, James. I really do.'

★　★　★

A while later, they drew apart again. Diana lay still with her eyes closed for a while before slowly sitting up, pulling her bag onto the bed and unzipping a small side compartment. She slid her fingers inside and drew out a small black-and-white photograph.

'Here she is. This is your daughter.'

He took the picture and angled it towards the advancing afternoon light that slanted through the bedroom windows. After a few moments, he gave a low whistle.

'My, oh my, so that's her . . . that's our little girl. How old is she in this?'

'It's a recent one,' Diana said. 'I took it about six weeks ago, so she'd just turned ten. Those are our villa gates behind her.'

He studied the photo closely. It showed Stella standing on one leg, the other tucked up behind her and held in her hand by the ankle. Her other arm was thrown extravagantly above and behind her, gesturing towards the villa's drive. She appeared to be singing, her mouth a perfect '0'.

She was wearing a knee-length summer dress, and white sandals buckled on to bare feet. Her blonde hair was inexpertly tied up in bunches, which James guessed she had attempted to do herself.

He turned to her mother and grinned. 'She looks quite a character.'

Diana smiled back. 'Oh, she is. She can be so funny, and quick, and she doesn't miss a trick.'

'Can I keep this?'

'Of course you can, darling. I'll get some more and give them to you when we next see each other.'

They stared at each other, as the implication behind her words sank in.

'Hmm,' he said at last. 'Isn't this what they call the vanishing point?' He pulled her to him, kissing the top of her head. 'What I mean is — well, if we look behind us, we can see how we got here. It's certainly a crooked road, but it all makes perfect, logical sense. But when we look ahead . . . ' He shrugged. 'It's a completely blank landscape, isn't it? Which way do we go now?'

They held each other for some time longer, before she replied.

'I have no proper idea. Not yet. But I do know one thing. I won't lose you again, I'm absolutely certain of that. Yesterday I was full of confusion and even fear. But that's all gone.'

She sat up in the bed, and took both his hands in hers. 'It's horribly complicated, James. But my father has an expression: 'If it wasn't complicated, it wouldn't be life'.'

He looked at her quizzically. 'Meaning?'

'He means that every kind of apparently intractable problem has a solution. One just has to be patient and discover what it is. And that's what we're going to do. We're going to solve this and everything is going to be all right. For everyone. You, me, Stella — even Douglas. You'll see.' She almost glared at him, defiant in her nakedness.

To her astonishment, and slight annoyance, he began to laugh.

'No, no,' he managed to gasp. 'Don't be cross with me!' He hiccuped, then brought himself under control.

'Girton girl, you're *incredible*! The fact is, Miss Diana Arnold . . . you haven't changed one bloody bit.'

51

Diana thought she would have just enough time to take a taxi to Villeneuve Loubet and rendezvous with her daughter at the funfair. James went out into the square outside the Colombe d'Or to arrange a cab for them both — 'I've got some business in Nice, I'll drop you off on the way' — while she dressed and frantically reapplied her make-up. The sexual flush had faded from her cheeks but her eyes sparkled as she applied mascara.

James had taken her virginity that first night, eleven years past, at the Dower House. It seemed like a lifetime ago. She had had three other men since — four, if you counted Douglas — but no one had ever made her feel the way James did.

She examined herself critically in the bathroom mirror. Did the afternoon show? She smiled. She felt exactly the same as she had done when she came down to breakfast at the Dower House, the morning after James and she first slept together. Then, she was sure her parents would be able to tell. Now, she wondered if Douglas would somehow notice a change in her at dinner tonight. The contentment that flowed through her body from sexual fulfilment must be obvious to anyone with eyes to see.

She wondered why she felt no guilt. It had never crossed her mind before to be unfaithful to Douglas; today she had betrayed him without a moment's consideration. She'd do it again, too, and soon.

It was strange, she thought, as she snapped shut her powder compact and poured everything back into her handbag. The thought of sitting down with Douglas at some point in the future and telling him everything; explaining how she couldn't possibly stay with him now, not now that her James had come back to her, seemed the most reasonable, uncomplicated thing in the world.

But what about Stella? How could she communicate any of this to her daughter?

Diana supposed she'd find a way eventually. But at the close of this extraordinary afternoon, and despite her fierce optimism with James just now, the task seemed quite beyond her.

★ ★ ★

Half an hour later, as their taxi was bumping down the steep hill that plunged in a series of dips and loops towards Villeneuve Loubet, James cleared his throat. He and Diana had been holding hands, her head on his shoulder, since leaving St Paul and the driver, after a sharp glance from James, had hastily adjusted his mirror so he could see nothing of the passengers behind him.

'Darling, I have to ask you something. I need a favour from you. It's not a small one, I'm afraid.'

Diana looked up at him. 'Well?'

He cleared his throat again. 'Remember I told you I'm about to do a deal here in Nice — a really important one?'

'Yes.'

'Good . . . Well . . . here's the thing, Diana. I'm a few francs short of what I need to set the whole thing up. I thought I had enough, but another chap's outbid me. It's extremely annoying. I can get the extra, obviously, but it'll take a week or so and the deadline's Friday, the day after tomorrow.'

Diana sat up straight. 'Yes, I see. How much do you need?'

He shrugged. 'It would only be a very short loan. I could pay you back in, say, a month to six weeks.'

'But how much is it?'

He appeared to calculate a figure in his head.

Diana blinked when he told her. 'My goodness. That is rather a lot.'

'I know, darling, but if there's one thing I've learned in Nice, it's that one can't accumulate if one doesn't speculate. Not that this is speculation,' he added quickly. 'Not at all. It's a sort of down payment; the price of entry to join this particular business club. Once you're on the inside, you've practically got a licence to print money.' He paused.

'But it's not all about me,' he continued. 'I employ a lot of people whose livelihoods depend on my pulling this off. They have families — children. I can't let them down.'

He looked at her. 'Well? What do you say? I'll quite understand if you can't manage it, of course.'

Diana shook her head. 'I can manage it. I have

my own bank account here. Douglas is very modern-minded about that sort of thing. He insisted on settling a large sum on me and Stella when he and I married. Then there's the trust money I got when I turned 21. Altogether, I must have at least what you need. Well, I did the last time I checked my bankbook.'

He managed to conceal his sudden excitement. 'And you'd lend it to me?'

Diana turned to face him. 'James, I love you. You're my first husband; you are my *real* husband. You were lost to me, but I've found you again. What's mine is yours. I know we're in an incredibly complicated situation, but I've already told you: I'm not going to lose you a second time. We're going to work this out. It won't be easy, but we will.'

She kissed him. 'Of course you can have the money.'

He returned her kiss for a long time, before finally breaking away.

'You're wonderful, Diana,' he whispered. 'Thank you. Thank you.'

She opened her handbag. 'Let's see, my chequebook should be in here somewhere.'

James told the driver to pull over while Diana wrote out the cheque. She filled in the date and the amount and then laughed. 'Who do I make it out to, James? What's your *nom de guerre?* Or is it a *nom de plume* these days? You haven't actually told me.'

James thought quickly. 'Well, I have one or two different business names, actually. Tell you what, leave that part blank. I'll decide which one to use later.'

By the time the taxi was dropping Diana at the entrance to the funfair, James had the cheque folded into his wallet.

At his suggestion, she had made it out for cash.

★ ★ ★

'Mummy! Mummy! We're over here!' Stella hopped from one foot to the other, waving both arms above her head. She and Maxine were in the short queue for the funfair's star attraction — a huge wooden Big Dipper topped with a garish neon sign: *Le Crazee Chat!!*

Diana hurried over to her daughter. Maxine, she noticed as she joined them, was looking a little green.

'Maxine doesn't *really* want to come on the Crazy Cat, Mummy,' Stella said breathlessly. 'She's being very brave, though, and she's pretending that she does. I've told her you hate rollercoasters too, so she's not to worry. I'm used to going on them by myself.'

One of the cat-shaped cars rattled past them on its final swooping descent to the exit platform. The occupants screamed in delighted terror as it whipped by.

'It's all right, Maxine,' Diana told her. 'You don't have to ride with her. I'll do it.'

Stella gaped. '*Mummy?*'

Diana grinned. 'Why not? It's about time I gave it a go, don't you think? Maxine, you go and

360

buy us some lemonades from the stall over there.'

The girl nodded with relief and slipped out of the queue. When she reached the lemonade stall, she looked back. Diana and Stella were climbing into one of the cars, laughing. Diana looked around and, noticing Maxine, gave her an exaggerated wave.

Maxine realised that she had never seen *madame* looking quite so alive, or so beautiful. She nodded to herself. This was the second afternoon that Diana had not returned home for lunch.

As she beadily eyed her employer now, she thought she could guess the reason why.

* * *

Douglas was back at the villa ahead of his wife and stepdaughter. He was surprised no one was home, before remembering that Diana had promised to take Stella to the funfair after lunch. He sighed. He would have loved to have gone with them. He knew how serious and stuffy he must seem to his 'girls'.

His oppressive, stifling upbringing had given him few examples of how to have fun. His subsequent career had been successful enough, but sometimes he felt he had been buried alive in paperwork and ledgers and consultants' reports. That was one of the reasons why he had been so keen to bring them all to the South of France. He'd hoped some of the glamour of the Côte d'Azur might somehow rub off on him; banish his quintessential dullness; make him a little more exciting as a husband.

But if anything, Diana had withdrawn from him since they arrived. They didn't make love nearly as often as he would have liked, and in recent weeks his wife had seemed locked into her own private world. She spoke little, and often went to bed before him.

Then there was the business of this so-called 'wine merchant' she'd bumped into yesterday. Douglas didn't like that one bit. He knew he'd been heavy-handed that morning, ordering Diana not to see the man again, and he'd heard the resentment in her voice as she agreed not to, but what was he to do? Nice was full of scoundrels.

He wandered into the *salon*. An envelope glimmered on the mantelpiece and he walked across the room to inspect it. *Diana* was written neatly on the front in black ink, and the reverse had been gummed closed. For a moment he contemplated opening it and reading the contents, but Douglas was an honourable man. He put the envelope back and drifted over to the drinks table.

He'd just poured himself a scotch when he heard the front door open and Stella's piping voice. 'Douglas? Douglas, are you home?'

'I'm in here,' he called.

She rushed into the room and embraced him before hopping up and down before him.

'You'll never *guess*, Douglas! Mummy joined us at the funfair and actually came on the Crazy Cat with me, and she was sick as soon as we got off! She's all right now but she keeps saying: 'I'll never go near that dratted thing again!' ' Stella doubled over laughing.

Douglas smiled at her, waiting for her to calm down. Then he kissed her forehead and said, 'I'm glad Mummy was able to join you at the fair. I wonder where she'd been before that?'

'Oh, having lunch with someone, Maxine said,' replied Stella, reaching for the soda siphon that rested on the drinks tray. 'Can I, Douglas?'

'Of course, dear.' He watched her as she squirted a jet of soda water into a glass. 'Did Mummy mention who she was with?'

Stella shook her head. 'She didn't say. Maxine said she'd bumped into an old friend.' Stella waggled her head and made a face. 'Anooother one!'

52

Diana rose from the dining table and stamped her foot. 'I *won't* be questioned like this, Douglas! I simply won't!'

Her husband looked anguished as he put his knife and fork to one side of his half-finished evening meal.

'All I was asking you is — '

'I *know* what you're asking and I understand the implication behind the question perfectly well.' She glared at him fiercely. Diana knew she was deliberately allowing her temper full rein: it helped mask the guilt that had engulfed her the moment she'd walked into the room and caught sight of his miserable face.

'Diana, please stop shouting. Stella will hear.'

She took a deep breath and forced herself to sit back down. 'Yes. Of course. But this is the second time today you've challenged my independence. Now, it seems, I am not to go to La Colombe d'Or for lunch with an old friend from Girton.'

'I said nothing of the kind! I merely observed that it was odd that for the second day running, you happened upon an old friend here. I — '

'Oh! Don't you know how you sound, Douglas? This is the South of France! St Paul is a huge tourist destination! It's odd that I *haven't* bumped into someone from England before now.'

He looked at her, defeated, before unwisely persisting: 'And this really was a woman friend, Diana? Not the man from yesterday?'

She was on her feet again, hurling her napkin to the floor. 'Oh, this is insufferable. Why don't you phone the restaurant? Go on, do it now. Ask them for yourself.'

'Don't be absurd. You know I'm not going to do anything like that. Of course I accept what you say. I'm sorry. It's just that recently things between us have been, well . . . different. Difficult.' He looked at his plate. 'Sometimes I worry that perhaps you feel you have made a mistake. In agreeing to marry me, I mean.'

The guilt that she had forced down with her extravagant anger threatened to rise again and overwhelm her.

'Now *you're* being absurd,' she told him as she walked quickly to the door. 'I can't stand this; I'm going to bed. Don't worry, I'll sleep in one of the spare rooms tonight. Goodnight, Douglas.'

He started to say something, but she closed the door behind her and almost ran to the stairs. This was dreadful, *dreadful*. She was turning into the kind of person she despised.

But Diana had only one thought as she collected her things from her bedside and moved them into a smaller room at the end of the passage.

She simply *must* talk to James.

★   ★   ★

365

Well, *that* was an awkward conversation, James Blackwell thought to himself as he replaced the receiver and went to his drinks tray, where he poured himself an extremely generous scotch. *Bloody* awkward, actually.

He scooped ice from the silver bowl next to the bottle and dropped it into the glass.

Thank God he'd asked Diana for as much as he had. It had barely been enough. As soon as he returned to his apartment from the bank, he'd bagged up the cash and summoned his most trusted courier to deliver it to an address in one of Nice's wealthiest districts.

Then he sat back and waited for the phone call. It came just after midnight, and surprised him not at all.

'*Where's the rest?*'

'I'm still collecting it. I sent you that ahead of the deadline to show good faith. I thought you'd be . . . encouraged.'

'*By a third of what you owe us? I'm not encouraged, I'm worried. And so should you be, monsieur. Some of us here are beginning to wonder if you really have the balls to operate at this level. Perhaps we should just take you over. If you're lucky, maybe someone will find you a job.*'

'You gave me until the end of the month. I think giving you thirty-three per cent ahead of that is fucking impressive, actually.'

'*Watch your language. The boss is listening in.*'

'Good. Then he can hear me tell you that you'll have the remaining amount, in full, on

366

time. And that's just the entry fee. You guys know I can deliver, week on week. You've seen my accounts. You know how I work. Even if you did take me over, you'd never run my business as profitably as I do. And I'll bring fresh ideas with me. So just show a little faith, OK?'

'*Don't hang up.*'

There had been a loud click as the line went dead and he knew they were discussing him. He chewed his bottom lip. Then the earpiece crackled again and the voice was back.

'*OK. The boss feels maybe I'm being a little hard on you. But nowhere near as hard as he says he'll be if you don't come through by the end of the month. Are we clear?*'

'Perfectly.'

Now he sat on his balcony, staring moodily out into the night. He couldn't see the Mediterranean from his apartment, but he could hear it, especially when it was late and the traffic quietened. Then the sound of waves crashing onto the pebbled beach filtered into the streets behind the Promenade des Anglais. Usually it soothed him, but not tonight.

He was in a cleft stick. When the Mafia had come sniffing around his business a few weeks ago, he wasn't surprised. He'd been expecting some kind of contact from them for a while; his operation was getting too big not to be noticed, and anyway, they were hand-in-glove with the police and had probably started picking up bits of information about him from them.

The Italians had been sticking their fingers in Nice's affairs for years, he knew that, of course, but it was the war that had given them their big break. With France out for the count and Italy Germany's new best friend, the Mafia had launched their own invasion across the border and ruthlessly driven out Nice's home-grown mob. Since then, their grip had tightened remorselessly on the city. They had a piece of everything, and now they wanted a piece of him.

As soon as he realised he was in their sights, he'd taken the initiative. He'd gone to the old don himself and made his pitch — fifty-fifty on his profits if he was allowed to keep running the business, a seat at the big table which would give him incredible access to new markets, and the organisation to take over his financial arrangements with the police.

He had reckoned it was a mutually beneficial arrangement, but two days after shaking hands on it, the other side had come back to him with their belated demand for a sweetener to seal the deal. Some sweetener. Where the hell was he going to find that kind of cash in the time left to him?

In truth, he'd thought Diana's money would buy him more time, not ratchet up the bloody pressure. Greedy bastards. He'd completely underestimated them. They were probably bent on taking him over anyway, and they'd deliberately set the bar almost impossibly high.

If he somehow came up with the goods, they'd let him in, he was certain of that. All part of their warped code of honour. But if he didn't, they'd walk all over him. He just might be allowed to

368

get out of Nice on condition he never returned. If he was lucky.

Jesus, what a mess. And after ten years of slog and graft, too. Maybe he should just cash in his chips and clear out. But the prospect of starting again was unthinkable. Where, anyway? Four hundred miles south, bordering the same stagnant sea, lay Naples. Naples was even more corrupt than Nice but the place was sewn up tight. He'd never find an opening there. He would probably be killed for even trying.

He tossed back his drink and was about to go to bed when his phone rang again. Probably one of his enforcers with a problem. He could do without it right now, but picked up anyway.

'*Oui?*'

'Darling?'

Christ, it was her. He looked at his watch. Past one. 'Diana! Where are you calling from? Is something wrong?'

The silence at the other end lasted so long he thought they'd been cut off. Then she spoke again.

'I have to see you. Tomorrow. I don't know what to do.'

'Where are you speaking from?'

'I'm in the kitchen. Douglas is upstairs asleep. We had a row. I have to see you. Can I?'

'Of course. Let's meet for coffee tomorrow morning in La Petite Maison. It's at the edge of the Old Town. Eleven o'clock. Do you know it?'

'Yes, I know it . . . James?'

'Yes, Diana?'

'You do love me, don't you?'

'Of course I do.'

'It's going to be all right, isn't it?'

'Yes, I promise. You yourself said today how complicated this all is, but that we'd work it out — and we will. Now get some sleep. Everything will look much better in the morning. It always does.'

'Yes — I know that. I — damn, I think I can hear Douglas on the stairs.' Her voice became a whisper. 'I'll have to pretend I've come down to make myself a drink or something. Goodnight, James.'

'Goodnight, Diana. Sleep well.' He replaced the receiver, thoughtfully.

Douglas.

The generous, and doubtless besotted, husband.

James Blackwell went to bed, the ghost of a fresh idea beginning to form.

53

Breakfast at the villa was a subdued affair. Stella looked from her mother to her stepfather and, with a child's bluntness, asked if they'd had a row.

'Just a silly one, darling,' Diana replied. 'And it was all my fault.' For the first time that morning, she looked directly at her husband opposite. 'I'm sorry, Douglas. I probably had a glass of wine too many at lunch yesterday and I should never have got on that stupid rollercoaster. I felt dreadful when I got home and I was in a foul temper. I was very unfair on you.'

Douglas looked relieved. 'I was pompous and irritating. No wonder you were cross.' He got up and came round to where Diana was sitting, and kissed her on the cheek. 'I'm sorry too.'

'*Yeuch!*' Stella stuck her tongue out. 'Soppy!'

Douglas leaned over and rubbed the end of her nose with his forefinger. 'There's never anything wrong with saying you're sorry, young lady. Nothing at all.' He turned to his wife. 'There's something I keep meaning to tell you — there's a letter for you on the mantelpiece in the *salon*. I noticed it last night, but with everything that happened, I forgot to mention it.'

He picked up his briefcase from beside his chair and walked to the kitchen door. 'Marseilles for me. I'll be back tomorrow evening. You'll both be all right?'

'More than all right,' Stella told him. 'I'm going riding for the whole day near Vence, remember? Mummy's dropping me off straight after breakfast. There'll be a picnic by a waterfall and everything.'

Diana's heart sank. She'd completely forgotten the arrangement, made the previous month with a riding school in the hills above the nearby market town. Stella, an accomplished rider, desperately missed her riding lessons back in England and had been looking forward for weeks to a day in the saddle. All the other girls — they were mostly girls — would be French, but Stella didn't seem to mind going on her own.

'I'll probably meet some of the people I'll be at school with when I start next term,' she had said airily. Diana and Douglas had marvelled at her casual confidence.

As soon as Donald had left and Stella was upstairs changing into her riding clothes, Diana telephoned James. Fortunately he was still at his apartment. She explained about the riding lesson — he said he knew the school concerned and that it was a good one — and they agreed to meet for lunch instead of coffee. Diana calmed down. She was still going to see him today after all.

★ ★ ★

Diana was in such a rush to get Stella to the stables that she grabbed the envelope from the mantelpiece without opening it and stuffed it in

372

her bag. She could read whatever was inside later.

In fact, she delivered her daughter to the little ranch in the hills above Vence well before time, and was safely in Nice by noon with an hour to kill before she was due to meet James. She toyed with the idea of going to see Armand and Hélène, but instead chose to walk along the Promenade from its eastern end, all the way past the Negresco and on to where the private beaches owned by the restaurants ended, and the long public shoreline began.

It was a hot day but the breeze coming off the sea was cooling and Diana began to feel her optimism return. She was glad she'd made up with Douglas. She was still certain that their marriage would have to end — the prospect of life without James was unthinkable now — but she resolved to behave with more fairness and kindness from now on. God only knew how she was going to break the news to Douglas, but self-indulgent, *faux* anger must play no part in it. None of this was his fault. If she felt guilt — which she did — that was a burden for her to carry, not to be transferred to him in histrionics like those of the previous evening.

As for Stella . . . Diana was no closer to knowing how to handle that side of the equation, and until she was, the status quo must remain. She supposed inspiration would strike at some point, but every imaginary conversation with Stella that she rehearsed now made her realise just how difficult it was going to be.

'*Stella, you know we thought that Daddy died*

in the war? Well . . . '

'Stella, *there's someone I've been wanting very much for you to meet . . . '*

'Darling, *you know that sometimes miracles can happen?'*

All awful, just awful. If only there was someone she could ask for advice, but twice-married widows whose first husbands returned from the grave were thin on the ground.

She turned round and headed back to La Petite Maison and the flower-market.

The flower market. Hélène.

Of course. Hélène may have been wrong about James being a figment of her imagination, but her counsel had been fundamentally wise and kind. With a sudden rush of hope, Diana realised she would be comfortable confiding everything to Hélène. She would not be judged. The woman was worldly — she was a war-widow too, and had a daughter — and shrewd. Diana felt instinctively that if anyone could think of the right way to introduce Stella to her father, it was the flower-seller.

First thing tomorrow, she would come down to Armand's café and ask Hélène's advice.

Twenty minutes later, still feeling a sense of relief from her decision and brimming with anticipation at seeing James again, Diana walked into the restaurant and was shown to her table. She looked at her watch. She was a quarter of an hour early.

She was about to ask a waiter to fetch her a

374

newspaper when she remembered the envelope in her bag.

★ ★ ★

Hélène was hurrying to the bank to deliver her morning's takings before they closed for lunch, when she saw Diana cross the road ahead of her and disappear into the doorway of La Petite Maison.

Hélène came to an abrupt halt. Had the Englishwoman read the letter yet? Surely not. If she had, Diana would have come straight to the flower-market that morning, Hélène was certain of it. Besides, even though she had only caught the briefest glimpse of her just now, Diana looked happy, even excited.

No, she had not read the letter.

Hélène was a woman of instinct and she knew with a calm certainty why Diana had come to this restaurant.

She was meeting *Le Loup Anglais*.

Hélène forgot about going to the bank. She spun on her heel and walked as quickly as she could back to the flower-market. Armand must come with her to La Petite Maison — now, this instant. Perhaps *Le Loup* had yet to arrive; there might still be a chance to speak to Diana alone.

She must hurry.

★ ★ ★

Diana dropped the final page of Hélène's letter onto the table in front of her and stared at her reflection in the mirrored wall opposite. The blood had drained from her face; her bright red lipstick was stark against the pallor of her cheeks.

She felt as if she had been physically struck over the head. Black spots danced before her eyes and she felt so dizzy she had to grip the edge of the table to keep herself upright.

Disjointed fragments of the letter kept flashing through her mind like lurid neon signs:

He will want to take advantage of you . . . one of the cruellest men on the Riviera . . . stabbed in the eye . . . do not believe any of the lies I am certain he will tell you.

She realised with dull horror that from the moment she had begun reading the pages, she had not doubted their veracity; not in the slightest. It wasn't just that she could think of no reason for Hélène to lie (nor Armand, who she saw had signed the letter too); it was as if Hélène's careful, deliberate sentences shed ever-strengthening light on something she now realised had been in plain sight all along, ever since James stepped from his taxi and she'd spun him around to face her.

That expression on his face — the fleeting, feral snarl — so swiftly replaced by . . . by what? A beautiful mask?

Later, there had been the craven behaviour of the Negresco's manager, and of the waiter there — not to mention the boy who'd served them yesterday at La Colombe d'Or. All three men were clearly terrified of James. Why hadn't she recognised their fear of him for what it was?

Well she had, of course — but she had allowed

376

James to explain it away. It was as if she'd been hypnotised — willingly so. She'd wanted to believe everything, anything, he said to her; how he lived in Nice now, why he'd gone there, what he'd had to do to survive.

Now, she replayed James's account of his actions the day he was shot down. How had she allowed herself to be persuaded to accept his justification of shooting the doctor? It was cold-blooded murder, obviously. And the bed-ridden old woman upstairs? Diana shuddered. She was certain that if she made enquiries in the village of . . . what was it? *Licques* — she would learn that a double murder had been committed in the doctor's house that afternoon.

Diana was overwhelmed by a devastating sense of loss. In its way, it was more painful than the day at the Dower House when she was told that James was dead. Hélène's neatly written pages had utterly dissolved the image of the husband she thought she had found again. That man had evaporated into nothingness in the time it took to read a letter.

A new and terrible question came unbidden to her. What if the James she had married; the James she had fallen in love with and been besotted by, had been a carefully crafted illusion, too? If he hadn't been shot down, and they had had some sort of married life together, how long might it have been before cracks began to appear in his smooth façade?

They had never really spent time together, had they? A few dates, and those days leading up to their wedding. If you put it all together, it wouldn't add up to much more than a week.

A whirlwind romance indeed. How could she ever have thought she knew him?

Such a silly girl. Such a ridiculously stupid girl.

Diana bowed her head. Her tears fell onto the white tablecloth where they formed dark, spreading circles.

A few moments passed. She heard steps behind her and turned to see Hélène and Armand walking over to her table. Both wore set, determined expressions.

'Diana!' called Hélène. 'We have sent you a —'

'Yes,' Diana said dully. She wiped her eyes with a napkin. 'I know. I've just read it.' Slowly, she stood up.

Hélène reached out to her, taking the younger woman's hands in her own. 'I am so, so sorry, my dear. This is a terrible thing for you to learn, terrible. You do not doubt us?'

Diana shook her head. 'No. No, I don't.' Her voice sounded thick and strange to her, as if she had not spoken for days.

Hélène looked at her, her eyes full of pity. 'Then you must be in much pain, I fear.'

'I don't know how to describe the way I feel . . . How did you know I was here, Hélène?'

'I saw you walk in. You are here to meet him, *oui?*'

Diana nodded miserably.

Armand spoke for the first time. 'Then we must leave at once. *Allons-y.*'

They were too late. The restaurant's revolving

door turned and James Blackwell entered the room. He didn't see them immediately, turning to the head waiter and asking for his table. The man gestured in their direction, and the next moment James's gaze fell on the three figures who were staring at him from across the room.

He cocked his head to one side, taking in the little tableau. Then he nodded to himself before crossing the floor to them, smiling faintly.

'Well, well,' he said, bowing slightly to Diana and Hélène. 'Not quite the *tête-à-tête* I was expecting, Diana.' He turned to the café owner. 'Armand. I had no idea you could afford to eat in restaurants like this. I feel it may be time to review our arrangement.'

Armand made no reply. James looked at Hélène and smiled engagingly at her. 'I don't think we've met, *madame*, but your face is familiar.'

Hélène regarded him without fear. 'You may have seen me in the flower-market, *monsieur*. I have a small stall there. Doubtless if it was a larger affair I would have come to your attention.'

James's smile broadened. 'Indeed you would. We'd be old friends by now, I think. Like Armand and me.'

Armand cleared his throat. 'We are not friends, *monsieur*.'

James frowned. 'No? Well, perhaps you're right. Business and friendship don't really mix, do they?'

For the first time, he looked directly at Diana, and her alone.

'Well, Diana? Would you mind telling me what's going on? I take it our lunch is cancelled. You don't look very pleased to see me, I must say.'

A faint but unmistakable tone of mockery in his voice sparked a new response in Diana. Her misery and dislocation were replaced by a surge of anger so sudden and unexpected that she struggled to speak. When words eventually came, she was surprised at how calm she sounded.

'Armand, Hélène — would you wait outside for me, please? I'll join you shortly. Don't worry, I'll be perfectly all right.' She indicated the only other occupied table, where four men in business suits sat quietly talking. 'There are others here.'

Reluctantly, the pair left the restaurant. When they'd gone, Diana turned to James, her eyes shining with fury.

'Have you spoken one word of truth to me, James? Ever? About anything? Anything at all?'

'Ah.' He folded his arms and sighed. 'I can see you've been got at, Diana. Your new friends have been telling you things about me, haven't they?'

'At least they've given you a name. You still haven't told me what you're called.'

'Well, I have a few names here, I told you that. Which one did they supply you with?'

She ignored the question.

'You've been deceiving me from the moment we met. You didn't want my money to help your businesses and keep people in their jobs. You've given it straight to the Mafia, haven't you? You're a gangster, James. An out-and-out criminal. I've heard about some of the things you've done.

You're disgusting. You disgust me.'

He looked at her steadily. 'You didn't find me so disgusting yesterday.'

Her blow surprised them both. Diana stepped back, breathing rapidly, the imprint of her palm and outstretched fingers livid on James's cheek. He shook his head quickly from side to side. 'Good for you, darling. That's the spirit.'

'Don't you dare call me that. Don't you dare call me *anything*. I never want to set eyes on you again. Who are you, James? What kind of a monster have you become? What did you think you were doing with me this week? Did you honestly think I wouldn't find out about you; that it wouldn't end like this? What was the *point*?'

He shrugged. 'Does there always have to be a point? Come on, Diana, we were both confounded to find each other again, and of course all the old feelings came back. We both gave in to them. You, every bit as much as me. And you did your share of the chasing, didn't you? It wasn't me calling *you* at one in the morning, was it? I didn't drag you kicking and screaming into bed in the middle of the afternoon. It's not my fault if you have a boring marriage.'

Diana moved as if to strike him again. 'Don't you dare talk about my marriage. Douglas is worth a thousand of you. He's a wonderful, decent man. He's not a murderer.'

James sighed again. 'I explained all that to you. I had no choice; the doctor was — '

Diana jabbed him hard in the chest with her

forefinger, aware that the thrilled businessmen were covertly watching the two of them from their table. A lovers' tiff. Who knew the English could be so passionate?

'I'm not talking about the poor man you shot in the back. But while we're on that subject, what *really* happened to his mother, James? You killed her too, didn't you? *Didn't you?*'

After the briefest of hesitations, he nodded. 'Yes. But I don't expect you to understand why.'

'You're bloody right there; I wouldn't, not if you spent a year justifying your sordid actions. But tell me, James: how many other people have you murdered since? Are we into double figures yet?'

He held both palms up. 'Sorry, Diana. I know confession is good for the soul but there is a limit.'

'Soul? That's a good one. You *have* no soul!'

He considered the point for a few moments. 'No, I don't think I do. We at least agree on that, Diana. I came to that conclusion myself a long, long time ago. Before we even met. First met, I mean.'

She gathered up her bag and stuffed Hélène's letter inside it.

'I can't bear to look at you a second longer. I can't stand to be in the same room as you, or breathe the same air as you. You revolt me. But I've one more question and then we're never going to speak again.'

'If it's about the money, I'll — '

She gave a bitter laugh. 'Save your breath,

James. I know I'll never see a centime of that again.'

Infuriatingly, she felt tears beginning to prick her eyes once more, but with an enormous effort, she managed to blink them back.

'When we first met — before the war, I mean — and when we married, did you love me at all? Or was I just a poor little rich girl, someone you wanted for her daddy's money? Tell me the truth, James. For once in your depraved life, try to do that.'

He nodded. 'Very well. I suppose I owe you that.'

He closed his eyes and stood in silence before her for so long that she thought he was playing another of his games. But as she was about to walk away, his eyes opened again.

'I didn't love you at first,' he told her calmly. 'You're quite right, Diana. I saw you as an opportunity. If your father hadn't been a wealthy man I would never have pursued you so . . . adroitly. *Wait.*' He caught her arm as she turned away, her face tight with the pain she couldn't conceal.

'Wait, Diana. I'm not finished. When I came back to you after Dunkirk, there was — I don't know . . . something different. Something I'd never felt before.

'I agreed with you just now — I don't have a soul. I don't think I was born with one, actually. But back then, that summer, just for a moment, I wondered. Something seemed to catch light inside me. Then I got shot down and whatever it might have been, quietly went out. If we'd not been parted . . . well, I do sometimes wonder if I might have found a different path. Because of you, Diana.'

He released her arm and gave a slight shrug. 'I'm afraid that's the best I can do.'

Abruptly, she put out her hand, and after a moment, he shook it. For some reason it seemed the most natural thing in the world for them to do.

'Goodbye, James.'

'Goodbye, Diana.'

In spite of herself, she could not help glancing back over her shoulder as she reached the revolving doors that led to the street.

He had taken her chair and was rocking gently back on it, staring at the restaurant's ceiling. He appeared to be lost in thought. Then, as if suddenly aware of her scrutiny, he turned and regarded her. His face was expressionless. After a moment he gave her an absent wave, more of dismissal than farewell.

Diana pushed through the doors and disappeared on to the busy pavement outside.

★ ★ ★

Behind her, James Blackwell resumed his gentle rocking back and forth.

54

A few minutes later, James Blackwell was back at his apartment. He checked his watch. There should definitely be enough time.

He swept his car keys from a marble-topped table — this was no job for a taxi — and walked quickly to the phone, dialling a number from memory. When the man at the other end picked up, James was brief.

'I want you to open up the other apartment — now, this afternoon. Get it ready for two people. And buy some food — enough for a few days. When you're finished, lock up and don't come back. I want it all done by four o'clock at the latest. Oh, and make sure all the shutters and blinds are closed.'

He hung up without waiting for a reply and headed for the lift that serviced the flats' basement car park.

* * *

Stella was beginning to wish she hadn't come. The stable had given her their fattest, slowest pony, and however firmly she kicked its flanks with her heels, it refused to break into even the vaguest semblance of a trot.

There were six other girls in the riding party. They were all French and friendly enough — one of them was Maxine's younger sister

Bernadette, whom she knew well — but once they set out for the waterfall and their picnic lunch, her pony stubbornly insisted on bringing up the rear and she couldn't join in the others' conversation. This was boring. Even the scenery was boring. The trail led through a rocky forest; the trees blocked any view of the mountains that surrounded them, the first stepping-stones to the Alps. They could be anywhere.

Stella wondered whether she should just turn around and go back to the stables. There was a telephone there and she could call her mother, or Maxine, and ask one of them to come and collect her earlier than planned. Even if they weren't in, there was plenty to keep her occupied until her mother arrived at five o'clock, as arranged. The stables had an annexe that served as a stud farm and she'd noticed a magnificent black stallion grazing in the paddock, with several colts larking around in the adjoining one.

Perhaps the owners would let her do some grooming, too.

She made up her mind. 'I'm going back to the stables,' she called after the others. 'À *bientôt!*'

One of the older girls who was leading the party stopped and carefully turned her pony round. She looked surprised.

'Why, Stella?' she called back. 'What's the matter?'

'It's this pony,' Stella replied as she slowly wheeled her reluctant mount in the opposite direction. 'He's so slow and lazy. I'm bored, that's all.'

The teenager nodded in sympathy. 'What

386

about your lunch?' She tapped her saddlebag. 'Don't you want it?'

'No, thanks.' She wasn't hungry yet.

'Well, all right. *Au revoir*, Stella.'

Stella waved goodbye and headed back down the winding trail. In a few moments, she was lost from view.

★ ★ ★

Diana used the telephone in Armand's café to call Douglas. Luckily, he was taking lunch at his desk.

'Darling, what a nice surprise. Why are you ringing?'

She took a deep breath. 'I need you to come back from Marseilles, Douglas. Today. Right now, if possible. I've been very, very foolish and I must talk to you. I need your advice, and — your forgiveness.'

There was a long silence before Douglas spoke again, so quietly that Diana could barely hear him.

'There's another man.'

Diana closed her eyes. She was burning with guilt.

'Yes. But only for a very short time, and not any more. It's over. Completely. But it's — it's nothing like you can possibly imagine, my dearest. It's terribly complicated and . . . unlikely. I still can't quite believe any of it; it's as if I've been trapped in some sort of grotesque fantasy and I've only just escaped.'

This time the silence lasted so long that she

387

thought he'd quietly replaced the receiver.

'Douglas . . . are you there?'

'Yes, of course. Do you still want to be my wife, Diana? I must know, here and now. I'll give you a divorce if you want.'

The question threw her off balance. She had expected many things — anger, coldness, even tears. Not this swift appraisal of the situation and the most logical of enquiries, asked calmly, even sympathetically.

How could she have done this to him?

'Yes. Yes, I do. Want to stay as your wife, I mean . . . but you may be the one asking for the divorce, Douglas.'

'Can't you tell me more about it now?' he asked in the same quiet tone. 'Is it about this man you've been having lunch with? Who is he?'

Diana hesitated. She desperately wanted to have this conversation face-to-face.

'When I tell you, you'll understand why you have to come home,' she said at last. 'You *will* come home, straight away, please, Douglas?'

'Yes, of course. I love you, Diana, whatever it is that you've done. But who is this man? You must tell me. Do I know him?'

Diana rested her forehead against the cool glass of the phone booth's window before replying.

'In a manner of speaking, yes, you do. You've known *of* him since first we met.'

He waited.

She pulled her head back from the glass and rubbed her eyes with the back of one hand. Suddenly, she felt extraordinarily tired.

'His name is James. James Blackwell. Douglas, it's my first husband. He's alive. He isn't dead at all.'

★ ★ ★

By the time Stella got back to the stables she was beginning to feel hungry, and regretted refusing the earlier offer of a packed lunch. Perhaps there would be something to eat at the office here.

She tied her morose pony to the hitching post and fetched it a bucket of water to drink. 'There. You don't deserve this, you lazy creature.'

The animal ignored her, flicking its ears as it drank.

To her disappointment, there was no sign of the stallion in his paddock and even the colts had disappeared. The place was almost eerily quiet. She went into the office and rang the little hand-bell that stood on the counter.

'Hello! Is anyone here?'

There was no reply, and after ringing the bell again, she wandered disconsolately outside. She was getting very hungry now. There must be someone around who could give her something to eat.

'Hello! *Hello!*' Her voice echoed off the corrugated-iron storage sheds that were dotted around the compound. She was about to call again, more loudly, when she heard the slamming of a gate in the main paddock behind the office, followed by the brisk clip-clop of horse's hooves. The next moment the black stallion appeared from behind the building, with the stables' owner, an athletic-looking middle-aged man, in the saddle. When he saw Stella, he pulled up his horse and stared at her in surprise.

'Mam'selle Stella? Quelle surprise!'

Stella began to explain but he waved her to be silent, breaking into good English.

'But how did you know to come back? I was coming to get you.'

Now it was Stella's turn to look surprised. 'What? I only came back because my pony was so slow.'

He nodded his understanding. 'Ah, now I see. Well, anyway, it is most fortunate, as your father has come to collect you. It seems something has occurred and you must go home earlier than expected.'

Stella was mystified. 'My father? You mean Douglas — he's my stepfather. But what is he doing here? I thought he was in Marseilles.'

The rider shrugged, and dismounted. 'It seems not. I told him to wait in his car while I rode out to find you.' He pointed over her shoulder. 'It is in the little car park behind those trees. The one where your mother left you this morning.' He looked at her. 'Have you had lunch?'

Stella shook her head. 'No, but it's all right, we can stop at a café or something on the way home.' She frowned. 'Nothing's happened, has it? Nothing bad, I mean?'

The man shrugged again. 'I think not. Your father — I am sorry, your stepfather — seems in pleasant spirits.' He smiled at her. 'And so would I be if I drove a car like his! I am very jealous.'

'Jealous?'

'Yes, of course! It is beautiful, so dashing and *sportif*. A young man's car. It suits your stepfather very well, I think.'

Stella looked at him in astonishment. Douglas could hardly be described as a young man. As for his car, it was a large and stately Rolls-Royce. Luxurious, certainly. No one would call it sporting.

What on *earth* was going on?

⋆ ⋆ ⋆

As he drove through the cobbled streets of Vence, James wondered if anyone at the stables up in the hills behind the town would know who he was.

He thought it extremely unlikely. His business was almost exclusively confined to Nice, with one or two newer operations in the neighbouring town of Cagnes sur Mer. He hardly ever went to Vence and when he did, he was not recognised. It was three or four miles from St Paul de Vence and the Colombe d'Or, where only the staff knew him anyway.

He was as anonymous here as the people taking their siestas behind the blue and green shuttered windows of the old stone houses that lined both sides of the narrow road.

He swung the long-nosed Jaguar XK120 towards Col de Vence and the riding school a couple of miles beyond it. The two-seater's powerful 3.5 litre engine gave a throaty roar as he accelerated past a farm truck, and he took the

391

next bend at speed. It felt good to be behind the wheel again. Taxis gave him a necessary anonymity on the daily rounds of his 'clients' in Nice, but being able to afford a coveted car like this was part of what pushed him ever onwards. In recent years he'd been able to afford practically anything he wanted. The apartment, for example. The fashionable artwork he was gradually acquiring. This car. But there was always room for more.

I'm not going to give any of it up, he thought grimly as the Jaguar tore through a dusty village, forcing an oncoming moped off the road, its rider's eyes bulging in terror. Not a single thing.

His back might be to the wall now, but he'd been here before. The day he was shot down. In the weeks afterwards. And when he'd first begun to establish himself in Nice, in the teeth of opposition from the local hoods and arm-twisters. None of it had ever been easy, but he'd always known how to take his chances when they came.

Diana was a perfect example. What an extraordinary turn of luck to run into her again, just when he needed such a huge lump sum — and her husband a multi-millionaire! Thank God for Douglas.

And thank God for Stella.

Between them, Douglas and Stella were going to buy him his ticket into the big time. And who knew? Maybe they'd be good for a shakedown further along the line. That was why he wouldn't ask Douglas for a centime more than he needed now.

No point in killing the golden goose.

The steep mountains that guarded the Alps were now rising before him, their bald heads baking under the sun in a clear blue summer sky. James shifted down a gear as the Jaguar's engine began to labour, and eased back on the throttle. No need to risk overheating.

He'd be there in less than ten minutes.

55

Diana was bewildered.

'What do you mean?' she asked the riding-school's owner. 'Stella's stepfather couldn't possibly have collected her at lunchtime. He was in Marseilles; I spoke to him on the telephone. He was in his office.'

The man shrugged. 'It is as I tell you, *madame*,' he said. 'Your daughter's father said there had been some unexpected event and he was to take her back home.' He looked at his watch. 'This would be about three hours ago, I think.'

Diana stared at him. 'It's not possible,' she said at last. 'Anyway, Stella doesn't have a father. He's ... dead. And her stepfather never describes himself as her father. What's more, she calls him Douglas.'

'Perhaps there has been some misunderstanding, *madame*.'

Diana thought hard. 'What sort of car was he in?' she asked eventually.

'Ah, that is most easy to remember. It was a very expensive black sports saloon — a Jaguar, I think. I was most impressed. And jealous.'

A terrible apprehension began to take hold of her.

'But my husband drives a Rolls-Royce. *Monsieur*, what did this man look like?'

When he described James Blackwell, Diana's world crumbled.

★ ★ ★

Stella walked towards the car. It was facing away from her. The top was down in the sunshine, and she could see a man with blond hair sitting in the driver's seat, his back to her. He was smoking a cigarette and looking towards the Alps proper that towered in the distance, the last remnants of the winter snows gleaming on their jagged peaks.

'*Monsieur?*'

The man turned around.

For a moment, Stella was confused. The face that now smiled at her own was extraordinarily familiar, but she couldn't put a name to it. She wondered for a moment if it was one of her teachers from England, before dismissing the thought. Her mind raced. Who *was* this?

'Hello, Stella.'

A crisp, pleasant voice she did not recognise. Stella moved a little closer to the car.

'Hello. I know you, don't I? But I can't remember your name.'

The smile widened, blue eyes crinkling slightly at the corners.

'That's quite all right, Stella. We've never met before. There's no particular reason you should recognise me — although I'm told on good authority that you keep my photograph by your bed.'

Stella gaped.

That face. The last one she saw every night.

The first one she set eyes on when she woke. For as long as she could remember.

That very morning, she had chatted to the man in the picture as she dressed in her riding clothes, telling him her plans for the day.

Here he was now, in front of her, his blond hair blowing in the warm breeze that rustled the leaves in the trees around them.

He smiled at her again, and took a puff of his cigarette. 'Yes. I think you know who I am now, don't you, Stella?'

Her dead father.

Alive.

Stella's hands were clenched in tight fists. Her breath came in rapid gasps as she fought against the swirling dizziness that threatened to overwhelm her.

He climbed out of the car and stepped carefully toward her. 'It's all right, Stella. I'm not a ghost. I'm your father, my dear. I'm alive. I've come back to you.'

She began to tremble, and spoke in a hoarse voice she did not recognise as her own. 'You can't be. You can't be my father. He's . . . *dead*.' Her hands flew to her mouth.

He spoke very gently. 'Yes, my dear. I know that you and everyone else has believed that for a very long time. Why shouldn't you? After all, my aeroplane was shot down and I never came home.'

Slowly, he extended an arm and touched her shoulder. She flinched, but did not step back from him.

'The thing is, I didn't die, Stella. I lived. It was

a kind of miracle, I think. And for all sorts of reasons, I couldn't come back to your mother. And as for you . . . ' He gave a short laugh. 'As for you, *ma petite*, I didn't even know you existed. Not until your mother told me about you a few days ago.'

Stella looked utterly bewildered. 'My *mother*? You've seen my mother? She knows you're alive as well?'

He nodded. 'Yes, she does. We met quite by accident the other day in the flower-market in Nice. She was as shocked as you are at first. And since then we've been trying to work out a way to tell you about me, and . . . well, this was her idea, actually.'

'What was her idea?'

'For me to meet you like this. We talked it all through this morning. Diana — I'm sorry, your mother — has gone to Marseilles to break the news to your stepfather, and I'm to take you home with me to my apartment. We can get to know each other a bit on the way, and . . . and your mother and Douglas will be along later.'

Stella was still trembling. 'I want my mother. Where is she?'

'I just told you — she's gone to Marseilles to speak to your stepfather. In fact, they're probably on their way back to Nice right now, so we should head off there ourselves. Come along, Stella.' He opened the Jaguar's passenger door for her. 'Hop in.'

She hesitated. 'But — I don't think . . . '

'I know, I know.' He gave her a kind smile. 'You've had a shock. You look exactly as your mother did when we bumped into each other. But she's very glad about it all now. I expect you've noticed how happy she's been of late.'

Stella thought about it. Her mother *had* seemed especially happy in recent days. She'd sung most of the way on the drive up here this morning; silly songs with ridiculous rhymes.

'Yes,' she agreed. 'She came on the roller-coaster with me.'

'Well, there you are then! Don't worry, Stella. You'll soon get used to this. Jump in. I want to know everything about you. Your mother says you're the best girl in the whole wide world.'

'And she and Douglas are coming to your apartment?' she asked him as she climbed uncertainly into the passenger seat.

'Absolutely.' He got behind the wheel. 'They might even be there when we arrive, waiting for us outside. Have you been in a sports car before, Stella?'

She shook her head. 'No.'

'Then this should be fun. Hold tight — this beats any old roller-coaster, I can promise you.' He gunned the engine and the sleek Jaguar roared out of the car park, gravel spraying from the rear wheels. A moment later, the car was speeding down the twisting road that led back to the coast.

Impromptu plans were often the best, James reflected as the car nudged 80mph. They left no time for doubting and questioning one's instincts.

And this one? This one was turning out to be the cleverest he could remember.

Diana took the villa's stairs two at a time. She'd driven back home like a madwoman and ignored a *gendarme*'s frantic hand signals to slow down as she raced through Vence. He'd probably got her number but she couldn't care less.

Now she ran into the master bedroom and frantically pulled out the bottom tray of her jewellery box.

It *had* to be in here.

Sure enough, hidden beneath a heavy double row of pearls was the scrap of paper James had given her with his address and phone number written on it. She hesitated. Should she simply drive straight there, or try calling him first?

Without making a conscious decision, she grabbed the bedside telephone and dialled zero.

'Come on, come *on*,' she muttered beneath her breath. 'Answer, damn you.'

At last the operator came on the line.

'Nice four-six-seven-three, please.' Diana could hear the tremble in her voice. After a moment she heard the ring tone, a repetitive and somehow rather dismal single beep. It went on for nearly a minute before the operator's voice returned.

'There's no answer, *madame*,' she said in English.

Diana slammed down the phone. She was heading back to the stairs when a man's voice floated up from the hall.

'Diana? Where are you? What's going on? You've left your car engine running.'

'DOUGLAS! Thank God you're here!' She practically threw herself downstairs and into his arms, clinging to him tightly.

'Hey, what's this? What's going on, Diana?'

'Oh, Douglas, he's taken her! He's got her somewhere!'

'What? Who's taken who? I don't understand.'

'*James!* He's taken Stella! We've got to find her, Douglas!' She pulled away from him. 'We've got to go there right now and — '

He held up his hands. 'Whoa there, Diana. Slow down. Calm yourself, my dear. I need to know exactly what has happened otherwise I'll be no use to you.'

He led her into the salon and made her sit down on one of the chaise longues, settling himself beside her.

'Now, begin from the beginning. Whatever's happened, you can take a few minutes to explain things calmly. Why do you think James has taken Stella? And when did you first run into him?'

She gulped. 'A few days ago. He got out of a taxi in the flowermarket, right in front of me. I nearly passed out, although to be honest, Douglas, I've suspected he was in Nice for some time. You see, I thought I glimpsed him in a cab back in April, but I'd begun to think I was deluded — that I'd imagined it. It turns out he survived being shot down — a complete fluke — and decided he couldn't face life in a POW camp or any more fighting. So he deserted. He's spent the last eleven years hiding in Nice. Since meeting him again I've been . . . we've been . . . '

Douglas put a hand on her shoulder. 'It's all

400

right, Diana, we can talk about that part later. Tell me about Stella.'

'Well, this morning I drove Stella to the riding school and then — I'm so sorry, Douglas — then I went into Nice to meet James.'

If Douglas was wounded by the information, he concealed it. 'And then?'

'I was early to the restaurant. I remembered that letter you told me about — the one on the mantelpiece. I had it with me in my bag and I decided to read it while I was waiting. It was from some friends of mine who work in the flower-market: Armand — I've told you about him — and a flower-seller called Hélène.' She paused, miserably.

'Well? What did it say?'

Diana bowed her head. 'It said I'd been a complete fool. Not in so many words, but that's what it meant. James has been telling me he's a legitimate businessman here in Nice, and I believed him.' She looked up.

'It turns out he's become a gangster, Douglas. He murders people, or has them murdered for him. Everyone's terrified of him. He runs a protection racket here and he's about to join the Nice Mafia. He tricked me into giving him money for a so-called business deal but he's given it straight to them; some kind of joining fee, I think.'

'I see,' he said quietly. 'How much did you give him?'

She told him and he winced. 'He must be a very persuasive man. You're nobody's fool, Diana.'

She looked at him gratefully. 'Anyway . . . as soon as I'd read the letter, he arrived. Obviously I confronted him and he didn't bother denying any of it. In fact, Douglas, I don't think he gave a damn one way or the other what I thought of him. I was finally seeing the real person I married all those years ago. I feel so *stupid*.'

She clutched her head in her hands. 'How could I have been so taken in? I never once glimpsed the real James — or if I did, I chose to ignore it. Apparently the locals call him *Le Loup Anglais*, but I don't think he's a bit like a wolf. This morning I felt I was in the presence of a snake — cold and calculating and unfeeling. He's vile, Douglas.'

He touched her cheek. 'Don't be too hard on yourself. You were just a girl when you married him. From what you've told me before, you barely knew him. But putting all that to one side, you still haven't told me why you think our girl is with this man.'

When she had finished describing that afternoon's events, Douglas sat deep in thought for several minutes.

'Do you think she went willingly?' he asked at length.

'I have no idea. Probably. He could charm the birds from the trees.'

'What does he look like now? Would she have recognised him, d'you think?'

Diana nodded vigorously. 'Yes, definitely. He's hardly changed at all. God knows what she must have thought when she set eyes on him.'

'Poor kid.' He stood up. 'Right, let's go find

her. I'm sure she's in no danger. He is her father, after all. He'll be playing some stupid game or other. Do you know where he lives?'

She got to her feet and handed him the note she had been clutching throughout the conversation. 'This is his address — and before you ask, Douglas, no, I haven't been there. In fact,' she closed her eyes before continuing, 'in fact, it only happened once. I know that even once is unforgivable, but it's the truth.'

To her horror she saw his face crumple and tears suddenly drop from his eyes. He made no sound.

'Oh God, Douglas, I am *so, so sorry*. Whatever have I done to you?' She threw her arms around him and held him until she felt him stiffen his shoulders and try to pull away. She released him and he cleared his throat.

'I'm all right, Diana. Really I am. Will be, anyway.' He took a large white handkerchief from his breast pocket and blew hard. 'These things can happen in any marriage, I know that,' he continued. 'And anyway, it's not as if you went off with any Tom, Dick or Harry, is it? He was once your husband.'

She stared at him. 'You're incredible, Douglas. I don't deserve you.'

He ushered her to the door. 'I don't know about that. But I'll tell you one thing. *You* certainly don't deserve *him*. Come on. Let's go get our girl.'

56

James had bought the second apartment some years earlier. He thought of it as his office; he preferred to do business there rather than in the much larger, more luxurious set of rooms behind the Promenade des Anglais. This was chiefly because of an incident that had taken place there just after the war. A 'client' behind with his payments had been summoned to a meeting, and by the end of the interview there was so much blood on an expensive Persian rug, James had had to have it destroyed. But the unmistakable acid aroma of fear had lingered for days and he decided he must separate home and business.

The 'office' comprised five smallish rooms — a kitchenette, lounge, two bedrooms and a bathroom. All were simply, even sparsely, furnished. The flat was in a slightly shabby, turn-of-the-century brick-built block not far from the railway station. There was no parking provided, and as the XK120 turned into the narrow street, James kept an eye open for a space. He found one fifty yards from his block, slid the Jaguar into it and switched off the ignition.

'Are Mummy and Douglas here yet?'

It was the first time Stella had spoken since they reached the outskirts of Nice. James could tell she was still uneasy; his attempts to jolly her along and draw her out had been pretty much blunted by her taciturn responses. He decided she was still in mild shock after being confronted with her long-dead father. He didn't blame the kid for that, but he didn't particularly care either. The main thing was he'd got her here, and once she was securely inside the flat, he could make his next move.

'No, I can't see them. Don't worry, they'll be here soon. Come on, let's go up.'

Stella obediently got out of the car and walked with her father towards the apartment block. He looked at her covertly as they went. In profile, he could see how much she resembled her mother. If Diana looked like a younger Vivien Leigh, her daughter had something of the rising American actress Elizabeth Taylor about her when she'd been a child star. There was the same, determined jaw that Diana had, and although mother and daughter's eyes were similarly shaped, Stella's were the colour of James's. The nose, too, was his.

But most of her similarity to her father, James decided, lay in her composure and bearing. There was a slight haughtiness about her; an unwillingness to reveal too much of herself or what she was thinking. He approved of that. She was certainly giving nothing away as they climbed the steps to the apartment block's front doors.

The concierge nodded coldly at them as they walked into the small entrance lobby. It was strange, James thought as he pressed the button for the lift. Nice's concierges, almost all old, wizened women like this one, were the only people who never seemed remotely afraid of him. Perhaps that was because they'd seen it all: the human tide that endlessly ebbed and flowed past their little cubicles held no surprises any more.

The lift stopped at the fourth floor and James led his daughter to the steel door that opened into his flat. He'd replaced the original wooden one as a basic security precaution. Not that any burglar in his right mind would think of breaking into this place.

Stella was disappointed when she stepped inside. The flat was dreary. A little entrance corridor opened onto the small sitting room, with a cheap sofa and armchairs, and a bare wooden table next to a door leading onto the tiny balcony. There were no books on the single shelf that ran the length of one wall.

Stella gave him a measured look before moving into the kitchenette. There was a knife block with three kitchen knives and three empty slots. The oven was tiny, *Baby Belling* stencilled on the door, and an ancient fridge hummed loudly in one corner. Stella opened it. It held three brown-paper carrier bags. She peered into them in turn. They contained milk, wine, bread and cheese. Stella closed the door again and went back into the *salon*, where James was waiting.

'You don't live here, do you.' It was a statement, not a question.

James nodded in agreement. 'Well observed, Stella. Your mother's right — you are indeed a clever girl.'

She stared at him for a few moments, sizing him up.

'They're not coming, are they? Mummy and Douglas. That was just a story.'

He was impressed. She was old beyond her years, this one. She was as bright as her mother and as wary as himself.

He smiled at her. 'I can see I can afford to be direct with you, Stella. Yes. You're quite right; they're not coming. Not just yet, anyway.' He motioned for her to sit. She ignored him.

'Why am I here? Why did you trick me?'

'Please sit down, Stella. I can explain everything.'

She chose the chair furthest from him.

'Good girl. Would you like a drink, or something to eat?'

'No. I want to know what's happening. If you don't tell me, I'll scream and someone will come. I can scream really loudly.'

He gave her a regretful smile. 'Firstly, Stella, no one will come. Look — the windows are double glazed. The front door is very thick too, but I expect you noticed that.'

'I did.'

'Good for you! Secondly, even if someone *did* hear you screaming, they'd pretend that they hadn't. There's been quite a lot of screaming in these rooms here over time, much of it far louder than anything you could manage, I assure you. My neighbours have learned that it's best not to interfere. In any case, there's no need to scream. I told you I'd explain things.'

She glared at him. 'I'm not afraid of you.'

407

'And neither do you look as if you are, Stella. Bravo. You're a chip off the old block.'

She said nothing.

He lit a cigarette and gestured with it towards the kitchenette. 'I'm going to pour myself a drink. Are you allowed wine at home?'

'Don't be stupid. I'm only ten.'

He grinned at that and went to the fridge. When he returned, he held a glass of rosé for himself and one of Vichy water for her. She looked at it suspiciously.

'Don't worry,' he told her. 'It's not poisoned. Take it.'

She placed it carefully on the floor by her feet, not taking her eyes off him. He could feel her contempt for him and silently applauded his daughter's spirit.

'Are you going to tell me what's going on or aren't you?' she asked. 'I suppose you feel ever so clever and proud of yourself, tricking a ten-year-old.'

He shook his head. 'No, I don't feel proud of that. But it was necessary, Stella, I'm afraid.' He paused for a moment, considering how much to tell her.

'OK, here's the thing. I owe some rather unpleasant men rather a lot of money. Your mother kindly gave me some to help me — just yesterday, as it happens — but I need quite a bit more.' He sipped his wine. 'This morning,' he continued, 'your mother was told some rather unfortunate facts about me, and I don't think she's going to lend me any more of her money, to be honest. So I decided — '

'You decided to kidnap me.'

He laughed. 'Excellent! I wish I'd known about you a long time ago, Stella. I think you and I would make a good team. Perhaps one day we shall.'

She stared out of the window in silence. James took his time, finishing his wine and cigarette before continuing: 'So, you're to stay here until your mother, or your stepfather, sees their way clear to lending me what I need. Then you can go home.' He stroked his chin and gazed at the ceiling, choosing his next words.

'But I'm afraid you can't remain in this room, Stella; I don't want you banging on the windows and waving and making all sorts of fuss. I have a bedroom all ready for you. There isn't a window, I'm afraid, but I doubt you'll be there for long. I have a feeling all this will be sorted out very soon. Come along.'

Stella stood. Her eyes glittered like her mother's had earlier that day, and for the first time that he could remember, James felt disconcerted. There was enough of himself in this child, he realised, to throw him off balance if he wasn't careful.

'I'll do what you say because I have to,' she told him evenly. 'You're bigger than me. But I hate you. I *hate* you! You're nothing like the father I thought I had. I thought my father was a hero. But you're just a cheat and a liar and a bully. I wish you *had* died. I wish I'd never set eyes on you. I bet Mummy does, too. You're a horrible, horrible man.'

He recovered his poise sufficiently to make an

409

ironic bow. 'All perfectly true, I'm afraid. I can only apologise, Stella, for my failings. Perhaps one day I can convince you that I have some good points too. And now, if you'd just . . . ' He gestured towards a bedroom door that led off from the *salon*. 'In there, please.'

She stalked past him and slammed the door behind her. The click of his key in the lock was followed almost at once by muted sobs from within.

He put his ear to the door.

They were not the sounds of defeat or fear.

James Blackwell's daughter was weeping in pure, undiluted rage.

★　★　★

'He's not here. Neither of them is.'

Douglas delivered the news to Diana as he slid behind the wheel of the Rolls-Royce, which he'd parked on the apron of the luxury apartments behind the Promenade des Anglais. He'd insisted she wait in the car while he went in to speak to the concierge. After a thick wad of francs was produced, the woman had shown him up to James Blackwell's empty apartment.

Now Diana gave a little wail. 'Oh God! Where can she be, Douglas? What is he doing with her? We have to go to the police!'

He started the engine and pulled out onto the road before speaking.

'From what you told me on the way here, I don't think that would do the slightest bit of good. He's got the *gendarmerie* in his pocket,

410

hasn't he? Anyway, he's Stella's father. He'd just say he was spending time with his long-lost daughter, and even if Stella told a different story, the police wouldn't pay any attention. I'm afraid we're on our own, Diana.'

She stared helplessly through the windscreen as they joined the evening traffic on the Promenade. 'What are we going to do?'

Her husband drove in silence for a minute. 'Right, here's my assessment,' he said finally. 'He's got a pressing debt to settle with the local Mafia, correct?'

* * *

Diana tried to think as calmly as she could. 'Yes. After my confrontation with him today, Armand and Hélène filled me in on a lot more detail. They say the word is that he has a very short time left to come up with the money, otherwise the Mafia will simply take his business from him. I suppose they might even kill him. He's under enormous pressure.'

'How do they know all this? I thought the Mafia were a secretive lot.'

'Not when they have an opportunity to show what they're capable of,' she replied. 'If they can be seen to stamp on *Le Loup Anglais* good and hard, they might even get some gratitude. Armand actually said he'd prefer dealing with the Mafia than with James, as they're more flexible. That tells you a lot about my first husband, doesn't it?'

'It certainly does. Well, it's obvious what's

411

happening now. You tumbled to the kind of chap he really is before he could get any more money from you, and — '

'But I don't *have* any more money,' she interrupted. 'I gave him just about everything in my account. He knows that.'

'That's exactly my point, Diana. However, he knows you're married to a wealthy man, doesn't he? He was probably planning to persuade you to 'borrow' my chequebook and make him out a cheque. Forge my signature, and so on.'

Diana was shocked. 'I would never have agreed to do that!'

'Of course you wouldn't. But in any case, he's lost that option completely, now that you know him for what he is. So he's grabbed Stella and you can bet your bottom dollar he'll be on the phone this evening suggesting a cosy little exchange. A nice big bag of cash in return for her. So we need to get back to the villa and take his call.'

He switched lanes and took the turn-off to St Paul de Vence, leaving the palm trees of the Promenade behind them and heading towards the pine-clad foothills that rose immediately behind the coastal plain. The sun was setting over the mountains to the west, and late-evening cloud over their summits was flushed pink. In a couple of hours it would be dark.

Diana was filled with a sudden premonition. What was happening now was incredible, but beyond this moment lay — what, exactly? Instinct told her that something was about to reach fulfilment; completion. An ending.

She knew it in her heart, irrefutably, and she shivered.

Douglas glanced towards her as the road began to rise into the hills. 'What are you thinking?'

Diana gazed at her lap. 'I'm thinking that I've put Stella in great danger, Douglas. If I hadn't been so stupid, if I'd told you everything in the first place, from the moment I thought I saw James, we wouldn't be here now, would we? I've been so selfish and foolish. And now, if you're right, and I pray that you are, we're being blackmailed. It's extortion pure and simple, isn't it? You're going to have to pay a huge ransom for Stella, and it's all my fault.'

He snorted. 'Pay that scoundrel? You've got it all wrong, Diana. I'm not going to give that creature my money. Not a single penny. He can whistle for it.'

★　★　★

The volcanic argument that erupted in the car intensified when they reached the villa. Diana had never felt so helpless and terrified and enraged in the same moment.

Douglas, however, was intractable. James, he insisted, had no intention of harming Stella. She was his own daughter, for God's sake. Even the Mafia didn't kidnap and murder their own children. This was all a ruse; the last throw of the dice by a desperate man. As soon as James realised that he, Douglas, had his number, Stella would be released unharmed and her father would seek another way out of his current difficulties. It was obvious. James Blackwell didn't know it yet, but he was going up a dead end.

Diana wanted to strangle him.

'Haven't you heard a *word* I've been telling you about him? He's a cold-blooded murderer, Douglas! He told me himself he doesn't think he possesses a soul! Stella is in terrible danger every minute she's with him, wherever they may be. You're talking about him as if he's some sort of businessman who makes rational decisions. He's nothing of the kind. I think he may be insane!'

They were on the marble stairs of the villa. Douglas was pale with anger, his sparse hair awry.

'And *I'm* telling *you* that Stella isn't in the slightest danger! This man is playing games with us in exactly the same way he's played games with you, Diana, right from the first day you met him all those years ago. I'm sorry, but I'm not falling for it. And don't you lecture me on business. That's my field. James Blackwell — James Blackguard, more like — is just another shark. I've been dealing with his type all my life. He's a chancer. But he *won't* harm his daughter. No father would.'

To his shock and astonishment, Diana reached out with both hands and gripped his ears, yanking them back and forth as hard as she could. He howled in pain.

'A chancer?' she screamed into his face. 'A *chancer*? What are you talking about, Douglas?

He's not some spiv on the make! He's one of the most feared men on the Riviera! He doesn't *know* Stella! He didn't even know she existed until this week! She's just a convenient bloody pawn in his hideous game! Can't you *see?*' She gave one last desperate heave before releasing him.

He rubbed his ears, panting, before managing: 'I see this as a time for cool heads, not a screaming match. That *bloody* hurt, Diana.' His Highland accent was more pronounced than she had ever heard it before.

He continued massaging his ears. 'Let's both calm down, shall we? This isn't achieving anything. Anyway, you haven't let me finish. I'm not going to tell him to go hang and slam the phone down on him, for Christ's sake.'

The unexpected blasphemy startled her. Douglas never took his Lord's name in vain. 'What do you mean?' she demanded.

He sighed. 'If you'd just simmer down, and give me a chance to explain — you haven't stopped yelling at me since we were in the car. And I've no idea what we're doing here on the stairs. Come away into the *salon*. I don't know about you, but I need a drink.'

* * *

Douglas took a gulp of scotch, and motioned to his wife to do the same.

'It's like this, Diana. The police here are no good to us, we both know that, so we have to fall back on our own resources. I propose stalling

415

when Blackwell phones and makes his demands. I'll tell him it'll take me time to get the money together; I'll feed him some rubbish or other. Meanwhile, I'll commission a private detective agency to find out his and Stella's whereabouts. I'll take care of it first thing in the morning. I know of two good bureaux down here, one in Nice, the other in Cannes. I've used them to check out a couple of companies I wasn't all that happy about doing business with. They're very good.'

He took another sip from his tumbler. 'Come to think of it, I'll hire them both and offer a bonus to the one that tracks the swine down first. I give it twenty-four hours before one or the other nails him. Then we can — '

Diana groaned and buried her face in her hands.

'Oh, Douglas — you're a good man, but you simply don't understand, do you? If the police are frightened of him, do you seriously think private detectives will have the guts to take him on? He *kills* people. If he doesn't do it personally — and trust me, he has, he's admitted it — he has others do it for him. I've told you all this.'

Her husband bristled. 'Well I'm sorry, but I think you're wrong. My plan has a great deal to commend it. You greatly overestimate this unpleasant fellow's capacities. And I must say, Diana, that I'm somewhat offended by your — '

'This is about Stella!' she exploded. 'My daughter! Stop being such a pompous prat, Douglas! I want you to give James *exactly* what he asks for, so we can get her back. Then you can

416

hire all the bloody private detectives you like to track him down, although God knows what they or you will do if they manage to do that. Ask him for my money back? Sue him? Have him roughed up? You have no idea what we're up against. Can't you *see*? It's he who holds all the cards.'

The phone began to ring. They both stared at it.

'*Please*, Douglas.'

He stepped towards the telephone table and picked up the receiver. 'Yes?' He listened intently.

When he replied, he was laconic, as though he were closing an inconsequential business deal.

'Yes, I think I can manage that, under the circumstances — although of course I shall require some form of guarantee, you understand. But I need a little time to organise the finances. Say, forty-eight hours?'

Another pause. Douglas again. 'Well, these things take time. I can — '

Diana saw his hand suddenly tighten on the receiver.

'What? But I'm trying to explain to you, I'm perfectly happy to do this, I simply require — What? What did you say?'

Diana saw her husband visibly pale.

'Now look, I'm not going to listen to these kinds of threats. I — NO! Don't hang up! What? Yes, she's here. Of course. One moment.'

He turned, shaken, to his wife. 'He wants to speak to you.' He held the telephone towards her, avoiding eye contact.

417

Diana crossed the room and snatched the receiver from him. 'James. It's me.'

'Diana. Your husband is a stupid prick. Tell him I know exactly what he's doing. I want the money tomorrow night without fail. I'll call again in the morning with the details. Once it's been handed over, Stella will be sent by taxi to the Negresco. You can pick her up there.'

'You bastard. How can you do this to her? She's your daughter! I insist on speaking to her — now!'

He sighed. 'I honestly couldn't give a tuppeny damn if she was the Queen of Sheba and I was her misbegotten old dad. Currently Stella's fine, trust me. And I'll make you a guarantee. If the money doesn't materialise at the time and place of my choosing, our daughter will be delivered by taxi to the Negresco.'

Diana's head swam. 'What? I don't understand you. You're confusing me. You'll give her back in *any* event?'

'Well, up to a point, Diana. Tell me, is Stella left-handed or right-handed?'

'*What*? What has that to do with anything? She's . . . she's right-handed. Why?'

She thought he was coughing, until she realised he was laughing.

'Then I'll play fair. If Dougal — dammit, *Douglas* — doesn't do his stepfatherly duty, it'll be our daughter's left hand that's delivered in a paper bag to the Negresco tomorrow night. I'll cut it off myself.'

The line went dead.

57

Douglas was shaken by his conversation with James and his eyes widened when Diana told him what he'd threatened. But he was a stubborn man.

'I know this is extremely distressing, but that's how he means it to be. He's all bluff, Diana. You have to face these types down.'

She closed her eyes.

'No, Diana, listen to me! I'm telling you, by this time tomorrow he'll have realised he's backing a losing horse and Stella will be safe home with us. But I understand how you must be feeling, so look, this is what I'll do. I'll go into Nice and Cannes right now, tonight, and get both those agencies on the case before midnight.

'I know you say they'll be frightened of him, but it's possible to buy courage, you know. I'll promise to make it worth their while. And heck, if necessary, I'll double whatever it is he pays the cops to look the other way. They'll look *his* way then all right, believe you me!' Douglas looked rather pleased with himself when he'd finished.

Diana balled her hands into tight fists in a tremendous effort of self-control.

'Douglas, *he just threatened to cut her hand off!* Please, pay him the bloody money!'

Douglas shook his head slowly, defiantly. 'He's all bluff,' he repeated. 'Stella's his daughter. He won't harm a hair of her head. My way is the right way, believe me. And I'll tell you why. If we pay him now, what's to stop him doing all this again one day, when he needs another fast buck? Hmm? Ask yourself that, my dear. We can't risk putting Stella through anything of the kind again.'

He paused. 'You'll thank me for this when she's back here safe and sound. I'm leaving now, Diana. I have a lot to arrange.' He left the room.

Diana ground her teeth in frustration. She couldn't think what to do. She had no money of her own to buy her daughter back. She felt completely powerless. Douglas was wrong, wrong, wrong. Everything she now knew about James convinced her that he did not make empty threats.

She heard the front door slam and a few moments later, the sound of the car leaving.

She began to pace the villa. How long had Stella been gone? Five, six hours? She looked at her watch. It was eight o'clock. Seven o'clock in England.

England. Of *course*.

She ran to the telephone.

★   ★   ★

On this warm June evening, Mr Arnold was sitting out on the lawn in the fading light, struggling to read the business pages of his evening paper. He glanced towards the ha-ha. Those blasted rabbits . . . nothing seemed to diminish their numbers, not myxomatosis, the disease transplanted from Australia that year that

420

had decimated the rabbit population in other parts of England; not his gardener's .22 rook-rifle, nor the snares he himself personally set along the rabbit-runs.

He could count about thirty of the lolloping creatures roaming the far end of the lawn, digging and burrowing in the flowerbeds that ran along its southern border. The plants were quite ruined. As for his vegetable patch, he'd surrendered that to them long ago. He clapped his hands. Several of the bunnies sat up like question-marks. Maybe he should go to the potting shed and fetch the rook-rifle. There was probably enough light left to shoot two or three before the others fled for cover.

At that moment, the phone began to ring in the house behind him. Oliver and Gwen had recently installed an extension in the garden room, so Mr Arnold took his time crossing the lawn to the French windows.

On the seventh ring he reached the instrument and picked up the receiver. 'Oliver Arnold.'

'Daddy!'

'Diana? It's about time. We thought you'd fallen into a bottomless pit.'

'Daddy, listen to me. I have to ask you something. And if you possibly can, just say 'yes'. It's incredibly important.'

The fear and urgency in his daughter's voice were palpable; he'd never heard her sound like this before. Dammit, he'd known something was wrong. He'd bloody well known it. He should have flown down to Nice weeks ago.

'It's all right, Diana. I'm here. I'm listening. Go ahead.'

'Can you raise a lot of money in cash by tomorrow morning, and have it here in France by tomorrow night? I'm sorry, I realise that will probably mean bringing it yourself.'

She told him how much.

Mr Arnold struggled to control the astonishment in his voice.

'What? I'm sorry, dear, I think I misheard you. How much did you say?'

Diana repeated the amount. 'And it's absolutely imperative it's here tomorrow — all of it.'

'What in heaven is this about?'

'It's about Stella. She's in great danger and Douglas — well, Douglas just doesn't realise it. That's why I've had to turn to you like this. But time is desperately short and you'll need to organise it all at once. There just isn't time for me to explain what's happened, it's too horribly complicated. You'll simply have to trust me.'

'I trust you, Diana. Give me a moment, please.'

He thought furiously. The figure she was asking for was not, in itself, a problem. Mr Arnold was extremely wealthy; he was generally regarded as the richest libel lawyer in London. He had many times the required amount in his personal savings account and in any case this was about his granddaughter.

What on earth was happening down there?

His mind racing, he remembered that the principal at his bank was Sir Richard Jobson, a personal friend. They'd been in the same regiment together during the First War. Mr Arnold was fairly certain he could persuade Sir Richard to release such an irregular sum in cash, even at this short notice. It would merely take a phone call.

So much for the money, then.

'Hang on, Diana. I'm still thinking this through.'

France by tomorrow night — that was the tricky part. It would mean travelling to Dover, taking the boat train, and catching the Nice Express at the Gare de Lyon in Paris. Even if he was at the bank when it opened at nine o'clock next morning, he'd never make Nice by tomorrow night. It just wasn't physically possible.

'I can get the money, Diana, I'm pretty certain of that,' he said at last. 'But I can't be in Nice until the day after tomorrow, at the earliest.'

The iron in her reply shook him. 'Sorry, Daddy, that won't do. You *have* to be here tomorrow night with the money.'

He fell silent again, momentarily defeated. Then he suddenly snapped his fingers.

'I think I've got it. Call me back in an hour. I have to telephone some people. And Diana?'

'Yes?'

'You will tell me what all this is about? Is Stella — '

'Stella is fine as we speak, I believe. And of course I'll tell you everything. But you have to sort the money and journey out first, Daddy; there simply isn't time to explain it all now. I doubt you'd believe it. I'm not sure I do myself.

The point is, we have to get her back.'

'Back? Back from where?'

'Do what you have to do, Daddy. There isn't a minute to spare. I'll explain everything when I call you back, I promise.'

He rang off, and pulled the telephone directory towards him. He only hoped the men he was about to call were at home.

★ ★ ★

An hour later it was arranged. Diana almost wept with relief when her father told her he thought he could meet her deadline after all.

'Sir Richard's going to meet me at the bank in person, so that's all right. But here's my brainwave, Diana. Remember Bunny Watson, and his weekend air trips to Le Touquet in the summer before the war? Well, he's branched out. These days he flies down as far as Lyon and Bordeaux. I've just spoken to him. He's a brick; says he'll fly me himself all the way to Nice tomorrow in one of his planes. We'll have to make a couple of extra fuelling stops, but with luck and a following wind he reckons we'll be landing there at around seven o'clock. Will that do?'

His daughter's sobs of relief were answer enough. Then, when she'd recovered, he said: 'Now that's settled, what's the situation with Stella? My heart's in my mouth here, Diana. She's obviously in difficulties. You all are.'

And Diana told her father about the return of James Blackwell.

Mr Arnold listened to her in growing astonishment. 'Why didn't you tell us he was alive as soon as you found out?' he managed, when she had finished.

'That's a part of the story that will have to wait, I'm afraid.'

'Yes . . . well, I think I can guess that bit, actually, Diana. But you're right, it can wait. First, we need to get Stella back from that bastard.'

★ ★ ★

Shortly before midnight, Oliver was rummaging for his passport inside the bedroom safe. 'Got it!' he announced triumphantly to his wife, who sat on their bed watching him. She was in a state of complete bewilderment.

'James Blackwell is *alive?*' she asked him for at least the third time. 'It simply can't be so, Oliver. Are you sure Diana hasn't lost her mind?'

Mr Arnold shook his head. 'No, she's lost her daughter.' He crossed the room and tossed his passport into the leather valise Gwen had packed for him. He spoke over his shoulder to her as he secured the buckles on the bag.

'I knew something was amiss down there. I've known it for weeks, as I've been trying to tell you. It all makes sense now. Diana was asking the strangest questions about James as long ago as April.'

He snapped the brass catches closed, then looked around him. 'I'm sure I've forgotten to pack something. I suppose it'll come to me.

425

Anyway, Gwen, Diana's only had time to give me the gist tonight, but it seems as if James was only ever one of the walking wounded. Not dead at all.'

'But how, Oliver? He was shot down.'

'He told Diana he got out of his plane at the last moment, and promptly deserted. He's been holed up in Provence ever since, and by the sound of things he's turned into the Devil's Disciple.'

'I can't believe it,' his wife said after a few moments. 'I've never thought of him as anything other than a hero, like John. You too, Oliver, come to that. But a deserter . . . ' She looked utterly bemused. 'And why in heaven's name would he abduct his own daughter?'

'I honestly don't know. It all sounds horribly confused. Something to do with the Nice Mafia and debts. The point is, Douglas won't stump up the ransom, even though he could afford it more than I can. It's the old puritan in him, I suppose; he doesn't think it right to reward evil and avarice under any circumstances whatsoever. I hesitate to pass judgement at this distance, but I think the man is being a total idiot.'

He looked around him. 'I've ordered a taxi to take me straight to London tonight. I'll sleep at the club and be at the bank when it opens and rendezvous with Sir Richard. Then I'll go straight to Croydon aerodrome and meet Bunny, bless him. Isn't he terrific to step into the breach like this?'

The doorbell rang. 'That'll be my taxi. Kiss me, Gwen, and wish me luck.'

He was hurrying down the stairs when he stopped and turned around. He had remembered what it was he'd forgotten to pack.

* * *

Stella sat up on her narrow bed. She was wide awake, and heard the quiet snick of the hall door being opened, and the dull thump as it closed again.

She had had only one visitor since she heard her father leave the flat.

At least three hours ago now, a thin man with greying hair had let himself into the bedroom. He hadn't spoken to her, but carefully placed a cardboard box and a chamber-pot on the floor. He nodded politely to her before leaving again, locking the door behind him.

She'd scrambled over to the box. It contained a ham sandwich, a bottle of water and an apple. Inside the chamber-pot was a roll of shiny toilet paper.

That was all.

Now she could hear low voices murmuring in the room beyond. A crack of light shone under her door. She slipped across, lay down and pressed her ear against it. It was no good. She couldn't make out what they were saying, although she was certain they were speaking in French. She scrambled away from the door and looked at the chamber-pot with distaste. Like it or not, she would soon have to use it.

She unwrapped her sandwich from its greaseproof paper. The insides of her cheeks prickled and her stomach growled. She realised she hadn't eaten since breakfast. Hunger overwhelmed her and she tore the bread and ham into rough chunks with her fingers, stuffing them into her mouth and washing them down with the bottle of water.

The apple followed, core and all.

Stella had sharp, white teeth. She sucked the remains of her supper from them and licked her lips.

Whatever the morning brought, she decided that, given half a chance, she would use those teeth on her father. She would bite him harder than he had ever been bitten before, by man or beast. She would teach him to trick her and kidnap her and lock her in a stifling room with a disgusting chamber-pot.

She would mark him. She would mark him for the rest of his life.

Not for the first time that night, Stella felt herself trembling. Not with fear, but with fury.

58

Diana was at Nice airport in time to see the little twin-engine aeroplane carrying her father touch down in the early-evening sunshine. She waited in the cramped wooden Arrivals hut while he went through Passport and Immigration, which were at the back of the shed. He saw her and smiled reassuringly as he had his papers stamped. Then he was taken aside by customs officials. Diana's heart sank.

If they found the money, it would be over before it had even begun.

The officers were about to inspect her father's bag, when he spoke quietly to the senior man, and reached inside his jacket. Diana thought she caught the glimmer of an envelope before it disappeared from view.

The next moment, Mr Arnold was being waved through and she was rushing into his arms.

'You did it! You did it! They didn't find the money?' She kissed his cheek and grabbed his arm, steering him outside towards the airport's tiny car park.

'Sshhh! Keep your voice down. Yes — well, they didn't find the money that matters, at any rate. Thank goodness I remembered what I call my travelling francs as I left the Dower House. The stuff from the bank is in the largest denominations we could find. That wouldn't have gone down well just now at all. So hello, Diana. What news?'

'I think everything's under control. Douglas was furious when I told him you were flying down with the money. He thinks we're being unutterably foolish. He's put his faith in a couple of private detective agencies. He's spent all day with them, trying to persuade them to take the job. I don't think he's having much luck. He's certainly no closer to finding out where Stella's being held.'

'Hmm, even so, he may have a point, you know.'

'No, he doesn't, Daddy! He doesn't *begin* to understand about James, what he's capable of. Here we are, this is my car. Get in. I want to show you something.'

Mr Arnold tossed his valise onto the back seat of the little Citroën as he settled into its front passenger seat. His daughter climbed in on the other side and rifled through the car's glove box.

'Here. Read this. It's from a great friend of mine. She has a stall in the flower-market. She was married to a Manchester man so her English is pretty good.'

By the time Diana had navigated her way on to the Promenade des Anglais, her father had finished reading Hélène's letter.

'I see.' He tilted his head back and gave a low whistle. 'I really never would have suspected this about James, I have to say. I've been thinking about him most of the way down here, trying to remember if he ever gave the smallest hint of what he was really like, even then. I can't think of anything at all. Can you?'

She shook her head. 'Nope. I thought he was wonderful. Sweet and funny and brave . . . it's extraordinary. D'you know what he told me the last time we met? He said he only pursued me because he saw me as an 'opportunity'.'

Mr Arnold looked across at her. 'I'm so sorry, my dear. But I don't see how any of us could have known any better. He was so charming and — well, convincing.'

'Convincing?' She gave a hollow laugh. 'He's convincing all right. Wait until you meet him later. Talk about the Two Faces of Janus.'

'What do you mean, when I meet him later? What about Douglas? Surely he'll admit defeat with his detectives and come home to help us out?'

Diana swerved over two lanes of evening traffic to position herself on a slip road that gave access to the Negresco. She took a moment to reply.

'I don't want him helping us out. I've told him that when he gets back from his pointless assignations, he's to keep right out of it. I'm in charge now.'

She pulled up outside the hotel and a uniformed valet hurried to park their car. 'Let's go inside, Daddy. We've a little time before it has to be done.'

Mr Arnold took his daughter's arm in his as they went up the steps to the lobby. 'And what exactly is to be done, Diana? I'm still rather in the dark, you know.'

'I'll explain inside,' she told him. They reached

431

the hotel's revolving door. 'But the top and bottom of it is that you're delivering the ransom, Daddy, and I'm collecting Stella.'

★　★　★

By the time Oliver and Diana had been served their drinks in the lounge of the Negresco, Mr Arnold was a little clearer.

'Let me be correct about this. I go to,' he consulted the card Diana had given him, 'this address in an hour, meet James, and give him the money.'

'Yes,' said Diana. 'He'll then make a telephone call, in front of you, ordering Stella's release. You will both stay in the room until the phone rings. It will be me, telling you that Stella has been delivered to me here in the hotel by one of his goons. Which means it's over. The whole rotten, revolting business will be over.'

'Hmm.' Mr Arnold sipped his drink. 'Will it, I wonder. What's to stop this odious man from persecuting you all again?'

His daughter stared at him. 'Surely he wouldn't. I mean, this is a unique situation, isn't it? Once he's got the money he needs to buy his way into the Mafia, we'll be shot of him, won't we? Come on, Daddy, he can't keep kidnapping Stella every time he needs a sack of money!'

'Perhaps not. I hope not. I definitely hope not.'

A bell-boy approached them. '*Madame?* The telephone for you.'

Diana jumped to her feet. 'This is it.'

Two minutes later she was back, her face

suffused with relief. 'I just spoke to Stella! She said she was fine, absolutely fine. Oh, thank God, thank God! James was running the whole conversation, obviously. He says he's leaving now for the address I gave you. It's his private club, apparently. He says he'll be there in five minutes, so you may as well leave now too.'

'Hang on,' said her father. 'Who's looking after Stella?'

'The henchman who'll bring her here. Stella said he brought her some food last night. It's extraordinary, Daddy, she doesn't seem frightened at all. Just furious.'

Mr Arnold stood up. 'Well, that's a good sign, anyway. So the next time you and I speak, Stella with be safe and sound here with you, correct?'

'Absolutely.'

'Did James say what I was to do when I get to the club?'

'I almost forgot! You're to ask at the desk for a Mr Walker, and you'll be shown up. James has taken a suite of rooms right at the top of the club so you won't be disturbed.'

'How thoughtful of him. Well, I'll see you both later, then. You're not to worry, Diana. Everything's going to be fine.' He kissed her cheek and walked to the taxi-rank outside the hotel.

He kept his bag close to his side.

★ ★ ★

The club was a few minutes' walk from where Stella was being held, and James moved swiftly

433

through the streets. His wrist was bandaged and throbbing painfully, and his face was marked with what looked like the bites of an animal.

Little cow. He'd taken the trouble to go into her room to reassure her that she'd soon be back with her mother, but the moment he entered she'd flown at him like a spitting cat, knocking him backwards through the doorway into the lounge. They'd rolled over and over on the floor, her jaws clamped to his wrist and her fingers trying to gouge his bloody eyes out. When he'd managed to get her off him she'd pretended to give up, only to come flying back at him under his guard, sinking her teeth into his cheek and nose. She was unbelievably strong for a ten-year-old, and a girl at that.

It was lucky one of his bagmen, Claude, had been with him or he might have had to do Stella some serious damage to get her under control. His man had managed to drag her away by the hair and manhandle her back into her cell. She'd still been kicking at the locked door when he left. The whole ruddy flat was shaking. He couldn't wait to be shot of her.

Next time — oh yes, there'd be a next time all right, especially after that little performance — he'd use the chloroform.

★ ★ ★

Mr Arnold knocked on the door of the suite. It was at the very top of the private members' club, tucked away behind some back stairs.

He turned to thank the man who had shown

434

him up, but he had already silently disappeared.

James Blackwell opened the door. 'Come in, Oliver.'

Mr Arnold was surprised — almost shocked — at how little the younger man had changed. He hesitated, gathering himself before entering the room. He noticed a bottle of champagne with two glasses set on a table in the centre of the room.

'Celebrating something, James?'

The other man turned from closing the door.

'Yes, actually. Thanks to you, tonight I get to join the most exclusive, powerful organisation in Nice. I'm going to be richer than even you soon, Oliver. The least I can do is offer you a drink. How are you, anyway? You're looking well. Younger than I was expecting.'

He extended his hand, but dropped it again after a few moments.

'As you wish, old boy. Just trying to be friendly. Would you wait a moment, please?'

James went to a telephone on the same table as the champagne and picked it up, jiggling the cradle with his forefinger. After a moment he spoke into the receiver.

'This is Walker. On no account whatsoever am I to be disturbed. I don't want anyone coming up here for the rest of the evening. I may spend the night here, and unless I specifically ring down for something, no one is to come up. Is that clear? Good.' He hung up.

'There. We shan't be interrupted.' He gestured to two armchairs on either side of an unlit fireplace, and the two men sat down opposite each other. 'You really *are* looking well, Oliver. Almost the same as when I last saw you. My wedding day.'

Mr Arnold made no reply. He looked calmly at James Blackwell, his arms folded quietly in his lap. There was nothing about the younger man that spoke to him of evil. Mr Arnold saw no signs of degradation or cruelty in the pleasant face opposite his. If James Blackwell had been in RAF uniform, he could almost have been the handsome young man Oliver had once welcomed to his table, and into his family.

James pulled the champagne bottle out of the silver bucket and began fiddling with the foil around the cork. He grinned at Mr Arnold. He just couldn't help it. This was all working out so perfectly.

'I expect you think I'm a bit of a swine, don't you?'

Mr Arnold smiled pleasantly in return. 'I think you're a total shit, actually.'

'*That's* the spirit!' James popped the cork. Foam poured out of the neck of the bottle, and as it subsided, James poured a little champagne into the twin glasses on the tray. 'Good for you, Oliver. Always speak as you find. You and your boy had that in common, did you know that? John always spoke his mind. I liked that about him. I always did.'

'If my son were here now, he'd do a lot more than tell you what he thought of you. He'd have you by the throat.'

James nodded sympathetically. 'Yes, I expect you're right there — but he's not here, is he? It's just you. With a bag full of money. For me.' James pushed one of the flute glasses across the table to Mr Arnold. 'What shall we drink to? I know. Absent friends.' He raised his glass.

Oliver left his own untouched. 'Can we get this over with?'

'Of course. May I see the money, please?'

Mr Arnold opened his bag and pulled out a heavy grey canvas sack. 'It's all in there.'

'Yes, but all the same, if I might just . . . ' James took out several blocks of banknotes at random and tore off their wrappers. He flicked through them, taking the occasional note out of its thick pile, and holding it up towards a naked light bulb that hung from the ceiling. Occasionally, he sniffed one of the notes.

'Yes, yes,' he said at last. 'This all seems to be in order. Thank you.' He picked up the phone and dialled for the operator. He gave a number, and after a moment, he said: 'Get her in a taxi. Go to the Negresco. Her mother's in the main lounge.'

He replaced the receiver and shrugged. 'And now we wait. Not that I really need to, Oliver, but I am a man of my word. So we wait for the beautiful Diana to telephone and say the indomitable Stella is safe and sound and back in the maternal embrace. And then we all go home and life goes on. Are you sure you won't have that drink now?'

'I'll wait for the call, thanks. And I'd rather we didn't speak.'

'As you wish.'

Both men sat in silence for several minutes,

437

Mr Arnold seemingly calm and relaxed, the younger man fidgeting and bored. He yawned occasionally, displaying perfectly white teeth.

At last the phone rang. James gestured politely to Mr Arnold, who picked up the receiver.

'Oliver Arnold.'

'It's me, Daddy. Stella's here. She's absolutely fine. She's a bit tired, but she's fine. We're going straight back to the villa. Are you all right at that end?'

'Yes, of course. Don't worry about me. All's well that ends well. I'll see you back at the house.' He replaced the phone on its cradle.

James was transferring the money from the canvas bag into a soft leather briefcase. 'Thanks again for this, Oliver. You did exactly the right thing, I want you to know that. If it had been left to that fool Douglas, who knows how things might have turned out.'

He stood up. 'I think we're all finished here, don't you? Can I get you a cab? I can have one here in a minute to take you up to St Paul de Vence.'

'I'll make my own way, thank you.'

'Suit yourself.' James hefted the briefcase under one arm. 'Goodness, this is heavy. I suppose this is goodbye, then.'

'Indeed it is, James.' But Mr Arnold remained seated. He pointed at the marks on the other man's face. 'By the way, what are those cuts? And why is your wrist bandaged?'

'Your granddaughter, old boy. She has a high spirit and sharp teeth. I was considerate enough to give her the good news of her impending release this evening, and this was my reward.' He rubbed his wrist ruefully. 'I won't hold it against her, though. I didn't take any nonsense from anyone when I was a kid, either.'

He made to leave the room, then hesitated and turned around.

'I know this is probably the last time we'll see each other, but oddly enough, it's been good meeting you again, Oliver. You know, if I hadn't been shot down that day, things might have been very different. I told Diana that.'

Mr Arnold gave a short laugh. 'I very much doubt it. You were a snake in the grass from the start, I realise that now. But this is certainly the last time we'll see each other, James.' He reached down into his valise and brought up the service revolver that he'd never quite got around to handing back in, cocking the hammer as he did so. The barrel pointed directly at the other man's head.

'How theatrical.' James burst out laughing. 'Are you going to say 'this is a stick-up' and grab your money back? Do you really think I can't take Stella, or Diana, any time I like, Oliver? Do you have *any* idea what I am capable of?'

Mr Arnold smiled at him, almost kindly. 'Oh, yes. I know exactly what you're capable of, James. That's the point. I have absolutely no intention of letting you threaten my daughter and granddaughter ever again. You really haven't given me any choice. I'm afraid I can't possibly let you leave this room.'

James looked incredulous, his eyebrows arching in genuine surprise.

'Good grief! You're actually threatening to kill me!' He threw back his head and roared with laughter again.

'Well, that raises an interesting point, James.' Mr Arnold nodded thoughtfully. 'You see — you're already dead, aren't you? James Blackwell died eleven years ago. He can't be killed twice. He no longer exists. You're a walking, talking ghost. One can't kill a ghost.'

James's smile faded slightly.

'I'm not a ghost here in Nice, Oliver. I'm quite the man of the moment. Flesh and blood. And I don't go under the name of Blackwell. I have serious contacts, associates. Kill me, and you'll be taking on forces far more powerful than you can begin to know.'

Now it was Mr Arnold who laughed.

'James, I know *exactly* who your associates are and they couldn't give a damn about you. If I hadn't turned up tonight with the money, they'd have stolen your business and probably killed you into the bargain. You're way out of your depth. This whole kidnapping scenario — your own *daughter*, for God's sake — it's pathetic. But I'm not here to punish you; I'll leave that to God.'

The revolver steadied.

James blinked. He licked his lips.

'Be that as it may . . . now look, Oliver. You need to think carefully. You're a civilised man; a lawyer, for heaven's sake. You couldn't possibly kill a fellow human being in cold blood. How would you live with yourself afterwards?'

James realised that a pleading note had

entered his voice and he strove to re-assert himself.

'Look me in the eyes. Go on, look at me! We're six feet away from each other. Could you really do it? I think not. Put your antique pistol down, Oliver, and let's both go home. You're an old man. Our business here is over and done. I'm no threat to your family. Not now.' He patted the bag. 'I've got what I came for.'

Mr Arnold sighed. 'James, I'm perfectly content to look you in the eyes. I was in the trenches for four years. I was in the tunnels *under* the trenches, groping and fighting and stabbing in the dark. I shot and knifed and strangled so many men, face to face, that I lost count of them. You do, after a while. One more death won't make any difference.'

James Blackwell stared blankly back at him.

Mr Arnold sighed again. 'To be perfectly frank, James, I've killed better men than you before breakfast.'

He pulled the trigger. The report was deafening in the small room and James Blackwell's brains exploded through the back of his head and showered the wall behind him. He toppled sideways and landed full length on the floor, his body giving a single, convulsive shudder. Then he was still.

Oliver Arnold picked up his champagne flute and drained it in one swallow. He removed the canvas money sack from the briefcase, and replaced it in his own valise, along with the gun.

James Blackwell's legs were partly blocking the door. Mr Arnold kicked them away.

He opened it and listened carefully for a moment. There was no sound of any approach. *Le Loup Anglais* had given specific instructions about not being disturbed.

Mr Arnold slid quietly from the room and closed the door behind him.

He'd killed better men before breakfast.

59

She knew the moment she saw his face.

'I didn't have any choice, my dear.'

Diana let her father into the villa and closed the door. 'But, Daddy — how did you . . . '

He briefly showed her the gun, before dropping it back in his bag.

'Dear God.'

'If I'd thought there was any other way, Diana, I promise I would have taken it.'

She shot the bolts at the top and bottom of the door before turning back to face him.

Oliver Arnold watched his daughter carefully. She was pale, and trembled slightly.

'He'd never have left us alone,' she said with sudden resolve. 'I'm glad he's dead. Really dead, this time. But how did you bring yourself to do it, Daddy? It must have been horrible.'

He leaned forward and gently kissed her forehead. 'That's a conversation for another time, my dear. Don't worry about me. As you can see, I'm quite all right. But what about you, Dee-Dee?'

She started. 'You haven't called me that since I was a child.'

'Haven't I? I suppose I'm feeling particularly protective of you tonight. After all, once you were so very much in love with him, and this week you were reunited, and I'm sure you must have . . . ' He gave an awkward shrug. 'I'm sorry.

I'm being presumptuous.'

'No. No, you're not,' Diana said quietly.

'Anyway,' he went on after a pause, 'then the awful business with Stella — and now tonight. You must feel very confused and angry, Diana. With me too, perhaps, after what I've just done.'

Diana put both hands on her father's shoulders, gripping so firmly he almost winced.

'No! Don't ever think that, not for one second! James was an evil, evil man. He kidnapped Stella, and he threatened to cut her hand off if we didn't pay him the money. He would have done it, too, I'm sure of it. His own daughter! If anyone was ever in league with the Devil, it was James Blackwell. You exorcised a demon tonight.'

She released him. 'Come on.'

They walked slowly into the sitting room, where Diana poured two large whiskies.

'I've behaved unutterably foolishly,' she confessed, as they both sank into comfortable chairs, 'from the first moment I suspected James was still alive. Although I do believe that he managed to sort of hypnotise me after we met again. Actually, I think he hypnotised all of us, right from the beginning, didn't he? John at Cranwell, you and Mummy at the Dower House, and me at Girton.'

Oliver nodded slowly. 'Yes. He had a remarkable facility for making one want to like him and believe in him. Even tonight he was . . . I don't know, Diana; it's very strange. I found myself wanting to give him the benefit of the doubt, even though I knew he was extraordinarily manipulative and dangerous. I

444

very nearly let him leave the room, you know. He was a very charismatic person.'

Diana sipped her scotch. 'He was. But I did my mourning a long time ago for him; the man I believed I knew and loved. It certainly wasn't the person you killed tonight. That was the real James Blackwell.'

Oliver loosened his tie and eased himself down in his chair, emptying his tumbler in one long steady swallow. 'Where's Stella?'

'In bed, fast asleep. She's absolutely exhausted.'

'I'll bet she is. And Douglas?'

'He's staying in Cannes tonight.'

Mr Arnold raised an eyebrow.

'We've come to a decision,' she said.

Epilogue

By the time the *gendarmes* were peering at James Blackwell's shattered skull, Oliver, Diana and Stella were back at the Dower House.

They'd left Nice on the first train to Paris and were crossing the Channel before the manager of James's club had plucked up the courage to gingerly tap on the door of his notorious client. If *Le Loup* said he wanted to be left undisturbed, you took him at his word.

It wasn't until nightfall that the manager discovered that nothing would ever disturb the Englishman again, and he called the police.

There was nothing to connect Mr Arnold or indeed anyone else to the killing, and detectives almost immediately wrote it off as a Mafia hit. There had been rumours for weeks that *Le Loup* was in the Italians' sights; clearly they had made their move.

'Let dog eat dog,' the head of the city's murder squad told his assistant. 'Close the file. No one gives a shit.'

James was buried in a dreary civic cemetery under his last assumed name of Peter Walker, even though police checks quickly established that his papers were false.

Le Loup's protection racket was quietly and efficiently taken over by the Mafia.

Before long, Nice forgot all about him.

Douglas had quickly realised how completely he'd underestimated James Blackwell's reputation. As Diana had predicted, the private detectives he sought to employ in Cannes had been slippery and evasive, even in the face of huge financial inducements. He simply could not persuade them to even begin looking for Stella.

By the time he'd called Diana to admit defeat, his stepdaughter was already home and tucked up in bed. Douglas felt foolish and emasculated.

'I think we need some time apart,' Diana had told him carefully. 'We've both got a lot of thinking to do. I'm going back to England with my father in the morning.'

★ ★ ★

Almost as soon as she arrived at the Dower House, Diana decided she would not go back to Nice. There was no need to rush through a divorce from Douglas, but it was clear to her that the marriage must be dissolved. She would admit her adultery, if Douglas allowed her to. Knowing him, he would insist on shouldering the blame.

In September, her daughter was enrolled into the same public school that her mother had attended. The girl calmly accepted the news that Diana and Douglas were to separate. She was genuinely fond of her stepfather, but he simply hadn't had enough time to properly establish himself in her world.

Within weeks of returning to Kent, Stella had comfortably slipped back into her old life with her mother and grandparents. In fact, she was even becoming a little bored, and so was thrilled to be told she was to begin a new adventure in the autumn.

For the first time in years, Diana had found her thoughts returning to Girton. Women had at last won the right to read for full degrees at the university, and Diana decided there was now a point in resuming her studies, if her old college would have her back. She wrote a tentative letter to Girton, and to her astonishment received an enthusiastic reply almost by return, suggesting she enrol the following month, the start of the new university year. With Stella away at boarding school, Diana felt there really was nothing to stop her completing her degree. She wrote back, accepting the offer of a place.

So it was that a few weeks later, on a sunny October morning, Mr Arnold's big green Humber swept under the familiar gate-house and past the neo-Tudor red brick and terracotta facades around Girton's grassy quadrangles. The car pulled into the same space that James Blackwell's battered sports car had occupied on a snowy day so long ago.

'Think you'll finish this time?' Oliver asked his daughter, smiling to show her he was not being serious.

Diana smiled back at him. 'I think so. Anyway, I'll have to set an example.' She nodded towards another new arrival who was stepping from her own parents' car. 'Look at her. I'm practically old enough to be her mother. I'm certainly dressed as if I were.' Diana looked ruefully down at her new tweed jacket and skirt, and plucked at the cuffs of a dark red woollen polo-neck.

Mr Arnold laughed. 'You look extremely stylish, my dear, as always — but yes, you'll probably end up being everyone's mother hen and unofficial tutor.'

Something in her face gave him pause.

'Of course.' He shook his head in amusement. 'I should have guessed. You're planning to stay on here when you've got your degree, aren't you?'

Diana nodded. 'Yes. I'm going to study for my doctorate. I want to lecture here. With any luck I'll have my PhD by the time Stella's ready to go to university herself. It'd be wonderful if she came here to Girton.'

'Well, it's a good enough plan to be going on with,' he told her. 'Come on, let's get your bags and find your room.'

They got out of the car and almost at once Diana gave a little cry.

'My goodness — it's just struck me! This is the exact spot where James parked his car when he came to see me here.'

Her father, about to heft two heavy cases from the boot, paused and squinted at her in the bright autumn sunshine.

'All right, Diana? Bad memories?'

'No, not at all,' she said firmly. 'I hardly ever think about him any more. Not since he . . . not since you . . . '

Oliver waited.

'In fact,' she went on, 'I realised the other day that my memories of him are getting fainter all the time. It's almost as if they've been drawn in vanishing ink.'

Mr Arnold hauled the big cases out and handed her a third, smaller one.

'How curious that you should put it like that,' he said. 'I thought more or less exactly the same thing, only the other day. He's just fading away, isn't he? I wonder why.'

They began walking together towards the building's entrance.

'I think I know,' Diana replied. 'It's because he never really existed, did he? Not as we thought we knew him.'

Father and daughter walked under the stone arches that led into her old familiar home.

She looked around her. 'This is real. You and I are real.'

The college clocks began to chime the hour.

'But James?' she continued. 'There's a poem, isn't there . . . how does it go? Oh, yes: *The other day upon the stair, I met a man who wasn't there.*

'That was James Blackwell, wasn't it? A man who never was.'

The two of them went to find her room.

We do hope that you have enjoyed reading
this large print book.

Did you know that all of our titles
are available for purchase?

We publish a wide range of high quality
large print books including:
Romances, Mysteries, Classics
General Fiction
Non Fiction and Westerns

Special interest titles available in
large print are:
The Little Oxford Dictionary
Music Book
Song Book
Hymn Book
Service Book

Also available from us courtesy of Oxford
University Press:
Young Readers' Dictionary
(large print edition)
Young Readers' Thesaurus
(large print edition)

For further information or a free
brochure, please contact us at:
Ulverscroft Large Print Books Ltd.,
The Green, Bradgate Road, Anstey,
Leicester, LE7 7FU, England.
Tel: (00 44) 0116 236 4325
Fax: (00 44) 0116 234 0205

FATHERS & SONS

Richard Madeley

Seven years before the Great War, ten-year-old Geoffrey Madeley was travelling to Liverpool with his family to take the ship to Canada to start a new life. But after their overnight stop on his uncle's farm, Geoffrey woke up to find that his mother, father and siblings had gone. In a heartbreaking betrayal, he'd been left behind. This child was Richard Madeley's grandfather. Shock waves would reverberate through the generations of Madeley boys, each struggling to cope with a tangled emotional inheritance. Starved of paternal affection, Christopher, Geoffrey's son, swore that for his son things would be different. But were they? And what kind of father did Richard become? *Fathers & Sons* is a journey into fatherhood in the most rapidly changing centuries in history.

THE GUEST LIST

Melissa Hill

When funny, kind and gorgeous Shane proposes, Cara is over the moon. Excitement, however, quickly turns to apprehension when it seems that everyone has a fixed idea of the perfect wedding and offers to 'help' with the planning. With tussles over the ceremony and the size of the guest list, sibling rivalry and insistent in-laws-to-be, Cara can see the vision she has of her big day being ripped to shreds. So she and Shane determine to make a stand and do things *their* way. But when they announce their plans for a beach wedding on a beautiful Caribbean island, there is uproar. Threats are made, family secrets are revealed, and things turn decidedly stormy. Will Cara and Shane manage to overcome all the obstacles? Or will their dream wedding turn into a nightmare?

THE COMPROMISE,

Zoë Miller

Childhood friends Juliet, Rebecca, Rose and Matthew grew up in a small village outside Dublin. Now privileged, wealthy and powerful, they appear to have it all. But when Juliet is involved in a suspicious accident and lies trapped between life and death at the bottom of a cliff, a secret that has been hidden for years threatens the seemingly perfect lives of the close-knit group. For the beautiful, fragile Rose, Juliet's accident draws unwanted attention to the sins of the past. For her husband, the ruthlessly ambitious Matthew, it removes a critical obstacle from the path of his political career. And as Rebecca discovers more about what happened to her friend, she begins to wonder if she ever knew the real Juliet . . .